Charles Percy Snow educated as a chemist and physicist at the universities of Leicester and Cambridge. After scientific research he turned to administration and then to writing and later held many important public posts and was made Baron Snow of Leicester.

Snow's first novel *Death Under Sail* was published in 1932. His successful novel sequence portraying English life from 1920 onwards is *Strangers and Brothers*. This sequence spans the life of its narrator, Lewis Eliot, barrister − and took over 30 years to write. Snow describes the rarefied worlds of academia, Cambridge, the Jewish community and Westminster. In addition to fiction, Snow also wrote several critical works including a biography of Trollope. He married the novelist Pamela Hansford Johnson in 1950 and died in 1980.

BY THE SAME AUTHOR
ALL PUBLISHED BY HOUSE OF STRATUS

GENERAL FICTION:

THE AFFAIR
A COAT OF VARNISH
THE CONSCIENCE OF THE RICH
CORRIDORS OF POWER
DEATH UNDER SAIL
HOMECOMINGS
IN THEIR WISDOM
LAST THINGS
THE LIGHT AND THE DARK
THE MALCONTENTS
THE MASTERS
THE NEW MEN
THE SEARCH
THE SLEEP OF REASON
TIME OF HOPE

NON-FICTION:

THE PHYSICISTS
TROLLOPE

C P SNOW

George Passant

HOUSE OF
STRATUS

This edition published in 2000 by House of Stratus, an imprint of
Stratus Books Ltd., 21 Beeching Park, Kelly Bray,
Cornwall, PL17 8QS

www.houseofstratus.com

Typeset, printed and bound by House of Stratus.

A catalogue record for this book is available from the British Library
and the Library of Congress.

ISBN 1-84232-422-5

CONTENTS

Part One – THE TRIUMPH OF GEORGE PASSANT

1	Firelight on a Silver Cigarette Case	3
2	Conference at Night	12
3	View Over the Gardens	19
4	A Cup of Coffee Spilt in a Drawing-Room	23
5	George's Attack	33
6	Results of a Celebration	43
7	Argument Under the Gaslight	52
8	George at the Centre of His Group	60

Part Two – THE FIRM OF EDEN & MARTINEAU

9	The Echo of a Quarrel	75
10	Roofs Seen from an Office Window	80
11	A Firm of Solicitors	86
12	Evening by the River	90
13	An Unnecessary Confession	96
14	The Last 'Friday Night'	102
15	Martineau's Intention	108
16	Walk in the Rain	115
17	A Slip of the Tongue	121
18	I Appeal	127
19	George Calls on Morcom	132
20	Two Progesses	139

Part Three – THE WARNING

21	News at Second Hand	145
22	Return from a Holiday	148
23	Sight of Old Friends	155
24	The First Inquiries	165
25	Conversations at Night	172
26	A Guilty Story	181

27 Conflict on Tactics   187
28 The Twenty-Ninth of December   193
29 Newspaper Under a Reading Lamp   198
30 George's Diary   204
31 Confidential Talk in Eden's Drawing-Room   225
32 Visit to George   231

Part Four – THE TRIAL

33 Courtroom Lit by a Chandelier   237
34 Dinner Party After a Bad Day   248
35 The Park Revisited   255
36 Martineau's Day in Town   261
37 Night With the Passants   270
38 Impressions in the Court   276
39 The Last Cross-Examination   283
40 Confession While Getliffe Prepares His Speech   294
41 Getliffe's Speech   304
42 Fog Outside Bedroom Windows   310
43 The Last Day   317
44 Walk into the Town   324

Part One

THE TRIUMPH
OF GEORGE PASSANT

1

Firelight on a Silver Cigarette Case

THE fire in our habitual public house spurted and fell. It was a comfortable fire of early autumn, and I basked beside it, not caring how long I waited. At last Jack came in, bustled by the other tables, sat down at mine, and said: 'I'm in trouble, Lewis.'

For an instant I thought he was acting; as he went on, I believed him.

'I'm finished as far as Calvert goes,' he said. 'And I can't see my way out.'

'What have you done?'

'I've done nothing,' said Jack. 'But this morning I received a gift – '

'Who from? Who from?'

'From young Roy.'

I had heard Roy's name often in the past two months. He was a boy of fifteen, the son of the Calvert whom Jack had just mentioned and who owned the local evening paper; Jack worked as a clerk in the newspaper office, and during the school holidays, which had not yet ended, the boy had contrived to get to know him. Jack, in his easy-natured fashion, had lent him books, been ready to talk; and had not discovered until the last few days that the boy was letting himself be carried in a dream, a romantic dream.

With a quick gesture Jack felt in his coat pocket and held a cigarette case in front of the fire. 'Here we are,' he said.

3

The firelight shone on the new, polished silver. I held out my hand, took the case, looked at the initials J C (Jack Cotery) in elaborate Gothic letters, felt the solid weight. Though Jack and I were each five years older than the boy who had given it, it had cost three times as much as we had ever earned in a week.

'I wonder how he managed to buy it,' I said.

'His father is pretty lavish with him,' said Jack. 'But he must have thrown away every penny – '

He was holding the case again, watching the reflected beam of firelight with a worried smile. I looked at him: of all our friends, he was the one to whom these things happened. I had noticed often enough how women's eyes followed him. He was ready to return their interest, it is true; yet sometimes he captured it, from women as from Roy, without taking a step himself. He was not handsome; he was not even specially good looking, in a man's eyes; he was ruddy-faced, with smooth black hair, shortish and powerfully built. His face, his eyes, his whole expression, changed like quicksilver whenever he talked.

'You haven't seen it all,' said Jack, and turned the case over. On this side there was enamelled a brilliant crest, in gold, red, blue and green; the only quarter I could make out contained a pattern of azure waves. 'He put a chart inside the case to prove these were the arms of the Coterys,' Jack went on, and showed me a piece of foolscap, covered with writing in a neat, firm, boyish hand. One paragraph explained that the azure waves 'are a punning device, Côte for Cotery, used by a family of Dorset Coterys when given arms in 1607 by James I.' I was surprised at the detail, the thoroughness, the genealogical references, the devotion to heraldry as well as to Jack; it must have taken weeks of research.

'It's quite possibly genuine,' said Jack. 'The family must have come down in the world, you know. There's still my father's brother, the Chiswick one – '

I laughed, and he let the fancy drop. He glanced at the chart, folded it, put it carefully away; then he rubbed mist from the case and studied the arms, his eyes harassed and half-smiling.

'You'd better send it back tonight,' I said.

4

'It's too late,' said Jack. 'Didn't you hear what I said – that I'm finished as far as old Calvert goes?'

'Does he know that Roy's given you a present?'

'He knows more than that. He happened to get hold of a letter that was coming with it.'

It was not till then that I realised Calvert had already spoken to Jack.

'What did the letter say?'

'I don't know. He's never written before. But you can guess, Lewis, you can guess. It horrified Calvert, clearly. And there doesn't seem anything I can do.'

'Did you manage to tell him,' I said, 'that it was an absolute surprise to you, that you knew nothing about it?'

'Do you think that was easy?' said Jack. 'Actually, he didn't give me much of a chance. He couldn't keep still for nerves, as a matter of fact. He just said that he'd discovered his son writing me an – indiscreet letter. And he was forced to ask me not to reply and not to see the boy. I didn't mind promising that. But he didn't want to listen to anything I said about Roy. He dashed on to my future in the firm. He said that he'd always expected there would be a good vacancy for me on the production side. Now he realised that promotions had gone too fast, and he would be compelled to slow down. So that, though I could stay in my present boy's job for ever, he would advise me in my own interests to be looking round for some other place.'

Jack's face was downcast; we were both sunk in the cul-de-sac hopelessness of our age.

'And to make it clear,' Jack added, 'he feels obliged to cut off paying my fees at the School.'

The School was our name for the combined Technical College and School of Art which gave at that time, 1925, the only kind of higher education in the town. There Jack had been sent by Calvert to learn printing, and there each week I attended a couple of lectures on law: lectures given by George Passant, whom I kept thinking of as soon as I knew Jack's trouble to be real.

'Well, we've got a bit of time,' I said. 'He can't get rid of you altogether – it would bring too much attention to his son.'

'Who'll worry about me?' said Jack.

'He can't do it,' I insisted. 'But what are we to do?'

'I haven't the slightest idea,' said Jack.

Then I mentioned George Passant's name. At once Jack was on his feet. 'I ought to have gone round hours ago,' he said.

We walked up the London Road, crossed by the station, took a short cut down an alley towards the noisy street. Fish and chip shops glared and smelt: tramcars rattled past. Jack was more talkative now that he was going into action. 'What shall I become if Calvert doesn't let me print?' he said. 'I used to have some ideas, I used to be a young man of spirit. But when they threaten to stop you, being a printer seems the only possible job in the whole world. What else could I become, Lewis?' He saw a policeman shining his lantern into a dark shop window. 'Yes,' said Jack, 'I should like to be a policeman. But then I'm not tall enough. They say you can increase your height if you walk like this – ' he held both arms vertically above his head, like Moses on the hill in Rephidim, and walked by my side down the street saying: 'I want to be a policeman.'

He stopped short, and looked at me with a rueful, embarrassed smile. I smiled too: more even than he, I was used to the hope and hopelessness, the hopes of twenty, desolately cold half an hour ago, now burning hot. I was used to living on hope. And I too was excited: the Cotery arms on the silver case ceased to be so pathetic, began to go to one's head; the story drifted like wood smoke through the September evening. It was with expectancy, with elation, that, as we turned down a side street, I saw the light of George Passant's sitting room shining through an orange blind.

At that time, I had known George for a couple of years. I had met him just through the chance that he gave his law lectures at the School – and that was because he wanted to earn some extra money, since he was only a qualified clerk at Eden & Martineau's, not a member of their solicitors' firm. It had been a lucky encounter for me: and

George had already exerted himself on my behalf more than anyone I knew.

This was the only house in the town open to us at any hour of night. Jack knocked: George came to the door himself.

'I'm sorry we're bothering you, George,' said Jack. 'But something's happened.'

'Come in,' said George, 'come in.'

His voice was loud and emphatic. He stood just over middle height, an inch or two taller than Jack; his shoulders were heavy, he was becoming a little fat, though he was only twenty-six. But it was his head that captured one's attention, his massive forehead and the powerful structure of chin and cheekbone under his full flesh.

He led the way into his sitting room. He said: 'Wouldn't you like a cup of tea? I can easily make a cup of tea. Perhaps you'd prefer a glass of beer? I'm sure there's some beer somewhere.'

The invitation was affable and diffident. He began to call us Cotery and Eliot, then corrected himself and used our Christian names. He went clumsily round the room, peering into cupboards, dishevelling his fair hair in surprise when he found nothing. The room was littered with papers; papers on the table and on the floor, a briefcase on the hearth, a pile of books beside an armchair. An empty teacup stood on a sheet of paper on the mantelpiece, and had left a trail of dark, moist rings. And yet, apart from his debris of work, George had not touched the room; the furniture was all his landlady's; on one wall there remained a text 'The Lord God Watcheth Us', and over the mantelpiece a picture of the Relief of Ladysmith.

At last George shouted, and carried three bottles of beer to the table.

'Now,' said George, sitting back in his armchair, 'we can get down to it. What is this problem?'

Jack told the story of Roy and the present. As he had done to me, he kept back this morning's interview with Calvert. He put more colour into the story now that he was telling it to George, though: 'This boy is Olive's cousin, you realise, George. And that whole family seems to live on its nerves.'

'I don't accept that completely about Olive,' said George. Olive was one of what we called the 'group', the collection of young people who had gathered round George.

'Still, I'm very much to blame,' said Jack. 'I ought to have seen what was happening. It's serious for Roy too, that I didn't. I was very blind.'

Then Jack laid the cigarette case on the table.

George smiled, but did not examine it, nor pick it up.

'Well, I'm sorry for the boy,' he said. 'But he doesn't come inside my province, so there's no action I can take. It would give me considerable pleasure, however, to tell his father that, if he sends a son to one of those curious institutions called public schools, he has no right to be surprised at the consequences. I should also like to add that people get on best when they're given freedom – particularly freedom from their damned homes, and their damned parents, and their damned lives.'

He simmered down, and spoke to Jack with a warmth that was transparently genuine, open, and curiously shy. 'I can't tell him most of the things I should like to. But no one can stop me from telling him a few remarks about you.'

'I didn't intend to involve you, George,' said Jack.

'I don't think you could prevent me,' said George, 'if it seemed necessary. But it can't be necessary, of course.'

With his usual active optimism, George seized on the saving point: it was the point that had puzzled me: Calvert would only raise whispers about his son if he penalised Jack.

'Unfortunately,' said Jack, 'he doesn't seem to work that way.'

'What do you mean?'

Jack described his conversation with Calvert that morning. George, flushed and angry, still kept interrupting with his sharp, lawyer's questions: 'It's incredible that he could take that line. Don't you see that he *couldn't* let this letter get mixed up with your position in the firm?'

At last Jack complained: 'I'm not inventing it for fun, George.'

'I'm sorry,' said George. 'Well, what did the sunket tell you in the end?'

George just heard him out: no future in the firm, permission to stay in his present job on sufferance, the School course cut off: then George swore. He swore as though the words were fresh, as though the brute physical facts lay in front of his eyes. It takes a great religion to produce one great oath, in the mouths of most men: but not in George's, once inflamed to indignation. When the outburst had spent itself, he said: 'It's monstrous. It's so monstrous that even these bellwethers can't get away with it. I refuse to believe that they can amuse themselves with being unjust and stupid at the same time – and at the expense of people like you.'

'People like me don't strike them as quite so important,' said Jack.

'You will before long. Good God alive, in ten years' time you will have made them realise that they've been standing in the road of their betters.' There was a silence, in which George looked at Jack. Then, with an effort, George said: 'I expect some of your relations are ready to deal with your present situation. But in case you don't want to call on them, I wonder – '

'George, as far as help goes just now,' Jack replied, 'I can't call on a soul in the world.'

'If you feel like that,' said George, 'I wonder if you'd mind letting me see what I can do? I know that I'm not a very suitable person for the present circumstances,' he went on quickly. 'I haven't any influence, of course. And Arthur Morcom and Lewis here always say that I'm not specially tactful in dealing with these people. I think perhaps they exaggerate that: anyway, I should try to surmount it in a good cause. But if you can find anyone else more adequate, you obviously ought to rule me out and let them take it up.'

As George stumbled through this awkward speech, Jack was moved; and at the end he looked chastened, almost ashamed of himself.

'I only came for advice, George,' he said.

'I might not be able to do anything effective,' said George. 'I don't pretend it's easy. But if you feel like letting me – '

'Well, as long as you don't waste too much effort – '

'If I do it,' said George, returning to his loud, cheerful tone, 'I shall do it in my own style. All settled?'

'Thank you, George.'

'Excellent,' said George, 'excellent.'

He refilled our glasses, drank off his own, settled again in his chair, and said: 'I'm very glad you two came round tonight.'

'It was Lewis' idea,' said Jack.

'You were waiting for me to suggest it,' I said.

'No, no,' said Jack. 'I tell you, I never have useful ideas about myself. Perhaps that's the trouble with me. I don't possess a project. All you others manage to get projects; and if you don't George provides one for you. As with you, Lewis, and your examinations. While I'm the only one left – ' he was passing off my gibe, and had got his own back: but even so, he brought off his mock pathos so well that he disarmed me – 'I'm the only one left, singing in the cold.'

'We may have to consider that, too.' George was chuckling at Jack; then the chuckles began to bubble again inside him, at a thought of his own. 'Yes, I was a year younger than you, and I hadn't got a project either,' he said. 'I had just been articled to my first firm, the one at Wickham. And one morning the junior partner decided to curse me for my manner of life. He kept saying firmly: if ever you want to become a solicitor, you've got to behave like one beforehand. At that age, I was always prepared to consider reasonable suggestions from people with inside knowledge: I was pleased that he'd given me something to aim at. Though I wasn't very clear how a solicitor ought to behave. However, I gave up playing snooker at the pub, and I gave up going in to Ipswich on Saturday nights to inspect the local talent. I put on my best dark suit and I bought a bowler hat and a briefcase. There it is – ' George pointed to the hearth. Tears were being forced to his eyes by inner laughter; he wiped them, and went on: 'Unfortunately, though I didn't realise it then, these manoeuvres seem to have irritated the *senior* partner. He stood it for a fortnight, then one day he walked behind me to the office. I was just hanging up my hat when he started to curse me. "I don't know what you're playing at," he said. "It will be time enough to behave like a solicitor if ever you manage to become one." '

George roared with laughter. It was midnight, and soon afterwards we left. Standing in the door, George said, as Jack began to walk down the dark street: 'I'll see you tomorrow night. I shall have thought over your business by then.'

2

Conference at Night

THE next night George was lecturing at the School. I attended, and we went out of the room together; Jack was waiting in the corridor.

'We go straight to see Olive,' said George, bustling kindly to the point. 'I've told her to bring news of the Calverts.'

Jack's face lit up: he seemed more uneasy than the night before.

We went to a café which stayed open all night, chiefly for lorry drivers working between London and the North; it was lit by gas mantles without shades, and smelt of gas, paraffin and the steam of tea. The window was opaque with steam, and we could not see Olive until we got inside: but she was there, sitting with Rachel in the corner of the room, behind a table with a linoleum cover.

'I'm sorry you're being got at, Jack,' Olive said.

'I expect I shall get used to it,' said Jack, with the mischievous, ardent smile that was first nature to him when he spoke to a pretty woman.

'I expect you will,' said Olive.

'Come on,' said George. 'I want to hear your report about your family. I oughtn't to raise false hopes' – he turned to Jack – 'I can only think of one way of intervening for you. And the only chance of that depends on whether the Calverts have committed themselves.'

We were close together, round the table. George sat at the end; though he was immersed in the struggle, his hearty appetite went mechanically on; and, while he was speaking intently to Jack, he munched a thick sandwich from which the ham stuck out, and stirred a great cup of tea with a lead spoon.

'Well then,' George asked Olive, 'how is your uncle taking it?'

We looked at her; she smiled. She was wearing a brilliant green dress that gleamed incongruously against the peeling wall. Just by her clothes a stranger could have judged that she was the only one of us born in a secure middle-class home. Secure in money, that is: for her father lived on notoriously bad terms with his brother, Jack's employer; and Olive herself had half-broken away from her own family.

She had taken her hat off, and her fair hair shone against the green. Watching her as she smiled at George's question, I felt for an instant that there was something assertive in her frank, handsome face.

'How are they taking it?' George asked.

'It's fluttered the dovecotes,' she said. 'I'm not surprised. Father heard about it this morning from one of my aunts. They've all done a good deal of talking to Uncle Frank since then.'

'What's he doing?' said George.

'He's dithering,' said Olive. 'He can't make up his mind what he ought to do next. All day he's been saying that it's a pity the holidays last another week – otherwise the best thing would be to send the boy straight back to school.'

'Good God alive,' said George. 'That's a singularly penetrating observation.'

'Anyway,' said Olive, 'the rest of the family seem to have worn him down. He'd made a decision of sorts just before I came along here. He's sending a wire to Roy's housemaster to ask if he can look after the boy – '

'Has that wire been sent?' George interrupted.

'It must have been, by now,' Olive replied.

'Don't you realise how vital that is?' cried George, impatient that anyone should miss a point in tactics.

Olive did not answer, and went on: 'That's all he's plucked up his courage to do. They couldn't bully him into anything stronger. He tries to talk as though Roy was just a bit overworked and only needed a change of air. If I'd performed any of these antics at his age, I should have been in for the biggest hiding of my life. But his father never could control a daughter, let alone a son.'

George was preoccupied with her news; but at her last remark he roused himself.

'You know it's no use pretending to believe in that sadistic nonsense here.'

'I never have pretended to believe in all your beautiful dreams, have I?' she said.

'You can't take sides with those sunkets against me,' said George.

His voice had risen. We were used to the odd Suffolk words as his temper flamed up. Olive was flushed, her face still apart from her full, excitable mouth. Yet, hot-tempered as they both were, they never quarrelled for long: she understood him by instinct, better than any of us at this time. And George was far more easy with her than with Rachel, who stored away every word he spoke and who said at this moment: 'I agree, oh! of course I agree, George. We must help people to fulfil themselves – '

She was the oldest of us there, a year or more older than George: Olive was the same age as Jack and me. When Rachel gushed, it was disconcerting to notice that, in her plump, moon face, her eyes were bright, twinkling, and shrewd.

'In any case,' George said to Olive, 'there's no time tonight to resurrect matters that I've settled with you long ago. We've got more important things to do: as you'd see yourself, if you realised the meaning of your own words.'

'What do you mean?'

'You've given us a chance,' said George. 'Don't you see, your sunket of an uncle has taken two steps? He's penalised Jack: in the present state of things he can do that with impunity. But he's *also* sent messages to a schoolmaster about his son. The coincidence ought to put him in a distinctly less invulnerable position.'

'He's taking it out of Jack,' she said. 'But how can anyone stop him?'

'It's not impossible,' said George. 'It's no use trying to persuade Calvert, of course: none of us have any standing to protest direct to him. But remember that part of his manoeuvre was to cut off Jack's fees at the School – ' he reminded us that this step would, as a matter of routine, come before the committee which governed the affairs of students at the School – a committee on which Calvert served, as the originator of the scheme of 'bursaries'. By this scheme, employers picked out bright young men as Calvert had picked out Jack, and contributed half their fees. The School remitted the rest.

'It's a piece of luck, his being on the damned committee,' said George. 'We've only got to present our version of the coincidence. He can't let it be known that he's victimising Jack. And the others on the committee would fight very shy of lending a hand.'

'Would they all mind so much about injustice?' said Rachel.

'They mind being suspected of injustice,' said George, 'if it's pointed out to them. So does any body of men.'

'It can't be pointed out,' said Jack.

'It can,' said George. 'Canon Martineau happens to be on the committee. Though he's not a deeply religious man like his brother,' George burst into laughter. 'I can see that he's supplied with the truth. Our Martineau will make him listen.' ('Our Martineau' was the brother of the Canon and a partner in the firm of Eden & Martineau, where George worked.) 'And also – '

'And also what?' said Olive.

'I've a complete right to appear in front of the committee myself. Owing to my position at the School. It would be better if someone else put them right about Jack. But if necessary, I can do it.'

We were confused. My eyes met Olive's; like me, she was caught up in the struggle now; the excitement had got hold of us, we wanted to see it through. At the same instant, I knew that she too felt sharply nervous for George himself.

There was a moment's silence.

'I don't like it,' Olive broke out. 'You might pull off something for Jack. It sounds convincing: but then you're too good at arguing for me.'

15

'And you're always too optimistic,' I said. 'I don't believe that the Canon is going to make himself unpleasant for a young man he's never met. Even if you persuaded his brother, and I don't think that's likely either.'

'I'm not so sure,' said George. 'In any case, that doesn't cripple us. The essential point is that I can appear myself.'

'And how are *you* going to come out of it?' Olive cried.

'Are you certain that it won't rebound on you, personally?' asked Jack. He had turned away from Olive, angry that she made him speak against his own interest.

'I don't see how it could,' said George.

From his inside pocket he took out a sheet of notepaper and smoothed it on the table. Olive watched him anxiously.

'Look here,' she said, 'you oughtn't to be satisfied with looking after your protégés much longer. We're not important enough for you to waste all your time on us. You've got to look after yourself instead. That means you'll have to persuade Eden and Martineau to make you a partner. And they just won't do it if you've deliberately made a nuisance of yourself with important people. Don't you see,' she added, with a sudden violence, 'that you may soon curse yourself for ever having been satisfied with looking after us?'

George had begun to write on the sheet of paper. He looked up and said: 'I'm extremely content as I am. I want you to realise that I'd rather spend my time with people I value than balance teacups with the local bellwethers.'

'That's because you're shy with them,' said Olive. 'Why, you've even given up going to Martineau's Friday nights.'

'I intend to go this Friday.' George had coloured. He looked abashed for the first time that night. 'And by the way, if I ever do want to become a partner, I don't think there should be any tremendous difficulty. Whatever happens, I can always count on Martineau's support.' He turned back to writing his letter.

'That's true, clearly. I've heard Martineau talk about George,' said Jack.

'You're not impartial,' said Olive. 'George, is that a letter to the committee?'

'It isn't final. I was just letting the Principal know that I might conceivably have a piece of business to bring before them.'

'I still don't like it. You're – '

Just then Arthur Morcom entered the café and walked across to Olive's side. He had recently started practice as a dentist in the town, and only met our group because he was a friend of Olive's. I knew that he was in love with her. Tonight he had called to take her home; looking at her, he felt at once the disagreement and excitement in the air.

Olive asked George: 'Do you mind if we tell Arthur?'

'Not as far as I am concerned,' said George, a little awkwardly.

Morcom had already heard the story of the boy's gift. I was set to explain what George was planning. I did it rapidly. Morcom's keen blue eyes were bright with interest, and he said 'Yes! yes!' urging me on through the last hour's conference; I watched his thin, fine-featured face, on which an extra crease, engraved far out on each cheek, gave a special dryness and sympathy to his smile. When I had finished, he said:

'I am rather worried, George. I can't help feeling that Olive is right.' He turned to Jack and apologised for coming down in the opposing camp. Jack smiled. When Olive had been trying to persuade George, Jack had been hurt and angry: but, now Morcom did the same thing, Jack said quite spontaneously: 'I bear no malice, Arthur. I dare say you're right.'

Morcom raised both the arguments that Olive and I had tried: would George's intervention really help Jack? and, more strongly, wasn't it an indiscreet, a dangerous move for George himself? Morcom pressed them with more authority than we had been able to. He and George were not close friends; neither was quite at ease with the other; but Morcom was George's own age, and George had a respect for his competence and sense. So George listened, showed flashes of his temper, and defended himself with his elaborate reasonableness.

At last Morcom said: 'I know you want to stop your friends being kept under. But you won't have the power to do it till you're firmly established yourself. Isn't it worthwhile to wait till then?'

'No,' said George. 'I've seen too much of that sort of waiting. If you wait till then, you forget that anyone is being kept under: or else you decide that he deserves it.'

Morcom was not only a more worldly man than George, he was usually wiser. But later on, I thought of George's statement as an example of when it was the unworldly who were wise.

'I shall soon begin to think,' said Morcom, 'that you're anxious to attack the bellwethers, George.'

'On the contrary,' George replied, 'I am a very timid man.'

There was a burst of laughter: but Olive, watching him, did not join in. A moment after, she said: 'He's made up his mind.'

'Is it any use my saying any more?' said Morcom.

'Well,' said George, with a shy smile, 'I'm still convinced that we can put them into an impossible position…'

3

View Over the Gardens

OUR meeting in the café took place on a Wednesday; two days later, on the Friday afternoon, Olive rang me up at the office. 'Roy has found something out from his father. George ought to know at once, but I can't get hold of him. It's his day at Melton, isn't it?' (The firm of Eden & Martineau had branches in several market towns: and George regularly spent a day a week in the country.) 'He must know before he goes to Martineau's tonight.'

Her voice sounded brusque but anxious; she wanted someone to see Roy, to examine the news. Jack was the obvious person, but him Roy was forbidden to meet. She asked me to go along to Morcom's as soon as I was free; she would take Roy there.

I walked to Morcom's flat in the early evening. The way led from the centre of the town, and suddenly took one between box hedges and five-storey, gabled, Victorian houses, whose red brick flared in the sunset with a grotesque and Gothic cosiness. But the cosiness vanished, when one saw their dark windows: once, when the town was smaller, they had been real houses: now they were offices, shut for the night. Only Martineau's, at the end of the New Walk, remained a solid private house. The one next door, which he also owned, had been turned into flats: and there Morcom lived, on the top floor.

When I went into his sitting room, Olive and Roy had just arrived. Olive had brought Morcom a great bunch of deep red dahlias, and she was arranging them on a table by the window. The red blazed as one looked down over the park, where the New Walk came to an end.

Olive put a flower into place: then, turning away from the bowl, she asked Morcom, 'Will they do?'

Morcom smiled at her. And he, the secretive and restrained, could not prevent the smile giving him completely away – more than a smile by Jack would ever do.

As though recovering himself, Morcom turned to Roy, who had stood quietly by, watching the interplay over the flowers. Morcom at once got him into conversation.

Happy because of Olive, Morcom was more than ever careful and considerate. They talked about books, and Roy's future; he was just beginning to specialise at school. They got on very well. As it happened, Morcom need not have been so careful; for Roy surprised us both by being entirely self-possessed, and himself opened the real topic.

'I'm sorry to give you all so much trouble, Mr Morcom,' he said. 'But I did think someone should know what they're doing about Mr Passant.'

He spoke politely, formally, in a light, musical voice: so politely that sometimes there sounded a ripple of mischief. His face was good-looking, highly-strung, and very sad for a boy's: but sad, I felt, as much by nature as by his present trouble. Once or twice he broke into a gay, charming smile.

'I've told Olive already – but last night someone visited my father unexpectedly. I got Mother to tell me about it this morning. It was the Principal of – what Jack used to call the School. He had come to tell Father that a Mr Passant might be trying to make a fuss. Mother didn't mention it, of course, but I guessed it was about Jack. And it was all connected with a committee, which I didn't understand at the time. But Olive explained it this afternoon.'

'I had to tell him what George decided to do on Wednesday,' said Olive.

'I shan't let it out,' said Roy. 'I shouldn't have told Olive what I found out this morning – if these things weren't happening because of me.'

I tried to reassure him, but he shook his head.

'It's my fault,' he said. 'They wouldn't have been talking about Mr Passant last night if it hadn't been for me.'

'Do you know anything they said?' I asked.

'I think the Principal offered to deal with Mr Passant himself. He was sure that he could be stopped from going any further.'

'How.'

'By dropping a hint to Mr Eden and Mr Martineau,' said Roy.

I looked at Morcom: we were both disturbed.

'You think that will soon happen?' I said.

'Mother expected the Principal to see them this morning. You see,' said Roy, 'they all seem more angry with Mr Passant than they were with Jack.'

He saw that our expressions had become grave.

'Is this very serious?' he said.

'It might be a little uncomfortable, that's all,' said Morcom lightly, to ease Roy's mind. But he was still watching us, and said:

'Do you mind if I ask another question, Mr Morcom?'

'Of course not.'

'Are you thinking that it has ruined Jack's chances for good?'

'This can't affect them,' I said quickly, and Morcom agreed.

'You mustn't worry about that, Roy,' Olive said.

Roy half-believed her; her tone was kind, she cared for him more than she had admitted on Wednesday night. He was still doubtful, however, until she added:

'If you want to know, we were thinking whether they can do any harm to George Passant.'

The boy's fears lifted; for a few moments his precocity seemed to leave him, and he teased Olive as though the other three of us were not still harassed.

'Are you fond of Mr Passant, Olive?' he asked, with his lively smile.

'In a way,' she said.

'Are you sweet on him?'

'Not in the least,' she replied. She paused, then said vehemently: 'But I can tell you this: he's worth twenty Jack Coterys.'

A little later, they went away. Before they left, Roy shook hands with us both; and, as Morcom and Olive were talking together, Roy said quietly to me: 'I'm being whisked off tomorrow. I don't suppose I shall see you again for a long time, Mr Eliot. But could you spare a minute to send me word how things turn out?'

From the window, Morcom and I watched them walk across the gardens.

'I wonder what sort of life he'll have,' said Morcom. But he was thinking, hopefully that night, of himself and Olive.

We stayed by the window, eating bread and cheese from his pantry, and keeping a watch on the road below; for we had to warn George before he arrived next door, on his visit to Martineau's at home.

4

A Cup of Coffee Spilt in a Drawing-Room

THE lamplighter passed up the road; under the lamp by Martineau's gate, the hedge top suddenly shone out of the dusk. Looking down over the gardens, Morcom was content to be quiet.

Just then, thinking how much I liked him, I felt too how he could never have blown so many of us into more richly coloured lives, as George had done. Where should we have been, if George had not come to Eden & Martineau's?

Where should we have been? We were poor and young. By birth we fell into the ragtag and bobtail of the lower middle classes. Then we fell into our jobs in offices and shops. We lived in our bed-sitting rooms, as I did since my mother's death, or with our families, lost among the fifty thousand houses in the town. The world seemed on the march, we wanted to join in, but we felt caught.

Myself, but for George, I might still have been earning my two pounds a week as a clerk in the education department, and wondering what to do with a legacy of £300 from an aunt. I should have acted in the end, perhaps, but nineteen is a misty age: while George gave me no rest, bullied and denounced me until I started studying law and reading for the Bar examinations. A month before Jack's crisis I had at last stopped procrastinating, and arranged to leave the office at the end of this September.

And so with the others in George's group – except Jack, who had been the unlucky one. George had set us moving, lent us money: he never seemed to think twice about lending us money, out of his income of £250 from the firm, together with an extra £30 from the School. It was the first time we had been so near to a generous-hearted man.

We became excited over the books he told us to read and the views he stood by, violent, argumentative, four square. We were carried away by his belief in human beings and ourselves. And we speculated, we could not help but speculate, about George himself. Olive certainly soon knew, and Jack and I not long afterwards, that he was not a simple character, unmixed, all of a piece. We felt, though, and nothing could shake us, that he was a man warm with broad, living nature; not good nature or bad nature, but simple nature; he was a man of flesh and bone.

I thought this, as I saw him at last walking in the lamplight, whistling, swinging his stick, his bowler hat (which he punctiliously wore when on professional business) pushed on to the back of his head.

I shouted down. George met us on the stairs: it did not take long to explain the news. He swore.

We went back to Morcom's flat to let him think it out. For minutes he sat, silent and preoccupied. Then he declared, with his extraordinary, combative optimism: 'I expect Martineau will get me to stay behind after we've finished the social flummeries. It will give me a perfect opportunity to provide him with the whole truth. They've probably presented us with the best possible way of getting it home to the Canon.'

But George was nervous as we entered Martineau's drawing room – though perhaps no more nervous than he always felt when forced to go through the 'social flummeries', even the mild parties of Martineau's Friday nights. He only faced this one tonight because of Olive's nagging; while the rest of us went regularly, enjoyed them, and prized Martineau's traditional form of invitation to 'drop in for coffee, *or whatever's going*' – though after a few visits, we learned that coffee was going by itself.

'Glad to see you all,' cried Martineau. 'It's not a full night tonight.' There were, in fact, only a handful of people in the room; he never knew what numbers to expect, and on the table by the fireplace stood files of shining empty cups and saucers; while in front of the fire two canisters with long handles were keeping warm, still nearly full of coffee and milk, more than we should ever want tonight.

Morcom and I sat down. George walked awkwardly towards the cups and saucers; he felt there was something he should do; he felt there was some mysterious etiquette he had never been taught. He stood by the table and changed his weight from foot to foot: his cheeks were pink.

Then Martineau said: 'It's a long time since you dropped in, George, isn't it? Don't you think it's a bit hard if I only catch sight of my friends in the office? You know it's good to have you here.'

George smiled. In Martineau's company he could not remain uncomfortable for long. Even when Martineau went on: 'Talking of my friends in the office, I think Harry Eden is going to give us a look in tonight.'

George's expression became clouded, stayed clouded until Martineau baited him in his friendly manner. The remark about Eden had revived our warning: more, it made George think of a man with whom he was ill-at-ease; but no one responded to affection more quickly, and, as Martineau talked, George could put away unpleasant thoughts, and be happy with someone he liked.

We all enjoyed listening to Martineau. His conversation was gay, unpredictable and eccentric; he had a passion, an almost *mischievous* passion, for religious controversies, and he loved to tell us on Friday nights that he had been accused of yet another heresy. It did not matter to him in the slightest that none of us was religious, even in any of his senses; he was a spontaneous person, and his 'scrapes', as he called them, had to be told to someone. So he described his latest letter in an obscure theological journal, and the irritated replies. 'They say I'm getting dangerously near Manichaeism now,' he announced cheerfully tonight.

George chuckled. He had accepted all Martineau's oddities: and it seemed in order that Martineau should stand in front of his fire, in his morning coat with the carnation in the buttonhole, and tell us of some plan for puzzling the orthodox. It did not occur to any of us that he was fifty and going through the climacteric which makes some men restless at that age. His wife had died two years before; we did not notice that, in the last twelve months, the eccentricities had been brimming over.

Like George, we expected that he would stay as he was this Friday night, standing on his hearthrug, pulling his black tie into place over his wing collar. I persuaded him to read a letter from a choleric country parson; Martineau smiled over the abusive references to himself, and read them in a lilting voice with his head on one side and his long nose tip-tilted into the air.

Then George teased him affectionately about his religious observances; which seemed, indeed, as eccentric as his beliefs. He had long ago left the Church of England, and still carried on a running controversy with his brother, the Canon; he now acted as steward in the town's most respectable Methodist congregation. There he went with regularity, with enjoyment, twice each Sunday; but he confessed, with laughter and almost with pride, that he reckoned to 'get off' to sleep before any sermon was under weigh.

'Did you manage to get off last Sunday, Mr Martineau?' said George.

'I did in the morning, George. But at night we had a stranger preaching – and there was something disturbing about his tone of voice.'

George beamed with laughter; he sank back into his armchair, and surveyed the room; it was a pleasant room, lofty, painted cream, with a print of Ingres' *Source* on the wall opposite the fireplace. For once, he did not want his evening in respectable society to end.

And Jack, who came in for half an hour, guessed that all was well. He had been warned by Olive that pressure might be used upon George; but George was so surprisingly at home that Jack's own spirits became high. He left early: soon afterwards the room thinned out, and only George, Morcom and I stayed with Martineau.

Then Eden came in. He walked across the room to the fireplace.

George had half-risen from his chair as soon as he saw Eden: and now stayed in suspense, his hands on the arms of his chair, uncertain whether to offer it. But Eden, who was apologising to Martineau, did not notice him.

'I'm sorry I'm so late, Howard,' Eden said affably to Martineau. 'My wife has some people in, and I couldn't escape a hand of cards.'

The dome of his head was bald; his face was broad and open, and his lips easily flew up at the corners into an amiable smile. He was a few years older than his partner, and looked more their profession by all signs but one: he dressed in a more modern, informal mode. Tonight he was wearing a comfortable grey lounge suit which rode easily on his substantial figure. Talking to Martineau, he warmed a substantial seat before the fire.

George made a false start, and then said: 'Wouldn't you like to sit down, Mr Eden?'

At last Eden attended.

'I don't see why I should turn you out, Passant,' he said. 'To tell you the truth, I don't really want to leave the fire.'

But George was still half-standing, and Eden went on: 'Still, if you insist on making yourself uncomfortable – '

Eden settled into George's chair. Martineau said: 'Will you be kind, George, and give Harry Eden a cup of coffee?'

Busily George set about the task. He lifted the big canister and filled a cup. The cup in hand, he turned to Eden: 'Will that be all right, Mr Eden?'

'Well, do you know, I think I'd like it white.'

George was in a hurry to apologise. He went to put the cup down on the table: Eden, thinking George was giving him the cup, held out a hand: George could not miss the inside of Eden's forearm, and the coffee flew over Eden's coat and the thigh of his trousers.

For an instant George stood immobile. He blushed from forehead to neck.

When he managed to say that he was sorry, Eden replied in an annoyed tone: 'It was entirely my fault.' He was vigorously rubbing himself with his handkerchief. Breaking out of his stupor, George tried to help, but Eden said: 'I can look after it, Passant, I can look after it perfectly well.'

George went on his knees, and attempted to mop up the pool of coffee on the carpet: then Martineau made him sit down, and gave him a cigarette.

Actually, if it was anyone's fault, it was Eden's. But I knew that George could not believe it.

Martineau set us in conversation again. Eden joined in. After a few minutes, however, I noticed a glance pass between them: and it was Martineau who said to George: 'I was very glad to see your friend Cotery tonight. How is he getting on, by the way, George?'

George had not spoken since he tried to dry Eden down. He hesitated, and said: 'In many ways, he's doing remarkably well. He's just having to get over a certain amount of trouble in his firm. But – '

Eden looked at Martineau, and said:

'Why, do you know, Passant, I meant to have a word with Howard about that very thing tonight. I didn't expect to see you here, of course, but perhaps I might mention it now. We're all friends within these four walls, aren't we? As a matter of fact, Howard and I happened to be told that you were trying to steer this young man through some difficulties.'

Eden was trying to sound casual and friendly: he had taken the chance of speaking in front of Morcom and myself, who had originally been asked to Friday nights as friends of George's. But George's reply was edged with suspicion: I felt sure that he was more suspicious, more ready to be angry, because of the spilt cup.

'I should like to know who happened to tell you, Mr Eden.'

'I scarcely think we're free to disclose that,' said Eden.

'If that is the case,' said George, 'at least I should like to be certain that you were given the correct version.'

'Tell us, George, tell us,' Martineau put in. Eden nodded his head. Hotly, succinctly, George told the story that I had heard several times by now: the story of the gift, the victimisation of Jack.

Martineau looked upset at the account of the boy's infatuation, but Eden leant back in his chair with an acquiescent smile.

'These things will happen,' he said. 'These things will happen.'

George finished by describing the penalties to Jack. 'They are too serious for no one to raise a finger,' said George.

'So you are thinking of protesting on his behalf, are you?'

'I am,' said George.

'As a matter of fact, we heard that you intended to take up the matter – through a committee at the School, is that right?'

'Quite right.'

'I don't want to interfere, Passant.' Eden gave a short smile, and brought his fingertips together. 'But do you think that this is the most judicious way of going about it? You know, it might still be possible to patch up something behind the scenes.'

'I'm afraid there's no chance of that. It's important to realise, Mr Eden,' George said, 'that Cotery has no influence whatever. I don't mean that he hasn't much influence: I mean that he has no single person to speak for him in the world.'

'That is absolutely true,' Morcom said quietly to Eden in a level, reasonable tone. 'And Passant won't like to bring this out himself, but it puts him in a difficult position: if he didn't try to act, no one would.'

'It's very unfortunate for Cotery, of course,' said Eden. 'I quite see that. But you can't consider, Morcom, can you, that Passant is going the right way about it? It only raises opposition when you try to rush people off their feet.'

'I rather agree,' said Morcom. 'In fact, I told Passant my opinion a couple of nights ago. It was the same as yours.'

'I'm glad of that,' said Eden. 'Because I know that Passant thinks that when we get older we like to take the course of least resistance. There's something in it, I'm afraid, there's something in it. But he can't hold that against you. You see, Passant,' he went on, 'we're all

29

agreed that it's very unfortunate for Cotery. That doesn't mean, though, that we want to see you do something hasty. After all, there's plenty of time. This is a bit of a setback for him, but he's a bright young chap. With patience, he's bound to make good in the end.'

'He's twenty,' said George. 'He's just the age when a man is desperate without something ahead. You can't tell a man to wait *years* at that age.'

'That's all very well,' said Eden.

'I can't bring myself to recommend patience,' said George, 'when it's someone else who has to exercise it.'

George was straining to keep his temper down, and Eden's smile had become perfunctory.

'So you intend to make a gesture,' said Eden. 'I've always found that most gestures do more harm than good.'

'I'm afraid that I don't regard this as a gesture,' said George.

Eden frowned, paused, and went on: 'There is another point, Passant. I didn't particularly want to make it. And I don't want to lay too much emphasis on it. But if you go ahead, it might conceivably raise some personal difficulties for Howard and myself – since we are, in a way, connected with you.'

'They suggested this morning that you were responsible, I suppose?' George cried.

'I shouldn't say that was actually suggested, should you, Howard?' said Eden.

'In any case,' said George, 'I consider they were using an intolerably unfair weapon in approaching you.'

'I think perhaps they were,' said Eden. 'I think perhaps they were. But that doesn't affect the fact.'

'If we were all strictly fair, George,' said Martineau, 'not much information would get round, would it?'

George asked Eden: 'Did you make these people realise that I was acting as a private person?'

'My dear Passant, you ought to know that one can't draw these distinctions. If you – not to put too fine a point on it – choose to make a fool of yourself among some influential people, then Howard and I will come in for a share of the blame.'

'I can draw these distinctions,' said George, 'and, if you will authorise me, I can make them extremely clear to these – to your sources of information.'

'That would only add to the mischief,' said Eden.

There was quiet for a moment. Then George said: 'I shall have to ask you a definite question. You are not implying, Mr Eden, that this action of mine cuts across my obligations to the firm?'

'I don't intend to discuss it in those terms,' said Eden. 'I've been talking in a purely friendly manner among friends. In my opinion you'd do us all a service by sleeping on it, Passant. That's all I'm prepared to say. And now, if you'll forgive me, Howard, I'm afraid that I must go and get some sleep myself.'

We heard his footsteps down the path and the click of the latch. George stared at the carpet. Without looking up he said to Martineau: 'I'm sorry that I've spoiled your evening.'

'Don't be silly, George. Harry Eden always was clumsy with the china.' Martineau had followed George's eyes to the stain on the carpet, and spoke as though he knew that, in George's mind, the spill was rankling more even than the quarrel. Martineau went on: 'As for your little disagreement, of course you know that Harry was trying to smooth the matter down.'

George did not respond, but in a moment burst out: 'I should like to explain to you, Mr Martineau. I know you believe that I should be careful about doing harm to the firm. I thought it over as thoroughly as I could: I'm capable of deceiving myself occasionally, but I don't think I did this time. I decided that it would cause a whiff of gossip – I admit that, naturally – but it wouldn't lose us a single case. You'd have made the same decision: except that you wouldn't have deliberated quite so long.' George was speaking fervently, naturally, with complete trust. I wished that he could have spoken in that way to Eden – if only for a few words.

'I'm a cautious old creature, George,' said Martineau.

'Cautious! Why, you'd bring the whole town down on our heads if you felt that some clerk, whom you'd never seen, wasn't free to attend the rites of a schismatic branch of the Greek Orthodox Church – in which you yourself, of course, passionately disbelieved.' George gave a friendly roar of laughter. 'Or have you been tempted by some new branch of the Orthodox lately?'

'Not yet,' Martineau chuckled. 'Not yet.'

Then George said:

'I expect you understood my position right from the start, Mr Martineau. After Mr Eden's remarks, though, I should like to hear that you approve.'

Martineau hesitated. Then he smiled, choosing his words: 'I don't consider you a man who needs approval, George. And it's my duty to dissuade you, as Harry did. You mustn't take it that I'm not dissuading you.' He hesitated again. 'But I think I understand what you feel.'

George listened to the evasive reply: he may have heard within it another appeal to stop, subtler than Eden's, because of the liking between himself and Martineau. He replied, seriously and simply: 'You know that I'm not going into this for my own amusement. I'm not searching out an injustice just for the pleasure of trampling on it. I might have done once, but I shouldn't now. You've understood, of course: something needs to be done for Cotery, and I'm the only man who can do it.'

5

George's Attack

THE meeting of the School committee was summoned for the following Wednesday. I knew before George, since the notice passed through my hands in the education office. And, by asking a parting favour from an acquaintance, I got myself the job of taking the minutes.

On Tuesday night, I thought that I might be wasting the effort: for a strong rumour came from Olive that Jack himself had pleaded with George to go no further. But when I saw George later that night, and asked, 'What about tomorrow?' he replied: 'I'm ready for it. And ready to celebrate afterwards.'

I arrived at the Principal's room at ten minutes to six the next evening. The gas fire was burning; the Principal was writing at his desk under a shaded light; the room seemed solid and official, though the shelves and chairs were carved in pine, in a firm plain style which the School was now teaching.

The Principal looked up as I laid the minute book on a small table; he was called Cameron, and had reddish hair and jutting eyebrows.

'Good evening. I am sorry that we have to trespass on your time,' he said. He always showed a deliberate consideration to subordinates; but from duty, not from instinct. At this time he probably did not know that I attended lectures at the School.

Then Miss Geary, the vice-principal, entered. 'It was for six o'clock?' she said. They exchanged a few remarks about School business: it was easy to hear that there was no friendliness between them. But the temperature of friendliness in the room mounted rapidly when, by the side of Canon Martineau, Beddow came in. He was a Labour councillor, a brisk, cordial, youngish man, very much on the rise; he had a word for everyone, including an aside for me – 'Minuting a committee means they think well of you up at the office. I know it does.'

'I suppose we're waiting for Calvert as usual,' said Canon Martineau, who had a slight resemblance to his brother, but spoke with a drier and more sardonic tang. 'And can anyone tell me how long this meeting is likely to last?'

'No meeting ever seems likely to last long until you've been in it a few hours,' said Beddow cheerfully. 'But anyway, the sooner we begin this, the sooner we shall get through.'

Ten minutes later, Calvert appeared, a small bald man, pink and panting from hurry. Beddow shook his hand warmly and pulled out a chair for him at the committee table.

'I hope you won't mind sitting by me,' he said. He chatted to Calvert for a few moments about investments; and then briskly, but without any implication that Calvert was late, said: 'Well, gentlemen, we've got a certain amount ahead of us tonight. If you don't object I think we might as well begin.'

The City Education Committee was made up partly from councillors and partly from others, like the Canon: in its turn it appointed this one, *ad hoc*: and so Beddow took the chair. He, with Calvert on his right and the Principal on his left, sat looking towards the door, on the same side of the committee table: the Canon and Miss Geary occupied the ends of it. I worked at the smaller table behind theirs, and within reach of the Principal and Beddow.

The Principal read the minutes (I was there purely to record) and then Miss Geary interrupted.

'Can we take No. 6 first, Mr Chairman?' No. 6 on the agenda read: 'J Cotery. Termination of Bursary.' 'I believe Mr Passant wishes to make a statement. And I noticed that he was waiting in the staffroom.'

'I suggest that the first three items cannot conveniently wait,' said the Principal promptly. Beddow looked round the table.

'I think the feeling of the meeting is for taking those three items first,' he said. 'I'm sorry, Miss Geary: we shan't waste any unnecessary time.'

The three items were, in fact, mainly routine – fees for a new course in architecture, scholarships for next year. The clock on the Principal's desk was striking the third quarter when Beddow said: 'That polishes off your urgent business, doesn't it? Well, I suppose we're obliged to get No. 6 over some time. Perhaps this would be a convenient opportunity to have Mr Passant in.'

The Principal said nothing. Beddow went on: 'But, before I do ring for him, I should like to say something that we all feel. We are all more than sorry that Mr Calvert should be put in the position of having to listen to criticism – criticism of whether he should continue to pay an employee's fees or not. Perhaps he'll let me assure him, as a political opponent, that he has the reputation of being one of the best employers in this city. We all know that he has originated the very scheme over which he is being forced to listen to – unfortunate criticism. Perhaps I can say that one of the compensations for educational work in the city is the privilege of meeting men like Mr Calvert – political opponents though they may be – round the same friendly table.'

The Principal produced a loud, deliberate 'Hear, hear.' Calvert gave a quick, embarrassed smile, and went on scribbling on the pad of foolscap in front of him.

Beddow rang the bell: George was shown in.

'Ah, sit down there, Mr Passant. I'm sorry we've had to keep you so long,' Beddow, with his brisk, friendly smile. His affability was genuine at the root, but had become practised as he found it useful. He pointed out a small cane-bottomed chair on the other side of the table. George sat down; he was isolated from the others; they all looked at him.

'I'll now ask the Principal,' said Beddow, 'to speak to this business of the bursary.'

'This is really a very ordinary matter, Mr Chairman,' said the Principal. 'The Committee is aware of the conditions on which our bursaries are awarded. Owing to the inspiration of our benefactor, Mr Calvert' – the Canon smiled across at Calvert – 'various employers in the town have co-operated with us in paying the fees of young men of promise. No one has ever contemplated that this arrangement could not be cancelled in any particular case, if there appeared adequate reason to the employer or ourselves. There are several precedents. The present case is entirely straightforward. Cotery, the man in question, has been sent here by Mr Calvert; his course normally would extend over three years, of which he has completed one. But Mr Calvert has decided that there is no likelihood of his being able to use Cotery in a position for which this course would qualify him; and so, in the man's own best interests, he considers that his bursary here should be discontinued. Several of these cases, as I say, have been reported to the committee in previous years. The committee has always immediately approved the employer's recommendation.'

'As the Principal has told us,' Beddow said, 'we have always taken these cases as a matter of form... But Mr Passant, I believe, is interested in this young man Cotery, and has asked permission to attend this business tonight. After the Principal's statement, Mr Passant, is there anything that you want to say?'

'Yes, Mr Chairman, there are some things that I want to say,' said George. He had nowhere to rest his hands: he pulled down his waistcoat. But he was not resentful and defensive, as he had been with Eden the Friday night before. Four out of these five were against him: always ready to scent enemies, he must have known. Yet, now it had come to the moment, his voice was clear, masterful, and strong.

'First, this committee is responsible for appointing Cotery and it is responsible now if his support is withdrawn. The only consideration which such a committee can act upon is whether a man is making good use of his opportunity. Cotery could not be making better. I sent a request to the Principal that a report from those supervising his work here should be circularised to the committee. If it has not arrived, I can say that they regard his ability as higher than anyone in their department for the last three years. You cannot ask more than that. If the committee allows itself to be coerced by an employer to get rid of such a man, it is showing itself singularly indifferent to merit. And it ought in honesty to declare that its appointments are governed, not partly but entirely, by employers' personal vendettas.'

George's voice rang round the room. Calvert's sounded faint by contrast as he broke in: 'I can't allow – I mean, personal considerations have nothing to do with it.'

'I should like to ask, through you, Mr Chairman,' said George, the instant Calvert finished, 'whether Mr Calvert maintains that personal considerations have not dictated his entire course of action?'

'I protest,' said the Principal.

'It's entirely a matter – the organisation of my firm, I mean, didn't happen to give room for another man of Cotery's age. I let him know – I think he realised during the summer. I certainly let him know.'

In the midst of George, Beddow and the Principal, all fluent in their different manners, Calvert was at a loss for words. His face was chubby and petulant, and quite unlike his handsome son's. His irritation seemed naïve and bewildered; but I felt a streak of intense obstinacy in him.

'I think,' said George, 'that Mr Calvert ought to be allowed to withdraw his last suggestion.'

'I have no intention of – No,' said Calvert.

'Then,' said George, 'who knew that you wouldn't have room for Cotery? and so intended to cut him off here?'

'No one, except Cotery and myself. I don't – it's not necessary to discuss my business with other people.'

'That is, no one knew of your intention until you wrote to the Principal some days ago?' said George.

'There was no need.'

'No one knew of your intention, in fact, until another incident had happened? Until after you told Cotery that you had forbidden your son – '

Beddow interrupted loudly: 'I can't allow any more, Mr Passant. I've got to apologise again' – he turned to Calvert – 'that you've been compelled to listen to remarks that, giving Mr Passant every shadow of a doubt, are in the worst possible taste.'

'I entirely concur,' said the Principal. It was clear that he and Beddow, at any rate, knew the whole sorry story. 'And, Mr Chairman, since a delicate matter has most regrettably been touched on, I wonder if Miss Geary would not prefer to leave the room?'

'Certainly not,' said Miss Geary; and settled herself squatly and darkly in her chair.

'I take it,' said George, 'that to punish a man without trial is in the best possible taste. And I refuse to make this incident sound ominous by brooding over it in silence. Mr Calvert either knows or ought to know that Cotery is absolutely innocent; that the whole matter has been ridiculously exaggerated; that it was nothing but a romantic gesture.'

'I believe that,' said Calvert. A glance of sympathy passed between them; for a second, they were made intimate by their quarrel. Then Calvert said obstinately: 'But it has nothing to do with it.'

'I am a little surprised,' said Canon Martineau, 'that Mr Passant is able to speak with such authority about this young man Cotery. I confess that his standing in the matter isn't quite so obvious – '

'I have the right to appear here about any student,' said George. Their hostility was gathering round him: but he was as self-forgetful as I had ever seen him.

The Principal seized a cue, and said: 'Mr Passant has, as it happens, a right to appear about students with whom he is not connected. In fact, Cotery never attended any of your classes, Mr Passant?'

'He presumably wouldn't have done so exceptionally well in printing,' George said loudly, 'if he had attended my classes in law.'

'Classes in law,' said the Principal, rising to a cautious, deliberate anger, 'which amount to two a week, this committee may remember. Like those given by twenty other visiting helpers to our regular staff.'

'The committee may also remember,' said George, 'that they can terminate the connection at a month's notice. That, however, does not affect the fact that I know Cotery well: I know him, just as I know a good many other students, better than anyone else in this institution.'

'Why do you go to this *exceptional* trouble?' asked the Canon.

'Because I am attached to an educational institution: I conceive that it is my job to help people to think.'

'Some of your protégés are inclined to think on unorthodox lines?' the Principal said.

'No doubt. I shouldn't consider any other sort of thinking was worth the time of a serious-minded man.'

'Even if it leads them into actions which might do harm to our reputations?' said the Principal.

'I prefer more precise questions. But I might take the opportunity of saying that I know what constitutes a position of trust: and I do not abuse it.'

There was a hush. Calvert's pencil scribbled over the paper.

'Well,' said Beddow, 'perhaps if – '

'I have not quite finished,' said George. 'I am not prepared to let the committee think that I am simply intruding into this affair. I am completely unapologetic. I repeat, I know Cotery well: you have heard my questions: I regard my case as proved. But I don't want to leave the committee under a misapprehension. Cotery is one out of many. You will be judged by what you make of them. They are better human material than we are. They are people who've missed the war. They are people who are young at the most promising time in the world's history. If they don't share in it, then it's because this committee and I and all we represent are simply playing the irresponsible fool with our youngers and betters. You may take the view that it's dangerous to make them think: that it's wiser to leave them in the state of life into which it has pleased God to call them. I refuse to take that view: and I shall not, while I have a foot in this building.'

He stood up to go.

Beddow said: 'If no one has anything more to ask Mr Passant...'

Until the door closed Beddow did not speak again, but his eyes moved from Calvert to the Canon.

'Well, Principal,' said Beddow, but his tone had lost (I was excited to notice) some of its buoyancy, 'I take it that you have made your recommendation.'

'I have, sir,' said Cameron emphatically.

'In that case, if no one has a motion, I suppose we accept the recommendation and pass on.'

Miss Geary leaned forward in her chair. 'Certainly not,' she said. 'We've been listening to a man who believes what he says. And I want to hear some of it answered.'

There was a stir round the table. They were relieved that she had spoken out, given them someone to argue against.

'Haven't we been listening,' said Canon Martineau, with his subtle smile, 'to a man who has a somewhat exaggerated idea of the importance of his mission?'

'No doubt,' said Miss Geary. 'Most people who believe in anything have a somewhat exaggerated idea of its importance. And I don't pretend that he made the best of his case. Nevertheless – '

She was speaking from a double motive, of course; her dislike for the Principal shone out of her: so did her desire to help George.

It was still one against four, if it came to a vote; but there was a curious, hypercharged atmosphere that even the absolute recalcitrants, Calvert and the Principal, felt as they became more angry. Over Beddow and Martineau certainly, the two most receptive people there, had come a jag of apprehension. And when, after Miss Geary had competently put the position of Cotery again, and Calvert merely replied stubbornly: 'He's known for months that I didn't intend to keep him here. Nothing else came into account. Nothing else – ' the Canon became restless.

'Of course,' he said, 'there are times when it's not only important that justice should be done. Sometimes it's important that justice should appear to be done. And in this case, unless we're careful, it does seem to me possible that our Mr Passant may make a considerable nuisance of himself.'

'I regret the suggestion,' said the Principal, 'that we should consider giving way to threats.'

'That isn't Canon Martineau's suggestion, if I understand it right,' said Beddow. 'He's saying that we mustn't stand on our dignity, even when we're being taught our business by a man like Passant. Because nothing would take the wind out of his sails like giving way a bit. And, on the other hand, it might do this young fellow Cotery some good if we stretched a point.'

'The Chairman has put my attitude,' said Martineau, 'much more neatly than I could myself.'

'I'm afraid that I still consider it dangerous,' said the Principal.

'Well,' said Beddow, 'if we could meet one condition, I myself would go so far as to stretch a point. But the condition is, of course, that we must satisfy Mr Calvert. We shouldn't think of acting against your wishes,' said Beddow to Calvert, in his most cordial and sincere manner.

Calvert nodded his head.

'I can't alter my own position,' he said. 'There's no future — I can't find a place for Cotery. I decided that in the summer. I don't bear him any ill-will — '

'I wonder,' Canon Martineau looked at Beddow with a sarcastic smile, 'whether this idea would meet the case? Cotery would normally have two more years: we pay half the cost, and Mr Calvert half. Mr Calvert, for reasons we all accept, can't go on with his share. But is there anything to prevent us keeping to our commitment, and remitting — may I suggest — not the half, but all Cotery's fees for just *one* year?'

'Except that it would be no practical use to the man himself,' said Miss Geary.

'No,' said Calvert. 'He needs the whole three years.'

'I'm not so desperately concerned about that,' said the Canon.

'He'd have to get the money from some other source. If he wanted to finish,' said Beddow briskly. 'I agree with the Canon. I think it's a decent compromise.'

Miss Geary saw that it was her best chance.

'If you'll propose it, Canon,' she said, 'I'm ready to second.'

'I deeply regret this idea,' said the Principal. 'And I am sure that Mr Calvert does.'

Canon Martineau and Beddow had judged Calvert more shrewdly, however, and he shook his head.

'No,' he said, 'I can't support the motion. But I shan't vote against it.' It was carried by three votes to one, with Calvert abstaining.

6

Results of a Celebration

I WENT straight from the committee to the Victoria, our public house, where George and Jack were waiting.

'Well?' cried George, as soon as I entered. I saw that Morcom was with them, sitting by the fire.

'It's neither one thing nor the other,' I said. I told them the decision.

'It's a pretty remarkable result for any sane collection of men to achieve. I never believed that you'd drive them into it. But it doesn't help Jack, of course.'

'Nonsense,' George shouted. 'You're as cheerful as Balfour giving the news of the Battle of Jutland. Your sane collection of men have been made to realise that they can't treat Jack as though he was someone who just had to be content with their blasted charity. Good God alive, don't you see that that's a triumph? We're going to drink a considerable amount of beer and we're going to Nottingham by the next train to have a proper celebration. In the meantime, I'm going to hear every word that they found themselves obliged to say.'

Jack smiled, raised his glass towards George, and said: 'You're a wonderful man, George.' Jack was shrewd enough to know already that, for himself, the practical value of the triumph was nothing: but it was his nature to rejoice with him who rejoices. (I was soon to see the same quality again in Herbert Getliffe.) He could not bear to spoil George's pleasure.

George lived through my description of the meeting before he confronted them and after he left. He was furiously indignant with Beddow's attempt to propitiate Calvert, more than with the Principal's: 'I suppose Cameron, to do him justice, is out to get benefactions for the institution. It's true that he's quite incapable of administering them, but we can't reasonably expect him to realise that. But what Beddow, who calls himself a socialist, thinks he's doing, when he tries to lick the feet of a confounded businessman – ' so George went on, drinking his beer, chuckling with delight at Miss Geary's interventions, reinterpreting the Canon's equivocal manoeuvres as directly due to the influence of Howard Martineau. 'The Canon must have worked out his technique. To come in on our side without letting it seem obvious,' said George. But he had no explanation of Calvert's naïve defence that he formed his decision about Jack long before the incident with his son.

'That's just incredible,' said George. 'If I'd wanted to invent something improbable, I couldn't have invented anything as improbable as that.'

Morcom said little; but he was amused by the change of sides, the choice of partners, before the vote. As I told the story, Jack illustrated it by moving glasses about the table; two glasses of beer representing the Canon and Beddow, a glass of water the Principal, a small square jug Miss Geary, and for Calvert Jack turned a glass upside down. When he moved them into their final places, George gave a loud satisfied sigh.

'They couldn't do anything else,' he said. 'They couldn't do anything else.'

Morcom looked at him with a curious smile.

'I doubt whether anyone else could have made them do it, George,' he said.

'I don't know about that,' said George.

'But, to come back for a minute to what Lewis said, they've still left Jack in the air, haven't they?'

'They've recognised his position. He's got time to turn round.'

'He's really in very much the same position,' said Morcom. 'It's important you should keep that in mind, for Jack's sake – '

'Arthur,' George cried, angrily and triumphantly, 'you tried to dissuade me from breathing a word to the bellwethers. You don't deny that, I suppose?'

'No,' said Morcom.

'And now I've done it, you're trying to deprive me of the luxury of having brought it off. I'm not prepared to submit to it. I've listened to you on most things, Arthur, but I'm not prepared to submit to it tonight.'

Half-drunk myself, I laughed. This was his night: I was ready, like Jack, to forget tomorrow. Yet, somewhere beneath my surrender to his victory, there crept a chill of disappointment. An hour ago, I had seen George in his full power and totally admired him; but now, knowing that Morcom was right, I was young enough to resent the contradiction between George in his full power and the same man sitting in this chair by the fire, shutting his eyes to the truth. He ought not to be sitting there, flushed, optimistic, triumphant, seeing only what he wanted to see.

'In fact,' shouted George, defiantly, 'you're not going to argue me out of my celebration. I dare say you don't want to come. But the others will.'

Jack and I were eager for it. We left Morcom sitting by the fire, and ran across to the station. The eight-forty was a train to Nottingham that we all knew; for half an hour the lights of farms, the villages, the dark fields, rushed by. The carriage was full, but George talked cheerfully of the pleasures to come and how he first met Connie at the 'club'; he was oblivious, as in all happiness or quarrels, to the presence of strangers; that night none of us cared.

We had a drink in a public house at the top of Parliament Street, and crossed over to another on the other side; it was a windy night, and the wind seemed very loud and the lights spectacularly bright. Jack, though he drank less than George and I, began demanding bowls of burning gold and going behind bars to help the maids: George kept greeting acquaintances, various men, whores, and girls from the factories out for a good time. He had met them on other night visits to Nottingham: for he went often, though he concealed it from Jack and me until we discovered by accident.

He knew the back streets better than those of our own town. He led us to the club by short cuts between high, ramshackle houses, and through 'entries', partly covered over, where George's voice echoed crashingly. One such entry led to a narrow street, lit only by a single street lamp at the mouth. At the door of a tall house at the end remote from the light, George rapped three times with the brass knocker.

A woman climbed up from the area and recognised George. She told him to take us upstairs, the top door was unlocked. We went up the four flights of creaking wooden stairs, and met a new, bright blue door which cut off the attic storey from the landing.

A gramophone was wailing inside. George marched in before us: the room was half-full, mainly of women; as soon as he entered, a group of them gathered round him. He was popular there; they laughed at him, they were after the money which he threw away carelessly at all times, fantastically so when drunk; but they genuinely liked him. They did him good turns, and took their troubles to him for advice. With them, he showed none of the diffidence of a visit to Martineau's respectable drawing-room; he was cheerfully, heartily enjoying himself, he liked being with them, he felt at home.

Tonight he burst into extravagance from the start. He saw Connie sitting with Thelma, her regular older friend; George put an arm round each of them, and shouted, 'Thelma's here! Of course, I insist that everyone must have a drink – because Thelma's here!'

Connie told him that he was silly, then whispered in his ear; his eyes brightened, and he took out a couple of notes for Thelma to buy drinks round. George shouted to some women across the room, and in the same breath talked in soft chuckles to Connie. She was fair and quite young, with a pretty, impassive face and a nice body. She pretended to escape from his arm: at once he clutched her, and she came towards him: the contact went through George like an electric current, and he shouted jubilantly: 'Make them have another drink, Thelma. Why shouldn't everyone have two drinks at once?'

Soon George and Connie had gone away. The rest of us drank and danced. The floor was rough; there was nothing polished about the 'club' except the bright blue door on the landing. The furniture was mixed, but all old; the red velvet sofas seemed like the relics of a gay house of the nineties; so did the long mirror with the battered gilding. But there were also some marble-topped tables, picked up in a café, several wicker chairs and even two or three soap boxes. One of the bulbs was draped in frilly pink, and one was naked. Women giggled and shrilled; and among it all, the 'manager' (whose precise function none of us knew) sat in the corner of the room, reading a racing paper with a cloth cap on the back of his head.

Now and then a pair went out. The gramophone wailed on, like all the homesick, lust-sweet longing in the world. The thudding beat got hold of one, it got mixed with the smell of scent. After one dance, Jack spoke to me for a moment.

'Jesus love me, I can't help it, Lewis,' he said with his fresh open smile. 'I'm going all randy sad.'

It was after one o'clock when the three of us gathered round one of the marble-topped tables. The room was nearly empty by then, though the gramophone still played. We should have liked to go, but there was over an hour before the last train home. So we sat there, sobered and quiet, ordering a last glass of gin to mollify the manager: and, of course, we talked of women.

'The first I ever had,' said George, 'happened on the night before my eighteenth birthday. She told me that she did it for a hobby. Afterwards, when I was walking home, it seemed necessary to shout, "Why don't they all take up a hobby? Why don't they *all* take up a hobby?" ' The words would have resounded boisterously three hours ago, when we entered that room; but now they were subdued. He was not randy sad, as Jack and I had been; this was a different, a deeper sadness. He knew the pleasure he had gained; and turning from it, he – whose pictures of the future usually glowed like a sunrise – felt all that he might miss.

'I should have wanted something better before now,' said Jack, 'if I'd been you.'

'It serves my purpose,' said George. 'I don't know about yours.'

Jack smiled. 'Why don't you try nearer home?'

'What do you mean?'

'I mean that some of the young women in our group would be open to persuasion. You'd get more happiness from one of them, George. Clearly you would.'

'That would destroy everything I want to do,' George said. 'You realise that's what you're suggesting? You'd put me into a position where people like Morcom could say that I was building up an impressive façade of looking after our group at the School. That I was building up an impressive façade — and that my real motive was to cuddle the girls on the quiet.'

Jack looked at George in consternation. For once in a quarrel, he had not raised his voice; yet his face bore all the signs of pain. Affectionately, Jack said: 'I want you to be happy, that's all.'

'I shouldn't be happy that way,' said George. 'I can look after my own happiness.'

'Anyway, for my happiness, I'm afraid I shall need love,' said Jack. 'Love with all the romantic accompaniments, George. The sort of love that makes the air seem a remarkable medium to be moving through. I'm afraid I need it.'

'I don't know whether I need it,' I said. 'But I'm afraid that I've got it.'

'Don't you ever want it, George?' Jack asked.

'Of course I want it,' said George. 'Though I shouldn't be prepared to sacrifice everything for it. But of course I want it: what do you think I am? As a matter of fact, I've been thinking tonight that I'm not very likely to find it.' He looked at me with a sympathetic smile. 'I don't know that I've ever been in love — at least not what you'd call love. I've made myself ridiculous once or twice, but it didn't amount to much. I dare say that it never will.'

It seemed strange that George, not as a rule curious about his friends' feelings, should have recognised from the start that my love for Sheila (which had begun that summer) would hag-ride me for years of my life. Yet that night he envied me. George was a sensual man, often struggling against his senses; Jack an amorous one, revelling in the whole atmosphere of love. In their different ways, they both that night wanted what they had not tasted. Saddened by pleasure, they thought longingly of love.

I said to Jack:'I think that Roy would have understood what we've been saying. It would have been beyond us at fifteen.'

'I suppose he would,' said Jack doubtfully.

'He's been in love,' I said.

'I still find it a bit hard to credit that,' said Jack.

'No one would believe me,' I said, 'if I told them that you were a very humble creature, would they?'

At the mention of Roy's name, George had become preoccupied; his eyes, heavy-lidded after the evening, looked over the now empty room; but that abstracted gaze saw nothing, it was turned into himself. Jack and I talked on; George sat silently by; until he said suddenly, unexpectedly, as though he was in the middle of a conversation: 'I accept some of the criticisms that were made before we started out.'

I found myself seized by excitement. I knew from his tone that he was going to bring out a surprise.

'I scored a point or two,' George said to Jack. 'But I haven't done much for you.'

'Of course you have,' said Jack. 'Anyway, let's postpone it. I'll see you tomorrow.'

'There's no point in postponing it,' said George. 'I haven't done much for you, as Lewis said before ever Morcom did. And it's got to be attended to. Mind you, I don't accept completely the pessimistic account of the situation. But we ought to be prepared to face it.'

Clearly, rationally, half-angrily, George explained to Jack (as Jack knew, as Morcom and I had already said, though not so precisely) how the committee's decision gave him no future. 'That being so,' said George, 'I suppose you ought to leave Calvert's wretched place.'

'I've got to live,' said Jack.

'Is it possible to go to another printer's?'

'I could get an identical job, George. With identical absence of future.'

'Well, I can't have any more of this fatalistic nonsense,' said George, irascibly, and yet with a disarming kindness. 'What would you do – if we could provide you with a free choice?'

'I could do several things, George. But they're all ruled out. They all depend on having some money – now.'

'Do you agree?' George asked me. 'I expect you know Jack's position better than I do. Do you agree?'

I had to, though I could foresee what was coming. If Jack's fortunes were to be changed immediately, he must have a loan. My little legacy had given me a chance: each pound at our age was worth ten to a man whose life was fixed. Jack was young enough to get into a profession – or 'to have a shot at that business we heard about the other day,' as he said himself.

'Yes,' said George. 'So in fact with a little money now, you're confident that you could laugh at Calvert and his friends?'

'With luck, I should make a job of it,' said Jack. 'But – '

'Then the money will have to be produced. I shall want you to let me contribute.' George's manner became, to stop Jack speaking, bleak and businesslike. 'Mind you, I shall want a certain number of guarantees. I shall want to be certain that I'm making a good investment. And also I ought to warn you straightaway that I may not be able to raise much money myself.' He went on very fast. 'I don't see why I shouldn't put my financial position on the table. It's all a matter of pure business. And I've never been able to understand how people manage to be proud about their finances. Anyway, even people who are proud about their finances couldn't be if they had mine. I collect exactly £285 per year. (Such incomes, because of the fall in the value of money, were to seem tiny within thirty years.) Of that I allow £55 to my father and mother. I'm also insured in their interest. I think if I decreased the £55 a bit, and added to the insurance, they oughtn't to be much upset. And then I could probably raise a fair sum from the bank on the policy – but I warn you, it's a matter of pure business. There may be difficulties.'

Neither Jack nor I fully understood the strange nature of George's 'finances'. But Jack was moved so that he did not recover his ready, flattering tongue until we got up to catch our train. Then he said: 'George, I thought we set out tonight to celebrate a triumph.'

'It was a triumph,' said George. 'I shall always insist that we won at that meeting.'

7

Argument Under the Gaslight

IT took some days for Jack to settle what he wanted to do (from that night at Nottingham, he never doubted that George would find the money): and it took a little longer to persuade George of it.

Those were still the days of the small-scale wireless business. An acquaintance of ours had just started one; Jack had his imagination caught. He expounded what he could make of it – and I thought how much he liked the touch of anything modern. He would have been a *contemporary* man in any age. But he was inventive, he was shrewd, he had a flair for advertisement; he persuaded us all except George.

George did not like it. He would have preferred to try to article Jack to Eden & Martineau. He asked Morcom and me for our opinions. We gave practically the same answer. Making Jack a solicitor would mean a crippling expense for George; and we could not see Jack settling down to a profession if he started unwillingly. His choice was far more likely to come off.

At last George gave way. Then, though Jack, as I say, never doubted that the money would be found, George faced a last obstacle; he had to tell his father and mother that he was lessening his immediate help to them.

For many men, it would have been easy. He could have equivocated; after all, the insurance provided for their future, and he had been making an extravagantly large contribution. But he never thought of evading the truth. He dreaded telling it, for he knew how it would be taken; their family relations were passionately close. But tell it he did, without any cover, three days after our visit to Nottingham.

A week later, when he took me to supper with them, they were still not reconciled to it. It was only Mr Passant's natural courtesy, his anxiety to make me feel at home, that kept them from an argument the moment we arrived.

Actually, I was not a stranger in their house. Until two years before, Mr Passant had been assistant postmaster at Wickham; then, when George got his job at Eden & Martineau's, Mr Passant transferred to the general post office in the town. For fear of their family ties George insisted on going into lodgings, while they lived in this little house, one of a row of identical little houses, each with a tiny front garden and iron railings, on the other side of the town. But George visited them two or three times every week; he took his friends to spend whole evenings with them; tonight we arrived early and George and his mother kissed each other with an affection open and yet suddenly released. She was a stocky, big-breasted woman, wearing an apron over a greyish dress.

'It's half the week since I saw you, old George,' she said: it was the overtones of her racy Suffolk accent that we noticed in George's speech.

She wanted to talk at once about the question of money. Mr Passant managed to stop her, however, his face lined with concern. In a huff, as hot-tempered as George, she went into the back kitchen, though supper would not be ready for an hour.

Mr Passant sat with us round the table in the kitchen. It was hot from a heaped-up fire, and gave out the rich smell of small living-rooms. Under the gaslight, Mr Passant burst into a breathless, friendly, excited account of how, that morning at the post office, a money order had nearly gone astray. He spoke in a kindly hurry, his voice husky and high-pitched. He said: 'Do you play cards, Mr – er – Lewis? Of course you must play cards. George, we ought to play something with him now.'

It was impossible to resist Mr Passant's enormous zest, to prevent him doing a service. He fetched out a pack of cards from the sideboard, and we played three-handed solo. Mr Passant, who had been brought up in the strictest Puritan discipline, was middle-aged before he touched a card; now he played with tremendous enjoyment, with a gusto that was laughable and warmed us all.

When we finished the game, Mr Passant suddenly got up and brought a book to the table.

'Just a minute, Mr – er – Lewis, there's something I thought of when I was playing. It won't take long, but I mustn't forget.'

The book was a Bible. He moistened a pencil in his lips, drew a circle round a word, and connected it by a long line to another encircled word.

I moved to give him more room at the table, but he protested.

'No, please, no. I just do a little preparation each night to be ready for Sunday, you know. I'm allowed to tell the good news, I go round the villages, I don't suppose George has told you.' (Of course, I knew long since that he devoted his spare hours to local preaching.) 'And it's easier if I do a little work every night. I'm only doing it before supper so that afterwards – '

George and I spread out the evening paper and whispered comments to each other. In a few moments Mr Passant sighed and put a marker into the Bible.

'Ready for Sunday?' said George.

'A little more tomorrow.' Mr Passant smiled.

'I suppose you won't have a big congregation,' George said. His tone was both intimate and constrained. 'As it's a slack time of the year.'

Mr Passant said: 'No, we can't hope for many, but that's not the worst thing. What grieves me is that we don't get as many as we used to. We're losing, we've been losing ever since the war.'

'So has the Church of England,' I observed.

'Yes, you're losing too,' Mr Passant smiled at me. 'It isn't only one of us. Which way are you going to win them back?'

I gained some amusement from being taken as a spokesman of the Church of England. I did not obtrude my real beliefs: we proceeded to discuss on what basis the Christian Churches could unite. There I soon made a mistake; for I suggested that Mr Passant might not find confirmation an insurmountable obstacle.

Mr Passant pushed his face forward. He looked more like George than I had seen him. 'That is the mistake you would have to understand before we could come together,' he said. 'Can't I make you see how dangerous a mistake it is, Mr – Lewis? A man is responsible for his own soul. Religion is the choice of a man's soul before his God. At some time in his life, sooner or later, a man must choose to stay in sin or be converted. That is the most certain fact I know, you see, and I could not bring myself to associate in worship with anyone who doesn't want to know it as I do.'

'I understand what you mean by a man being responsible for his soul.' George rammed tobacco into his pipe. 'That's the basis of Protestantism, naturally. And, though you might choose to put it in other words' – he looked at me – 'it's the basis of any human belief that isn't completely trivial or absurdly fatalistic. But I never have been able to see why you should make conversion so definite an act. It doesn't happen like that – irrevocably and once for all.'

'It does,' said Mr Passant.

'I challenge it,' said George.

'My dear,' said Mr Passant, 'you know all sorts of matters that I don't know, and on every one of these I will defer to your judgment or knowledge, and be glad to. But you see, I have been living amongst people for fifty years, for fifty-three years and a half, within a few days, and as a result of that experience I know that their lives change all of a sudden – like this – ' he took a piece of paper out of his pocket and moistened his pencil against a lip; then he drew a long straight line – 'a man lives in sin and enjoyment and indulgence for years, until he is brought up against himself; and then, if he chooses right, life changes altogether – *so*.' And he drew a line making a sharp re-entrant angle with the first, and coming back to the edge of the paper. 'That's what I mean by conversion, and I couldn't tell you all the lives I've seen it in.'

'I can't claim the length of your experience,' George's tone had suddenly become hard, near anger, 'but I have been studying people intensively for several years. And all I've seen makes me think their lives are more like this – ' he took his father's paper under the gaslight, his hand casting a blue shadow; he drew a rapid zigzag. 'A part of the time they don't trouble to control their baser selves. Then for a while they do and get on with the most valuable task in sight. Then they relax again. And so on another spurt. For some people the down-strokes are longer than the up, and some the reverse. That's all I'm prepared to admit. That's all you need to hope, it seems to me. And whatever your hopes are, they've got to be founded in something like the truth – '

Mr Passant was breathless and excited:

'Mine is the truth for every life I've seen. It's the truth for my own life, and no one else can speak for that. When I was a young man I did nothing but run after enjoyments and pleasures.' He was staring at the paper on the table. It was quiet; a spurt of rain dashed against the window. 'Sensual pleasures,' said Mr Passant, 'that neither of you will ever hear about, perhaps, much less be tempted with. But they were pleasures to me. Until I was a young man about your age, not quite your age exactly.' He looked at George. 'Then one night I had a sight of the way to go. I can never forget it, and I can never forget the difference between my state before and since. I can answer for the same change in others also. But chiefly I have to speak for myself.'

'I have to do the same,' said George.

They stared at each other, their faces shadowed. George's lips were pressed tightly together.

Then Margaret, George's youngest sister, a girl of fourteen, came in to lay the supper. And Mrs Passant, still unappeased, followed with a great metal tray.

Supper was a meal both heavy and perfunctory. There was a leg of cold overdone beef, from which Mr Passant and George ate large slices: after the potatoes were finished, we continued with the meat alone. Mrs Passant herself was eating little – to draw George's concern, I thought. When her husband tried to persuade her, she merely smiled abruptly. His voice was entreating and anxious; for a moment, the room was pierced by unhappiness, in which, as Mr Passant leaned forward, George and the child suddenly took their share.

Nothing open was said until Margaret had gone to bed. From halfway up the stairs, she called out my Christian name. I went up, leaving the three of them alone; Margaret was explaining in her nervous, high-pitched voice that her candle had gone out and she had no matches. She kept me talking for a few moments, proud of her first timid attempt to flirt. As she cried 'Goodnight' down the stairs, I heard the clash of voices from below. The staircase led, through a doorway, directly into the kitchen; past the littered table, George's face stood out in a frown of anger and pain. Mr Passant was speaking. I went back to my place; no one gave me a glance.

'You're putting the wrong meaning on to us,' the words panted from Mr Passant. 'Surely you see that isn't our meaning, or not what we tried to mean.'

'I can only understand it one way,' George said. 'You suspect the use I intend to make of my money. And in any case you claim a right to supervise it, whether you suspect me or not.'

'We're trying to help you, that's all. We must try to help you. You can't expect us to forget who you are and see you lose or waste everything.'

'That amounts to claiming a right to interfere in my affairs. I've had this out too many times before. I don't admit it for a single moment. If I make my own judgment and decide to spend every penny I receive on my own pleasures, I'm entitled to do so.'

'We've seen some of your judgment,' said Mrs Passant. George turned to her. His anger grew stronger, but with a new note of pleading: 'Don't you understand I can't give way in this? I can't give way in the life I lead or the money I spend. In the last resort, I insist of being the judge of my own actions. If that's accepted, I'm prepared to justify the present case. I warn you that I've made up my mind, but I'm prepared to justify it.'

'You're prepared to keep other people with your money. That's what you want to do,' said Mrs Passant.

'You must believe what I've told you till I'm tired,' George shouted. 'We're only talking about this particular sum of money I propose to use in a particular way. What I've done in the past and what I may do in the future are utterly beside the point. This particular sum I'm not going to spend on a woman, if that's what you're thinking. If you won't believe me –'

'We believe that, we believe that,' Mr Passant burst out. George stared at his mother.

'Very well. Then the point is this, and nothing but this; that I'm going to spend the money on someone I'm responsible for. That responsibility is the most decent task I'm ever likely to have. So the only question is whether I can afford it or not. Nothing I've ever learned in this house has given me any respect for your opinions on that matter. Your only grumble could be that I shan't be discharging my duty and making my contribution here. I admit that is a duty. I'm not trying to evade it. Have I ever got out of it except for a day or two? Have I ever got out of it since I was qualified?'

'You're making a song about it. By the side of what we've done,' she said.

'I want an answer. Have I ever got out of it?'

She shook her head.

'Do you suggest I shall get out of it now?'

She said, with a sudden bitter and defenceless smile: 'Oh, I expect you'll go on throwing me a few shillings. Just to ease your mind before you go off with the others.'

'Do you want every penny I earn?'

'If you gave me every penny,' she said, 'you'd still only be trying to ease your mind.'

George said in a quietened, contrite tone: 'Of course, it's not the money. You wouldn't worry for a single instant if my salary were cut and I couldn't afford to find any. I ought to know' – his face lightened into an affectionate smile – 'that you're just as bad with money as I am myself.'

'I know that you can afford to find money for these other people. Just as you can afford to give them all your time. You're putting them in the first place – '

'It's easy to give your money without thinking,' said Mr Passant. 'But that's worse than meanness if you neglect your real duties or obligations – '

'To hear you talk of duties,' Mrs Passant turned on him. 'I might have listened to that culch if I hadn't lived with you for thirty years.'

'I've left things I ought not to have left,' said Mr Passant. 'You've got a right to say that.'

'I'm going to say, and for the last time,' George cried, 'that I intend to spend this money on the realest duty that I'm ever likely to find.'

Mrs Passant said to her husband: 'You've never done a mortal act you didn't want. Neither will he. I pity anyone who has to think twice about either of you.'

8

George at the Centre of His Group

IT was all settled by the beginning of October. Just three weeks had passed since George first heard the news of Jack's trouble. Now George was speaking as if those three weeks were comfortably remote; just as, in these same first days of October, he disregarded my years in the office from the moment I quit it. Even the celebratory weekend at the farm was not his idea.

The farm was already familiar ground to George's group. Without it, in fact, we could not have become so intimate; nowhere in the town could we have made a meeting place for young men and women, some still watched by anxious families. Rachel had set to work to find a place, and found the farm. It was a great shapeless red-brick house fifteen miles from the town, standing out in remarkable ugliness among the wide rolling fields of High Leicestershire; but we did not think twice of its ugliness, since there was room to be together in our own fashion, at the price of a few shillings for a weekend. The tenants did not make much of a living from the thin soil, and were glad to put up a party of us and let us provision for ourselves.

Rachel managed everything. This Saturday afternoon, welcoming us, she was like a young wife with a new house.

She had tidied up the big, low, cold sitting-room which the family at the farm never used; she had a fire blazing for us as we arrived, in batches of two and three, after the walk from the village through the drizzling rain. She installed George in the best armchair by the fire, and the rest of us gathered round; Jack, Olive and I, Mona, a perky girl for whom George had a fancy, several more of both sexes from the School. The entire party numbered twelve, but did not include Arthur Morcom, for George was happiest when it was kept to his own group.

This afternoon he was filled with a happiness so complete, so unashamedly present in his face, that it seemed a provocation to less contented men. He lay back in his chair, smoking a pipe, being attended to; these were his friends and protégés, in each of us he had complete trust; all the bristles and guards of his defences had dropped away.

Cheerfully he did one of his parlour tricks for me. I had been invited for tea in a neighbouring village; I had lived in the county twenty years to George's two, but it was to him I applied for the shortest cut. He had a singular memory for anything that could be put on paper, so singular that he took it for granted; he proceeded to draw a sketch map of the countryside. We assumed that each detail was exact, for no one was less capable of bluffing. He finished, with immense roars of laughter, by drawing a neat survey sign, a circle surmounted by a cross, to represent my destination; for I was visiting Sheila's home for the first time, and George could not recover from the joke that she was the daughter of a country clergyman.

Then, just as I was going out, a thought struck him. Among this group, he was always prepared to think aloud. 'I'm only just beginning to realise,' said George, 'what a wonderful invention a map is. Geography would be incomprehensible without maps. They've reduced a tremendous muddle of facts into something you can read at a glance. Now I suspect economics is fundamentally no more difficult than geography. Except that it's about things in motion. If only somebody could invent a dynamic map – '

Myself, having a taste for these things, I should have liked to hear him out. But people like Mona (with her sly eyes and soft figure and single-minded curiosity about men) listened also: listened, it occurred to me as I walked over the wet fields, because George enjoyed his own interest and took theirs for granted.

When I returned, the room was not so peaceful. I heard Jack's voice, as I shook out my wet coat in the hall; and as soon as I saw him and Olive sitting together by the table, I felt my attention fix on them just as all the others' were fixed. George, sunk into the background, watched from his chair. It was like one of those primitive Last Suppers, in which from right hand and left eleven pairs of eyes are converging on one focus.

Yet, so far as I could tell, nothing had happened. Jack, some sheets of paper in front of him, was expanding on his first plans for the business: Olive had joined him at the table to read a draft advertisement. They had disagreed over one of his schemes, but now that was pushed aside, and Olive said: 'You know, I envy you! I envy you!'

'So you ought,' said Jack. 'But you haven't so much to grumble at, yourself.'

'I suppose you mean that I needn't work for a living. It's true, I could give up my job tomorrow.'

'You wouldn't get so much fun out of that,' said Jack, 'as I did out of telling your uncle that I had become increasingly dissatisfied with his firm — '

Olive smiled, but there was something on her mind. Suddenly I guessed (recalling his manner at Martineau's the night before) that Morcom had proposed to her.

'It's true,' Olive said, 'that my father wouldn't throw me out. I could live on him if I wanted. He probably expects me to be at home, now his health's breaking up. It's also true, I expect, that I could find someone to marry me. And I could live on him. But I envy you, being forced to look after yourself: do you understand that?'

'I don't think you're being honest,' said Jack.

'I tell you, Jack, it's bad luck to be born a woman. There may be compensations — but I'd change like a shot. Don't you think I'm honest about that?'

'I think you ought to get married,' said Jack.

'Why?'

'You wouldn't have so much time to think.'

Jack then became unexpectedly serious.

'Also you talk about your father wanting you at home. It would be better for you to get free of him altogether.'

'That doesn't matter.'

'It does.'

'I tell you I've got a lot of respect for him. But I've got no love.' She turned towards Jack: the light from the oil lamp glinted on the brooch on her breast.

'You understand other people better than you do yourself,' said Jack.

'What should you say if I decided – I don't think I ever should, mind you – that I ought to put off thinking of marriage yet awhile, and stay at home?'

'I should say that you did it because you wanted to.'

'You think that I want to stay at home, preserving my virginity and reading the monthly magazines?' she cried.

Jack shrugged his shoulders, and gave his good-natured, impudent, amorous smile. He said: 'Well, part of that could be remedied – '

She slapped his face. The noise cracked through the room. Jack's cheek was crimson. He said: 'I can't reply properly here – ' but then Rachel intervened.

'I'll knock your heads together if there's any more of it,' she said. 'Olive, you'd better help me lay the supper.'

The meal gleamed in bright colours on the table – the red of tomatoes, russet of apples, green of lettuce, and the red Leicestershire cheese. George, as always at the farm, made Rachel take the head of the table and placed himself at her right hand. Gusts of wind kept beating against the windows and whining round the house. The oil lamp smoked in front of us at table, and candles flickered on the mantelpiece. The steam from our teacups whirled in the lamplight; we all drank tea at those meals, for George, with an old-fashioned formality that amused us, insisted that our drinking and visits to Nottingham should be concealed from the young women – though naturally they knew all the time.

The circle from the lamp just reached the edge of the table. We were all within it, and the shadow outside, the windy night, brought us together like a family in childhood. Olive's quarrel with Jack lost its sting, and turned into a family quarrel. George basked as contentedly as in the afternoon, and was as much our centre.

With great gusto he brought out ideas for Jack's business; they were a mixture, one entirely unrealistic and another that seemed ingenious and sound. Then he made a remark about me, assuming casually and affectionately that I was bound to do well in my examination in the summer. He cherished our successes to come – as though he had them under his fingers in the circle of lamplight.

Olive looked at him. She forgot herself, and felt anxious for him. She cried sharply: 'Don't forget you can't just watch these people going ahead.'

'I don't think you need worry about that,' said George.

'I shall worry, George. You'll find as they get on' – she indicated us round the table – 'that you *need* recognition for yourself. To be practical, you'll need that partnership in the firm.'

'Do you think I shall ever fret so much about a piece of respectable promotion?'

'It's not just that –' but, though she stuck to it, she could not explain her intuition. Others of us stepped in to persuade him; no one spoke as strongly as Olive, but we were concerned. George, gratified but curiously embarrassed, tried to pass it off as a joke.

'As I told you at the café,' he said to Olive, 'when we were going into action about Jack – it shouldn't be so difficult. After all, even if I did perform actions which they don't entirely approve of, I certainly do most of the work, which they approve of very much: Martineau being given to religious disputation, and Eden preferring pure reflection.'

'That isn't good enough,' said Olive.

'Very well,' said George at last. 'I'll promise not to let it go by default. It will happen in time, of course.'

'We want to see it happen,' said Olive. Her eyes were bright and penetrating while she thought only of George. Now they clouded.

'George,' she said, 'I want you to give me some advice.'

'Yes.'

'You heard what I said to Jack. Things at home aren't getting any easier. Possibly I ought to give up the next two or three years to my father. But you know all about it. I just want an answer to this question – ought I to clear out at any price?'

'This is a bit complicated,' said George. 'You know I don't approve of your parents. We'll take that for granted. If you could bring yourself to get away, I think you would be happier. What exactly are you thinking of doing?'

'I might get a better job,' she said, 'and live away from home. Or I might get married soon.'

George stayed silent for a moment. A good-natured smile had settled on his face. He said: 'Getting a job to make yourself really independent wouldn't be as easy as you imagine. Everyone knows what I think of your capabilities, but the fact is, girls of your class aren't trained to be much use in the world.'

'You're right,' said Olive.

'You're given less chance than anybody. It's a scandal, but it's true. To be honest, I don't think it would happen if women weren't in the main destined for their biological purpose. I dare say you could live on your present job. But living in abject poverty isn't much fun. Anyone who's ever tried would have to tell you that. I'm afraid you might begin to be willing – to get wrapped in your family again.'

Everyone was struck by the caution and the moderate tone of his advice: in fact, George, who could take up any other free idea under heaven, never had an illusion about the position of women. Olive inclined her head.

'I'm glad you're speaking out,' she said. 'And marriage?'

George said slowly: 'Escaping even from a family like yours is no reason for marriage. The only reason for marriage is that you are certain that you're completely in love.'

'Perhaps so,' said Olive, 'perhaps so. I don't know.' She sat silently for an instant. Then she smiled at him. 'Anyway, it's more important for you to get established,' she said, as though there was a link between them.

George did not reply, and Olive fell into silence. The windows rattled in the wind. Rachel sighed opulently, and said: 'We've never had a night here quite like this. George, don't you think we ought to remember this Saturday? We ought to make it a festival, and come over here to keep it in October every year.'

The sentiment welled from her; and she gave the rest of us an excuse to be sentimental.

A few moments later I said: 'Some of us are starting. Where we shall have got to, after a few of Rachel's festivals – '

'Good God alive,' George burst into triumphant laughter, 'you don't expect me to choose this day of all days to lose faith in the future, do you?'

The next night, after supper, George and I were alone in the room. The others had gone into the town by the last bus: George was staying another night in order to call at the Melton office in the morning, and I could stretch myself in my new liberty.

We made another pot of tea. 'There's something I should like to show you,' George said suddenly, with a friendly but secret smile. 'I want you to inspect my exhibit. Just to round off the weekend. It is exactly the right night for that.'

He put a small suitcase on the table. This he unlocked and produced a dozen thick folios, held together in a clip-back case.

'You've heard me mention this,' he said. 'I'm going to let you read a few entries about Jack Cotery's affairs. I assume you'll keep them to yourself, naturally.'

It was his diary, which he had kept for years.

He searched through one of the folios, detached pages and handed them to me. At another, more important, moment in George's life, I was to read much of the diary. The appearance of the pages, years later, altered little from when he began it at eighteen. They were all in his clerkly and legible hand; in a wide left-hand margin he printed in capitals (sometimes after the entries were made, usually when a folio was completed) a sort of sectional heading, and another at the top of the page.

Thus:

COMFORT WITH THE GROUP
FRIDAY, AUG. 23

I could not let today pass by without writing. It was a day of hard work in the office; Eden listened to my summary and is well and truly $\quad$ launched on the co-operative case. I screwed myself PLEASURES $\quad$ up to spend a couple of hours at Martineau's this OF ONE DAY $\quad$ evening; it is not long since I left him and, as so often, felt stronger by his influence. But, above all, I passed a memorable evening with my friends...

'That entry is just to acclimatise you,' said George. In fact, there were pages of rhapsody over the group; rhapsody in a florid, elaborate and youthful style, which nevertheless could not keep one from believing his enthusiasm; and mixed with the rhapsody, more self-reproach and doubt than his friends would have expected then.

At first sight much of it seemed unfamiliar; for it was bringing home (what at that age I hadn't seen directly) some of the ways in which he appeared to himself. I read:

For I feel these people (these protégés of mine, if they will let me call them that) are gradually renewing their grip on my affections, my thought, my visions, although I have only visited them occasionally. The last weekend was full of drunken nights, of decrepit nights. I went to Nottingham, finding money drip away as usual... I was still on the hunt and finished at Connie's, as in duty bound. Then I realised once again that no other girl of the past year is fit to take her place. I just had time for a huzzlecoo; then I went back on the last train.

It left me in a mood of headache and despair...

And another day:

I felt very depressed this evening. I arrived at one of those moods when the world seemed useless – when effort seemed in vain; the

THEY ARE REMOTE   impossibility of moving mountains had overwhelmed me with my little faith. A chance remark by Olive on the purposelessness of the group had suddenly awakened me to their lack of response, to the lack of response of all of them; to their utter remoteness from me...

Then there was another entry over which I thought a good deal in the next few months.

MORCOM AND MY WORLD
TUESDAY, SEP. 3

Today Morcom entertained me to lunch. He was charming and considerate – the perfect host. He has so much that I fear I shall never acquire, taste and polish and *savoir faire*, while MORCOM RAISES A I am still uncultivated except in my one or PROFOUND QUESTION: two narrow special regions. If only he would WHAT SHOULD THE abandon his negative attitude and join my GROUP MEAN? attempts! He and I would be the natural alliance, and there is no limit to what we could achieve among the Philistines in this town. He with his strength and command and certainty. I with my burning hopes. When he went out of his way to be pleasant today and issued this invitation, I could scarcely contain my hopes that he was about to throw in his weight on my side. Yet apparently, if ever he possessed it, he withdrew from any such intention, and, indeed, he dropped one or two hints which made me examine myself anew, distressed me profoundly, and caused me, as before, to distrust his influence on some of my closest friends.

Morcom had criticised, sensibly and much as Olive did later, George's devotion to our group. He had said, in short, that it was not close enough to the earth to satisfy a man of power for long. On paper George answered the criticisms, so elaborately that he showed his own misgivings: and finished:

And what else lies in my powers? The gift of creation, worse luck, was not bestowed on me: except, I dare sometimes think, in the chance to help my protégés, beside whom all the artistic masterpieces of the world seem like bloodless artifices of men who have never discovered what it is to live. I must concentrate on the little world: I shall not get esteem, except the esteem which I value more than any public praise; I shall get no fame, except some gratitude which will soon be forgotten; I shall get no power at all. But I shall do what with all your gifts, Morcom, you may never do: I shall enjoy every moment of every day, and I shall gain my own soul.

In the first pages he showed me, Jack played very little part; there was a word in August:

I am still enjoying the fruitful association with Jack Cotery as much as ever. I have never been so lucky in my friends as I am now.

Then the idea of helping Jack came into the forefront of the diary, and continued there for weeks. There were descriptions of days which I remembered from another side: our first telling him the news, his attack on the committee (written with curious modesty), the visit to Nottingham, his resolve to find money for Jack.

Jack himself is easily disposed of. He is obviously the most gifted person I have a chance of helping. It is a risk, he may fall by the wayside, but it is less risky than with any other of the ISSUES unfortunates. Morcom mustn't think he is the only OF JACK person to spot talent. We mustn't forget that I first discovered that in spite of his humorous, lively warmth, there is a keen and accomplished edge to Jack's mind.

Jack's flattery, however, he mentioned, to my surprise:

We must perhaps remember that Jack is not completely impartial just now, though I should repudiate the suggestion if it were made...

And the opposition by his mother, he described a little oddly:

QUIET EVENINGS AT HOME, WITH INTERMISSIONS There had been little visible sign of misunderstanding or incompatibility, but one or two needless scenes.

But there was one thing which astonished me, more than it should have done, since, when I myself rejected George's advice about becoming a solicitor, there must have been similar entries about me. I knew that he had been angry at Jack preferring to experiment in business instead of accepting George's scheme of the law. Until I read George's entries, though, I could not have realised how he felt deserted, how deeply he had taken it to heart.

Cotery wantonly destroyed all my schemes for him...after destroying his feeble case for this fatuous project, I went away to consider closely the reasons for this outburst. It is fairly clear that he is not such a strong character COTERY REVEALS as I tried to imagine. He may have been subject FEET OF CLAY to underhand influences. I must not blind myself to that; and no doubt he is reacting to his complete acceptance of all I stand for. But, though understandable, such liability to influence and reaction are the signs of a weak character; and it is abundantly certain that I shall have to revise parts of my opinion of him. He will never seem the same again...

Then, a week later, there came the last entry he showed me that night:

I REACH EQUILIBRIUM ON THE COTERY BUSINESS
FRIDAY, SEP. 28

I have settled the difficulty about Cotery at last. I do not withdraw a word of my criticism, either of the wisdom of his course or the causes behind it. In a long and, on whole, KERNEL OF profitable conversation with Morcom, I COTERY'S BEHAVIOUR forced him to admit that I had been unfairly treated. Morcom is, no doubt, regretful of using his influence without either thought or knowledge. Apart from that, Jack seems, in short, to be handicapping himself at the outset because of an unworthy reaction against me. But that doesn't dispose of my share in his adventure.

I have decided that I owe it to myself to PROPER ATTITUDE maintain my offer...he must be helped, as UNAFFECTED though he were acting more sanely...I talk about freedom, about helping people to become themselves; I must show the scoffers that I mean what I say, I must show that I want life that functions on its own and not in my hothouse. I have got to learn to help people on *their* terms. I wish I could come to it more easily.

As for the money, I shall cease worrying and hope THE PRACTICAL that finance will arrange itself in the long run. I shall PROBLEM carry through this offer to Jack Cotery; then I shall wait and see, and, somehow, pay.

Part Two

THE FIRM OF
EDEN & MARTINEAU

9

The Echo of a Quarrel

THE winter was eventful for several of us. Olive, as she had foreshadowed that Saturday night at the farm, told Morcom that she could not marry him; she began to spend most of her time at home, looking after her father. Morcom tried to hide his unhappiness; often, he was so lonely that he fetched me out of my room and we walked for hours on a winter night; but he never talked of his own state. He also tried to conceal something else which tormented him: his jealousy for Jack Cotery. It was the true jealousy of his kind of love; it was irrational, he felt degraded by it, yet it was sharp and unarguable as a disease. Walking through the streets on those bitter nights, he could not keep from fearing that Jack might *that very moment* be at the Calverts' house.

Although Morcom was older than I was, too much so for us to have been intimate friends, I understood something of what he was going through, for it was beginning to happen to me. In time, I lost touch with him, and never knew what happened to him in later life. Yet, though I was closer to the others that year, he taught me more about myself.

Meanwhile, Jack himself had plunged into his business. One bright idea had come off: another, a gamble that people would soon be buying a cheap type of valve set, engrossed him all the winter and by spring still seemed to be about an even chance.

But George remained cheerful and content, in the middle of his friends' concerns. He was sometimes harassed by Jack's business, but no one found it easier to put such doubts aside; the group occupied him more and more; he spent extra hours, outside the School, coaching me for my first examination; he was increasingly busy at Eden & Martineau's.

The rest of us had never envied him so much. He was sure of his roots, and wanted no others, at this time when we were all in flux. It was not until the spring that we realised he too could be threatened by a change.

On the Friday night after Easter, I was late in arriving at Martineau's. Looking at the window as I crossed the road, I was startled by a voice from within. I went in; suddenly the voice stopped, as my feet sounded in the hall. Martineau and George were alone in the drawing-room; George, whose voice I had heard, was deeply flushed.

Martineau welcomed me, smiling.

'I'm glad you've come, Lewis,' he said, after a moment in which we exchanged a little news. George stayed silent.

'Everyone's deserting me,' Martineau smiled. 'Everyone's giving me up.'

'That's not fair, Mr Martineau,' George said, with a staccato laugh.

Martineau walked a few steps backwards and forwards behind the sofa, a curious, restless mannerism of his. 'Oh yes, you are.' Martineau's face had a look at once mischievous and gentle. 'Oh yes, you are, George. You're all deciding I'm a useless old man with bees in his bonnet who's only a nuisance to his friends.'

'That simply is not true,' George burst out.

'Some of my friends haven't joined us on Friday for a long time, you know.'

'That's nothing to do with it,' said George. 'I thought I'd made that clear.'

'Still,' Martineau added inconsequently, 'my brother said he might drop in tonight. And I'm hoping the others won't give us the "go-by" for ever.' He always produced his slang with great gusto; it happened often to be slightly out-moded.

The Canon did not come, but Eden did. He stayed fairly late. George and I left not long afterwards. In the hall George said: 'That was sheer waste of time.'

As we went down the path, I looked back and saw the chink of light through the curtains, darkened for an instant by Martineau crossing the room. I burst out: 'What was happening with Martineau before anyone came in? What's the matter?'

George stared ahead.

'Nothing particular,' he said.

'You're sure? Come on –'

'We were talking over a professional problem,' said George. 'I'm afraid I can't tell you anything else.'

Outside the park, under a lamp which gilded the chestnut trees, I saw George's chin thrust out: he was swinging his stick as he walked. A warm wind, smelling of rain and the spring earth, blew in our faces. I was angry, young enough to be ashamed of the snub, still on edge with curiosity.

We walked on silently down to the road where we usually parted. He stopped at the corner, and I could see, just as I was going to say an ill-tempered 'Goodnight,' that his face was anxious and excited. 'Can't you come to my place?' he said abruptly 'I know it's a bit late.'

Warmed by the awkward invitation, I crossed the street with him. George broke into a gust of laughter, good-humoured and exuberant. 'Late be damned!' he cried. 'I've got a case that's going to keep me busy, and I want you to help. It'll be a good deal later before you get home tonight.'

When we arrived in his room, the fire contained only a few dull red embers. George, who was now in the highest of spirits after his truculence at Martineau's, hummed to himself, as, clumsily, breathing hard, he held a newspaper across the fireplace; then, as the flames began to roar, he turned his head: 'There's something I've got to impress on you before we begin.'

He was kneeling, he had flung off his overcoat, one or two fair hairs caught the light on the shoulders of his blue jacket; his tone, as whenever he had to go through a formal act, was a trifle sententious and constrained (though he often liked performing one).

'What are you going to tell me?' I said, settling myself in the armchair at the other side of the fire. There was a smell of charring; George's face was tinged with heat as he crumpled the paper in the grate.

'That I'm relying on you to keep this strictly confidential,' he said, putting on a kettle. 'I'm laying you under that definite obligation. It's a friendly contract and it's got to be kept. Because I'm being irregular in telling you this at all.'

I nodded. This was not the first of the firm's cases I had heard discussed, for George was not always rigid on professional etiquette; and indeed his demand for secrecy tonight served as much to show me the magnitude of the case as to make sure that I should not speak. It was their biggest job for some time, apart from the routine of conveyancy and so on in a provincial town. A trade union, through one of its members, was prosecuting an employer under the Truck Act.

Eden had apparently realised that the case would call out all George's fervour. It was its meaning as well as its intricacy that gave George this rush of enthusiasm. It set his eyes alight and sent him rocking with laughter at the slightest joke.

As he developed the case itself, he was more at home even than among his friends at the Farm. There, an unexplained jarring note could suddenly stab through his amiability; or else he would be hurt and defensive, often by a remark which was not intended to bear the meaning he wove into it. But here for hours, he was completely master of his surroundings, uncriticised and at ease; his exposition was a model, clear and taut, embracing all the facts and shirking none of the problems.

George himself, of course, was led by inclination to mix with human beings and find his chief interest there. There is a superstition that men like most the things they do supremely well; in George's case and many others, it is quite untrue. George never set much value on these problems of law, which he handled so easily. But, whatever he chose for himself, there was no doubt that, of all the people I knew in my youth, he was the best at this kind of intellectual game; he had the memory, the ingenuity, the stamina and the orderliness which made watching him arrange a case something near an aesthetic pleasure.

As he finished, he smacked his lips and chuckled. He said: 'Well, that reduces it to three heads. Now let's have some tea and get to work.'

We sat down at the table as George wrote down the problems to which he had to find an answer; his saucer described the first sodden circle on a sheet of foolscap. I fetched down some books from his shelves and looked up references; but I could not help much – he had really insisted on my coming in order to share the excitement, and perhaps to applaud. On the other side of the table George wrote with scarcely a pause.

'God love us,' George burst out. 'If only' – he broke into an argument about technical evidence – 'we should get a perfect case.'

'It'll take weeks,' I said. 'Still – ' I smiled. I was beginning to feel tired, and George's eyes were rimmed with red.

'If it's going to take weeks,' said George, 'the more we do tonight the better. We've got to get it perfect. We can't give Eden a chance to make a mess of it. I refuse to think,' he cried, 'that we shan't win.'

In the excitement of the night, I forgot the beginning of the evening and the signs of a quarrel with Martineau. But, as George gathered up his papers after the night's work, he said: 'I can't afford to lose this. I can't afford to lose it personally – in the circumstances,' and then hurried to make the words seem innocuous.

10

Roofs Seen from an Office Window

MOST nights in the next week I walked round to George's after my own work was done. Often it was so late (for my examination was very near, and I was reading for long hours) that George's was the only lighted window in the street. His voice sounded very loud when he stood in the little hall and greeted me.

'Isn't it splendid? I've got another argument complete. You'd better read it.'

His anxiety, however, was growing. He did not explain it; I knew that it must be caused by some trouble within the firm. Once, when Martineau was mentioned, he said abruptly: 'I don't know what's come over him. He used to have a sense of proportion.' It was a contrast to his old extravagant eulogies of Martineau, but he soon protested: 'Whatever you say, the man's the only spiritual influence in the whole soulless place.'

Then tired over the case, vexed by this secret worry, he was repeatedly badgered by the crisis in Jack's business. For a time Jack had taken Morcom's advice, and managed to put off an urgent creditor. He did not confide the extent of the danger to George until a promise fell through and he was being threatened. George was hot with anger at being told so late.

'Why am I the last person who hears? I should have assumed I ought to be the first.'

'I didn't want to worry you.'

'I suppose you don't think it's worrying me to tell me now in the middle of as many difficulties as anyone ever had?'

'I couldn't keep it back any longer,' said Jack.

'If you'd come before, I should have stopped you getting into this absurd position.'

'I'm there now,' said Jack. 'It's not much comfort holding inquests.'

Several nights in the middle of the case, George switched off to study the figures of the business. They were not over-complicated, but it was a distraction he wanted to be spared: particularly as it soon became clear that Jack was expecting money to 'set it straight'. George discovered that Morcom had heard of this misfortune a week before; he exploded into an outburst that lasted a whole night. 'Do you think I'm the sort of man you can ignore till you can't find anyone else? Why don't you let other people finish up the business? There's no need to come to me at all.' He was half-mollified, however, to be told that Morcom's advice had only delayed the crisis, and that he had volunteered no further help.

Affronted as he was, George did not attempt to throw off the responsibility. To me in private, he said with a trace of irritated triumph: 'If I'd asserted myself in the first place, he'd have been settling down to the law by now.' But he took it for granted that he was bound to set Jack going again. He went through the figures.

'You guaranteed this man – ?'

'Yes.'

'What backing did you have?'

'It hasn't come off.'

In the end George worked out that a minimum of fifty pounds had to be provided within a month. 'That will avoid the worst. We want three times as much to consolidate the thing. I don't know how we shall even manage the fifty,' George said. As we knew, he was short of money himself; Mrs Passant was making more demands, his sister was going to a different school; he still lived frugally, and then frittered pounds away on a night's jaunt.

It surprised me how during this transaction Jack's manner towards George became casual and brusque. Towards anyone else Jack would have shown more of his finesse, as well as his mobile good nature. But I felt in him a streak of ruthlessness whenever he was intent on his own way: as he talked to George, it came almost to the surface.

I mentioned this strange relation of theirs to Morcom, the evening before I went to London for my examination: but he drove it out of my head by telling me he was himself worried over Martineau.

There was no time for him to say more. But in the train, returning to the town after the examination, I was seized by the loneliness, the enormous feeling of calamity, which seems lurking for us – or at any rate, all through my life it often did so for me – when we arrive home at the end of a journey. I went straight round to George's. He was not in, although it was already evening. His landlady told me that he was working late in the office; there I found him, in his room on the same floor as those which carried on their doors the neat white letters 'Mr Eden,' 'Mr Martineau'. George's room was smaller than the others, and in it one could hear trams grinding below, through the centre of the town.

'How did you get on?' George said. Though I felt he was wishing the inquiries over so that he could pass on to something urgent, he insisted on working through my examination paper.

'Ah,' George breathed heavily, for he had been talking fast, 'you must have done well. And now we've got a bit of news for you.'

'What is it? Has anything gone wrong?' I was full of an inexplicable impatience.

'I've got the case absolutely cut and dried,' said George enthusiastically. I heard his explanation, which would have been interesting in itself. When he had finished, I asked: 'Anything new about Martineau?'

'Nothing definite.' George's tone was uncomfortable, as though the question should not have been put. 'By the way,' he added, 'Morcom rang up to ask if he could come in tonight and talk something over. I believe it's the same subject.'

'When?' I said. 'When is he coming?'

'Well, as a matter of fact, quite soon.'

'Do you mind if I stay?' I said.

'There's a slight difficulty,' said George. He added: 'You see, we've got to consider Morcom. He's inclined to be discreet – '

'He's already spoken to me about it,' I said, but George was unwilling until I offered to meet Morcom on his way.

When I brought him back, Morcom began: 'It's rather dull, what I've come to you about.' Then he said, after a question to me: 'But you know a good deal about Martineau, George. And you're better than I am at figures.'

George smiled, gratified: 'If that's what you want, Lewis is your man.'

'All the better,' said Morcom. 'You can both tell me what you think. The position is this. You know that Martineau is my landlord. Well, he says he can't afford to let me keep on my flat. It seemed to me nonsense. So I asked for an account of what he spends on the house. I've got it here. I've also made a note of what I pay. That's in pencil; the rest are Martineau's figures. I want to know what you think of them.'

George was sitting at the table. I got up and stood behind him, and we both gazed for some minutes at the sheet of notepaper. I heard George's breathing.

'Well?' said Morcom.

'It's not very – careful, is it?' said George, after a long hesitation.

'What do you say?' Morcom said to me.

'I should go further,' I said. 'It's either so negligent that one can hardly believe it – or else – ' I paused, then hurried on: 'something like dishonesty.'

'That's sheer fatuity,' George said. 'He's one of the most honest people alive. As you both ought to know. You can't go flinging about accusations frivolously against a man like Martineau.'

'I didn't mean it like that. I meant, if one didn't know him and saw that account – '

'It's a pity,' said George, 'that you didn't say that.'

'How do you explain the figures?' Morcom asked.

'I reject the idea of dishonesty,' George said. 'Right from the beginning; and if you don't, I'm afraid I can't continue with the discussion.'

'I shouldn't believe it. Unless there turned out nothing else to believe,' Morcom said.

George went on: 'I grant it might have been dishonest if Lewis or I had produced an account like that. But we shouldn't have done it with such extraordinary clumsiness. Anyone could see through it at a glance. He's put all sorts of expenses down on the debit side that have got as much to do with his house as they have with me.'

'I saw that,' said Morcom.

'That proves it wasn't dishonesty,' George was suddenly smiling broadly. 'Because, as I say, a competent man couldn't have done it without being dishonest. But on the other hand a competent man wouldn't have done it so egregiously. So the person who did it was probably incompetent and honest. Being Martineau.'

'But is he incompetent?'

'He's not bad at his job,' George admitted slowly. 'Or used to be when he took the trouble. He used to be pretty good at financial things – '

Morcom and I leapt at the same words.

'Took the trouble?' said Morcom. 'When has he stopped? What do you mean?'

'I didn't want to say anything about this.' George looked upset. 'You'll have to regard it as in absolute confidence. But he's been slacking off gradually for a long time. The last month or two I've not been able to get him to show any kind of recognition. I tried to make some real demands on him about the case. He just said there were more important things. He's become careless – '

'That was what you were quarrelling about,' I cried out. 'That Friday night – do you remember? I found the two of you alone.'

'Yes,' said George, with a shy grin. 'I did try to make one or two points clear to him.'

'I heard him,' I said to Morcom, 'before I left the gardens.'

Morcom smiled.

84

'I don't know what is possessing him,' said George. 'Though, as I told him the night we had our disagreement, I can't imagine working under anyone else.'

'It's a pity for his sake,' I said, 'but the most important thing is — what does it mean to you?'

'Yes,' said Morcom. 'We haven't much to go on yet.'

'You'll tell me if you get any news,' said George.

'Of course.'

They were enjoying this co-operation. They each found that pleasure we all have in being on the same side with someone we have regularly opposed.

George walked to the window. It was almost nine, and the summer night had scarcely begun to darken. George looked over the roofs. The buildings fell away in shadow, the roofs shone in the clear light.

'I'm glad you came round,' said George. 'I've been letting it get on my nerves. It doesn't matter to you so much. But it just possibly might upset all the arrangements I have built up for myself. I've always counted on his being perfectly dependable. He is part of the scheme of things. If he's going to play fast-and-loose — it might be the most serious thing that has happened since I came here.'

11

A Firm of Solicitors

THE firm of Eden & Martineau had been established, under the name of G J Eden, Solicitor, by Eden's father in the eighties. It was a good time for the town, despite shadows of depression outside; by the pure geographical chance of being just outside the great coal- and iron-fields, it was beginning to collect several light industries instead of a single heavy one. And it was still a country market and a centre for litigious farmers. The elder Eden got together a comfortable business almost from the beginning.

His son became junior partner in 1896; Martineau joined when the father died, ten years later. Through the next twenty years, down to the time when George was employed, the firm maintained a solid standing. It never obtained any unusual success in making money: a lack of drive in the Edens seemed to have prevented that. The firm, though well thought of in the town, was not among the most prosperous solicitors'. It is doubtful whether Harry Eden ever touched £3,000 a year.

From the moment he entered it, George bore a deep respect for the firm, and still, nearly three years after, would say how grateful he was to Martineau for 'having somehow got past the opposition and wangled me the job'. His pride in the firm should not have surprised us, though it sometimes did. It seemed strange to notice George identifying himself with a solid firm of solicitors in a provincial town – but of course it is not the Georges, the rebels of the world, who are indifferent to authority and institutions. The Georges cannot be indifferent easily; if they are in an institution, it may have to be changed, but it becomes part of themselves. George in the firm was, on a minor scale, something like George in his family; vehement, fighting for his rights, yet proud to be there and excessively attached.

In the same way, his gratitude to Martineau and his sense of good luck at ever having been appointed both showed how little he could take himself and the firm for granted. As a matter of fact, there was no mystery, almost no manoeuvring, and no luck; they appointed him with a couple of minutes' consideration.

The only basis for the story of Martineau's manoeuvres seemed to be that Eden said: 'He's not quite a gentleman, of course, Howard. Not that I think he's any the worse for that, necessarily,' and Martineau replied: 'I liked him very much. There's something fresh and honest about him, don't you feel?'

At any rate, George, who was drawn to Martineau at sight, went to the firm with the unshakeable conviction that there was his patron and protector.

Eden, George respected and disliked, more than he admitted to himself. It was dislike without reason. It was an antipathy such as one finds in any firm – or in any body of people brought together by accident and not by mutual liking, as I found later in colleges and government departments.

About the relations of Eden and Martineau themselves, George speculated very little. Their professional capacity, however, he decided early. Martineau was quite good while he was at all interested. Eden was incompetent at any kind of detailed work (George undervalued his judgment and broad sense). Between them, they left a good deal of the firm's work to George, and there is no doubt that, after he had been with them a couple of years, he carried most of their cases at the salary of a solicitor's clerk, £250 a year.

With Martineau to look after his interests George felt secure and happy, and enjoyed the work. He did not want to leave; the group at the School weighed with him most perhaps, but also his comfort in the firm. He was not actively ambitious. He had decided, with his usual certain optimism – by interpreting some remark of Martineau's, and also because he thought it just – that he would fairly soon be taken into partnership. Martineau would 'work it' – George had complete faith. Meanwhile, he was content.

And so the first signs of Martineau's instability menaced everything he counted on.

It was the first time we had seen him anxious for his own sake. We were worried. We tried to see what practical ill could happen. I asked George whether he feared that Martineau would sell his partnership; this he indignantly denied. But I was not reassured, and I could not help wishing that his disagreement with Eden last autumn, the whole episode of the committee, was further behind him.

I talked it over several nights that summer with Morcom and Jack; and also with Rachel who, for all her deep-throated sighs, had as shrewd a judgment as any of us. We occupied ourselves with actions, practical prudent actions, that George might be induced to take. But Olive, her insight sharpened by the lull in her own life, had something else to say.

'Do you remember that night in the café – when we were trying to stop him from interfering about Jack?' she said. 'I had a feeling then that he was unlucky ever to come near us. He'd have done more if he'd have gone somewhere that kept him on the rails. Perhaps that's why the firm is beginning to seem important to him now.'

She went on: 'I admire him,' she said. 'We shall all go on admiring him. It's easy to see it now I'm on the shelf. But he's getting less from us – than we've all got from him. We've just given him an excuse for the things he wanted to do. We've made it pleasant for him to loll about and fancy he's doing good. If he hadn't come across such a crowd, he'd have done something big. I know he's been happy. But don't you think he has his doubts? Don't you think he might like the chance to throw himself into the firm?'

Even at that age, Olive had no use for the great libertarian dreams. Perhaps her suspicions jarred on Rachel, who was, like me, concerned to find something politic that George might do. We suggested that it would do no harm to increase Eden's goodwill. 'Just as an insurance,' Rachel said. We meant nothing subtle or elaborate; but there were one or two obvious steps, such as getting Eden personally interested in the case and asking his advice now and then – and taking part in some of the Edens' social life, attending the parties which Mrs Eden held each month and which George avoided from his first winter in the town.

George was angry at the suggestions. 'He wants me to do his work for him. He doesn't want to see me anywhere else – ' and then, as a second line of defence: 'I'm sorry. I don't see why I should make myself uncomfortable without any better reasons than you're able to give. I am no good at social flummery. As I think I proved, the last time you persuaded me to make a fool of myself. I should have thought I'd knocked over enough cups for everyone's amusement. I tell you I'm no good at social flummery. You can't expect me to be, starting where I did.'

Dinner at the Edens' was an ordeal in which the right dress, the right fork, the proper tone of conversation, presented moments of shame too acute to be faced without an overmastering temptation. As he grew older he was making less effort to conquer these moments.

'You can't expect me to, starting where I did.' That was one motive – I knew – why he built up a group where he was utterly at ease, never going out into the uncomfortable and superior world.

None of us could move George to cultivate Eden's favour. We pressed him several times after he returned from vague but disturbing conversations with Martineau. He said: 'I'd rather do something more useful – which meant engross himself in the case. Through the uncertainty, it had come to assume a transcendental importance in his mind. Sensibly, Eden was letting him argue it in the court.

Throughout June and July, George worked at it with extraordinary stamina and concentration. I saw him work till the dawn six nights running, and although I made up sleep in the mornings and he went to the office, he was fresher than I each evening and more ready for the night's work to come.

12

Evening by the River

UNTIL just before the final hearing of the case, George was searching for money to salvage Jack's business. It was a continual vexation; he did not endure it quietly. 'This is intolerable,' he shouted, as his work was interrupted. 'Intolerable!'

I had, in fact, used it as an argument for getting Eden's interest. Even in the Calvert trouble, Eden had shown a liking for Jack; and it would have been easy, I argued – if George were on friendly terms with Eden – to explain the position and secure an advance of salary for Jack's sake.

Instead, George was harassed by petty expedients. He borrowed a few pounds from Morcom and Rachel, pawned his only valuable possession, a gold medal won at school, increased his overdraft by ten pounds, up to the limit allowed by his bank.

George managed to raise nearly sixty pounds in all, a few days before Jack's grace expired.

'Well, here it is,' he said to Jack. He was sitting in his room for one of his last nights' work on the case. 'You can thank heaven you didn't need any more. I don't know how I could have scraped another penny.'

'Thank you, George,' Jack said. 'Saved again. It won't happen any more, though.'

'I warn you I'm just helpless now,' George said.

'I'll pay it back by the end of the year. I expect you think that I shan't,' Jack said. 'But, you wouldn't believe it, but I'm more confident after this collapse than I was at the start.'

George stared down at his papers.

'There is one other thing.'

'Yes, George?'

'I don't know whether you realise how near you have been to – considerable danger.'

'I don't know what you mean.'

'I mean something definite. Your methods of getting hold of some of that stock were just on the fringe of the law. You didn't know, I expect, but if you hadn't met your bills and they had sued – you stood an even chance of being prosecuted afterwards.'

'I was afraid you were worrying over those figures,' said Jack. 'You're seeing more than is really there, you know.'

'I don't propose to say another word,' George said. 'The whole thing is over. I want you to know that I don't retract anything I've said about expecting you to make a tremendous success. You were unlucky over this affair. You might just as easily have been gigantically lucky. It was probably a bigger risk than you were justified in taking. Perhaps it's wiser not to attempt long-range prophecies. They're obviously the interesting things in business; but then, you see, I'm still convinced that successful business is devastatingly uninteresting. But if you don't reach quite as far, you'll simply outclass all those bloated stupid competitors of yours. It's unthinkable that you won't. I refuse to waste time considering it.' His eyes left Jack, and he began studying one of his tables of notes. 'I'm afraid I shall have to neglect you now. I've got to make certain of smashing them on Thursday.'

The last hearing of George's case took up a July afternoon. I sat in the old Assize Hall, where the Quarter Sessions had been transferred this year. The hall was small, intimate, and oppressive in the summer heat. Thunder rolled intermittently as George made his last speech, aggressive, closely packed with an overwhelming argument. He was more nervous than in his attack on the School committee.

The judge had been a little short with him, provoked by his manner. Eden, who allowed George complete charge in the later stages, sat with his lips in a permanent but uneasy smile. When George was given the case, in words slightly peremptory and uncordial, Eden shook his hand: 'That was an able piece of work, Passant. I must say you've done very well.' Then Martineau, who had not attended a hearing throughout the case, entered, was told the news, and laughed. 'You'll go from strength to strength, won't you, George? You'll be ashamed of being seen with your old friends – '

When they had gone, I stayed alone with George while he packed his papers: he bent his head over the desk and made a neat tick on the final page; he was smiling to himself. We went together to a café by the river; when we sat down at the little table by the window, he said, with an exultant sigh: 'Well, we've pulled that off.' A happy smile spread over his face. 'This is one of the best occasions there have ever been,' he said.

'I've never seen anyone look quite so jubilant,' I said, 'as when you got the verdict.'

George shook with laughter.

'I don't see why anyone shouldn't look pleased,' he said, 'when you damned well know you've done something in a different class from the people round you.' His voice calmed down. 'Not that I ever had any serious doubts about it.'

'Not last week?' I said. 'Walking round the park?'

'You can't expect me not to have bad moments,' George said. 'I didn't get a reasonable chance to have any faith in myself until – not long ago. Being as shy as I am in any respectable society doesn't help. I've never got over my social handicaps. And you realise that I went through my childhood without anyone impressing on me that I had ability – considerable ability, in fact.' He chuckled. 'So you can't expect me not to have bad moments. But they're not very serious. Fortunately, I've managed to convince myself – '

'What of?'

'That I'm capable of doing something useful in the world and that I've found the way of doing it.'

Contentedly he leaned back against the wall, and looked beyond me through the window. It was a cloudy evening, but the sky was bright towards the west; so that in the stream that ran by the café garden the clouds were reflected, dark and sharply cut.

'It was extremely important that I should be a success in the firm,' George went on. 'I regard that as settled now. They couldn't do without me.'

'Do they realise that?'

'Of course.'

'Are you sure?'

George flushed. 'Of course I am. I'm not dealing with cretins. You heard yourself what Martineau said an hour ago.'

'You can't rely on Martineau.'

'Why not?'

'In his present state, he might do anything. Sell his partnership and go into the Church,' I smiled, stretching my invention for something more fantastic than the future could possibly hold.

'Nonsense,' said George. 'He's a bit unsettled. People of imagination often have these bouts. But he's perfectly stable, of course.'

'You've forgotten what Morcom said the other night?'

'I've got it in its right proportion.'

'You were desperately anxious about him. A few days ago. You were more anxious than I've seen you about anything else.'

'You can exaggerate that.'

'So you expect everything to be always the same?'

'As far as the progress of my affairs goes,' said George, 'yes.'

I burst out: 'I must say it seems to me optimism gone mad.'

But actually, when George was shelving or assimilating the past, or doing what was in effect the same, comfortably forecasting his own future, I was profoundly moved by a difference of temperament: far more than by a disinterested anxiety. At that age, to be honest, I resented George being self-sufficient, as it seemed to me, able to soften any facts into his own optimistic world. He seemed to have a shield, an unfair shield, against the realities and anxieties that I already felt.

Also, for weeks I had been working with him, sympathising with his strain during the case, arguing against the qualms which oddly seemed to afflict him more than they would a less hopeful man. It had been easier to encourage him over the doubtful nights than to sit isolated from him by this acceptance of success, so blandly complete that the case might have been over a year ago and not that afternoon. And so, guiltily aware of the relief it gave me, I heard my voice grow rancorous. 'You're making a dream of it,' I said, 'just to indulge yourself. Like too many of your plans. Do you really think it's obvious that Martineau will stay here for the rest of his life?'

'I don't see what else he's going to do,' said George, smiling. But I could detect, as often when he was argued against, a change in tone. 'In any case,' he said, with his elaborate reasonableness, 'I don't propose to worry about that. He's done almost everything I required of him. He's stayed in the firm long enough for me to establish my position. He's given me the chance, and I've taken advantage of it. It doesn't matter particularly what happens now.'

George's face suddenly became eager and happy.

'You see,' he said, 'I have the right to stay here now. I could always have stayed before. Even Eden would never have seriously tried to get rid of me, whether Martineau was there or not. But I couldn't really be entirely satisfied until I'd established to myself the right to go on as I am. I've never had much confidence, and I knew it would take a triumph to prove to myself that I've a right to do as I please. That's why this is so splendid. I'm perfectly justified in staying, now.'

In my resentful state, I nearly pretended to be mystified. But I thought of Olive's premonition; and I was captured by his pleasure in his own picture of himself. One could not resist his fresh and ebullient happiness.

'The people at the School?' I said.

'Obviously,' said George. 'What would happen to everyone if I went away?'

I replied, as he wanted:

'One or two of us you've affected permanently,' I said. 'But the others – in time they'd become what they would have been – if you'd never come.'

'I won't have it,' said George. 'Good God above, I won't have it.' He laughed wholeheartedly. 'Do you think I'm going to waste my time like that? You're right, it's exactly what would happen. And it's simply inconceivable that it should. I refuse to contemplate it,' he said. 'We must go on as we are. God knows, there isn't much freedom in the world, and I'm damned if we lose what little there is. I've started here, and now after this I can go on. I tell you, that's why this mattered so much to me.'

I looked across the table; his eyes were shining in the twilight, and I was startled by the passionate exultation in his voice. 'You've understood before, I've found the only people to whom my existence is important. How can you expect anything else to count beside that fact?'

His voice quietened, he was smiling; the evening light falling from the window at my back showed his face glowing and at rest.

13

An Unnecessary Confession

WITH the success behind him, George remarked more often about a partnership 'being not too far away'. For the first time, he showed some impatience about his own future: but he was no longer worried over Martineau. Both Morcom and I began to think he was right; during July and August, I almost abandoned my fear that Martineau might leave and so endanger George's prospects in the firm.

Martineau's behaviour seemed no more eccentric than we were used to. He was still doing everything we wanted of him; we went to Friday nights, we saw him walking backwards and forwards between the sofa and the window, his shadow leaping jerkily into the summer darkness. It was all as it had been last year; just as with any present reality, it was hard to imagine that it would ever cease.

We smiled as we heard him use a mysterious phrase – 'the little plays'.

'Of course, the man's religion is at the bottom of it all,' said George, back into boisterous spirits which were not damped even when Olive had to leave the town; her father's health had worsened, and she took him to live by the sea. George compensated himself for that gap by his enormous pride in Jack's and my performances; for my examination result was a good one, and Jack at last had achieved a business coup.

It added to Jack's own liveliness. He was warmed by having made a little money and by feeling sure of his flair. And it was like him to signalise it by taking Mrs Passant to the pictures – her who was suspicious of all her son's friends, who had denounced Jack in particular as an unscrupulous sponger. Yet he became the only one of us she liked.

It was also Jack who brought the next news of Martineau. One evening in September, George and I were walking by the station when we saw Jack hurrying in. He seemed embarrassed to meet us.

'As a matter of fact,' he said, 'I can't wait a minute. I'm staying at Chiswick for the weekend – my mother's brother, you know.'

'There's no train to London for an hour, surely,' said George. Jack shook his head, smiled, and ran into the booking hall.

'Of course there's no train at this time.' George chuckled to me. 'He must be after a woman. I wonder who he's picked up now.'

The following day was a Saturday; at eight George and I were sitting in the Victoria; I mentioned that at exactly this time last year, within three days, Jack had been presented with a cigarette case. George was still smiling over the story when Jack himself came in.

'I was looking for you,' he said.

'I thought you were staying with your prosperous uncle,' said George.

Jack did not answer. Instead, he said:

'I've something important to show you.'

He made us leave the public house, and walk up the street; it was a warm September night, and we were glad to. He took us into the park at the end of the New Walk. We sat on a bench under one of the chestnut trees and looked at the lights of the houses across the grass. The moon was not yet up; and the sky, over the cluster of lights, was so dense and blue that it seemed one could handle it. Jack pointed to the lights of Martineau's. 'Yes, it's about him,' he said.

He added: 'George, I want to borrow your knife for a minute.'

With a puzzled look, George brought out the heavy pocket knife which he always carried. Jack opened it; then took a piece of paper from his pocket, unfolded it, and pinned it to the tree by the knife blade.

'There,' he said. 'You'd have seen plenty of those last night – ' if we had gone with him to a neighbouring village.

It was too dark to read the poster in comfort. George struck a match, and peered in the flickering light.

The sheet was headed *'Players of the Market Place'* and then, in smaller letters, *'will be with you on Thursday night to give their LITTLE PLAYS*. Titles for this evening, *The Shirt, Circe*. Written by us all. Played by us all. There is no collection,' and in very large letters 'WE WOULD RATHER HAVE YOUR CRITICISM THAN YOUR ABSENCE.'

It was a printed poster, and the proofs had been read with typical Martineau carelessness: so that, for instance, 'evening' appeared as 'evenini', like an odd word from one of the lesser-known Latin tongues, Romanian or Provençal.

The match burnt down to George's fingers. He threw it away with a curse.

Jack explained that the 'little plays' purported to carry a religious moral: that they were presumably written by Martineau himself. Jack had watched part of one – 'painfully bad', he said.

George was embarrassed and distressed.

'We can't let him make a fool of himself in public. We must calm him down,' he said. 'He can't have lost all sense of responsibility.'

'He's just kept enough to hide these antics from us,' said Jack. 'Still, I found him out.' Then he laughed, and to my astonishment added: 'Though in the process, of course, I managed to let you find me out.'

'What do you mean now?' said George, uninterested by the side of his concern for Martineau.

'I made that slip about the train.'

'Oh,' said George.

'And, of course, I remembered as soon as I spoke to you last night. I've always told you that my father's brother lived in Chiswick. Last night I said it was my mother's. After you'd noticed that, I may as well say that I've got no prosperous uncles living in Chiswick at all. I'm afraid that one night – it just seemed necessary to invent them.'

Jack spoke fast, smiling freshly in the dusk. Neither George nor I had noticed the slip: but that did not matter; he wanted to confess. He went on to confess some more romances; how he had wrapped his family in mystery, when really they were poor people living obscurely in the town. I was not much surprised. He was so fluid, I had watched him living one or two lies; and I had guessed about his family since he took pains to keep any of us from going near their house. I still was not sure where he lived.

He went on to tell us that one of his stories of an admiring woman had been imaginary. That seemed strange; for, more than most young men, he had enough conquests that were indisputably real. Perhaps he felt himself that this was an inexplicable invention – for he looked at George. The moon was just rising, and George's face was lit up, but lit up to show a frown of anger and incomprehension.

'I suppose it must seem slightly peculiar to you, George,' said Jack. 'But you don't know what it is to be obliged to make the world a trifle more picturesque. I'm not defending myself, mind. I often wish I were a solid person like you. Still, don't we all lie in our own fashion? You hear Martineau say, "George, I'm sure the firm's always going to need you". You'd never think of departing from the literal truth when you told us the words he'd said. But you're quite capable, aren't you, of interpreting the words in your own mind, and convincing yourself that he's really promised you a partnership? While I'm afraid that I might be obliged to invent an offer, with chapter and verse. Lewis knows what I mean better than you do. But I know it makes life too difficult if one goes on after my fashion.'

He was repentant, but he was high-spirited, exalted. 'Did you know,' he went on, 'that old Calvert told the truth at that committee of yours? He had warned me a month or two before that there wasn't an opening for me in the firm.'

'I didn't know,' said George. 'Otherwise, I shouldn't have acted.'

'I can say this for myself,' said Jack, 'that the Roy affair brought him to the point.'

'But you let me carry through the whole business under false pretences,' George cried. 'You represented it simply to get an advantage for yourself – and make sure that I should win it for you under false pretences?'

99

'Yes,' said Jack.

'No,' I said. 'That was one motive, of course. But you'd have done it if there'd been nothing George could bring off for you. You'd have done it – because you couldn't help wanting to heighten life.'

'Perhaps so,' said Jack.

'I should never have acted,' said George. He was shocked. He was shocked so much that he spoke quietly and with no outburst of anger. I thought that he sounded, more than anything, desperately lonely.

He stared at Jack in the moonlight. At that moment, their relation could have ended. Jack had been carried away by the need to reveal himself; he knew that many men – I myself, for example – would accept it easily; he had not realised the effect it would have on George. Yet, his intuition must have told him that, whatever happened, they would not part now.

George was seeing someone as different from himself as he would ever see. Here was Jack, who took on the colour of any world he lived in, who, if he remembered his home and felt the prick of a social shame, just invented a new home and believed in it, for the moment with his whole existence.

While George, remembering his home, would have thrust it in the world's face: 'I'm afraid I'm no good in any respectable society. You can't expect me to be, starting where I did.'

That was his excuse for his diffidence's and some of his violence, for his constant expectation of patronising treatment and hostility. In that strange instant, as he looked at Jack, I felt that for once he saw that it was only an excuse. Here was someone who 'started' where George did, and who threw it off, with a lie, as lightly as a girl he had picked up for an hour: who never expected to find enemies and felt men easy to get on with and easier to outwit.

George knew then that his 'You can't expect me to, starting where I did' was an excuse. It was an excuse for something which any man finds difficult to recognise in himself: that is, he was by nature uneasy and on the defensive with most of his fellow men. He was only fully assured and comfortable with one or two intimate friends on whose admiration he could count; with his protégés, when he was himself in power: with women when he was making love. His shame at social barriers was an excuse for the hostility he felt in other people; an excuse for remaining where he could be certain that he was liked, and admired, and secure. If there had not been that excuse, there would have been another; the innate uneasiness would have come out in some other kind of shame.

That aspect of George, he shared with many men of characters as powerful as his own. The underlying uneasiness and the cloak of some shame, class shame, race shame, even the shame of deformity, whatever you like – they are a combination which consoles anyone like George to himself. For it is curiously difficult for any human being to recognise that he possesses natural limitations. We all tend to think there is some fundamental 'I' which could do anything, which could get on with all people, which would never meet an obstacle – '*if only I had had the chance*'. It was next to impossible – except in this rare moment of insight – for George to admit that his fundamental 'I' was innately diffident and ill-at-ease with other men. The excuse was more natural, and more comforting – '*if only I had been born in gentler circumstances.*'

George stood up, plucked his knife out of the tree and handed the poster to Jack.

'Thank you for taking that trouble about Martineau,' he said. 'I know you did it on my account. You'll let me know the minute you discover anything fresh, of course. We've got to help one another to keep him from some absolutely irretrievable piece of foolishness.'

14

The Last 'Friday Night'

FOR some time we heard no further news. Friday nights went on in their usual pattern. But one day in November, when I was having tea with George, I found him heavy and preoccupied. I tried to amuse him. Once or twice he smiled, but in a mechanical and distracted way. Then I asked:

'Is there a case? Can I help?'

'There's nothing on,' said George. He picked up the evening paper and began to read. Abruptly he said, a moment later: 'Martineau's letting his mania run away with him.'

'Has anything happened?'

'I found out yesterday,' George said, 'that he was asking someone to value his share in the firm.'

'You actually think he's going to sell?' I said.

'I shouldn't think even Martineau would get it valued for sheer enjoyment,' said George. 'Unless he's madder than we think.'

His optimism had vanished now.

'I thought he was a bit more settled,' I said. 'After he was headed off the plays.'

'You can't tell with him,' said George.

'Whatever can he be thinking of doing?'

'God knows what he's thinking of.'

'There may be enough to live on,' I suggested. 'He might retire and go in for his plays and things – on a grandiose scale. Or he might take another job.'

'It's demoralising for the firm,' George broke out. 'I never know where I'm going to stand for two days together.'

'You've got to forgive him a lot,' I said.

'I do.'

'After all, he's in a queer state.'

'It's absolute and utter irresponsibility,' said George. 'The man's got a duty towards his friends.'

George's temper was near the surface. He went to the next Friday night at Martineau's; and sat uncomfortably silent while Martineau talked as gaily as ever, without any sign of care. Then, as for a moment Martineau left the room, George came over to Morcom and myself and whispered: 'I'm going to tackle him afterwards. I'm going to ask for an explanation on the spot.'

When, at eleven, the others had gone, George said rapidly: 'I wonder if you could spare us a few minutes, Mr Martineau?'

'George?' Martineau laughed at the stiffness of George's tone. He had been standing up, according to his habit, behind the sofa: now he dropped into an armchair and clasped his fingers round his knee.

'We simply want to be reassured on one or two matters,' George said. 'Sometimes you are an anxiety to your friends, you know.' For a second, a smile, frank and affectionate, broke up the heaviness on George's face. 'Will you allow me to put our questions?'

'If I can answer,' Martineau murmured. 'If I can answer.'

'Well then, do you intend to give up your present position?'

'My position!' said Martineau. 'Do you mean my position in thought? I've had so many,' he smiled, 'that some day I shall have to give some of them up, George.'

'I meant, do you intend to give up your position in the firm?'

'Ah,' said Martineau. Morcom leant forward, half-smiling at the curiously naïve attempt to hedge. 'It'd be easier if you hadn't asked – '

'Can you say no?'

'I'm afraid I can't – not a No like yours, George.' He got up from the chair and began his walk by the window. 'I've asked that question to myself, don't you see, and I can't answer it properly. I can't be sure I've made up my mind for certain. But, perhaps I can tell you, I sometimes don't feel I have any right to remain inside the firm.'

I had a sense of certainty that the hesitation was not there: I felt that he was speaking from an unequivocal heart. Whether he knew it or not. I wondered if he knew it.

'Right,' said George. 'Of course you have a right. According to law and conventional ethics and any conceivable ethics of your own. Why shouldn't you stay?'

'It isn't as straightforward,' Martineau shook his head with a smile. 'We touched on this before, George. I've thought of it so often since. You see, I can't forget I've got some obligations which aren't to the firm at all. I may be wrong, but they come before the firm if one has to choose.'

'So have I,' said George. 'But the choice doesn't arise.'

'I'm afraid it does a little,' Martineau replied. 'I told you, I shouldn't be able to stop the things that I feel I'm called for most. I can't possibly stop them.'

'No one wants you to,' said George.

Martineau rested his hands on the sofa.

'But I haven't been able to see a way to keep on with those – and stay in the firm.'

'Why not?'

'Because I oughtn't to be part of a firm and doing it harm at the same time, surely you agree, George? And these other attempts of mine – that I can't give up, they're damaging it, of course.'

'You mean to say the firm's worse off because of your – ' George shouted, stopped and said, 'activities?'

'I'm afraid so.'

'What's the evidence?'

'One or two people have said things.' Martineau stared at the ceiling.

'Have they said, plainly and definitely, that they think the firm's worse off than it was a couple of years ago?'

'They haven't said it in quite so many words, but – '

'They've implied it?'

'Yes.'

'Who are they?'

'I forget their names, except – '

'Except who?'

'Harry Eden said something not long ago.'

'Then Eden's a fool and a liar and I shall have pleasure in telling him so to his face,' George was shouting again. 'He wants to get rid of you and is trying a method that oughtn't to take in a child. It's simply nonsense. This is a straightforward matter of fact. The amount of business we did in the last nine months is bigger than in any other twelve months since I came. And we did more last month than during any similar time. It's only natural, of course. Anyone but Eden would realise that. And even he would if he hadn't a purpose of his own to serve. We're bound to have more cases, considering the success we had not long ago.'

'What do you mean?' Martineau, who had been frowning, inquired.

'It's only reasonable to imagine,' George said in a subdued voice, 'that the case in the summer had something to do with it.'

'Oh yes,' Martineau became passive again.

Morcom said: 'Do you think George is wrong, Howard? Do you really think the firm is suffering?'

His voice sounded cold and clear after the others.

'I think perhaps we're talking of different things,' said Martineau. 'I'm sure George's figures are right. I wasn't thinking of it quite in that way. I mean, I believe, I'm doing – what shall I say? – a kind of impalpable harm – just as the work I'm trying to do outside the firm is impalpable work. Which doesn't prevent it' – he smiled – 'being the most practical in the world, in my opinion.'

'I want to know,' George's voice was raised, 'what do you mean by impalpable harm to the firm?'

They argued again: Martineau became more evasive, and once he showed something like a flash of anger.

'I'm trying to do the best thing,' he said. 'I'm sorry you seem so eager to prevent me.'

'That's quite unfair.'

'I hoped my friends at any rate would give me credit for what I'm trying.' Then he recovered his light temper. 'Ah well, George, when you do something you feel is right, you'll know just what to expect.'

'Have you definitely made up your mind', said Morcom, 'to sell your share in the firm?'

'I can't say that,' said Martineau. 'Just now. I will tell you soon.'

'When?'

'It can't be long, it can't possibly be long,' Martineau replied.

'Next Friday?' I asked.

'No, not then. I shan't be in that night.'

Since any of us knew him, he had never missed being at home on Friday night. He announced it quite casually.

'I'll see you soon, though,' he said. 'I'll tell George when we can arrange one of our chats. It's so friendly of you to be worried. I value that, you don't know how I value that.'

In the street there was a mist which encircled the lamps. For a moment we stood outside the park gate; I felt a shiver of chill, and an anxious tension became mixed with the night's cold. Morcom said: 'We'd better go and have a coffee. We ought to talk this out.'

We walked down the road towards the station, chatting perfunctorily, our footsteps ringing heavily in the dank air. We went – there was nowhere else in this part of the town at night – to the café where we held the first conference about Jack.

'Can we do anything?' Morcom asked, as soon as we sat down. 'Have either of you any ideas?'

'He must be stopped,' said George.

'That's easy to say.'

'If only he could be made to recognise the *facts*,' George said.

'That doesn't help.'

'Of course it would help. The man's simply been misled. By the way,' George added with an elaborately indifferent smile, 'I thought you might have taken the opportunity to enlighten him. About the importance of the work I've done for them. Particularly the case.'

I saw a light, a narrowed concentration, in Morcom's eyes; I was on edge. I expected him to be provoked by the insistence and say something like, 'I could have explained, George, how important the case seems to you.' Morcom hesitated, and said:

'I would. But it wouldn't have been useful to you – or to him.'

'That's absurd,' George burst out. 'If he could really see.'

'It wouldn't make the slightest difference.'

'I refuse to accept that.'

'Don't you see,' Morcom leaned forward, 'that he's *bound to leave*?'

I knew it too. Yet George sat without replying. He seemed blind: he was a man himself more passionate and uncontrolled than any of us, but now he was not able to see past his own barricade of reasons, he was not able to perceive the passions of another.

'You must recognise that,' Morcom was saying. 'You don't think all these arguments matter to him? Except to bolster up a choice he's already been forced to make. That's all. I expect it pleases him' – he smiled – 'to be told how much he's giving up, and how unnecessary it is. It's just a luxury. As for affecting him, one might as well sing choruses from *The Gondoliers*. He's already made the decision in his mind.' He smiled again. 'As far as that goes,' he added, 'he may already have made it in fact.'

'You mean he's actually sold his share?' George said.

'I don't know,' said Morcom. 'It's possible.'

'To some bastard,' said George, 'who happens to have enough money to make a nuisance of himself to other people. Who'll disapprove of everything I do. Who'll make life intolerable for me.'

15

Martineau's Intention

I WALKED past Martineau's, the following Friday night. The drawing room window was dark: Martineau, so George thought, was visiting his brother, the Canon. Next day, when I was having supper with Morcom, George sent a message by Jack: Martineau wanted to see us tomorrow (Sunday) afternoon: we were to meet at George's.

'Martineau's getting more fun out of all this than anyone else,' said Jack. 'Like your girl' – he said to Morcom – 'when she decided to sacrifice herself. Blast them both.' He could speak directly to Morcom about Olive, as no one else could; and he went out of his way to ease Morcom's jealousy. 'How is she, by the way? No one else ever hears a word but you.'

'She seems fairly cheerful,' said Morcom.

'Blast her and Martineau as well. Send them off together,' said Jack. 'They deserve each other. That'd put them right if anything could.' His face melted into a mischievous, kindly grin. I had heard him say the same, with even more mischief, about Sheila.

When I arrived at George's the next day, he was smoking after the midday meal. His shout of greeting had a formal cheerfulness, but I could hear no heart behind it.

'You're the first,' he said.

'Martineau *is* coming?'

'I imagine so,' said George. 'Even Martineau couldn't get us all together and then not turn up himself.'

We sat by the window, looking out into the street. The knocker on the door opposite glistened in the sun.

Soon there were footsteps down the pavement. Martineau looked in and waved his hand. George went to let him in.

'Come in,' I heard George saying, and then, 'Isn't it a beautiful day?'

Martineau sat down in an armchair opposite the window; his face, lit by the clear light from the street, looked tranquil and happy. George pushed the table back against the wall, and placed two chairs in front of the fire.

'Have you seen Morcom lately?' he said to Martineau. 'I sent him word.'

'He may be just a little late,' Martineau said. 'He is having lunch with' – he smiled at George – 'my brother.'

'Why's that?' George's question shot out.

'To talk over my little affair, I'm afraid,' Martineau answered. 'I've never made such a nuisance of myself before – ' his laugh was full of pleasure.

'What does your brother think of it?'

'Very much the same as you do, George. He rather took the line that I owe an obligation to my relatives.' Martineau stared at the ceiling. 'I tried to put it to him as a Christian minister. I pointed out that he ought to sympathise with our placing certain duties higher than our duties to relatives. But he didn't seem to agree with my point of view.'

'Nor would any man of any sense,' said George.

'But is sense the most important thing?' Martineau asked 'For myself – '

'I refuse to be bullied by all these attacks on reason. I'm sorry, Mr Martineau,' said George, 'but I spend a great deal of my own time, as you know perfectly well, in activities that don't give me any personal profit whatever; but I'm prepared to justify them by reason, and if I couldn't I should give them up. That isn't true of what you propose to do, and so if you've got any respect for your intellectual honesty you've got no option but to abandon it.'

'I'm afraid I don't see it like that.' Martineau moved restlessly; his eyes met mine and then looked into the fire.

'There is no other way of seeing it,' said George.

(Many years later, near the end of George's life, I had to recall that justification of his.)

Through the uproar of George's voice I thought I had heard a knock at the door; it came again, now. I got up, and brought Morcom in. He spoke directly to Martineau.

'Eden's made a suggestion – '

'Where have you been?' George interrupted.

'Having lunch with Eden and Howard's brother.'

'I'm afraid,' Martineau broke in, 'I've been rather guilty this afternoon. I was trying to break it gently, you see, George. You must forgive me!'

'I'd better be told now.'

'Well, I spent all the early part of last week thinking over everything that had been said,' Martineau began. 'It was very difficult with so many friends that I really respect – you must believe that I respect your opinion, George – with so many friends – disapproving so much. But in the end I felt that I had to let them disapprove. The way I'd come to did really seem to be the only way.' He smiled. 'It does still.'

George had flushed. Morcom was looking at Martineau.

'So I told Harry Eden on Monday afternoon,' Martineau went on. 'He said he'd like to see my brother. That's why I arranged for them to meet.'

'You'd arranged that a week ago. So you'd made up your mind then,' George burst out.

'Not quite made up.' For a moment Martineau looked a little distraught. 'And in any case I felt I should like to have his advice, whether I had decided or not, you see. And Eden thought he'd feel easier if he could talk to one of my relatives, naturally.'

'I was brought in,' Morcom said, 'because Martineau hasn't any close friends of his own age in the town. You were ruled out because you were in the firm yourself, George. So Eden asked me in.'

110

To me, it was natural enough. Morcom at twenty-eight was a man who seemed made for responsibility; and most people thought of him as older.

'I suppose it's understandable,' George said. 'But if you've made up your mind' – he looked at Martineau – 'however fantastic it seems to everyone else, why should Eden become so officious all of a sudden? It's simply a matter of selling your share. I should have thought even Eden could have done that without family conferences.'

There was a pause. Martineau said, his voice trailing off: 'There is one matter that isn't quite – '

'It's this,' said Morcom. 'Martineau doesn't want to sell his share. He insists on giving it up to Eden.'

We sat in silence.

'It's raving lunacy,' George cried out.

'George! You won't be the last to call it that kind of name.' Martineau laughed.

'I'm sorry,' said George, heavily. 'And yet – what else can you call it?'

'I should like to call it something else.' Martineau was still laughing. 'I should like to call it: part of an attempt to live as I think I ought. It's time, George, it's time, after fifty years.'

'*Why* do you think you ought?'

'The religion I try to believe in – '

'You know you're doubtful whether you can call yourself a Christian.'

'This world of affairs of yours, George,' Martineau was following another thought – 'why, my chief happiness in your socialism is that one ought to give up all one has to the common good. It's always been a little of a puzzle how one can fail to do that in practice and keep the faith.'

George was flaring out, when I said: ' "Give it up to the common good" – but you're not doing that. You're giving it to Eden.'

'Ah, Lewis!' Martineau smiled. 'You think at least I ought to dispose of it myself?'

'I should have thought so.'

'Don't you see,' he said, 'that I can't do that? If I admit I have the power to dispose of it, why then I haven't got rid of the chains. I've got to let it slide. I mustn't allow myself the satisfaction of giving it to a friend' – he looked at George – 'or selling it and giving the money to charity. I'm compelled to forgo even that. I must just stand by as humbly as I can and be glad I haven't got the power.'

I looked at Morcom and George. We were all quiet. It was in a flat, level voice that George said: 'No doubt Eden hasn't raised any objections.'

'That's not fair,' said Morcom. 'He's behaved very well.'

Martineau looked cheerfully at George. He still enjoyed a thrust at his partner's expense.

'He's a good fellow,' he said lightly.

'I prefer to hold to my own opinion.'

'He's behaved well,' said Morcom again. 'Better than you could reasonably expect. He refused to do anything at all until he'd seen Martineau's brother. He said today that he doesn't like it and that he won't sign any transfer for three months. If anything happens to make Martineau change his mind during that time, then Eden wants the firm to go on as before. And if it doesn't, well, he said he was a businessman and not a philanthropist, and so he wasn't going to make gestures. He'll just take the offer. He's very fond of Martineau, he's as sorry as anyone else that this has happened – '

'I wish,' Martineau chuckled, 'everyone wouldn't refer to me as though I were either insane or dead.' We all laughed, George very loudly.

'It's good of him,' said Martineau. 'But I'm afraid he might as well save the time. I consider that it isn't mine any longer, you see. For – it isn't decided by a form of law – '

Soon afterwards Martineau left. When I heard the door click outside, I said: 'Whatever's going to become of him?'

On George's face injury struggled with concern: he shook his head. Morcom said: 'God knows.' But, at that time, even our most fantastic prophecies would not have approached the truth.

'The first thing,' said George, 'is to satisfy ourselves that he can find a living. We can't take any other steps until we're sure of that.'

'Apparently he told his brother he was going to earn enough by various methods. Which he wouldn't give any details of,' said Morcom. 'I simply don't know what he means.'

'Though how he reconciles giving up his share,' said George with an impatient laugh, 'and earning a living in any other way, is just beyond me. I suppose consistency isn't his strong point. Oh God!' he broke out, 'don't you find it hard to realise that this has *happened*?'

'Of course he won't starve,' Morcom said. 'That's one comfort. There is plenty of money in the family. In fact, that's one of his brother's chief anxieties. That they'll have to support him. The Canon's a hard man, by the way. I don't think I like him much.'

'Not so much as you like Eden, I suppose,' George said.

Morcom paused slightly: 'Nothing like,' he said.

The strain between them was showing in every word. I said hastily: 'What's he going to do with the house? Does he own it or not?'

'He's got some scheme for turning it into a boarding house,' said Morcom. 'With his housekeeper in charge.'

'That means we've had the last "Friday night",' I said. 'I shall miss them,' I added.

'You have to realise,' said Morcom deliberately, 'that he's cutting himself away from his present life. That means cutting himself away from us as much as from the firm. You have to understand that. He doesn't want to see much of us again.'

Suddenly George burst into gusts of laughter. I found myself grow tense, watching him shake, seeing the tears that came so easily.

'I've just thought,' he wiped his eyes, then began to laugh again as helplessly. 'I've just thought,' he said at last in a weak voice: 'Martineau's position is exactly this. He thinks a man couldn't hold his share in the firm if he's either a Christian or a socialist. So he gives it up, being neither a Christian nor a socialist.'

It was a typical George joke, in its symmetry, in the incongruity that would strike no one else. But he had been laughing more for relief than at the joke. Soon he was saying, quite soberly:

'We've been assuming all the time that everything's settled. We haven't given ourselves a chance to do anything in the matter.'

'Of course we can't do anything,' said Morcom.

'I don't know whether I accept that completely,' said George. 'But if so we shall have to set to work in another direction.'

I did not know what those words foreshadowed; I was easier in mind than I had been that afternoon, to see his spirits enlivened again.

16

Walk in the Rain

AFTER he went away from George's, none of us saw Martineau for weeks. There were some rumours about him; he was said to have bought a share of a small advertising agency, and also to have been seen in a poor neighbourhood visiting from house to house. Several times at Eden's we talked of him and speculated over his next move. The whole episode often seemed remote, as we sat in the comfortable room, hung with a collection of Chinese prints, and heard Eden say: 'These things will happen.' He said it frequently, with a tolerant and good-humoured smile.

Now that 'Friday nights' no longer existed, he had suggested that we call on him instead. He changed the day to Sunday, explaining that Friday was inconvenient for him, as his wife entertained that night. His real reason, I thought later, was a delicacy we did not appreciate enough. He gave us good food and drink, and the conversation was, more often than not, better than at Martineau's. The liking I had formed for Eden after casual meetings strengthened now. It was difficult to remember that this was the man whom George so much disliked.

Though by this time I knew something of George's antipathies, I tried to argue him out of this, the most practically important. It seemed more than ever urgent for him to gain Eden's approval. He protested angrily, but was less obdurate than in the summer. One Sunday I persuaded him to come to the house, and he was nervously silent apart from a sudden quick-worded argument with Eden upon some matter of political history; it was the first time I had seen that drawing room disturbed. When Morcom and I disagreed with Eden, it meant only one of his good-humoured aphorisms, followed by a monologue that did not lead to controversy.

George said, as he stopped outside the gate to light a pipe: 'I hope you're satisfied now.'

In the match light, he was smiling happily. To him, I suddenly realised, for whom most meetings and most people were full of unknown hostility, the night had been a success.

'You must go again,' I said.

'Naturally,' said George. 'After all, I've truckled for three years, in the firm. I must say, though, that he went out of his way to be civil tonight.'

It began to rain heavily, and we got on a tram-car. As it moved towards the town, we pieced together the rumours about Martineau. Often George guffawed: 'Fancy having one's goods advertised by Martineau,' he burst out. 'And fancy giving up,' he chuckled, 'a perfectly respectable profession to take up one more disreputable by any conceivable standards in the world. The only advantage being that it's almost certain to fail.' He laughed and wiped his eyes. 'Oh, Good God in Heaven, whatever is the point? Whatever does he think is the point?'

Suddenly George said, without any introduction: 'I think we've exaggerated this upheaval in the firm.'

I shook my head, and said: 'I am quite certain of one thing.'

'What's that?'

'That, whatever happens, Martineau will never come back to the firm. I'm sure that's true. It's unpleasant for you. But you must resign yourself – '

George said: 'I did that weeks ago. I assumed it as soon as Martineau disappeared.'

'Then what did you mean?' I said. 'About the upheaval in the firm being exaggerated. Whatever could you mean?'

'Oh,' said George. 'I decided, as I said, that Martineau could be ruled out. He obviously wouldn't be any further help. But what I meant was, I couldn't see why Eden shouldn't do as much for me as Martineau ever did. And I began to realise there were reasons why he should do a great deal more.'

'At once?'

'I don't see why he shouldn't be taking steps to make me a partner. Fairly soon.'

'Is that likely?' (I was thinking: this ought to have been foreseen.)

'I don't see why not.'

The tram was rattling to a stop: I rubbed the window with my sleeve. The rain had ceased, though it was dripping from the roofs. We were near the railway bridge, by some old mean streets.

'Look here,' said George. 'I've got a bit of a head. Let's walk from here.'

The gutters were swirling as we got off. George said: 'I don't see why not. After all, he'll be gaining enough by this business. He can afford to take a partner without any capital. He would have to get someone in my place, naturally. But Eden would still be better off by a very decent amount, compared with what he has been. With the advantages of having me as a partner.'

'Those being? I mean, from Eden's point of view?'

We were walking under the bridge. Our footsteps echoed, and I shivered in the cold. George's voice came back.

'The first is one we all tend to forget. That is, there is such a thing as ordinary human justice. Eden can't be too comfortable if I'm doing more work than the rest of the firm put together – which I have been doing for the last two years – and getting the money, which doesn't matter so much, and having the position, which matters a great deal, of a fairly competent clerk.'

'Are you sure he realises that – altogether?'

'If he doesn't,' said George, 'it's simply because he doesn't want to see. But even then – it must be perfectly obvious.' He walked along, looking straight ahead. 'The other reason is what plain blunt practical men would consider a great deal more important. That is, Eden doesn't know anything about half the cases we have to deal with. You know perfectly well, we've got a connection in income tax and property law and other kinds of superior accountancy. Well, Martineau could cope with those before he began to be troubled with doubt' – he chuckled – 'and even lately he could give people the impression that he knew something about it. Well, Eden simply couldn't. He's grotesquely incompetent at any piece of financial detail. In three or four years he'd have ruined our connection. It'd be too ridiculous, he's bound to realise it.' He went on, very quickly, as though to dismiss any argument: 'No, so far as I can see, there's only one possible reason for his not taking me in, and that is, he hasn't much sympathy for my general attitude.

'But I can't believe he'd let that outweigh everything else,' George went on. 'There are limits, you can't deny there are limits. And also he's shown signs recently that he's coming round. I think it'll be all right. Anyway we must see it *is* all right. You realise,' he said, 'that Eden can be influenced nowadays.'

'How?'

'I should have thought it was obvious.'

'How?'

'Morcom, of course,' George said. 'Obviously Eden's very much impressed with him for some reason. You noticed how he sent for him for that rather absurd conference with the Martineau's. And Morcom sees him very often – '

'Only on Sundays.'

'I've seen them in the town.' George frowned. 'It's absolutely patent that Morcom counts for a great deal with him. Well, we've got to take advantage of that.'

'He can't – '

'I know what you're going to say,' said George. 'I know as well as you do that Morcom doesn't approve of most of the things I do. I realise that and I've considered it. And I've decided I've a right to demand that he forgets it. He must talk to Eden about me. It's too important to let minor things stand in the way.' He paused, and then turned to me. Before, he had been looking straight ahead down the dark street. 'You mustn't know anything about this. Not even to Morcom. I'll deal with him myself.' Then his voice suddenly became friendly, and he talked as though he was pleasantly fatigued.

'It's important that Eden should take me in,' he said. 'I don't want to stay there as a subordinate and watch myself getting old.'

'That won't happen,' I said.

'I don't know,' said George. 'Things have never fallen in my lap.'

I had a rush of friendship for him, the warm friendship which sometimes at this period I was provoked into forgetting.

'It's time they began,' I said.

'It isn't that I'm not ambitious,' said George. 'I am, you know, to some extent. I know I'm not as determined as you've turned out to be – but matters never shaped themselves to give ambition a chance. I had to take the job here, there wasn't any alternative to that. When I got here, I couldn't do anything different from what I have done. Of course, I got interested in making something of people at the School. But I couldn't help myself.'

'Yes,' I said.

'It's important from every point of view that I get promoted,' he said quickly. 'For the group as well. If I'm really going to do much for anyone. I haven't got the money. I'm often powerless. I nearly was about Jack. God! how crippled one feels when there's someone who only wants money to give them a start.'

'You'd be worse off than you are now.' I smiled. 'Giving it away.'

George's own smile grew vaguer.

'There's another possibility,' he said. 'I don't know, but I may feel some time that I've done as much as I can with the School. After all, the present people will go away in time. I don't know that I shall want to get interested in any more.'

It was the first time I had heard him permit such a suggestion.

'I may want to do something useful in a wider field,' said George. 'And for that, I must be in with Eden. The group's all very well in its way, but its success is inside oneself, as you've said before now. As one gets older, perhaps one isn't pure enough to be satisfied with that.'

I tried to laugh it off. 'Martineau seems to be satisfied pretty easily,' I said. 'If his success isn't inside himself – '

George laughed. Then he said: 'I may even want to get married.'

Although a wish, it was no clearer than the others. It was one of many wishes springing from the unrest, the hope, that brought to his face a happy and expectant smile.

17

A Slip of the Tongue

I WAS upset by that talk with George.

He was mistaken, I knew, when he suddenly discovered that he was ambitious. If he had been truly ambitious, I should not have been so concerned; for, when this partnership failed him, he would have found something else to drive for. While George valued it more acutely, precisely because he did not usually care – just as a man like Morcom, not easily surrendered to love, may once in his life long for it with a passion dangerous to himself.

George at this moment longed for the place and security to which, for years, he had scarcely given a thought.

But that was nothing like all. I realised that Olive had been right. Months before, by a lucky guess or clairvoyance, she had divined something more important. 'I think he sometimes knows he was unlucky to get amongst us. Sometimes he wants to get away,' she said. He was trying to break from his present life, the School, the little world, the group. Jack's confession might have weakened him – but Olive felt it long before, long before his most vehement declaration of faith, that night in the café by the river. I believed that she was right.

However much he was satisfied by the little world he had built up, he was able to think of breaking free. Perhaps he half realised the danger, the crippling danger to himself. Anyway, he seemed to know that for just these months there was a chance to break loose *from his own satisfaction.* He also seemed to know that, if this failed, he would never bring himself to the point again.

Hearing George express his want for a respectable position, a comfortable middle-class income, the restraints of a junior partner in a firm of solicitors in a provincial town, I could not help being moved. Knowing the improbability, knowing above all this new suspicious faith in Morcom's influence, I was afraid. There was only a short time before Eden's period of grace ran out; it need not be final, but it would deprive George of his hopes.

I heard nothing, until a fortnight later, when Morcom and I were on our way towards Eden's. Abruptly Morcom said: 'George thinks Eden will offer him a partnership.' I exclaimed.

'He stands exactly as much chance as I do,' said Morcom. He gave a short laugh, and talked about George's unrealistic hopes. Then I said: 'They're quite fantastic, of course. But that doesn't prevent him believing in them. It doesn't prevent him attaching as much importance to them as you might to something reasonable. Surely that's true.'

'I expect it is,' said Morcom. His voice sounded flat, his manner despondent and out of spirits. 'Anyway,' he said, 'I can't do anything. Eden will settle it completely by himself.'

'You might sound him,' I said.

'It's a lot of trouble simply because George believes the world revolves round him,' said Morcom.

'If he knew it had been mentioned –' I said. 'You see,' I added, filled with an inexplicable shame as well as anxiety, 'he's always got a dim feeling that you're antagonistic. If that grows, it's going to make life unpleasant.'

Morcom's face, as we came near a street lamp, looked drawn. I was surprised that the statement should have affected him so much. 'All right,' he said. 'I'd better try tonight.'

For most of the evening I sat listening to Eden's anecdotes, laughing more easily to make up for my impatience. The room was warm, there was a fire blazing, stoked high in the chimney: Eden was sitting by its side in his customary armchair, in front of which stood the little table full of books and pipes and a decanter. He wore a velvet smoking jacket. Morcom sat opposite to him. I in the middle: behind Morcom, the light picked out the golden lines in one of the Chinese pictures.

At last there was a lull. Eden filled his glass. Morcom was leaning forward, the fingers of one hand tight over his knee.

'By the way, the time you gave Martineau to make up his mind – it'll be over soon, won't it?'

'I hadn't thought of it just lately.' Eden sipped, and put down his glass. 'Why, do you know, I suppose it will.'

'There's no chance of his coming back,' said Morcom.

I added: 'None at all.'

'I'm afraid you're right,' said Eden. It was a comfortable fear, I could not help thinking. 'It's a queer business. It's one of the queerest things I've ever struck.'

'What are you going to do about it? About the firm, I mean?' The questions were sharp. I could feel Morcom, as I was myself, responding to a slight, an amiable unwillingness in Eden's manner.

'I dare say it will go on,' Eden smiled. 'When once you've really started, it's not a difficult proposition to keep going, you know.'

'You're not thinking of filling – Martineau's place?'

'I needn't make any decision yet,' Eden said. 'There isn't any hurry, of course. But my present belief is that I shan't take another partner. I'm an old-fashioned democrat in affairs of state' – he smiled – 'but the older I get, the more I believe smaller things ought to be controlled by one man.'

'I can believe that,' said Morcom. 'But it's a lot of work for one man.'

'There's plenty of responsibility,' said Eden. 'But that's the penalty of being in control. No one wants it, but it's got to be shouldered. As for the detailed work, I shan't do any more than I'm doing now. I can trust the staff for anything in the way of routine. And to some extent I can trust Passant to work on his own.'

'He is very capable?' said Morcom.

123

'Very capable. Very capable indeed.' Eden was talking affably, but his lips had no tendency towards their smile. 'So long as he's working under someone *level-headed*. I know he's a friend of you two. I'm speaking as I shouldn't, you mustn't let it go beyond these four walls. But Passant's a man who'd have a future in front of him if only he didn't spoil himself. He's got a brilliant scholastic record, and though that isn't the same as being able to take your coat off in an office, he's done some good sound work for the firm. An outsider might think that I ought to give him a chance in a year or two to buy a share in the firm. But unless he takes himself in hand I don't believe I shall be able to do it. I couldn't feel I was doing the right thing.'

'Why not?'

'You'll be sure not to let this go any further?' Eden looked at us. 'Though a hint from you' – he glanced at Morcom – 'on your own account wouldn't be amiss. The trouble about Passant is – he's rackety. He's like a tremendous number of young men of your generation. There's nothing to keep him between the rails.'

I suddenly could hear, among the moderate ordinary words, a dislike as intense as that which George bore him.

'I know you can say that's a matter for the man himself. It's no one else's business how he lives. He's a grown man, he's free to choose his own friends and his own pleasures. If he wants to spend his spare time with these young men and girls he collects together, no one's going to stop him. But' – Eden shook his head – 'it's got to be remembered when you're thinking of his position here. I mightn't mind – except that they take up too much of his time – but the great majority of our clients would. And it's very hard to blame them. When you see a man night after night sitting in cafés with hordes of young girls, and you haven't much doubt that he's pretty loose-living all round; when you hear him laying down the law on every topic under heaven, telling everyone how to run the world: when above all you find him making an officious nuisance of himself in matters that don't concern him, like that affair of Calvert's: then you have to be an unusually tolerant man' – Eden leaned back and smiled – 'to feel very happy when you pay the firm a visit and find he's your family solicitor.'

'Particularly if he insists on telling you that you ought to follow his example,' Morcom said. 'And that you ought to bring your daughter just to show there's no ill-feeling.'

Involuntarily, I smiled myself. Then I stared in dismay at Morcom, while Eden continued to laugh. I was thinking, more bitter in my reproaches because I might have committed it myself, that the gibe was less than deliberate. It was one of those outbursts, triumphantly warm on the tongue, whose echo afterwards makes one wince with remorse. It was one of those outbursts that everyone is impelled to at times, however subtle and astute. In fact, I was to discover, the more subtle and astute one was, the more facilely such indiscretions came. Until, like the politicians I knew later, one disciplined oneself to say nothing spontaneous at all.

But that was not the whole of it, I knew, as I listened to Eden's slow and pleasant voice again. For while we listen to a friend being attacked, there are moments of sick and painful indignation, however untrue the charge: and, at other moments such as those when we make Morcom's joke – however untrue the charge – we find ourselves leaping to agree. We find ourselves, ashamed and eager with the laugh, on Eden's side. Again, until we have hardened our characters, eliminated the trendiness along with the free-flowing.

'After all,' Eden was saying, 'Martineau can't have done us any good. People might respect him if they understood what he was getting at – but they don't want a saint, they want a sensible solicitor. We've got to win a certain amount of confidence back. We couldn't afford another Martineau. I'm afraid Passant would cause a bigger hostility even that that.'

'He's far more competent,' Morcom insisted.

'I suppose he is,' slowly Eden agreed.

'He's in a different class intellectually,' Morcom leaned forward. 'He's got an astounding mental energy. You ought to remember that when you talk of him wasting time. He's capable of amusing himself till midnight and then concentrating for five or six hours.'

'And be worn out next day.' Eden looked a little disturbed.

'No, he'd be tired. But not too tired to work. He's got a curious loyalty. Which we should naturally see more of than you would. He'd never do anything deliberately to harm the firm. Even for his beliefs – which are very real. That affair of Calvert's: he only did it because of his beliefs. He is rather a remarkable man.'

The sentences were rapped out, jerkily and harshly. Eden's face was calm and kindly as he listened, his head thrown back, his eyes looking down so that one saw a half-closed lid.

'Perhaps he's too remarkable,' Eden said, 'for a solicitor in a provincial town.'

When we left, it was late, the cars had stopped, we had to walk through the cold still night. We were both silent; I looked at the stars, without finding the moment's ease they often gave. As we parted, Morcom spoke: 'It would have done no good, whatever I said.'

18

I Appeal

I SAW none of them for several days. As it happened, I was sleeping badly and in a state of physical malaise. I stayed in my room, goading myself to work with an apprehension never far from my mind.

At last, on an evening in the week that Eden's period ran out, I was driven to visit Martineau. I had not been out for days.

I had heard that his advertising agency was run under the name of a partner called Exell. It took me some time to find their office; it was a tiny room on the fifth storey of an old block of buildings, at the corner of the market place. Martineau sat there alone, and greeted me with a cheerful cry.

'So nice to see you,' he said. 'This is where we keep body and soul together.'

He was dressed untidily in an old grey suit: but the habitual buttonhole still gleamed white and incongruous on his breast.

'Can we do anything for you, Lewis? There must be something we can do.'

'I'm sorry,' I said. 'I only came to talk.'

'Nearly as good,' said Martineau. 'Nearly as good. But I must show you one or two of our little schemes – '

He was so full of them that nothing could stop him describing them, fervently and happily. There were several: from one or two he did make a small income for some time: one I had cause to remember afterwards. They had bought a local advertising paper, which appeared weekly. It was sold at a penny, circulated among shopkeepers in the town, and carried some suburban news. Martineau had published some religious articles in it; he read them aloud enthusiastically, before asking me: 'Have you come for anything special, Lewis?'

'It's dull and private,' I said.

'Fire away,' said Martineau.

As it was cold in their room, however, I took him out to a café. When I explained that I was not well, Martineau said: 'You do look a bit under the weather!'

And when we went into the café lounge, he looked round with his lively curiosity, and said: 'Do you know, Lewis, I've not been in one of these big cafés for years.'

I was too strung up to pay attention then, but later that remark seemed an odd example of the geographical separations of our lives. For nearly two years I had seen Martineau each week. Yet the territory we covered – in a town a few miles square – was utterly different: draw his paths in blue and mine in red, like underground railways, and the only junction would be at his house.

We sat by a window: in the marketplace, as I glanced down, the light of a shop suddenly went out.

'You remember what Saturday is?' I said.

'I don't think I do,' Martineau reflected.

'It's the day Eden said he'd accept your share in the firm – if you didn't change your mind.'

'He's an obstinate old fellow.' Martineau smiled. 'I told him he could have it months ago – and he wouldn't believe me. Ah well, he'll have to now.'

'Yes, I know,' I said quickly. 'There's something important about all this. Which may be a calamity to some of your friends. And you can stop it. Shall I go on?'

'You're trying to persuade me to come back?' He laughed.

'No,' I said. 'Not that now. I want to ask – something a good deal less.'

'Go on, Lewis,' he said. 'Go on.'

'It's about your partnership,' I said. 'George has set his heart on having it himself.'

'Oh,' said Martineau. 'I can see one or two difficulties.' His tone was curiously businesslike. 'He didn't behave very wisely over Calvert, you know.'

'*You* can't hold that against him,' I cried.

'Of course I don't,' said Martineau quickly. 'But he's very young yet, of course.'

'It wouldn't have mattered about his age,' I said. 'If he'd the money to buy a partnership somewhere.'

'I believe that's true,' said Martineau.

'It's entirely a matter of money. Of course, he hasn't any.'

'You're sure he really wants to be tied down like that?'

'More than anything in the world. Just at this minute.'

'He used to put – first things first,' said Martineau.

'He still does, I think,' I said. 'But he's not entirely like you. He wants the second things as well.'

'Well done, well done,' he said. Then as he quietened down into a pleased smile, he said: 'Well, if old George really wants to go in, I do hope Eden asks him. George deserves to be given what he wants – more than most of us.'

The affection was, I had always known, genuine and deeper than for any of us. It was as unquestionable as Eden's dislike of George.

'Except,' said Martineau, 'that perhaps none of us deserves to be given what we want.'

'Eden certainly won't ask him,' I said. 'He's said as much.'

'Such a pity,' said Martineau. 'I'm sorry for George, but it can't be helped.'

I was as diffident as though I were asking for money for myself. Of all men, he seemed the most impossible to plead with for a favour: for no reason that I could understand, except a paralysis of one's own will.

'It can be helped,' I said. 'You can help it.'

'I'm helpless.' Martineau shook his head. 'It's Eden's firm now.'

129

'You needn't give your share to him. You can give it to George instead.'

Very gently, Martineau said: 'You know how I should like to. I'd like to do that more than most things. But haven't I told you already why I can't? You know I can't – '

'I know you said you were giving up everything – and it's being false to yourself to hold on to your share. Even in this way. Can't you think again about that?'

'I wish I could,' said Martineau.

'I wouldn't ask you if it weren't serious. But it's desperately serious.'

Martineau looked at me.

'It's George I'm asking you for. This matters more for George's well-being than it does for all the rest of us put together. It matters infinitely more to him than it does to you.'

'I don't believe George cares as much for ordinary rewards – '

'No. That is trivial by the side of what I mean. I mean this: that George's life is more complicated than most people's. He may make something of it that most people would approve. Even that you might yourself. Or he may just – squander himself away.'

'Perhaps you're right,' said Martineau.

'I can't explain it all, but I'm convinced this is a turning point. If George doesn't get this partnership, it may do him more harm than anything we could invent against him. I'm only asking you to avert that. Just to take a nominal control for George's sake. Can't you allow yourself an – evasion in order not to harm him more than he's ever been harmed? I tell you, this is critical for George. I think he sometimes knows himself how critical it is.'

There was a silence. Martineau said: 'I'm sorry, Lewis. I can't do it, even for that. I can't even give myself that pleasure.'

'So you won't do it?'

'It's not like that. I can't do it.'

'Of course you could do it,' I burst out, angry and tired. 'You could do it – if only you weren't so proud of your own humility.'

Martineau looked down at the table.

'I'm sorry you should think that.'

I was too much distressed to be silent.

'You're proud of your humility,' I said. 'Don't you realise that? You're enjoying all this unpleasantness you're inflicting on yourself. All this suffering and neglect and squalor and humiliation – they're what you longed for, and you're happy now.'

Martineau's eyes looked, smiling, into mine and then aside.

'No, Lewis, you're a little wild there. You don't really think I relish giving up the things I enjoyed most?'

'In a way, I think you do.'

'No. You know how I used to enjoy things, the ordinary pleasant things. Like a hot bath in the evening – and looking at my pictures – and having a little music. You know how I enjoyed those?'

I nodded.

'I've given them up, you know. Do you really think I don't miss them? Or that I actually enjoy the things I have now in their place?'

'I expect there's a difference.'

'You must try to see.' Martineau was smiling. 'I am happy, I know. I'm happy. I'm happier because I've given up my pleasures. But it's not because of the actual fact of giving them up. It's because of the state it's going to bring me to.'

19

George Calls on Morcom

I SPENT the weekend alone in my room: on Sunday I felt better, though still too tired to stir. I could do no more, I worked all day and at night sat reading with a convalescent luxury. But on Monday, after tea, that false calm dropped away as I heard a tread on the stairs. George came in – a parody of a smile on his lips.

'They've arranged it,' he said. He swore coldly. 'They've managed it very subtly. And insulted me at the same time.'

'What's happened?'

'I went to remind Eden today that the time had lapsed.'

'Was that wise?'

'What does it matter whether it's wise or not? Did the man think he could keep me in suspense forever? I'd got a perfect right to go and ask him what he had decided about the firm.'

'And he told you – '

'Yes, he told me.' George laughed. 'He was very genial and avuncular. He was quite glad to tell me. He went so far as to reassure me – I wasn't to be afraid the change would make any difference to my position. The swine had the impertinence to hint that I thought of myself like any office boy in danger of being dismissed. That's one of the pleasant features of the whole business: Eden having the kindness to say he wasn't going to dismiss me. He even went so far as to mention that he and Martineau had both had a high opinion of my ability, and that I'd done good work for the firm. That was the second insult. And the third was when he said I might have slightly more work to do under the new arrangement: so he proposed to give me an extra twenty-five pounds a year.'

'He meant it good-naturedly.'

'Nonsense,' George shouted. 'If you say that you're merely associating yourself with the insults. It was completely deliberate. He knew he could go as far as he wanted. And he knew, if he insulted me with an offer like that, I had to accept it. But I don't think I left him under the illusion that I accepted it very gratefully.'

'What did you say?'

'After he'd made it quite clear that he intended to do nothing for me, I didn't see any reason why I shouldn't let him know that he was acting atrociously. So I inquired point blank whether he had considered asking me into the firm. Anyway, I had the satisfaction of making him feel ashamed of himself. He said he had thought about the matter – very carefully – very carefully.' In the middle of George's violence, I saw his eyes were bewildered. 'And although he'd like to very much for many reasons, he thought the present time wasn't very opportune. I told him there would never be a more opportune one. Then he tried to stand on his dignity and said he proposed not to discuss it now. I asked him when there would be an opportune time and when he proposed to discuss it. He hedged. I kept at him. In the end he said it wouldn't be until he saw how I developed in the next few years. I asked him what he was implying. He said it was too embarrassing for us both for him to discuss it with me there and then, but that he'd had a few words about it with a friend of mine. He might be able to give me a fairer idea. You realise who that is?' George's voice filled the room.

'Morcom, I suppose,' I said.

'I shall go and get things straight with Morcom,' George said.

'Wait until tomorrow.'

'Why should I wait? I only want to explain a few things.'

'Look here,' I said. 'I was there one night when Morcom was trying to defend you – '

'I don't believe it,' said George. 'You'd better come. I don't want you to be deluded. In any case, I'm going there now.'

When we had walked through the back streets, I was in one of those states of fatigue, almost like extreme well-being, when one is lighter than the dark streets round one, the rain, and the rushing wind; the glowing windows of the shops by the tramlines at the bottom of the road seemed like the lights scattered round a waterfront.

Across the road from Morcom's new lodgings, the trees smelt mustily in the rain: the window (I hoped to see it in darkness) was a square of tawny light, and Morcom let us in himself.

'Good,' he said, with a smile of pleasure.

'I'm afraid,' said George, following him into the room, 'I've only come for a short talk.'

Morcom turned quickly at the tone. 'Sit down,' he said.

'I should like you to explain,' said George, 'something that Eden said to me this afternoon. I don't expect it's necessary to tell you that he refuses to take me into the firm. He suggested you might be able to tell me the reason better than he could himself.'

'Lewis knows as much as I do,' Morcom said.

'Eden mentioned you by name,' said George.

'He'd no right to throw this on me.'

'That's irrelevant,' George said. 'I'm not interested in Eden's behaviour. I've seen enough of that. I want to know the conversations you've had about me.'

'The only time I've heard him speak of you at any length,' said Morcom, 'was' – he looked at me – 'that Sunday. A fortnight ago. I said what you asked me – and tried to find out what he thought of you. I didn't tell you the result because I thought it would hurt you. If you must have it – he admitted rather reluctantly that you'd got ability, but he didn't think you're reliable enough to be in a responsible position and he's afraid you'd be a danger to the firm.'

'What sort of danger?'

'Roughly that your present way of life would put clients off. It was also pretty clear that it put him off.'

'What does he know of my way of life?'

'A fair amount,' said Morcom.

'He had the impertinence to mention the Calvert incident. I suppose he knows about the people at the School.'

'He couldn't very well help it.'

'I don't see why he should imagine anyone disapproving of that.' George's voice was penetrating and subdued, as though he were keeping it low by will alone.

'Simply because he thinks you get the young women together in order to seduce them.'

'That's the kind of cheap suspicion a man like that would have. I suppose you didn't tell him the truth? Did you deny it?'

Morcom flushed. 'I did what I could.'

'Eden didn't give me that impression.'

'It's certainly true,' I broke in. 'Arthur was as near being rude as I ever heard him.'

As I looked at Morcom, we could not forget one remark in another sense.

'Even if that's true,' said George, 'you gave different impressions on other nights.'

'Do you seriously mean,' Morcom suddenly broke out, 'that I've been blackguarding you in private?'

'Eden said that most people who knew me thought I was good at deceiving myself. Who said that if you didn't? Do you mean to say that you never dropped those *other* hints – to Eden about my behaviour?'

'If you want me to pretend that I've treated you as an entirely sacred subject in conversation with Eden or anyone else,' Morcom said, 'I'm afraid I can't. It isn't so easy for an outsider to believe in your divine inspiration, you realise.'

'You mean I'm a megalomaniac?'

'At times, yes.'

'That's an honest remark at last. It's a relief.'

Morcom raised himself in his chair: 'We oughtn't to quarrel. Let's leave this now.'

135

There was a silence; then George said: 'No, one honest remark isn't enough. It's time some more were made. This has been going on too long already.

'You don't think I've been completely taken in, do you?' George went on. His voice was getting louder now. 'I've credited you with every doubt I could until now. But it wouldn't be charitable to doubt any more, it would merely be culpable madness. Even when I was giving you the benefit of the doubt, I was all but certain you had been working against me at every single point.'

'This is sheer mania,' Morcom said.

'Mania? I dare say you call it mania to be able to see a connection between some very simple events. Do you call it mania to remember that you discouraged me from taking any steps about Jack Cotery? – one of the few effective things I've managed to do in this town. You wouldn't believe it when I brought it off. You went on to advise him to go into business against my judgment – that might have been disastrous for me. You don't deny that you tried to take Olive away. With slightly more success. Though not quite as much as you set out for. You hung round her as soon as you realised she was valuable to me.'

One side of Morcom's mouth was drawn in.

'Or that you discouraged Jack Cotery and Eliot from everything I believed and wanted to do? You did it very subtly and carefully. The great George joke, the silly amiable old ass, with his fatuous causes, just preaching nonsense that might have been fresh fifty years ago, and then cuddling one of the girls on the quiet. Fortunately they had too much independence to believe you altogether – but still it left its mark – '

'Of course not – ' I said.

'I can give you plenty of proof of that. Principally from Jack's behaviour.' George turned on me, then back to Morcom. 'And when you'd finished on my friends you tried to stop my career. You encouraged Martineau in his madness, you didn't stop him when he might have been stopped. You let him go ahead with the little plays, blast them to hell. You made suggestions about them as though they were useful. You let him think it was right to allow the firm to go to Eden, and you carefully kept him away from thinking of giving it over to me. Then you made really certain by this business with Eden. I'll admit you've been thorough. That's about all I will admit for you. It's the meanest deliberate attempt to sin against the human decencies that I've come across so far.'

George stopped suddenly: the shout seemed to leave a noise in the ears when his lips were already still.

'I'm not going to argue with you,' said Morcom. 'It isn't any good telling you that quite a lot of things happen in the world without any reference to yourself. It's possible to talk to someone like Martineau about his life without thinking of you for a single instant. But you're pathologically incapable of realising that. It's out of your control – '

'In that case, the sooner we stop pretending to have human intercourse the better. I don't much like being victimised; I dislike even more being victimised by someone who pretends that I'm not sane.'

'The only thing I should like to know,' Morcom said, 'is why you thought I should flatter you – by all these exertions.'

'Because we've always stood for different things,' George cried. 'And you've known it all the time. Because I stand for the hopeful things, and you for their opposite. You've never forgiven me for that. I'm doing something to create the world I believe in – you're sterile and you know it. I believe in human nature. You – despise it because you think all human nature is as twisted as your own. I believe in progress, I believe that human happiness ought to be attained and that we are attaining it. You're bitter because you couldn't believe in any of those things. The world I want will come and you know it – as for yours, it will be inhabited by people as perverted as yourself.'

Morcom sat with his eyes never leaving George's, his arms limp at his sides.

'Good God above, do I wonder you hate me?' George shouted on. 'You've got everything that I needed to make me any use. You could have done everything – if only you could bear to see someone else's happiness. As it is, you can only use your gifts against those who show you what you've missed. You try to get your satisfaction by injuring people who make you feel ashamed. Well, I hope you're satisfied now. Until you find another victim.'

20

Two Progresses

THE winter passed. George spent less time with me than formerly; partly because I was working intensively for my final examination in the summer – but also it was now Jack who had become his most confidential friend.

As soon as Eden's decision was made, George had thrown himself into the interests of the group. Several young men and women from the School had been added to it; George talked of them all more glowingly than ever. On the few occasions I went out to the farm that winter, I felt the change from the group which George first devoted himself to. George and Jack, I know, formed parties there each weekend.

George never visited Eden's house again, after the Sunday night when we walked back in the rain. I scarcely heard him mention Eden or the firm; and at Eden's the entire episode of Martineau and George was merely the subject of comfortable reflections.

It was Eden, however, who told me in the early spring that Martineau was making another move, was giving up the agency. He had found some eccentric brotherhood, not attached to any sect, whose members walked over the country preaching and begging their keep. This he was off to join.

'Ah well,' said Eden, 'religion is a terrible thing.'

We heard that Martineau was due to leave early one Saturday morning. I went along to his house that day and outside met George, who said, with a shamefaced smile: 'I couldn't very well let him go without saying goodbye.'

We had to ring the bell. Since the house had been transformed, we did not know where Martineau would be sleeping. The bell sounded, emptily, far away; it brought a desolation. At last his housekeeper came, her face was hostile, for she blamed us for the catastrophe.

'You'll find him in his old drawing-room,' she said. 'And if things had been right you'd never have had cause to look for him at all.'

He had been sleeping in the drawing-room, in one corner. A rough screen where the sofa used to be; in the bend of the room, between the fireplace and the window, where we used to sit on the more intimate Friday nights, a bed protruded, and there was an alarm clock on the chair beside it. The Ingres had been taken down, the walls were bare, there was a close and musty smell.

Martineau was standing by the bed, packing a rucksack.

'Hallo,' he cried, 'so glad you've come to see the last appearance. It's specially nice that you managed to find time, George.'

His laugh was wholehearted and full of enjoyment, utterly free from any sort of sad remembrance of the past. He was wearing an old brown shirt and the grey coat and trousers in which I had last seen him; he had no tie, and he had not shaved for days.

'Could I possibly help you to pack that?' said George.

'I've always been better with my hands than with my head,' said Martineau. 'But still, George, you have a shot.'

George studied the articles on the bed. There were a few books, an old flannel suit, a sponge bag and a mackintosh.

'I think the suit obviously goes in first,' said George, and bent over the bed.

'This is a change from the old days in the firm,' said Martineau. 'You used to do the brainwork, and I tried on the quiet to clean up the scripts you'd been selecting as ashtrays.'

George laughed. He could forget everything except their liking: and so (it surprised me more) could Martineau.

'How is the firm, by the way?' asked Martineau.

'As tolerable as one can reasonably expect,' said George.

'Glad to hear it,' said Martineau indifferently, and went off to talk gaily of his own plans. He was going to walk fifteen miles today, he said, down the road towards London, to meet the others coming from the east.

'Will there be any chance of seeing you here? On your travels?' said George.

'Some time,' Martineau smiled. 'You'll see me when you don't expect me. I shall pass through some time.'

He went to the door, called 'Eliz-a-beth,' as he used to when he wanted more coffee on a Friday night. He ran down the stairs and his voice came to us lilting and cheerful: we heard her sobbing. He returned with a buttonhole in his shirt. When we had left the garden and turned the corner, out of sight of the house, he smiled at us and tossed the buttonhole away.

Just before we said goodbye, George hesitated. 'There's one thing I should like to say, Mr Martineau. I don't know what arrangements you are making with your connections here. As you realise, they're not people I should personally choose to rely on in case of difficulties. And you're taking a line that may conceivably get you into difficulties. So I thought I ought to say that if ever you need money or anything of the sort – I might be a more suitable person to turn to. Anyway, I should like you to keep that in mind.'

'I appreciate that, George.' Martineau smiled. 'I really appreciate that.'

He shook our hands. We watched him cross over the road, his knapsack lurching at each stride. Up the road, where the houses rested in the misty sunshine, he went on, dark between the trees, until the long curve took him out of sight.

'Well,' said George.

We walked the other way, towards the town. I asked if I should meet him out of the office at midday, as I often did on Saturdays.

'I'm afraid not,' said George. 'As a matter of fact, I thought of going straight over to the farm. I don't suppose you can allow yourself the time off, can you? But Jack is taking over a crowd by the one o'clock bus. I want to work in a full weekend.'

Part Three

THE WARNING

21

News at Second Hand

I TOOK my final examination in May 1927, two months after Martineau's departure; and went into chambers in London in the following September. For several years it was only at odd times that I saw George and my other friends in the town.

Some of that separation was inevitable, of course. I was making my way; it was then that I entered the chambers of Herbert Getliffe, who turned out to be as lively, complex and tricky as Jack himself; there was the long struggle with him (amusing to look back upon) before I emerged to make a decent living at the Bar. And in the process I formed new friendships, and got to know new worlds. That occupied me for a great part of those years; but still I need not have seen so little of George. It was natural for people as shrewd as Rachel to think that I was forsaking my benefactor and close friend of the past.

It was natural; but it was the opposite of the truth. Not by virtue, but by temperament, I was at that age, when I was still childless, bound by chains to anyone who had ever really touched my life; once they had taken hold of me, they had taken hold for good. While to George, though he enjoyed paying me a visit, I became incidental as soon as I vanished from the group. And before long he was keeping from me any news that mattered deeply to him. Yet I could feel that he was going through the most important time of his life.

From various people I heard gossip, rumours, genuine news of his behaviour. Olive sometimes wrote to me; and she was intimate with

George again, when, after her father's death in 1930, she came into some money and returned to live in the town. Her letters were full of her own affairs: how she finally decided not to marry Morcom, though for a few months they lived together; how his old jealousy at last justified itself, for she had fallen in love with Jack and hoped to marry him. In the middle of these pages on herself, frequently muddled and self-deceiving, there occurred every now and then one of her keen, dispassionate observations upon George.

Materially, he was not much better off. Eden paid him £325 a year now; he still lectured at the School. But there was one surprising change – so surprising to me that I disbelieved it long after I ought to have been convinced. He had joined, as a concealed partner, in some of Jack's money-making schemes.

They had actually bought the agency and the advertising paper from Martineau and his partner Exell, a year or so after Martineau joined his brotherhood. When Olive returned, the three of them had invented more ambitious plans, and in 1931 raised money to buy the farm and run it as a youth hostel.

These stories were true enough, I found: and they appeared to be making some money. As Olive wrote: 'Of course, with Jack and me, we're just keen on the money for its own sake. But I still don't think anyone can say that of George. He gets some fun out of working up the schemes – but really all he wants money for is to leave him freer with his group.'

George had come, more thoroughly as each year passed, to live entirely within his group of protégés. He still carried young people off their feet; he still gave them faith in themselves; he was still eager with cheerful, abundant help, thoughtless of the effect on himself. Jack was only one out of many who would still have been clerks if they had not come under his influence. And there were others whom he could not help practically, but who were grateful. Olive quoted Rachel as saying: 'Whatever they say, he showed us what it's like to be alive.'

That went on: but there was a change. This was a change, though, that did not surprise me. It had been foreshadowed by Jack years ago, that night of our celebration in Nottingham. When I heard of it, I knew that it had always been likely; and I was curiously sad.

I heard of it, as it happened, from Roy Calvert, whom I met at a dinner-party in Cambridge. He was then twenty-one, polished and elegantly dressed. He talked of his cousin Olive. He was acute, he already knew his way about the world, he had become fond of women and attractive to them. He mentioned that George was attracting some gossip. George was, in fact, believed to be making love to girls within the group.

Roy had no doubt. Nor had I. As I say, it made me curiously sad. For I knew what, in earlier days, it would have meant to George.

I thought of him often after that piece of news. I had no premonition of danger; that did not reach me until a year later, until Morcom's call in the summer of 1932. But I often wished that George's life had taken a different curve.

During one case which regularly kept me late in chambers, so that I walked home through a succession of moonlit nights, those thoughts of George would not leave me alone. He was a man of more power than any of us: he seemed, as he used to seem, built on the lines of a great man. So I thought with regret, almost with remorse, walking in London under the moon.

I wished that I had been nearer his own age: I might have been more use to him: or that I had met him for the first time now.

Time and time again, I thought of him as I had first known him.

22

Return from a Holiday

IT was one of the last days of the Trinity term of 1932 when Morcom visited me. I had just arrived in my chambers, after an afternoon in court.

'I was passing through on my way back,' he said. 'I thought I'd call – '

He had been sailing, he was tanned from the sea; but his face was thinner, and a suspense seemed to tighten his voice.

We had dinner, and then I asked if anything was wrong.

'Nothing much,' said Morcom. He paused. 'As a matter of fact,' he said, 'I'm worried about the people at – ' He used the name of the town.

'Is there any news?' I asked.

'No news,' he replied. 'I've been away from them. I've been able to think. They'll finish themselves with a scandal,' he said, 'unless something is done.'

'What sort of scandal?'

'Money,' he said. 'At least, that seems to be the dangerous part.'

'What do you mean?' I said.

'Rumours have been going round for months,' he said. 'I couldn't help hearing them. As well as – private knowledge. When I got away, I realised what they meant.'

'Well?'

'There's no doubt they've been working up some frauds. I've known that for some time. At least I knew they were pretty near the wind. I've only just begun to think that they've gone outside the law.' He paused again. 'That's why I came in tonight.'

'Tell me what you're going on.'

'I don't think I'm wrong,' said Morcom. 'It's all sordid. They've been spending money. They've invented one or two schemes and persuaded people to invest in them. On a smallish scale, I expect. Nothing very brilliant or impressive. They've done the usual tricks – falsified their expectations and got their capital from a few fools in the town.'

I was invaded by a strange 'professional' anxiety; for, although exact knowledge of a danger removes some fears, it can also sharpen others. A doctor will laugh, when another young man comes to him fearing heart disease – but the same doctor takes an excessive care over the milk his children drink. So I remembered other frauds: quickly I pressed Morcom for the facts.

What had happened? What were their schemes? What had been falsified? What was his evidence? Some of his answers were vague, vague perhaps through lack of knowledge, but I could not be sure. At times he spoke with certainty.

He told me, what I had already heard from Olive, of the purchase of Martineau's advertising agency, and the organisation of the farm and another hostel. But he knew much more; for instance, that Miss Geary – who had taken George's part in the committee meeting years ago – was one of the people who had advanced money.

'You may still be wrong,' I said, as I thought over his news. 'Stupidity's commoner than dishonesty. The number of ways people choose to lose their money is remarkable – when everyone's behaving with perfect honesty.'

Morcom hesitated.

'I can't tell you why I'm certain. But I am certain that they have not behaved with perfect honesty.'

'If you're right – does anyone else know this?'

'Not for certain. As far as I know.' He added: 'You may have gathered that I see very little of any of them – nowadays.'

His manner throughout had been full of insistence and conviction; but it was something else which impressed me. He was angry, scornful, and distressed; that I should have expected: but, more disquieting even than his story, was the extraordinary strain which he could not conceal. At moments – more obvious in him than anyone, because of his usual control – he had been talking with hysterical intensity. At other moments he became placid, serene, even humorous. I felt that state was equally aberrant.

'You haven't told me,' I said, 'who "they" are? Who is mixed up in this?'

'Jack,' he began. I smiled, not in amusement but in recognition, for about the whole story there was a flavour of Jack Cotery – 'and George,' Morcom went on.

I said: 'That's very difficult to believe. I can imagine George being drawn to a good many things – but fraud's about the last of them.'

'I don't know,' said Morcom indifferently. 'He may have wanted the money more than usually himself – '

'He's a man of conscience,' I said.

'He's also loose and self-indulgent,' said Morcom.

I began to protest, that we were both using labels, that we knew George and it was useless to argue as though he could be defined in three words; but then I saw Morcom ready to speak again.

'And there's Olive Calvert,' said Morcom.

I did not reply for a second. The use of her surname (for as long as I remembered, she had been 'Olive' to all our friends) made me want to comfort him.

'I should have thought she was too sensible to be let in.' I made an attempt to be casual. 'She's always had a sturdy business sense.'

Morcom's answer was so quiet that I did not hear the words for certain, and, despite my anxiety, I could not ask him to repeat it.

As we walked away from the restaurant, Morcom tried to talk of indifferent things. I looked at him, when we had gone past the lamp in a narrow street. In the uneven light, faint but full of contrast as a room lit by one high window, his face was over-tired. Yet tonight, just as years before, he would take no pity on his physical state; he insisted on walking the miles back to my flat. I had to invent a pretext to stop on the way, at a nightclub; where, after we had drunk some whisky, I asked:

'What's to be done?'

'You've got to come in – and help,' said Morcom.

I paused. 'That's not too easy. I'm very much out of touch,' I said. 'And I don't suppose they'd like to tell me this for themselves. I can't say you've spoken to us – '

'Naturally you can't,' said Morcom. 'It mustn't be known that I've said a word. I don't want that known.'

'In that case,' I said, 'it's difficult for me to act.'

'You understand that anything I've said is completely secret. Whatever happens. You understand that.'

I nodded.

'You've got to stop them yourself. You've done more difficult things,' he said. 'Without as much necessity. You've never had as much necessity. It comes before anything else, you must see that.'

'You're sure you can't take control yourself?'

'I can only sit by,' he said.

He meant, he could do nothing for her now. But I felt that he was shutting himself away from release. With a strain that was growing as acute as his own, I begged him to act.

'It's the natural thing,' I said. 'It would settle it – best. You've every reason to do it – '

He did not move.

'See her when you go back. You can still make yourself do that.'

'No.'

'See George, then. It wouldn't be difficult. You could finish it all in a day or two – '

'I can't. There's no use talking any further. I can't.'

He suddenly controlled his voice, and added in a tone light and half rueful: 'If I did interfere, it would only make things worse. George and I have been nominally reconciled for years, of course. But he would never believe I wasn't acting out of enmity.' He was smiling good-naturedly and mockingly. Then his manner changed again.

'If anything's to be done, you've got to do it,' he said. 'They're going to be ruined unless you come in.'

'I can't help thinking you're being too pessimistic,' I said, after a moment. 'I don't believe it's as inevitable as all that.'

'They've gone a long way,' said Morcom.

'It's possible to go a long way in making dishonest money,' I said, 'without being any the worse for it. Still, if I can be any use – '

Then I made one last effort to persuade him to act himself. I looked into his face, and began to talk in a matter-of-fact, callous manner: 'But I shall be surprised if you're not taking it too tragically. First of all, they probably haven't managed anything criminal. Even if they have, we can either finish it or get them off. It's a hundred to one against anything disastrous happening. And if the hundredth chance came off, which I don't believe for a moment, you'd be taking it too tragically, even then. I mean, it would be disastrous, but it wouldn't be death.'

'That's no comfort.'

'I don't mean it wouldn't be unpleasant. I was thinking of something else. I don't believe that being convicted of swindling would be the end of the world for either of us. It's only ruin – when people crumble up inside, when they're punishing themselves. Don't you agree? You ought to know through yourself just now – in a different way. If you went back and protected them – if you weren't forcing yourself to keep away – you would be happier than you are tonight.'

There was a silence.

'You know perfectly well,' he said, 'that everything you've said applies to George. It would be ruin for him. In his own eyes, I mean, just as you've been saying. And the others – she's not a simple person – ' He paused. 'And there's more to it than the offence. You've got to realise that. It means the break-up of George's little world. It also means that the inside of the little world isn't going to be private any longer. You know – that isn't all high thinking nowadays.'

I remembered what Roy had told me, and what I had gathered for myself.

'Yes,' I said.

For a few moments he broke into a bitter outburst unlike anything I had heard from him – against idealists who got tangled up with sensuality in the end. His words became full of the savage obscenity of a reticent man. Then he stopped suddenly.

'I'm never fair to that kind of indulgence,' he said, in his ordinary restrained tone. 'They seem to me to win both ways. They get the best of both worlds.'

Then he said: 'That isn't a reason for leaving them alone.' But he would not let himself help them. I accepted that now, and we discussed the inquiries that I might make. Soon he insisted that he must return to the town by the last train; I remembered that, not long after his arrival, he had agreed to stay the night.

The morning after that visit, I wrote to George, asking if he could stay with me in London: I was too busy to leave. I had no reply for several days: then a letter said that he and 'the usual party' were on holiday in the North. I could do nothing more for the time being, and in August, a fortnight after Morcom called, went with Sheila, now my wife, to our own holiday in France.

There I thought over Morcom's story in cold blood. He had heard something from Olive – that was clear. And still loving her, he could make a trivial fact serve as a flare-up for his own unspent emotion. He wanted to worry about her – and had seized a chance to do it on the grand scale.

That must be true: but I was not satisfied. Then often I consoled myself, as one always would at such a time, by thinking 'these things don't happen'. Often I thought, with genuine composure, 'these things don't happen'.

In the end I cut our holiday short by a few days, telling myself I would go to the town and set my mind at rest. Across the sea, in the mist of the September evening, I felt the slight anxious ache that comes, lightly and remorselessly – as I noticed after an examination – no, earlier than that, when I was a child – whenever one has been away and is returning home. I was no more depressed than that, no more than if I had been away for a few days and was now (on a cool evening, the coast in sight) on my way home.

23

Sight of Old Friends

GEORGE wrote, when I suggested paying him a visit: 'We shall be out at the farm that weekend. If you can come over, I'll organise it immediately. You can meet some of the original party and some of the new blood that we've brought on – '

Neither there nor in the rest of the letter was there any symptom of uneasiness. It sounded like George for so long, absorbed and contented in the little world.

On the Saturday afternoon a week after my return, I arrived at Eden's house. About a year previously, just as I was beginning to earn a living at the Bar, he had sent me a couple of cases, and since then several invitations to 'stay in your old haunts'. In the drawing-room, where we had argued over Martineau's renunciation, Eden received me cordially and comfortably. He was in his armchair, lying back in golf suit and slippers after an afternoon walk.

'You've done very well,' he said. 'You've done very well, of course. But I heard you were off colour last year. You must take care of that,' he said. 'You won't get anywhere without your health. And unless you learn to be your own doctor by the time you're thirty, you never will afterwards.'

I had always enjoyed his company; he was hospitable and considerate.

'If you want to talk to your friends while you're staying here, just consider the study upstairs as your private property.' He got talking about 'those days', his formula of invocation of his youth; and it was later after dinner than I intended when I caught the bus to the farm.

As I walked across the fields, lights were shining from several of the farm windows. George came to the door.

'Splendid,' he said, with his hand outstretched. 'I was wondering whether you'd lost your way.' In his busy, elaborate fashion he took my coat. 'I knew you wouldn't stay any longer at Eden's than decency compelled you.' The door of one room was open, and there was a hubbub of voices: a smell of fresh paint hung in the hall, and I noticed that the stand and chairs were new.

George whispered: 'There are one or two people here you don't know. They'll be a bit awkward, of course. You'll be prepared to make allowances.' He led the way, and, as soon as we were inside the room, shouted in his loud voice, full of friendly showmanship: 'I don't think you've all met our guest. He used to come here a few years ago. You've all heard of him – '

The room was fogged with smoke and on the air there floated the smell of spirits; some bottles glistened on the table in the light of the two oil lamps, and others lay in the cushions near the radio set. There was the first dazzling impression of a group of unknown faces, flat like a picture without perspective. I recognised Rachel in one of the window-seats, sitting by Roy Calvert, and a girl whom I remembered meeting once.

'You'll have to be introduced all round,' said George from behind, as I went to talk to Rachel. She had aged more than any of us, I was thinking; lines had become marked under her eyes, in the full pale cheeks. Her voice as she said: 'Well, Lewis!' was still zestfully and theatrically rich.

As George took me round the room, Roy caught my eye for a moment. I wondered what he was doing there.

I was introduced to a couple of youths on the sofa, both under twenty: a girl and young man in the opposite window-seat to Roy.

'Then here's Daphne,' said George. 'Miss Daphne Jordan – ' he added a little stiffly; she was quite young, full-breasted, with a shrill and childish voice. George's manner bore out the rumours that she was his present preoccupation. Her face was plump, square at the cheekbones; her upper lip very short, and eyes an intense brown, sharp and ready to stare up at mine.

'What are you doing, George?' she said. 'Why don't you give the poor man a drink?'

'I'm sorry, won't you have something?' George said to me, and with a gust of laughter for the girl: 'I'm always being nagged,' he said.

I went back to the window, near Roy and Rachel. Roy whispered: 'Don't you think Daphne is rather a gem?' He was a little drunk, in the state when he wanted to exaggerate anyone's beauty. 'She is quite a gem,' he said.

With a deep, cheerful sigh, George sank into the chair opposite the fire. Under the heavy lids, his eyes roamed round, paternal, possessive, happy; Daphne curled up on a hassock by his chair, one of her hands staying on the arm.

'What were you saying about Stephen Dedalus – ' George said loudly to the young man in the window, 'before' – he paused – 'Eliot came in?'

George was not concealing his pride, his paternal responsibility, in being able to ask the question. It was his creation, he was saying almost explicitly, that these people had interests of this pattern. Half-smiling, he looked at me as the conversation began; he laughed uproariously at a tiny joke.

Then my attention caught a private phrase that was being thrown across the argument, one of the new private phrases, that, more than anything, made me feel the lapse of time. 'Inside the ring' – it bore no deep significance that I could see, but somehow it set alight again the anxieties and suspicions which had, in the freshness of arrival, vanished altogether. What had been happening? Nothing pointed to any dealings with money – except the actual material changes in the house. The demeanour of the party had changed from my time; then George, with the odd stiffness at which we had always laughed, was worried if the women drank with us. There was a quality of sexual feeling in the atmosphere, between many of the pairs and also, in the diffuse polyvalent way of such a society, between people who would never have any kind of relation; just as Rachel years ago had not loved, but been ready to love George, so I saw some other flashes of desire through the idealist argument. But that too, as it must be in any close society, was always present; I remembered evenings, four or five years ago, with Olive, Jack, George, Rachel and some others, when the air was electric with longing.

Daphne was laughing into George's face, after he finished one of his tirades. Clumsily he ran his fingers through her hair. Of all George's fancies this was the most undisguised. One could not see them without knowing that Roy was right.

I had been there about an hour when there was a noise of feet in the hall, and Olive came in, with Jack Cotery behind her.

At once she came across to my chair and took my hands.

'It must be years since I saw you,' she said. Her eyes were full and excited; she was over twenty-eight now, it crossed my mind. Her face had thinned a little into an expression which I could not define at that first glance. As she turned to bring Jack towards me, the strong curve of her hips was more pronounced than when I last met her, the summer she left the town.

'We didn't think you'd be here so early,' she cried. Then, catching someone's smile, her eyes flew to the clock on the mantelpiece: it was after eleven, and she looked at me before breaking into laughter.

'Good to see you,' Jack began, a little breathless and embarrassed in the greeting, until, in a moment, his old ease returned. He took me to one side, and began chatting humorously, confidentially, as though to emphasise that he had a special claim upon my attention. 'Life's rather crowded,' he chuckled when I asked him about himself. 'I've always got something going to happen, you know. I'm just getting on top of it, though. Clearly I am.'

The room had become noisy again. The others were drinking and talking, leaving us in our corner. Over Jack's shoulder, I saw Olive watching us with a frown as she talked to George. Jack was inquisitive about one of my cases. 'If I'd been on the jury, you'd never have got him off – '

Olive came and took us each by the arm.

'A few of us are going into the other room,' she said. 'We can't talk with everyone about.'

They had been quarrelling. Jack looked displeased, as she led us into the other sitting-room. It struck cold as we entered; she lit the lamp and knelt down to put a match to the fire.

'It won't be warm enough,' said Jack. 'We'd better go back.'

Olive looked up.

'No,' she said violently. Jack turned aside; his cheeks reddened.

George came in, bottles clinking in his hands, and Daphne carried the glasses. Rachel followed them.

'Oh, isn't the fire going?' she said. 'I thought you two had been here all night – ' then she broke off abruptly.

George's attention at last became diverted. He gazed at her from the tumblers into which he had been pouring gin.

'It isn't cold,' he said. 'The fire will soon be through.' He was placating the inanimate world, as he always had done, never willing to admit the worst of his surroundings.

Olive stood by the fire. The rest of us brought up chairs, and she whispered a word to Jack. She was restless with excitement; a tension had grown up in the room, a foot tapping on the floor sounded very loud. She broke out, inclining her face to me with a quick smile: 'What are you here for, anyway?'

'To have a look at you.'

'Lewis, is that true?'

'What do you mean?'

'I had a feeling,' she said, 'when I saw you tonight – that there was something else behind it. I don't believe it's just a casual visit, is it now?'

I did not speak for a moment. In the presence of Rachel and Daphne I could not be frank.

'As a matter of fact,' I said, 'I was a little worried about some of you.'

'What about us?'

'I heard something – by accident – that made me think you might be taking some silly risks.' I paused. 'Some silly financial risks.'

I expected George to interpose, but it was Olive who answered. She exclaimed: 'Who told you that?'

'No one,' I said. 'I only had the faintest suspicion. I worked it out from something your cousin Roy happened to say. He said it quite innocently, you realise.'

'He says a good deal that isn't innocent.' Olive laughed, frankly and good-naturedly.

I said: 'Look here, I want you to tell me if there's anything in it. I've seen enough money lost, you know.'

Again it was Olive who answered. 'I'm sorry to disappoint you. There's nothing to tell.'

Jack began to talk of my practice, but in a moment Olive interrupted.

'You're not to worry about us,' she said. 'You understand? You can worry about our souls if you like.'

Suddenly she ceased to be competent and masterful, and her voice went hysterically high.

'We've changed since your time,' she said to me. 'Haven't we changed?'

'We all have,' I said.

'That's no good. That's just playing with me,' she said. 'We've changed, I tell you. We're not the same people. Don't you see that?'

George shifted in his chair.

'There's something in it, but it's an exaggeration put like that,' he said. 'You've all developed – '

'We've all developed!' Olive cried. 'As though you'd nothing to do with it. As though you haven't been more responsible than any of us.'

'I accept that,' said George loudly. 'You don't think I should pretend not to accept it. I'm proud of it. I'm prouder of it than anything else in my life.'

'You mean to say you're proud of having us – '

'I'm proud that you're the human being you are. And the same of Jack. And all the others. As well,' said George, 'as of Lewis, here.'

'I've had more to do with myself than you have, George,' Olive broke out, 'and I should laugh at the idea of being proud.

'Yet I've been complacent enough,' she went on. 'God knows how I found any reason for it. I've never done an unselfish action in my life without feeling complacent for being such a whirl of compassion. Oh, I know I looked after my father for years – don't you think I was smug with myself for doing it?'

'If you're going down to that level,' I said, 'we are all the same. You oughtn't to be savage with yourself – just with all people.'

'Just with life,' said Rachel. 'Good God, girl, you've done more than most. You've had a man madly in love with you.'

'Do you think,' she cried, 'I ought to be glad of that?' She hesitated. 'That was the one time,' she said, 'when I thought I might do something unselfish.'

'When?' cried Rachel.

'When I lived with him,' said Olive.

'Why, you were in love with him,' Daphne said, after a moment's silence.

'I never was,' said Olive. She swept an arm round. 'They know I never was.'

'Why then?' George leaned forward. 'For all those months – '

Olive said: 'I did it out of pity.'

Everyone was quiet; I looked into her eyes, and saw her glance fall away. Suddenly George laughed.

The strain had broken down: Jack was whispering to Olive, his eyes and hands eloquent and humorous; Daphne was sitting on the arm of George's chair. I could feel that only my presence was keeping them from a wilder eirenicon; friend as I was, I was also a foreign influence, unfamiliar enough to keep the balance between decorum and release. My own nerves frayed (for I too had been played on by the undersweep of passion), I was glad when Olive rose to go to bed. Soon George and I were left alone.

We filled our glasses, settled into the easy chairs by the fire, and talked casually for a few minutes.

'It's a long while,' said George comfortably, 'since we came down here together.' I was touched by the sentimentality, unselfconscious and unashamed; perhaps, I thought, it came the easier to George, for, in spite of all his emotional warmth, he was less bound to the past than any of us, far less than Morcom or myself. Perhaps to those like him, solid in the core of their personalities, four-square in themselves, feeling intensely within the core but not stretching out tentacles to any other life, it is easier to admit the past – because it does not matter much, as he showed in our separation. While to Morcom, tied inseparably to a thousand moments of the past, it came too near the truth to acknowledge its softening hand, except by a smile of pretended sarcasm.

After that remark, we argued amiably; George had lost little of his buoyant appetite for ideas. I enjoyed his mental gusto for its own sake, and also because it was impeding the purpose which brought me there.

'We had some rather good talk tonight,' he said, after a time, with the change of his manner to an elated but uneasy defence that still covered him when he talked of the group: 'Didn't you think so?'

'Yes. I confess – '

'Of course you've got to remember the relevant circumstances,' said George hurriedly. 'The kind of people they would have been if they had been left to their own devices. You've got to remember that. Not that they're not an extremely good collection. They're better than they've ever been, of course. We've had some reorientations. I've reconsidered some of my opinions.'

'Still,' I said, 'I was glad to see some of the old gang. Particularly Olive. Though I thought she was too much upset – '

'Oh, I don't know,' George replied. 'She's had something to put up with, you know. You can't deny that she was magnificently frank about it – she got the whole affair in its right proportion. There aren't many people who'd do that.'

Obstinately he repeated: 'She was magnificently frank.'

'I could find another name for it,' I said. 'But still, I wasn't thinking of her being upset by a love affair. I thought there might possibly be some other cause.'

A frown, or something less (the fixity with which he would at any time have heard a criticism), came into his face.

'What else could be the matter with her?'

'I didn't know her circumstances, since her father died. I thought – perhaps – money – '

'Ridiculous,' George interrupted. 'Completely ridiculous. Her father left her a hundred and fifty a year of her own – and the reversion of the rest of the money when her mother dies.'

'It can't be that, then,' I said. 'I just felt there might be trouble.'

'With no justification at all.'

'Everything is all right?'

'As a matter of fact,' said George, 'I wondered why you were asking about our affairs.'

'I was worried.'

'I think I should have been approached first.'

I half-expected a burst of anger; but instead his manner was more formal than exasperated.

'If I could have got you alone before she spoke – '

'I was prepared to believe that might be the reason.'

'You understood what I meant to ask?'

'I gathered it.'

'George, I can speak out with you. I meant – it's easy to get into financial tangles that are dangerous. If so, you could trust me to help, couldn't you?'

'I know exactly what you meant.'

'Will you let me ask the same question – now?'

'I've got nothing to add.' Each reply had been stiff and distant.

'I can't do this again, you know.'

'Naturally.'

'Everything's completely well with them? With yourself?'

'I'm happier than I've ever been in my life,' George raised his voice. I put in a question about his position in the firm.

'I've dismissed that business for the time being. I had to make a deliberate choice between the successes I considered important – and the successes' – he laughed – 'that an ordinary man with his little house and his little motor car would consider important. I decided that I couldn't achieve them both, and so I was prepared to sacrifice the trivial ones. Just as you – have sacrificed some successes that I should consider essential. You've repressed all your social sense – well, I should simply have found it impossible to make a spiritual hermit of myself. Even – if it does give the Edens of this world a chance to humiliate me for ever.'

As I had often done when George was talking, I listened to the different levels of self-explanation. I heard nothing that bore on the apprehension. After we had talked on for a few moments, I said: 'The trouble about these choices – I'm not saying that you oughtn't to have made this one – is that you couldn't help yourself.'

'I could certainly help myself – '

'Anyway it does mean a certain practical inconvenience. Money and so on. How's that treating you?'

George's face opened in a chuckle. 'I'm harassed sometimes, as you might expect. I haven't borrowed from you recently, but you mustn't imagine you're completely immune.' He passed on to stories of the group in the last years. He got up to close the windows for the night: he said in a quiet voice: 'I've gained more from the last year or two than all the rest of my life. I know you all think I'm incapable of any sort of change. You haven't noticed that I'm more suggestible than any of you.' He looked over the fields, in the darkness. 'I've had my effect on these people – and they don't think it, but they've had an effect on me. And I'm better and happier because it's happened that way.'

24

The First Inquiries

MORCOM was away that weekend. I asked Roy to tell him that I had been in the town, and had called on George and Olive.

Through the autumn, a busy time for me, I was often uneasy. The visit had not brought anything like reassurance; but there seemed nothing I could do. As the months passed, though, I began to feel that my anxieties had run away with me. I heard nothing more until a Friday night in December.

I was tired after a day's work, lying on my sofa with a novel, which, when those moments came to have a significance they did not then possess (through the memory of action, so to speak, which is halfway between involuntary memory – recalled for instance by a smell – and that which we force back), I remembered as Thomas Wolfe's first book. The telephone bell rang. It was a trunk call, and among the murmurs, clangings, and whispers of the operation, I had the meaningless apprehension that sometimes catches hold as one listens and waits.

Then I heard Roy's voice: 'Is that, you, Lewis?'

The words were precise and clear, isolated in sound.

'Yes.'

'You should come down tonight. There's a train in half an hour. It would be good if you caught that.'

'What's the matter?'

'You should come at once. Morcom and I are certain you should come at once. Can you?'

'Can't you tell me? Is it necessary?'

'Yes.'

'Can't you tell – ?'

'I'll meet you at the station.'

Through the carriage window the lights of villages moved past. As my anger with Roy for leaving me uncertain became sharper, the lights became circled in mist and passed increasingly slow. We stopped at a station; the fog whirled under its lamps. At last the platform. The red-brick walls shone in the translucency; as I got out, the raw air caught at the throat.

Roy went quickly by, missing me in the crowd. I caught him by the arm. He turned and his face was serious and excited.

'Well?' I said.

'They're inquiring into some of George's and Jack's business. They questioned them this afternoon – and took away the accounts and books.'

It sounded inevitable as I heard it. It sounded unlike news, it seemed something I had known for a long time.

'I couldn't say it on the telephone,' Roy was talking fast, 'my parents were too near.'

We went into the refreshment-room on the platform. Roy's tumbler of whisky rattled in his fingers on the marble table, as he described the last few hours. Morcom heard from Jack, saw Roy immediately and insisted that he let me know. Then Roy called at George's office, a few minutes before he telephoned to me. George had said: 'Yes, they've had the effrontery to ask me questions,' and stormed.

'He was afraid though,' said Roy. 'He was anxious to prove that they parted on civil terms.'

'Morcom didn't know the best thing to do,' he said. 'He had no idea of the legal side. So you had to be fetched.'

'I'd better see George at once,' I said.

'I've arranged for him to meet you in my study,' said Roy. 'It's quicker than his lodgings.'

Actually, George's rooms were nearer. It was a strange trick for Roy to fix this meeting in his father's house. Yet he was as concerned as I.

His study reminded me that he was the only son of a prosperous family. It was a room more luxurious than one expected to find in the town: and then, again unexpectedly, the bookshelves of this spoilt young man were packed with school and college prizes. I was looking at them when George entered. He came from the door and shook hands with a smile that, on the moment, surprised me with its cordiality, its show of pleasure.

When the smile faded, however, the corners of his mouth were pulled down. Our range of expression is small, so that a smile in genuine pleasure photographs indistinguishably from a grimace of pain; they are the same unless we know their history and their future.

'This is an unpleasant business,' he said.

'Yes. But still – '

'One's got to expect attacks. Of course,' George said, 'this happens to be particularly monstrous.'

Roy made an excuse, and left us.

'We ought to go into it,' I said. I added: 'We don't want to leave anything to chance. Don't you think?'

'It's got to be stopped.'

'Yes. Can't you tell me what they wanted? It'd be useful to both of us.'

George sat down by the writing-desk. His fingers pushed tobacco into his pipe, and his eyes gazed across the room.

'It's absurd we should have to waste our time,' he said in an angry tone. 'Well, we may as well get it over. I'll organise the facts as we go along.' He began to speak more slowly than usual, emphasising the words, his tone matter-of-fact and yet deliberate with care.

'Jack Cotery made a suggestion over four years ago – ' George thought for a second and produced the year and then the month.

'He'd been considering the advertising firm that Martineau went into. He produced some evidence that if it were run more efficiently it could be made to pay. There was a minor advertising paper attached, you remember, called the *Arrow*. I talked to Martineau when he came back to clear up his affairs. That was the summer of 1928. The paper reached a fairly wide public; some thousands, he convinced me of that. Jack's case was – that if we could raise the money and buy Exell out, we could pay interest on the loan and make an adequate profit. I saw nothing against it – I see nothing to make me change my view' – George suddenly burst out – 'I can't be expected to live on a few pounds a week and not look round for money if I can get it without sacrificing important things. You know well enough that nothing's ever made me take money seriously. I've never given much attention to it. I've never made any concessions for the sake of money. But I'm not an anchorite, there are things I could buy if I had money, and I'm not going to apologise for taking chances when they meant no effort and no interruption to my real activities.'

'Of course,' I said.

'I'm glad you accept that,' George said as his voice quietened. I knew that, at moments, I or anyone must be numbered with the accusers now; it was strange to feel how he was obliged to justify the most ordinary contact with the earth. 'So on that basis I was ready to co-operate. Naturally, I hadn't any capital of my own. I was able to contribute about fifty pounds, chiefly by readjusting all my debts. Anyway, my function was to audit the accountancy side, and see how good a property it was – '

'You did that?' I said.

'There wasn't much evidence, which isn't surprising when you think of the two partners. There were a few books kept incompetently by Exell and the statement by Martineau. The statement was pretty definite, and so we considered it and proceeded to action. Olive raised a little. Her father wasn't dead then, so she couldn't do much. By the way, you might as well understand that this business has been consistently profitable. On a small scale naturally, but still it's brought in a pleasant addition to my income. And we met all our obligations.

Even in the worst weeks when our patriotic or national government was doing its best to safeguard the liberties of the British people.'

The habitual sarcasm left him, after months of use, as easily and unthinkingly as a 'Good morning'.

'I had very little to do with the financial backing. Jack undertook the whole responsibility for raising that. I should have been completely useless at getting businessmen to part with their money, of course – ' He gave a quick, slightly abject smile. 'On the other hand, I can produce their names and the details of the contracts that Jack made with them. We didn't consider it necessary to form a company; he simply borrowed a number of separate sums from various people, and made definite terms about paying them for the risk.'

'They lent it on the security of the firm, I suppose,' I said.

'Yes. It was a series of private loans for a purpose which everyone understood. It's the sort of arrangement which is made every day. The man who was here this afternoon,' he said, 'pestered me for an hour about the details. Incidentally he was unnecessarily offensive to me. That was before he came to the other scheme. It was a long time before I could make him understand they were slightly different. The position was' – he shifted in his chair – 'that Jack produced another idea when Olive's father died. That meant she had a little surplus capital – I mentioned it to you when I saw you last – and it was easy to see modifications in the technique. We'd acquired a little money and a certain amount of experience. So it was possible to think of something on a larger scale. Particularly in the special circumstances of my having a crowd of people that needed to be together. The idea was to buy the farm and one or two other places; then we could use the farm itself for our own purposes. There was no reason why the money we spent shouldn't come back to ourselves in part – and when we weren't using the place, we could let it out as a youth hostel or whatever people call them who haven't the faintest idea of helping people to enjoy their youth.'

'So you did it?'

'Yes. Jack and Olive were in it. I couldn't appear – but it was understood that I was to advise.'

'Jack brought in the money again?'

'Naturally,' said George. 'He collected some fairly large sums from various quarters. I'll make you a list. He's incredibly good at persuading them to part. He's so good that once I found it inconvenient – '

'How was that?'

'Actually,' George hesitated, 'I had to stop him taking it from some of my people.'

'Some of the group? Rachel and the – '

'Jack tried with this young man – Roy.' George looked round the study. 'But he was too cautious. Jack had persuaded Rachel, though; and someone else.'

I said: 'Why did you stop him?'

'I should have thought it was obvious enough. There's bound to be a certain amount of risk in this sort of project. I wasn't going to have it fall on people I was responsible for and who couldn't afford it.'

'One could bring out the fact – significantly.'

'I'm prepared to account for it.'

His voice was harsh and combative: I paused.

'How's this scheme going?' I asked.

'Not as well as the first,' George said slowly. 'It's not had long yet. It's perfectly healthy.'

'What has started the inquiries, then?' I said.

'It's impossible to say. I've been active enough in this place to make a good many people willing to see me disgraced.'

I wondered: was that true or the voice of the persecuted self? the self that was the other side, the complement, of his devotion and unselfseekingness.

'But did they know of these dealings?'

'We tried to keep them secret,' George said. 'None of the initial arrangements can possibly have got out.'

'What were the police looking for?'

'As far as I gathered from the lout who came this afternoon – the obvious thing for them to imagine. Misleading the people who supplied the money. The charge they're trying for is money by false pretences or conspiracy, I suppose. They might put in conspiracy so as to use all their evidence against each of us.' Though he was wincing as he spoke, I could not help noticing that his thought was clear and competent, as it had been all that night; his summary of their ventures could hardly have been better done; he was not detached at any time, there was no man less detached, he was in distress, afraid and resentful, and yet anyone – without my affection and concern – would have admired the stamina and precision of his mind.

Then to my amazement his face cleared and he laughed, shortly, not from his full heart, but still as though the distress had abated.

'It's scarcely likely they'll ever have the opportunity to make a charge.' It came to me like the fantastic optimism with which he sustained himself years ago, during Martineau's departure. I replied: 'So you're completely confident? You don't think it'll go any further?'

Remorsefully, I saw the half-laugh drain away; his voice was flat, with no pretence or anger left: 'If it does, I don't know how I'm going to face it.'

I said: 'As a matter of fact, have you done it?'

For an instant he sat without moving. Then slowly he shook his head.

25

Conversations at Night

ROY, quiet and self-effacing, brought in a tray of drinks and again left us alone.

'By the way,' I said, 'does Eden know about these – inquiries?'

'I've not told him.'

'Oughtn't you to?'

'It's obviously quite unnecessary,' George said. 'If these policemen have the sense to keep quiet, there's no reason why he should know. And if – we have to take other circumstances into account, Eden can be told quickly enough. I see no reason to give him the pleasure until it's compulsory.'

'I think he ought to be told,' I said. 'This isn't too large a town, you know. Eden comes across people in the Chief Constable's office every day.'

'That would be a breach of privilege.'

'Yes,' I said. 'But it happens – and it would be wiser for you to tell Eden than for someone who doesn't know you.'

His face was heavy and indrawn.

'You see,' I tried to persuade him, 'there's a good deal that can be done, if they want to inquire any further. You know that as well as I do. If Eden gives me authority, I could stop quite a few of their tricks. If you heard of anyone in your present position – the first advice you'd give, of course, would be for them to arrange with a solicitor –'

George said: 'I don't propose to discuss the matter with Eden.' He added: 'You can tell him yourself if you're so anxious.'

'You give me permission?' I said.

'I suppose so.'

When Roy rejoined us, I left them talking and telephoned Eden. He said he would expect me before eleven, and pressed me to stay in the 'usual room'.

George showed no curiosity when I said that I should not see him again until the morning.

Sitting in Eden's drawing-room, stretching my hands to the fire, I told him the events of the afternoon. He had begun by saying amiably: 'We had another conference about some of your friends here before.'

Eden nodded his head, his lips together, as I told him of their speculations. I finished by saying: 'It may not come to it, I don't know. But we ought to be prepared for a charge.'

'These things will happen,' he said. 'Ah well! these things will happen.'

'What do you think?' I said.

'You're right, of course we've got to be prepared,' he was speaking without heat, with a slight irritability. 'I must say they've been very foolish. They've been foolish whatever they've been doing. They oughtn't to try these things without experience. It's the sort of foolishness that Passant would go in for. I've told you that before –'

'He's one of the biggest men I've met. That still holds after meeting a few more. He's also one of the ablest,' I said in the only harsh words that had passed between Eden and myself, making a protest wrung from me years too late.

His deliberation broken for a moment, Eden said: 'We won't argue about that. It isn't the time to argue now. I must consider what ought to be done.' He laughed without any warmth. 'I can't instruct you myself,' he said slowly, going back to a leisurely professional manner. 'But I can arrange with someone else to act for Passant. And I shall give instructions that you're to be used from the beginning. That is, if this business develops as we all hope it won't –'

The phrase rolled off smooth with use, as he addressed me with the practised cordiality – different from his ordinary familiar manner – into which the disagreement had driven him. It was not until I spoke of visiting Jack Cotery before I went to bed, that he became fully at ease again.

'I'm sorry he's mixed up in this,' Eden said. 'He ought to have gone a long way. I haven't seen much of him the last few years.' He was genuinely distressed. He went on: 'And you want to find out what's been happening to him? I expect you do.' He gave me a latchkey. 'You can keep it until this is all over. You'll have to be down here pretty frequently, you know.' Then I said goodnight and he smiled. 'Mind you don't wear yourself out before it properly begins.'

The streets were clearer, but still dank with fog. A tram-car came down the lonely road, going on its last journey to the centre of the town; its light was reddened in the mist. What had happened? Through these stories and suspicions, what had happened? If George was lying (I could not be certain. He might be bound to the others – he might be masking some private guilt) how had he found himself in that kind of dishonesty? – which of all of us, careless as he was of money, self-deceiving as he could be in thought, I should have considered him the least likely to commit. And as well as these doubts, there was a sense, not flickering in questions in the mind, of conflict and fatality; of these lives, the people I had once known best, going as they had to go, each life alone, as it were, walking the dark streets. So, in loneliness, they had come to this.

For a time I could not find the street in which Jack lived. He had given up his flat, George said; he had returned to his parents' house. I had never been there in the past. When I first knew him, it was one of his mysteries to mention that he could not invite us to his house – and then, after his self-revelation that night in the park years ago, I had not expected to be asked.

Now, when at last I discovered it, I smiled, in spite of my errand. For the street, as I made my way down the faces of the houses, peering at the numbers in the diffused lamplight, seemed the perfect jumping-off place for daydreams of magniloquence: and, on the rebound, when he repented of those, just as good a place to let him imagine himself among the oppressed and squalid.

The houses were a neat row from the beginning of the century. Their front doors gave onto the street and the paint on most smelt fresh as I went close; it was a row of houses such as artisans lived in by thousands throughout the town; it was a frontier line of society, the representative street of the highest of the working class and the lowest of the middle. Few windows were lighted at this time of night.

I came to Jack's number. There was a light in the window, shining thin slats of gold between the Venetian blinds. I knocked softly on the door; a movement came from inside. The door opened slowly. A voice, light, querulous, said: 'Who's there?'

I answered, and he flung the door open.

'What on earth are you doing here?'

'I'm afraid I've come to worry you,' I said. 'I expect you've had enough for one day.'

'I was just going to bed.'

'I'm sorry, Jack. I'd better come in.'

Then my eyes, dazzled after the darkness, gradually took in a room full of furniture. A tablecloth, carrying some used plates and a dish, lay half over the table. A saucepan of milk was boiling on the hob.

'I have to live here occasionally. It gives them a bit of pleasure.' Jack pointed upstairs. He was wearing a new, well-cut suit. His eyes were excessively bright. I nodded, then threw my overcoat on a chair, and sat down by the fire.

'And so you're after my blood as well.' A smile, mischievous and wistful, shot through his sullenness. As I replied, telling him I had been with George, it was replaced by an injured frown.

'He must have told you everything,' said Jack. 'It's no use me going over it all again.'

'It may be the greatest use.'

'Then you'll have to wait. I'm tired to death.' He poured out the boiling milk into a tumbler. This, ignoring me, he placed on the hearth. I remembered once laughing at him at the farm, when he went through this ritual of drinking milk last thing at night; he had produced pseudoscientific reasons for it. He had always shown intense concern for his health. It was strange to see it now.

I pressed him to talk, but for a long time he was obstinate. I told him that I should be George's lawyer, if it came to a trial – and his, if he would have me. He accepted that, but still would not describe his interview in the afternoon. I said once again: 'Look, Jack. I tell you we've got to be ready.'

'There's plenty of time.'

'As I say, they'll be making inquiries while we do nothing.'

Suddenly he looked up.

'Will they have gone to Olive yet?'

'Probably,' I said.

'She was visiting a cousin. She won't get back to the town today. I suppose I ought to see her before they do. Clearly,' said Jack.

Then, for the first time, he was willing to talk of their businesses. He did it sketchily, without George's command. He finished up: 'I can't imagine why they expect to find anything shady. It's – it's quite unreasonable.' Then he said: 'Incidentally, I told the chap this afternoon, and I don't mind telling you, that if you search any business you'll find something that's perfectly legal but doesn't look too sweet. He took the point.' Jack looked at me. 'I'll show you what I mean, sometime, Lewis. It's all legal, but you'd expect me to try a piece of sharp practice occasionally, wouldn't you? I've never been able to resist it, you know. And it's never worth the trouble. One's always jumpy when one's doing it, and it never comes to anything worthwhile.'

I was certain that the 'sharp practice' had nothing to do with the suspicions: I did not follow it up. We were both silent for a moment:

Jack pulled out a case and offered me a cigarette. I thought I recognised the case, and Jack said, with his first smile since I tried to question him: 'Yes. It's the famous present.' His smile stayed as he ran a finger along the initials. 'I like having something permanent to remind me exactly who I am. It gives me a sort of solidity that I've always lacked.'

We both laughed. Then Jack said quietly: 'I simply cannot understand what these people expect to find. It's simply unreasonable for them to think they might pull out a piece of dishonesty. Why, if there'd been anything of the kind, I could have covered it up ten times over. If I'd had to meet every penny a month ago, I could have covered it completely. I happened to have an extra offer of money to tide me over any difficulty just about that time.'

'Who from?'

'Arthur Morcom.'

I exclaimed.

'Why ever not? Oh, you were thinking of his keeping away because of Olive. I don't see why he should.' He hesitated. 'As a matter of fact,' he said, 'he made the same offer this afternoon.'

'It's not useful now,' I said.

'It might be extremely useful,' said Jack. Then he took back the words, and said: 'Of course you're right. I can't use money until they give up these inquiries.' He broke off: 'You know' – he showed, instead of the fear and resentment I had seen so often in his face that night, a frank, surprised and completely candid look – 'these inquiries seem fantastic. They ask me about something I've said years ago – what I told people about the profits of the agency and so on. I just can't believe that what I said then might ruin everything now. Even if I'd done the dishonest things they believe I've done – which I've not – I'm certain that I still couldn't believe it. All those actions of mine they ask about – they're so remote.'

Yes, that was honest. On a different occasion, I had been through the same myself.

When I left, I walked straight to Morcom's. It was after one o'clock, but I had to speak to him that night. As it happened, he was still up. From the first word, his manner was constrained. He asked me to have a drink without any welcome or smile. I said straight away:

'I've just come from Jack's. He tells me that you offered him money this afternoon.'

'Yes.'

'Don't you see it might be dangerous?'

'What do you mean?'

'If Jack skips now, they'll take George for certain. For him, it's inevitable disaster. If you make it possible for Jack to go – and, well, it's crossed his mind. He's no hero.'

'That is true,' said Morcom, still in a cold, disinterested tone.

'I had to warn you tonight,' I said.

'Yes.'

After a silence, I said: 'I'm not too happy about them.'

'I'm not surprised,' said Morcom. 'I told you this was likely to happen. I thought you wouldn't be able to stop it. I might as well say, though, that I rather resent you considered it necessary to tell people that I was paralysed with worry. I dislike being made to look like a nervous busybody. Even when it turns out to be justified.'

'I said nothing.'

'Jack said that he heard I was very worried. I mentioned it to no one but you.'

Casting back in my mind, I was beginning to reassure myself: then, suddenly I remembered asking Roy to send word at any sign of trouble – because of Morcom's anxiety.

Morcom said: 'You know?'

'I'm sorry,' I said, 'I mentioned it to Roy Calvert. It was my last chance of getting the whole truth. I made it clear – '

'I told you in confidence,' said Morcom.

I took refuge in being angry with Roy. I knew that he was subtle and astute about human feelings – yet he had been so clumsily indiscreet. But I ought to have known that he, like many others, was in fact, subtle, astute – and indiscreet. The same sensitiveness which made him subtle, which gave him antennae to reach another's feelings, also caused this outburst of indiscretion. For it was from the desire to please in another's company, Jack's or George's, that he produced the news of Morcom's concern – from the same desire to share an emotion with another which is the root of all the deepest subtlety, the subtlety, which, whatever it is used for ultimately, arises from a spontaneous realisation and knowledge of another.

Just as, ironically, Morcom himself had once broken into a graver indiscretion in Eden's drawing-room.

It is one of the myths of character that subtlety and astuteness and discretion go hand in hand by nature – without bleak experience and the caution of age, which takes the edge both from one's sensitiveness and the blunders one used to make. The truth is, if one is impelled to share people's hearts, the person to whom one is speaking, must seem, must be, more vivid for the moment than anyone in the world. And so, even if he is irrelevant to one's serious purpose, if indeed he is the enemy against whom one is working, one still has the temptation to be in a moment's conspiracy with him, for his happiness and one's own against the rest. It is a temptation which would have seemed, even if he troubled to understand it, a frivolous instability to George Passant. But, for many, it is a cause of the petty treasons to which they cannot look back without shame.

Morcom was speaking with a restrained distress. Some of it I should have expected, whatever the circumstances, if he heard that he was being discussed in a way he felt 'undignified'. But tonight that was only the excuse for his anger. He was suffering as obviously as George. His cold manner was held by an effort of self-control; he was trying to shelve the anxiety in a justified outburst. Yet his anxiety was physically patent. With a mannerism that I had never seen him use before, he kept stroking his forehead as though the skin were tight.

We talked over the inquiries. Information must have been laid, I said, a week or two ago. I went on: 'Jack told me that he could easily have raised money just before that time. If there had been any call. He said you made your first offer then – is that true, by the way?'

'I ought to have done it in the summer,' said Morcom. 'I suppose it came too late. But I couldn't resist doing it at last. I've always had a soft spot for Cotery, you know.'

That was true: it had been true in the days of his bitterest jealousy. It was true now. He was filled with remorse for not having tried to help them until too late.

In a moment he asked me: 'What are the chances in this case?'

'It's impossible to say. We don't even know they've got enough to prosecute on.'

'What's your opinion?'

I paused: 'I think they'll prosecute.'

'And then?'

'Again I don't know.'

'I'd like to have your view.'

'Well,' I said, 'if you remember it's worth very little at this stage – I think the chances are against us.'

'Look,' he said, 'I can't do anything in the open. I've got to tell you that again. I insist that nothing I've said shall be repeated to anyone else. For any reason whatever. That's got to be respected.'

'Yes.'

'But if I can help in private – ' he said. 'You've got to ask. Whatever it is. Remember, whatever it is. You aren't to be prevented by any sort of delicacy about dragging up my past.'

He had spoken very fast. I answered: 'I shall ask. If there's any possible thing you can do.'

'Good.'

'There may be – practical things. We shall probably want money.'

'I should like to give it.'

26

A Guilty Story

WHEN I arrived at George's lodgings the next afternoon, I found his father just on the point of leaving. Mr Passant said, with the old mixture of warmth and hesitation: 'It's not – Lewis?' He had aged more than anyone I knew. His breathing was very heavy.

'I'm glad you're helping us, Lewis,' he said. He began to talk hurriedly, about the inquiries. His eyes were full of puzzled indignation against the people who had instigated them. 'You'll help us deal with them,' he said. 'They've got to learn that they suffer if they let their spite run away with them.' It was not that he did not know' of the danger of a prosecution. George had been utterly frank. But injured as he was, Mr Passant was driven to attack.

'At the end, when it's the proper time, you'll be able to go for compensation against them,' he said. 'The law must provide for that.'

During these outbursts, George was quiet, once augmenting his father's with an indignation of his own. For a moment they looked at each other, on the same side, the outer anxiety pressing them close. But when Mr Passant said, tired with his anger: 'It's a great pity they were ever given the excuse, Lewis – '

George said: 'We've had all this out before.'

'After it's over,' said Mr Passant, 'I still want to think of you yourself.'

George replied: 'I can't alter anything I've already said.'

Both their faces were strained as they parted. Without a word upon his father's visit, George came to the table and brought out his papers. He sat by me through the afternoon and evening, helping me arrange the facts.

The extraordinary precision of his memory might have been laughable in another context. But now I heard his voice on the edge of shouting, when from time to time he burst out: 'It's ludicrous for them to try to manufacture a case like this. We've got an answer for every single point the swine bring up. Do they think I decided to take over Martineau's paraphernalia simply for the pleasure of cooking the figures? When it was perfectly easy for him to check them? A man who'd been used to figures all his life. The suggestion's simply monstrous. If I'd wished to swindle in that particularly fatuous way, I should have chosen someone else – '

'He'd gone away, though, before you took over – '

'Nonsense. That is simply untrue. We bought Exell out in November '28' – he gave the exact date – 'Martineau had been in the town all July. He came back for a couple of weeks continuously the next January. Settling up his house and his other affairs. He could have investigated at any time. Do they think that a man in his senses – whatever else I may be, I suppose they'd give me credit for that – would take a risk of that kind?'

Yet several times I returned to Martineau's statement, in particular the figures of the *Arrow*.

'It seems such a tremendous lot,' I said.

'I thought it was rather large,' George said.

There was a silence.

'I'd have thought if they could reach as wide a public as that,' I went on, 'they'd have made more of a show of it themselves.'

'Jack's magnificent at making things go,' said George. 'He's full of ideas. I left that side to him. It's probably the explanation.' He stared at the paper. 'In any case, I don't think we shall get very far by speculating on Exell's and Martineau's incompetence.'

We continued through the accounts, on to the other business, the farm and its companions. There was, in fact, little written down. Most of the data were supplied by George, without delay or doubts, almost as though he was reading them from some mental sheet.

When at last I had completed my notes, George said: 'You may as well look at these. They're not strictly relevant, but I suppose you'd better see them. I'm sorry I haven't my proper diary here.' He gave me a twopenny notebook; it contained, in his neat hand, an account of his income and expenses, recorded in detail for several years. It struck me as strange he should keep this record of his money, over which he was so prodigal (I later found out that it was not complete or accurate, in contrast to the minute thoroughness of his diary). And I was mystified by his giving me the book. For a time, the statements told me nothing – a slight increase in expenditure for the last eighteen months, several entries reading – 'by cheque from J C, £10'. Then my eyes caught an entry: 'D at farm £1'; often, most weekends for some time back, the same words recurred.

'Do you pay for yourself at the farm?' I asked. 'I thought – '

'No.' He turned round from the bookshelves. 'I pay for those I take with me.'

'Of course,' I said. 'I ought to have – '

'Go back a few months.' His voice was unfriendly. At the beginning of the year, I found, as well as the entries about D (whom I knew to be Daphne), another series with a different letter, occupying other dates, thus:

> D at farm £1 Jan. 17.
> F at farm £1 Jan. 24.
> D at farm £1 Jan. 31.

The two sets D and F ran on together over several months. I looked up. His expression was angry, pained, and yet, in some way, relieved.

'I don't expect you to understand,' he said. 'I'm not excusing myself, either. I didn't break the rules I'd constructed for myself until I'd fallen abjectly in love: but I repeat, I'm not making that an excuse. I should have come to it in the end. I should have found my own happiness in my own way. I refuse to be ashamed of it; but there is one impression I shouldn't like you to get. Particularly you, because you saw me at the start. Now things may conceivably crash round me, I don't want to let you think that I retract one single word of what the group has meant to me. I don't want you to think I spoilt it all – because, when the rest of them were enjoying their pleasures, I saw no reason for not taking mine.'

'I shouldn't think so,' I said.

As I spoke, his face lightened and looked grateful. Every word in his self-justification carried its weight of angry shame.

'Do you remember how we compared notes on being in love – after a celebration in Nottingham?' said George. 'I hadn't fallen in love then, and I envied you the experience. Do you know, I still didn't fall in love until I was twenty-eight? That must be late for a man who has never been able to put women out of his mind for long. And I suffered for it. She was a girl called Katherine – you never met her – and she was absolutely unsuitable for a man like me. It was trying to find compensation elsewhere that I started with – ' he pointed to the F on the accounts. Both she and Daphne were members of the School and of George's group. 'But I insist, I don't give that as an excuse. I should simply have taken a little longer, but I should have come to the same point in the end. And I don't expect you to understand, but I'm capable of being fond of two women at once. So I kept on with her after I became attached to Daphne. I expect you to think it sordid – but we're not made in the same way.

'As a matter of fact,' he added, his truculence replaced by an almost timid simplicity, 'I discovered that I was hurting someone by the arrangement, so I had to give it up.'

So Daphne was too strong-willed for him; I could imagine her pleading in her child's voice, her upper lip puckered, pleading jealousy, caring nothing for her pride if she could get her own way, older in a fashion at twenty than George would ever be.

Going back through the figures, I found another set which occurred some time after the other began. 'Not. £1 11s 6d.' The amount was constant, and as I went further back, the entry came frequently, never less often than once a fortnight. The sum baffled me, although I guessed the general meaning. I asked him.

'A return to Nottingham, drinks and a woman,' George said. 'I kept to Connie's crowd for a long time, and it always used to cost the same.'

I laughed.

'I remember you used to spend twice as much on drinks round the club.'

'I suppose I did,' said George. 'I forgot to put those down.'

Then he said: 'It was years before I could imagine that I might find something better.'

'And now?'

'It may surprise you to know that I've been happier with Daphne than I've ever been in my life. I am more in love with her than I was with Katherine: I'm not a man who can worship the unattainable for long. This happens to be love for both of us, and it's the first time I've known it. When I realised it properly, I thought it was worth waiting thirty-three years for this.'

His voice became once more angry and defensive. 'After all that I've thought it necessary to show you,' he said pointing to the pocketbook, 'I expect you to laugh at what I say – but I can't believe that I shall know it again. And I'm compelled to think of the position I shall be in when these inquiries are over. I may not be able to inflict myself on her – '

'I don't think she'd leave you,' I said.

'Perhaps not,' said George, and fell into silence. At last he said: 'Just before you arrived, I told my father exactly what I've told you.'

'Why in God's name?'

'It might have come out in public. I considered that it was better I should tell him myself.'

'When I used the same argument about letting Eden know yesterday – '

'I don't recognise a connection with Eden,' said George. 'This was utterly different. I felt obliged to tell my father two things. He had a right to know that I might be providing malevolent people with a handle against him. I said I found that was the thing I could tolerate least of all.'

'What else did you say?'

'I had to say that, apart from the intolerable effect on him, I wasn't ashamed of anything I'd done. He naturally didn't believe that I had swindled: but he was hurt about my life with women. I had to tell him that I saw no reason to repent for any of my actions.'

27

Conflict on Tactics

A CASE, down for the next Tuesday, sent me back to London on Sunday night. For some days I heard nothing from the town; I rang up each night, but there was no news; and then, one morning in chambers, a telegram arrived from Hotchkinson, the solicitor who was managing the case for Eden: 'Three clients arrested applying for bail this morning.' It was now the middle of the month. I was not appearing in a London court until January; I decided to stay at Eden's until the first hearing was over.

When I arrived in the town, I was told they had been arrested late the night before. The warrant was issued on information sworn by someone called Iris Ward. The name meant nothing to me; but it added to Rachel's misery as soon as she heard it. 'It will seem to George – ' she said. 'You see, she was once a member of the group.'

They had spent the night in prison. That morning they had come before a magistrate: the charges were conspiracy to defraud against the three of them on two counts, the agency and the hostels; and also individual charges of obtaining money by false pretences against each on the two counts again. Nothing had been done except hear evidence of arrest and grant bail. The amount was fixed at £250 for each, and independent sureties of £250. This we had provided for in advance. Eden had arranged for two of his friends to transmit money raised by Morcom, Rachel, Roy Calvert and myself. For George and Jack, we had also been compelled to provide their personal surety; for

Olive, a friend of her uncle's had been willing to stand. The next hearing was fixed for 29 December.

I knew it would be good professional judgment to hold our hand in the police court on the twenty-ninth and let the case go for trial. I wanted to persuade them of this course at once; so I arranged to meet them at George's that same night.

When I got there, George was alone. I was shocked by his manner. He was apathetic and numbed; he stared at the fire with his unseeing, in-turned gaze. I could not stir him into interest over the tactics.

He was in a state that I could not reach. As he stared at the fire I waited for the others to come. I had scarcely noticed anything in the room but his accounts, the last evening I spent there; now I saw that, while everyone else was living more luxuriously, this sitting-room had scarcely altered since I first set foot in it.

Then Olive came in.

She said: 'I told you not to worry. You see how right I was.'

'It might have been better if you had told me the truth – ' I was seeing her for the first time since the inquiries, but I was immediately at ease with her.

'I didn't know – ' Then she realised that George was sunk into himself, and she tried to restore his defiance.

'It's nasty finding a traitor, George.' With her usual directness, she went straight into his suffering. 'But a man like you is bound to collect envy. The wonder is, there's not been more.'

She used also a bullying candour.

'We may have weeks of this. We mustn't let each other forget it.'

I felt she had done this before. And, as George was fighting against the despair, her instinct led her to another move.

She said: 'It's not going to be pleasant, is it? The twenty-ninth. You know, I simply couldn't realise what it would be like. Being ashamed and afraid in public. Until this morning. Yet sometimes it seemed perfectly ordinary. I felt that, last night in jail. Of course, it hasn't properly begun to happen yet. I only hope I get through it when it really comes.'

'You'll be better than any of us,' George said.

'I hope I shan't let you down,' she said. 'You see' – she suddenly turned to me – 'you can't believe how childish you find yourself in times like this. This is true, it happened this morning. I could face the thought that the worst might come to the worst. We might get twelve months. Then I felt a lump in my throat. I hadn't been near crying before, since it all began. Do you know why I was now? It had just occurred to me they might have had the decency to put it off until Christmas was over.'

She achieved her purpose; for George, with the curious rough comradeship that he had always shown towards her, made an effort to encourage her.

As soon as Jack entered, I was able to discuss the tactics. I argued that we must keep our defence back: there was no chance of getting the case dismissed in the police court: we should only give our points away.

In fact there was really no alternative: as a lawyer as able as George would have been the first to see. But tonight George broke out: 'You've got to defend it in the police court. It's essential to get it dismissed out of hand.'

Several times he made these outbursts, damning the prosecution as 'ludicrous', attacking it from all angles – as he had done since the alarm began. Some of his attacks were good law, and I had learned from them in my preparation of our case; some were fantastically unreal, the voices of his persecuted imagination. Tonight, however, there seemed another reason in the heart of his violence.

Jack detected the reason before I did. He interrupted George brusquely; I felt, not knowing whether I was right, that some of their meetings had gone like that, when the three of them were actually conducting their business.

Jack asked a few masterful, businesslike questions: 'You think there's no option? We've clearly got to let it go for trial?'

'Yes.'

'There's no possible way of arranging it now?'

'It's practically certain to be sent on.'

'Everyone else thinks the same? Eden and the others?'

'Yes.'

'I entirely disagree,' said George.

Jack turned on him.

'We know what you're thinking of,' said Jack. 'You're not concerned about getting us off. You just believe that will happen. What you're frightened of – is that your private life may be dragged out. And your precious group. The whole thing for you is wrapped up with your good intentions. You ought to realise that we haven't got time for those now.'

Jack had spoken freshly, intimately, brutally; George did not reply, and for minutes sat in silence.

Jack walked up and down the room. He talked a good deal, and assumed that the tactics were settled.

'If I'd had the slightest idea the hostels would come back on us – I could have worked it out some other way,' he said. 'It would have been just as easy. There was no earthly reason for choosing the way I did. If anyone had told me there was the faintest chance that I was letting us in for this – *waiting* – '

'You needn't blame yourself. More than us,' said Olive.

'I'm not blaming myself. Except for not looking after everything. Next time I do anything, I shall keep it all in my hands.'

'Next time. We've got a long way to go before then,' said Olive.

'I'm not so sure,' said Jack. He sat down by her side.

She looked at him with the first sign of violent strain she had shown that night. I knew she feared that he was thinking of escape: as I had feared the moment he spoke of Morcom's offer.

'We can make something of it,' she said.

'I suppose we can.'

'You're afraid there's a bad patch to go through first?'

'I shan't be sorry when it's over.' He laid a hand on her knee, with a gesture for him clumsy and grateful. He was dominating the room no longer. He said: 'I always told you I should get into the public eye. But I didn't imagine it on such a grand scale.'

It surprised me that he, as much as George, was full of the fear of disgrace. Often of disgrace in its most limited sense – the questions, the appearance in the dock, the hours of being exposed to the public view. They would be open to all eyes in court. Jack could imagine himself cutting a dash – and yet he showed as great a revulsion as George himself.

'Anyway, we've got some time,' said Jack. 'When are the assizes, actually?'

Then George spoke: 'I can't accept the view that this is bound to go beyond the police court. I have thought over your objections, and I refuse to believe that they hold water.'

'We've told you why you refuse to believe it,' said Jack casually. But there came an unexpected flash of the George of years before. He said loudly: 'I don't regard you as qualified to hold an opinion. This is a point of legal machinery, and Lewis and I are the only people here capable of discussing it. I don't propose to give you the responsibility.'

'Jack is right,' said Olive. 'You're thinking of nothing but the group.'

'I'm thinking of ending this affair with as little danger as possible to all concerned,' said George. 'It's true that I have to take other people into account. But, from every point of view, this ought to be settled in the police court. Of course, wherever it's tried, if they understood the law of evidence, our private lives are utterly irrelevant. But in certain circumstances they might find an excuse to drag them into the court. In the police court they can't go so far. Lewis can make them keep their malice to themselves.'

'Is that true?' said Olive.

I hesitated.

'I don't think they will bring it up there. They will be too busy with the real evidence.'

'You're still quite certain that, even if we show our defence, they'll clearly send us for trial?' said Jack.

'You're exaggerating the case against us,' said George. 'And even if you weren't, it's worth the risk. I admit that I want to save other people from unpleasantness as well as myself. But since you're so concentrated on practical results' – he said to Jack – 'I might remind you that our chances are considerably better if that unpleasantness is never raised.'

Olive asked: 'Do you agree?'

'If there were a decent chance of finishing it in the police court,' I said, 'of course George would be right. But I can't believe – '

'You can't pretend there's no chance of finishing it,' George said. 'I want you to give a categorical answer.'

The others looked at me. I said: 'I can't say there's no chance. There may be one in ten. We can't rule it out for certain.'

'Then I insist that we leave the possibility open. I reject the suggestion that we automatically let it go for trial. If you see a chance, even if it's not absolutely watertight, we shall want you to take it.' George raised his voice, and spoke to the other two in the assertive, protective tone of former days: 'You've got to understand it's important for both of you. As well as myself. You realise that the prejudice against us might decide the case.'

'So long as they get us off the fraud – ' Jack said.

'I've got to impress on you that the sort of prejudice they may raise is going to be the greatest obstacle to getting us off the fraud,' George said. 'You can't separate them. That's why I insist on every conceivable step being taken to finish it before they can insult us in the open.'

Olive said to me: 'George is convincing me.'

I said: 'I can't go any further than this: if there's any sign of a chance on the twenty-ninth, I'll go for it. But I warn you, there's not the slightest sign so far.'

Jack said: 'If we let you do that, it isn't for George's reasons. You realise that?' he said to George. 'You can't expect – '

George said: 'I intend to be listened to. I've let you override me too easily before. This time it's too important to allow myself to be treated as you want.'

28

The Twenty-Ninth of December

THEY appeared before the magistrates' court in the town hall on 29 December 1932.

In the week before, I had gone over the whole case with Eden and Hotchkinson. I explained to them that, if the unlikely happened and a chance opened, I might risk going for an acquittal on the spot. They both disagreed; I knew that they were right and that they thought I was losing my judgment; for I could not give them the real reason. I was contemplating a risk which, on the legal merits of the case, I should never have taken.

Eden was puzzled, for he knew that I had the case analysed and mastered. It was not an intricate one, but slightly untidy in a legal sense. It depended on a few points of fact, not at all on points of law.

The substance of the case was this: the evidence of fraud over the agency was slight, apart from one definite fact, the discordant information upon the circulation of the *Arrow*. The evidence over the farm and hostels was much stronger, but with no such definite fact. There were several suspicious indications, but the transactions had been friendly, with no written documents except the receipts. (The largest loans were two sums of £750 each from acquaintances of Jack's, and £500 from Miss Geary.)

There existed no record of the information which was supposed to have been given. This was, so the prosecution were to claim, deliberately untrue in two ways: (1) by the receipts of the hostels being falsely quoted – those of the farm itself, by manipulating the figures of the money spent there by George and his friends from '24 to '31; (2) by Jack pretending to have managed such hostels himself and giving details on that authority.

The prosecution could produce, over the farm business, several consistent and interrelated stories. The total effect was bound to be strong. But they did not possess an indisputable *concrete* piece of evidence.

It was that singularly which threw the story of the *Arrow* into relief. When Jack had approached people to borrow money to buy the agency, George had proved its soundness by showing them a definite figure for the circulation. He had put this figure on paper; and his statement had come into the hands of the prosecution. They were out to show that it was deliberately false.

That figure was the most concrete fact they held. Apart from it, they might have omitted the count of the agency altogether.

I have anticipated a little here. We did not possess the structure of the case so completely when we went into the police court on the twenty-ninth.

Before we had been there an hour, I knew, as any lawyer must have known, that we had no choice. It would go for trial; we were compelled to reserve our defence.

The man opposite built up a case that, although we could have delayed it, was not going to be dismissed. During the morning, everyone began to realise that nothing could be settled; Olive told me later that she felt a release from anxiety – as soon as she was certain that this could not be a decisive day.

The prosecution ran through their witnesses. The first was one of the four whom Jack had induced to lend money to buy the advertising firm, a slow-voiced man with kindly and stupid brown eyes.

'Mr Cotery made a definite statement about the firm's customers?' asked T—, the prosecutor.

'Yes.'

'He mentioned the previous year's turnover?'

'Yes.'

'Also the number of advertisers the firm were agents for?'

'Yes.'

After other questions, he asked whether Jack referred to the circulation of Martineau's advertising paper.

'Yes.'

'Can you reproduce that statement?'

'I made a note of it at the time.'

'Will you give me the figures?'

He read them out. The figure of the circulation sounded unfamiliar: I remembered it in George's account as 5300; now it appeared as 6000. I looked up my own papers and found that I was right.

'Didn't those figures strike you as large?'

'They did.'

'What did Mr Cotery say?'

'He said they'd be larger still now Mr Martineau had disappeared and his religious articles would be pushed out of the paper.' There were some chuckles.

'Did you ask for some guarantees?'

'Yes.'

'Will you tell us exactly what you did?'

'I asked Mr Cotery if he could show me what these figures were based on. So he introduced me to Mr Passant, who told me that he was a solicitor and had a good deal to do with figures and had known the former owner of the agency, Mr Martineau. He said he had received a statement from Mr Martineau giving the actual circulation. It was not 6000. Mr Cotery had been a little too optimistic, it was just over 5000. He offered to show me his notes of this statement. And if I were doubtful he promised to trace Mr Martineau, who had gone away, and get him to write to me.'

'Did you take advantage of that offer?'

'No.'

'Why not?'

'I didn't see any reason to. I had known Mr Cotery for some time, I felt sure it was all above board. I could see Mr Passant knew what he was talking about.'

The other witnesses followed with the information that T— had foretold in his speech; similar stories to the first, some including Olive. Then an accountant brought out some figures of the agency's business, in particular those of the *Arrow*: 'What was the average circulation in the year 1927?'

'Eleven hundred per week. So far as I can tell. The books are not very complete.'

'What would you say was the maximum possible for that year? Making every allowance you can?'

'Perhaps fifteen hundred.' This had been threatened in the speech.

They brought up witnesses against the farm. It was at this stage we realised for certain the legal structure of the case. Essentially the story was the same. George had taken a less prominent part, Olive substantially more. The information which Jack had given his investors was more complicated, not easy to contradict by a single fact; but several men attacked it piece by piece. Jack had asked advice about the business from a man who ran a hostel himself in another part of the country; the accounts he had given second-hand of this interview were different from the other's remembrance of it. The statistics of visitors to the farm before 1929 were compared – though here there were some uncertainties – with those given by George and Jack to several witnesses.

At lunch time I said to George: 'If we defend it today – it is bound to go for trial.'

He argued bitterly, but his reason was too strong in the end.

'You'd better play for safety,' he said. 'Though I still insist there are overwhelming advantages in getting it wiped off now.'

'If we try that,' I said, 'there'll be a remand for a week or two. We shall have to show our hand. And they'll still send the case on.'

'If these magistrates were trained as they ought to be,' said George, 'instead of amateurs who are feeling proud of themselves for doing their civic duty, we could fight it out.'

He turned away. 'As it is, you'd better play for safety.'

I told Eden and Hotchkinson. Eden said: 'I always thought you'd take the sensible view before it was too late.'

When the prosecution's case was finished I made the formal statement that there was no case to go before the jury, but that the nature of the defence could not be disclosed.

The three were committed for trial at the next assizes; bail was renewed for each of them in the same amounts.

29

Newspapers Under a Reading Lamp

THE local papers were lying on a chair in Eden's dining-room when I got back from the court. Under the bright reading lamp, their difference of colour disappeared – though I remembered from childhood the faint grey sheen of one, the yellow tinge in the other. On both of the front pages, the police court charge flared up.

There was a photograph of Olive. 'Miss Calvert, a well-known figure in town social circles, the daughter of the late James Calvert, J P'... 'Mr Passant, a qualified solicitor and a lecturer in the Technical College and School of Art'...a paragraph about myself. The reports were fair enough.

Everything in them would inevitably have been recorded in any newspaper of a scandal in any town. They were a highest common factor of interest; they were what any acquaintance, not particularly friendly or malign, would tell his friends, when he heard of the event. But it was because of that, because I could find nothing in the reports themselves to expend my anger on, that they brought a more hopeless sense of loneliness and enmity.

'Allegations against Solicitor.' The pitiful inadequacy of it all! The timorous way in which the news, the reporters, the people round us, we ourselves (for the news is merely our own voice) need to make shapes and counters out of human beings in order not to endanger anything in ourselves. George Passant is not George Passant; he is not the man rooted in as many complexities as we are ourselves, as bewildering in action and yet taking himself as much for granted as we do ourselves; he is not the man with his own private history, desires, mannerisms, perversities like our own, cowardice and braveries, odd habits of mind different from ours but of the same family, delights and, like us all, private oddities in love – a man of flesh and bone, as real as ourselves. He is not that; if he were, our own identity and uniqueness would have gone.

To most of the town tonight George is 'a solicitor accused of fraud'. 'I hope they get him'; a good many men, as kind-hearted as any of us can ever be, said at the time that I was reading. We are none of us men of flesh and bone except to ourselves.

Should I have had that reflection later in my life? Maybe I should have thought it over-indulgent. For in time behaviour took on a significance to me at least as great as inner nature. It was a change in me: not necessarily an increase in wisdom, but certainly in severity: a hardening: not a justification, but a change.

Excusing myself from dinner, I went to George's. He was alone listening to the wireless by the fire. 'Hallo,' he said. His cheeks were pale, and the day's beard was showing. He seemed tired and lifeless.

'I didn't know whether anyone would come round,' he said.

Jack and Olive entered as we were sitting in silence. Although there was a strained note in his laugh, Jack came as a relief.

'We'd better do something,' he said. 'It isn't every day one's sent for trial – '

'You fool,' cried Olive and put her arm round his waist.

Soon the room was crowded. Roy came in, Daphne, several of those I had seen at the farm in September. They had made a point of collecting here tonight. George whispered to Daphne for a while, and then, as the others addressed him with a pretence of casualness, he said: 'I didn't expect you all.' He was embarrassed, uncontrollably grateful for the show of loyalty.

Jack laughed at him. 'Never mind that. We've got to amuse them now they're here. This has got to be a night.'

A girl replied with a sly, hungry joke. There was a thundery uneasiness. The air was full of the hysteria of respite from strain, friendliness mixed with the fear of persecution and the sting of desire. We left the room, and packed into Olive's car and Roy's and another young man's. In the early days none of us thought of owning a car. We were poorer then; but now even the younger members of the group were not willing to take their poverty so cheerfully for granted.

We drove to a public house outside the town. The streets were still shining with the lights of Christmas week; a bitterly cold wind blew clouds across the sky; the stars were pale. As Olive drove us past the last tramlines, she took a corner very fast, swerved across the road, so that for a second we were blinded in a headlight, and then brought us away by a foot – a flash of light and the road again.

'Silly,' Olive cried.

In this mood, I thought, she could kill herself without it being an accident. Once or twice in our lives, we all know times when some part of ourselves desires to turn the wheel into a crash; just as we shiver on a height, feel the deathwish, force ourselves from the edge.

At the public house they were quickly drunk, helped by their excitement; Olive and Jack danced on the bar floor, a rough whirling apache dance. Everyone was restless. As the night passed, some of them drove to another town, but before midnight almost the entire party had gathered in Rachel's flat.

'They can't do much harm now,' said Rachel. 'It's a good job there's somewhere safe for them to come.' The flat took up the top storey of an unoccupied house near the station. Rachel had become secretary of her firm, and it was her luxury to entertain George's friends, while she watched them with good-natured self-indulgence.

Olive and I stayed in the inner room. Through the half-open sliding doors we saw some of the girls and heard George's voice throwing out drunken and passionate praise. Jack came to Olive.

'When are we going home?'

'Not yet,' she said. She was smiling at him. Her words were as full of excitement as George's. 'You want to stay, don't you?'

He laughed – but suddenly I felt that he had become dependent on her. He went back, and from our sofa she could see him caressing a girl, and at the same time attracting the attention of the room.

Olive's eyes followed him.

'I don't mind that as much as I did once,' she said to me. She added: 'He isn't as drunk as the rest of us. He never has liked drinking, you know. He's as – temperate as Arthur. It's queer they both should be.' She went on talking quickly about Morcom, among the noise of the other room.

'You know,' she went on, 'I never felt he was such a strong man as the others did. I liked him, of course.' Then she said: 'He wasn't my first lover, perhaps you don't know that. You knew me best when I was still frightened of my virginity, didn't you? Strange how strong that was. But it wasn't strong enough – ' She looked into the room with a half-smile. 'Jack seduced me one night – '

'When?' I had not known.

'Before my father died.'

'Were you attached to Jack, then? I didn't think – '

'I was always fond of him, of course. But not in the way that's got hold of me since,' she said. 'No, it just happened – we met in London somehow. He never was a man to fail for want of trying. I had one or two weekends with him, afterwards. At odd times. You know how erratic he used to be. It didn't matter much, just for once he'd think it might be a good idea.'

'And you?'

'Sometimes I refused. In the end, I was driven back, though. I suppose one's always driven back. Then I didn't see him for a long time.'

'What about Arthur, then?'

'I'd thought a lot of him. I'd heard from him all the time we were away. Then when I came back, he wanted me more than ever. Just then I didn't see why not.'

She paused. 'You've no idea how hard a time it was. He was jealous, madly jealous at times. Of anyone I seemed to like. And I couldn't help it, I kept playing on it. There were times when he was so jealous that he only got any rest when we were sleeping together. I drove him to that. He wanted me not really to make love – just to be sure of me.

And I couldn't help the little hints, that would set him off tearing himself with suspicion – '

'I know,' I said.

She said: 'He used to treat me rough now and then. I didn't mind that, sometimes I want it. You've guessed that, haven't you? But even then I couldn't believe the will was there.' She went on: 'We didn't reach happiness. We both deteriorated, we were both worse people. Counting it all up, I don't know who got hurt more. I can't bear to think of his life just then; jealousy going on and on. It was like that in the old days, of course. Funny that he was always more jealous of Jack than anyone else. Even when there was no reason for it in the world.'

'And so you left him and went to Jack?' I said.

'It was bound to hurt him – more than if I had gone to anyone else,' she said. 'But that had nothing to do with it. I tell you, I was really in love for the first time in my life.' She added: 'You've seen me with Jack. I want you to tell me that I'm not deceiving myself.'

'I know you love him – '

'But you think it isn't simple – even now?' She broke out. 'I'll confess something. When I went to Jack – I was certain that I belonged to him – I *still* wondered whether it was because of Arthur. That kept coming back. You imagine, it came back when Jack was after a new girl, when I wanted him and felt ashamed of myself. But I'm certain that I belong to him more than ever. It would have happened, if I'd never let Arthur come near me. I know it isn't simple, it isn't just a love affair. I expect he would prefer to have picked up one of those girls in there. I've had too many nights when I've wanted to break it off – and still been making plans for keeping him. But neither of us had any choice – '

Olive's nerves were tightened with fatigue, fear, the laughs of hysterical enjoyment from the outer room. But she was exhilarated by putting Jack off, sitting within a few yards of his drunken party, and then confiding how much she needed him. She had thrown off any covering of self-pity, however. She seemed stronger than any of us. She was still cherishing some petty sufferings, as she had always done. Her longing for humility was real, but it sprang from the depth of her intense spiritual pride. No one could have mistaken – under the surface of her restless nervousness, full of the day's degradation – still warmed and roused by Jack's voice, tired as she was – that she was speaking from an inner certainty of herself.

'If he quits before the trial, mind you, Lewis – ' she began.

I exclaimed.

'You know that he's thought of that?'

'Of course I know,' said Olive. 'I'm not blind when I love. He's thought of getting abroad. On the whole, I don't think he'll try.'

'If he did?'

'I should run after him. As soon as he cricked his finger. Whether he cricked his finger or not.'

I thought of George's safety: when she asked, 'How easy is it – for us to get abroad?' I kept the details out of my answer.

Just then I heard George's voice above the rest. The partition had slid further back, and from our room we could see him; he was half-lying on a sofa with Daphne on his knee, one arm round her; in the other hand he held a glass. He had begun to sing at the top of his voice, so violently his hand shook and the spirit kept spurting out.

Daphne jumped from his knee, and stood behind the sofa, trying to quieten him. He sang on: the words were so loud that I could not disentangle them, but it sounded like one of his father's hymns.

'There's George,' said Olive.

She watched him.

'Some people once thought there might be something between us. They were stupid. We've never had the slightest feeling for each other.' She went on: 'I know what you were afraid of a minute ago. If Jack flew, I should be ready to desert George. That's true. Yet he's been close to me – in a way I've never understood.'

She got up, and walked into the other room. Some of them looked in Jack's direction, expecting her to go there. But she went and stood by George. I had not seen her touch him, not once in those years. Now she dropped on her knees by the sofa, and took his hand in hers.

30

George's Diary

I LEFT them at three o'clock. Some hours later, when I was still in bed, a telephone message came from the hospital: would I go to the children's clinic at once? Morcom was on duty there, he urgently wanted to see me. The streets were filling up as I went out; out of the shops, women bustled by, their cheeks pink in the frost. The indifference of the scene, the comfort, like a Breughel picture, only brought out my anxiety. It was an actual relief to see Morcom's face, meeting me with a look of question and acute strain.

He could ask nothing; a nurse was in the room, and a batch of boys, round the age of twelve or so. As I watched, it was his gentleness which fascinated me. They responded to him immediately, with shrill, high, squealing laughs. With the nurse he was sharply efficient: but, as he talked to the boys, his manner became natural and self-effacing, so that they gathered round him, their nervousness gone, chaffing him. Some of them had noticed his pallor: 'Have you got a headache, Mr Morcom?'

'Were you out on the spree last night, Mr Morcom?'

Then, as he took me into his office, his expression changed.

'Were you with them last night?'

I nodded.

'What do they think?'

'They've a good idea what the chances are.'

'Has George?' asked Morcom.

'Yes.'

'You talked of Jack escaping, the first night this began. Why don't you suggest it to George?'

I hesitated.

'It wouldn't be easy,' I said.

'Easy! You of all people talk of it not being easy – when you know what the alternative is.'

'I know – '

'But you won't go to George.'

'I can't,' I said.

'It's his fault,' said Morcom. 'It's that madman's fault.'

'It's no use blaming anyone now.'

'What do you mean?'

'It's too late to talk about George's fault. Or yours. Or mine for not stopping it,' I said.

'Yes,' said Morcom.

'If you had gone back that night and taken care of them, this might never have happened. That night you warned me, and I begged you to go back. If you had only been able to forget your self-respect,' I said.

My voice had gone harsh like his; he heard me say what he was continually thinking; he was relieved. His face became softened. He said, in a casual, almost light-hearted tone: 'That wouldn't have been so easy, either.' He paused, then said: 'The only thing is, what's to be done? There's still some time.'

'I don't think there's anything you can do,' I said. 'They will have to wait for the trial.'

'You'll be busy with the case?'

'Yes.'

'You're lucky.' Then he said: 'I've not asked you before. But are you as likely to get them off – as anyone we could find?'

'No,' I said. 'If we could afford to pay.'

'I ought to have been told that. I'll give the money – '

'I've thought it out – as dispassionately as I can,' I said. 'I don't think the difference is worth the money. For one reason. Money may be more important afterwards. If we've spent every penny – '

'You mean, if they're convicted – '

'We've got to be ready,' I said.

That afternoon, when I was sitting alone in the drawing-room at Eden's, Daphne visited me. She talked of the previous night.

'It was rather an orgy, wasn't it?' she said. 'Of course, you didn't see it after it really began – ' She mentioned a common acquaintance, and said: 'Of course, it would have sent her away for good, wouldn't it? But then she's "upright". I can't help respecting her, you know, when I'm not relapsing like last night.' Then she said: 'But I'm being silly, wasting your time. In the middle of this horror. It's as bad as going mad last night. But that happened because we were in this mess, didn't it?'

The shrewdness shot through the prattle of her talk, and her eyes, often flirtatious, were steady and sensible. 'That's just why I've come up to see you now. I'm getting a bit worked up.'

'Go on.'

'You're easy to talk to, aren't you?' she said (coquettishness returned for a second; her upper lip puckered). 'I shan't be terribly helpful, you know. It's just to get it off my chest. But anyway, it's like this. When George first thought of making passes at me he wanted me to know the awful secrets of his life. He was certain that I should be shocked,' she went on. 'I oughtn't to laugh at him, poor dear. He was serious about it. It must have been a struggle. When he decided it was the right thing to do, he went ahead – though he fancied he was taking a risk. He really believed he might lose me.' She smiled.

'Well, do you know what he did?' she said. 'He insisted on giving me his diary. It's a staggering document. I expect I enjoyed the pieces he thought I'd mind. But there are some I can't always laugh away. I've brought it along.' (She had placed a small despatch case on the floor.) 'I want you to look at it for me – ' She sat on the arm of my chair; the arrangement of the first page, as her finger pointed out an entry, seemed identical with those George himself showed me years ago.

First she made me read a series of passages about the agency; quite soon after they bought it, it seemed that George was troubled about the circulation of the *Arrow* – 'it cannot conceivably have reached the figure that Martineau gave me in good faith'. The set of entries went on for several pages: neither of us spoke as I read it.

'That's all about that business,' said Daphne. 'I don't know what it means. But I couldn't rest till you'd seen it. I thought you might need it for the case – ' then she broke off. 'Will you read some more? While I'm here?'

There was little else directly bearing on the case in the entries Daphne selected. I saw only a few perfunctory references to his job at Eden's, and little more about the 'enterprises' with Jack and Olive. On the whole, I was surprised that they had seemed to matter so little.

Daphne, in fact, had not brought the diary only to ask about the case. I was not even certain what she inferred from the first entries she had pointed out. Sensibly, she had determined to reveal them to me as his lawyer. Whether she thought George guilty, I did not know. But she was obviously affected by other parts of his confessions.

She was deeply fond of him, and in a youthful, shrewd and managing way she was trying to plan their future life. She felt lost, as she read some passages which a more completely experienced woman might have found alien. Actually Daphne, though lively and sensual, was also sentimental and full of conventional dreams. In imagination, she was contriving a happy marriage with George.

I hesitated. Then I thought she had enough natural insight to stand something of the truth. I tried to explain some of the contradictions in his life as honestly as I could. I regretted it, for I hurt her; and she said goodbye, still convinced that she knew him better than I.

She left the entire diary with me, from 1922 to the month before the preliminary inquiries. I went on reading it for hours. To any intimate of George's, who accepted by habit the strange appearance of his life, it would have been moving. To me, it carried the irretrievability of the past, along with a life close to one's own in affection and pity – and so far away that it brought a desolation of loneliness.

I looked back for the first reference to the group, and read again the early 'justification' which he had shown me that night at the farm, in 1925. There was much more about the School and his friends in that tone, for years afterwards. In 1927, soon after his disappointment in the firm, he was writing:

The family have at last partially got rid of their conception of me as selfish – and he in particular appreciates my care and devotion, in his eagerness to give the world its due. Olive has gone, Mona has just become engaged, many of them have gone: but there are others, there are some closer to me than there have ever been. I find I have been writing of them all this holiday. If anything can be inferred from these expressions of my feelings, I have been useful to these people at the School. There are signs that freedom is life. And three years ago I was groaning inwardly at my distance from my friends. I was watching them from afar.

Then, still explaining to himself the divisions of his emotional life, he returned to the town, and for several weekends in Nottingham and London passed an 'equinox' of sensuality.

This randy fit is going on too long. Last night I could not resist taking the train to London. I was inflamed by the vision of one of our prettiest s—f—s, I found my little girl of 1921, older and more dilapidated, but with the same touching curve of the lips.

Tonight it was still on me. I took the familiar train to Nottingham. I found a pair of old friends in the first pub and spent a half-hour of pleasure looking at Pauline's face; but they were booked, and I was not in a mood to award free sherry for ever, so I moved on. I have hazy recollections of hordes of women that I kissed. I finished up drunk in the train three or four hours ago. And as we came to the scattered lights outside the town, I thought that everything worthwhile in my life I had invested in this place.

It was in the following autumn that they bought the agency. George's references to the group in the next two years became far more varied: at times impatient, moved by Jack, 'urging me on to his own freedom. Wanting me to destroy the only thing I have ever made. Yet he is a lover of life, he has given me his warm companionship for years, he looks into the odd corners of living' (17 November 1928).

During that autumn, also, a girl called Katherine Faulkner entered the society – usually referred to in the diary as K. For some time she was only mentioned casually.

A NEW VENTURE
16 OCTOBER 1928

Today Jack, Olive and I took over the agency, that curious stage in Martineau's mad progress. It is to be hoped it does well. Money is a perpetual nuisance: why should I, who care so little for it, have it always dragging round my neck? I have hopes that Jack will win us new comforts. Of course, I am not as optimistic as they all think. I remember his bad luck and bad management with that absurd first attempt of his. But he is still capable of success: it is time we had the luck on our side.

CONTRACT SIGNED

2 DECEMBER 1928

Jack is busy and active and full of ideas. A little money has come in already. Today it struck me as strange that Jack, of all my friends, should have been close at my side for the longest time. He was indulging in one of his new attacks on the group. 'Why don't you see what people really want?' He does not trouble to conceal that he includes me among them. He does not pretend to share my hopes nowadays: he would like me to follow him with his suburban girls. Yet all this sadistic nonsense of his does not seem to interrupt our alliance.

JACK AGAIN

4 DECEMBER 1928

Jack brought in a friend tonight who made a fierce emotional case for immortality. Lewis, in the old days, would have shrugged his shoulders, but I enjoyed the talk. On the train ARGUMENT afterwards, going to this petty little case – I'm tired of being foisted off with Eden's drudgery – I remember that it was the first argument with a stranger for many months.

The group is taking up all my energy – more even than it did in the first flush of youthful zeal, religious years that are not quite repeated now. If Jack were not obsessed with his own pleasures, he would see how that answers his attacks.

6 DECEMBER 1928

I thought it was perhaps a mistake not to keep a tiny fraction of my interests away from the 'little world'. I sometimes wish that Lewis were here for a day of two. So on the train I read A FEW HOURS some calculus with immense excitement. Why SNATCHED wasn't I told about these things at school? Also FOR MYSELF 'Clissold'; Wells is childish in politics, but there are moments when he feels for the whole common soul of man.

Yet I have found little time for anything outside the group now.

During the next few weeks, he wrote those entries about the circulation which Daphne had showed me at first. I put them aside to think over again.

22 FEBRUARY 1929

I appeared before the School Committee, asking for money for the brightest man since Lewis' day. It was a horrible fiasco. Cameron was unnecessarily offensive. The cleric Martineau scored at COLLAPSE my expense. I am not so effective as I used to be. I can still hear that grotesque display, and I feel like blinding all the damned night through.

1 MARCH 1929
I COME TO GRIPS AGAIN

Things have not been perfect. I have not quite the usual satisfaction of work well done. The débâcle of my appearance before the committee, another storm of lust, Jack's contempt for the 'hole-and-corner' way in which I indulge my passions, have all played their part. Jack hints also that Olive has begun an affair with Morcom of all

TOO EASILY
DOWNCAST

people, to whom I have scarcely spoken a private word for months. It may take her away from our little business venture, and it's a piece of wanton irritation. However, I ought to be able to ignore it.

The sight of K, smiling at the farm, a different person from what she was three months ago, is enough to remove any memories of Olive as anything more than a friendly, competent person, who is some help to Jack and myself.

After a walk in the beautiful rain-sodden evening, I have felt again the essential urge to live among these people. My course is set and my mind made up. Jack's friendship is valuable, but his influence must be despised. I see it clearly now.

2 MARCH 1929

K and the others made this the most perfect weekend I have ever known. They were alive, we were all on terms of absolute confidence. I was overwhelmed with happiness, unqualified happiness, such happiness as comes unawares and only in rare moments. I was bathed in the warmth of joyous living, so that any trouble seemed incredible.

18 APRIL 1929

Next weekend, so I have just heard, some clod has rented the farm and we cannot be accommodated. Why in heaven should I be denied what is my food and life by the sheer inconsequent whim of some unknown fool?

Although he did not admit it for some months, it was probably about this time that he became engrossed in Katherine – in love with her, perhaps. Never before, at any rate, had any girl in the group meant as much: Mona, now married to an acquaintance of Jack's, had only been one of many 'fancies'. In the diary about this date he dismissed her: 'She was a bright little thing. I could have slept with her if my theory had permitted it – I suppose Jack did not feel any scruples'. There had been another girl, Phyllis, who had by this time finished her training as an elementary schoolmistress, and taken a job in the county; George had toyed half-heartedly with the idea of marrying her, a couple of years back.

But Katherine moved him far more deeply: she came upon him when he was trying to maintain all his ideals over the 'little world'.

I never met her, or knew much of her, except that she was very poor and possessed the delicate and virginal beauty which most excited George. He struggled against recognising the passion. After that outburst over the farm, he tried to miss the group's meetings there. He found himself in one of his whirls of womanising, unusually long drawn out.

RELAPSES
7 MAY

Somehow I have not got the School and the group in my bones as I used to have. This is strange after the promise of a month ago. I am in a tangle of desires, scattering money more frantically than ever did. I met Winnie in Oxford Street: she is one of the nicest girls I have managed to know. Curious – her face comes and goes. Why? (Peggy's went long since. Dorothy's went, also the Cambridge girl, and the Bear Street one. It needs some effort to recall Hilda.)

FACES IN LONDON

(The names were all of women he had picked up on the streets.)

21 MAY

I am still a libido, though I get some joy from life. No moralising; things happen well when they do happen. Last night it was the old crowd in Nottingham. Some of the old hands are in trouble. Connie owes to a moneylender, poor soul. Thelma sees financial ruin coming. I told her that the 'good wife and mother stunt' is off. Why am I so attracted by prostitutes? I finished up with Pat, Connie's successor and the best of all.

3 JUNE

I have wrestled with repentance. Late though it be, I am wholly in love with the group again. I came back to a weekend at the farm —

RETURN TO THE GROUP

my first for a month — with extraordinary gratitude that they should receive me with a show of happiness and admiration. Jack was not there, and I am ashamed to say that made me easier in mind. They seem to respect me. Little do they know that I am really the prodigal son.

4 JUNE

I think I am in love with K. I cannot write until I have thought it out.

6 JUNE

I still cannot see my way clear. For hours I have rehearsed renunciatory speeches to myself. Yet I know I shall never make them. About one thing I must be certain, now and whatever happens in the future; nothing must impair any single person near me. I am beginning to think I have never been in love before — in my purely selfish life, it is the greatest thing that has happened. But that is a trifle beside the people I can still look after. If I neglect that work, there is nothing left of me except an ordinary man and a handful of sensations.

10 JUNE

I met K by accident tonight. She shook hands as we parted. Her touch is like no other touch. In the whispering air I rode home to a quiet house.

From the diary one gained no clear impression of K. She was probably a complex and sensitive person, easily hurt and full of self-distrust. Her relation with George was strained and unhappy, almost from the beginning: 'the only time I have been utterly miserable over a woman,' he wrote. With the odd humour that came less often in his diary than in speech, he added on 24 July: 'K let me hold her hand: but that may have been because there was no feeling in her arm'.

His distress and 'longing' (a word which entered frequently that summer) drove him more completely into the group. He resigned from the one or two organisations in the town to which he still belonged – five years before, he had taken part in many. He kept protesting against 'extra work for Eden'. 'I am a solicitor's clerk. I do not consider I am under any obligation to do more than a competent solicitor's clerk usually does. He has no call on me outside office hours.'

He ceased to mention his law lectures, in which he used to take so great a pride.

The same summer – Daphne, who was then nineteen, and Freda (the F of the accounts which George showed me early in the investigation) joined the group.

8 SEPTEMBER 1929

Last night saw what may be – what ought to be – the concluding stage in the K business. She let everyone see what she thought of me. Perhaps she will not come near us again. Jack, Rachel and Olive came to see me tonight. Rachel was all sympathy, and Olive did not disguise her own affair. When Rachel had gone, however, Olive got down to some of the agency's accounts. They are rather good, though the trickle of money does not relieve my financial doldrums. It gives Jack a living, though. He was fine and high-handed about K. Either I ought to make love to her, he insisted, or she ought to be thrown out. I think that he was being genuinely warm-hearted, he was thinking only of my peace of mind.

But it is all very well for them to brandish their freedom. They have got to realise that I am in a different position. They say I have created the position and difficulty for myself. That makes it all the more essential.

14 SEPTEMBER

The meek don't want the earth. Yet I have thought of her all day. Is it possible that she is anxious not to give herself away too cheaply? Or does she simply hate and despise me?

If I am not to have her, let me clear the lumber out of my heart and regain the old freedom. If I could only fall in love with Rachel – but this K business spoils every other relation.

17 SEPTEMBER

Martineau called in for an hour or two. He still wanders on his lonely, meaningless crusade, and remains his gentle self. I told him the agency was going adequately on. He did not seem interested. In the circumstances, I thought it unnecessary to say more. The family this evening asked me for more money: finance will soon be disastrous again.

28 SEPTEMBER

Perhaps K has gone for good. I have never been in so many troubles. I am baying at the moon. Sometimes the group itself seems like a futile little invention of my own. I am thoroughly despondent. The root of the trouble is a discontent which is not confined to me. There is money, which still harasses me. Apart from K, I begin to think the major cause of my present discontent lies in ambition. It will not be so easy to die in obscurity as I once thought.

3 OCTOBER

K is in a state of semi-return. Last night was the second weekend running in Nottingham, but if K comes back I need not go again. Pat's face is too often a disembodied smile, wickedly turned up, saying 'all right' or 'whisky'.

11 OCTOBER

We have had a good weekend at the farm. The people there were all living more abundantly than if I had never happened. I have despaired too easily. I still believe in them and myself, in spite of occasional tremors. In any case, what else could there be in life?

13 OCTOBER

K's essence still comes between me and everything. Yet tonight I was infuriated by a blasted business acquaintance of Olive's disregarding my presence and ignoring my intelligence. I cannot admit inferiority. It is an essential to my present poise that I should be supreme in intellect over anyone I meet.

17 OCTOBER

K is hardly apologetic over her refusal to attend another farm party. She would not explain, and now avoids me. I transferred a little of my affection to Freda, whose smile is sometimes like a faint reflection.

23 OCTOBER

K looked through me with cold eyes. I can't pretend that I still have any hope.

(later the same night)

I shook myself out of this absurd and humiliating affair and took the train to Nottingham. Pat was as delightful as ever a girl of this kind could be – and, damn it, I like these girls better than any others.

30 OCTOBER

One of the best parties we have had, and sometimes I have managed to put K out of mind. The group is far better, I am afraid, with Jack not present.

Freda told me that my 'half-closed' eyes were (*a*) concerning K and Jack,* and (*b*) to Rachel's feeling about me. As for Rachel, she chose her way and I am sure she likes it best.

---

* This seems to have been quite baseless.

3 NOVEMBER

I find myself longing, as I never longed before. For all my fantasies, I do not suppose I should take her as a mistress, even if she would let me near her. I could not help walking the streets round her house, in the hope of seeing her by accident. I walked through a gathering fog, getting for a moment a feeling of exultation as I sped through the mist, weaving my dreams. Of course I did not see her: I went back to the old café, played four games of draughts, then came home and raved.

That was a couple of hours ago. Since then I have been reading some of the diaries of recent years. It has brought back some of the pleasure and hope I have gathered from these people. Some of them have gone before now, without being helped. But others are free people, a nucleus of friends, thinking and acting and living as no other group I am likely to know again.

That is my achievement, and nothing can take it from me. Jack and Olive, for all their faults and defections: Lewis Eliot, away in London – Phyllis and – and – and – : they're all different for having known me and from my being able to spend my devotion. Well, that must go on – whatever distracts me by the way. Are there many men who have twenty better lives to their credit?

So let us not be sad. Personal misery is grotesque: and who am I to complain of losing one when there are so many to occupy my life? Really, I do not often worry about myself at all.

But the passion lasted – different from any in his life, and nearer to others' experience. The same pattern of unhappiness, desire for freedom and return to K, ran through the diary for months.

13 DECEMBER

I take too little notice of people about me. By this wretched affair, I have hurt Rachel. Apart from business I scarcely ever see Olive. I am vexed with ever-absent money, tension about K, no fame. But K seems to have hinted to Jack that she would like to be reconciled:

which news filled me with wild joy, though I was intensely annoyed by Jack's remark – 'She may think you too mad and dangerous.'

I am a little afraid of Jack at times.

This afternoon Freda said of K and me: 'When you take a dislike to a person, imagination does the rest.'

5 JANUARY 1930

I wish I could feel for Freda instead of K. Sometimes I think I could: at least I could get comfort from her. But there again I should have other problems to face. I cannot control myself all these years, resist being laughed at by Jack, only to crash all my aspirations by my own deliberate action.

Anyway the question does not arise. With K it is an ache, a slow corroding pain.

I went off to see Pat, sick at heart. I had quite a pleasant time with her.

14 JANUARY

Tonight K broke her silence. I saw her quite by chance in Rachel's flat – who, good soul, made a sarcastic remark and then went out. K began to talk. She did not apologise. After making myself incredibly late for everything else that evening, I went. But not before I had seen her smile, and felt a happiness that seemed unsensuous and perfect.

At times, by the way, she was wearisome and showed signs of being shallow – but I could hardly think of that.

The after effect has been to make me dream of Freda.

MY HAPPIEST DAY
15 JANUARY

REALISING IT It is very difficult to think of her as tangible.

The reconciliation and their 'ethereal' relations continued all that spring. It occupied much of the diary; for the rest he wrote far less of the constructive side of the group – with occasional reiterations that it was still 'my major interest'.

Instead, he became more explicit about his 'sensations' – to begin with, the nights in Nottingham and London were minutely described. Then: 'Jack and I are narrowing our attention to the libido. It is a long time since we talked of our friends in any other way. For myself, I still cannot limit my interest as he does in his frank fashion. Yet no man has lived more freely than Jack. I know they have often thought him a superficial person by the side of some of us. Perhaps that is not just.'

24 MARCH

Tonight Jack told me some of the stories of his conquests. Some I knew, of course; Mona, in the old days, and —. But Olive! I was astonished at that – though now it makes her Morcom adventure (which is probably ending) more explicable. And he made other hints – I was angry, I told him he had betrayed any decent code of friendship. But I cannot only be jealous. Haven't I inveighed, time after time, against irrational conventions? I must think of his behaviour in the light of reason.

4 APRIL

Last night at the farm I arranged that Freda and I be left alone. And, of course, I made love to her. I felt an altogether marvellous delight – more of the mind than the flesh perhaps, but that was to be expected.

Today I am still in a state of joy – but sometimes now quite easy. I must reassure myself once for all. No one is a penny the worse. It will not interfere with my influence with them, for none of them will know. I am prepared to believe that I could not bring them on as in the past, if this were common property. For many of them, the news would be altogether bad. But for Freda, by herself, it can have done nothing but good. She was longing for the substance of freedom, not only the words. She is older than twenty, in everything that matters: she wanted to begin a life that will be different from all that I have tried to rescue her out of. I am now a completer means of escape. That is all.

Yet tonight I am not altogether tranquil. The years of the group, the continual presence of K – it all seems strange and not entirely real. I used to think I should not stay in this town for long. Now I am past thirty. I have been at Eden's nearly nine years. Sometimes it seems too long a time.

1 JUNE

It has proved unnecessary to keep my change of attitude secret from the group. I must readjust some of my old values – founded probably on the family and my early upbringing. I am now convinced that it is easy to combine the greatest mental activity with a general view more like Jack's than mine. We are all the better for real freedom. No unnecessary internal restraints – and one has more appetite for constructive good. Of course there are times when I cannot always live up to what seems intellectually established: then I have hankerings after the old days.

4 JUNE

Daphne was at a Whitsun party at the farm, which was remarkable for the afterglow it left.

30 JUNE

Money is desperately short again. The trickle from the agency is lessening. I shall have to borrow. What does that matter in this *fin-de-siècle* time?

15 JULY

The high meridian of freedom is on us now. In our nucleus of free people, anyway – and sometimes I think on the world.

7 AUGUST

I tried uselessly to explain to the family some indication of my changed views. With no result, except great fatigue and bitter distress – though they could not understand all my statements. I am more worn than I have been for years. Old habits are the strongest: and still, at my age, nothing tires me to the heart so much as a family quarrel.

2 SEPTEMBER

K came unexpected to the farm this Saturday. After tea – Daphne, Iris R (Mona's half-sister, who used to be a 'regular' and has now come back) and several others were there – K began to talk to me, then stopped. Suddenly I saw tears running down her face. It upset me a little, though not as much as a possible absence of Daphne or Freda.

DAPHNE ALONE
9 SEPTEMBER

This makes a pale shadow of all the others. Words are too soft for some delights…coloured seas and ten million gramophones.

23 SEPTEMBER

There is sometimes too much indiscretion. In a hostile world, a scandal would be dangerous. We cannot ignore it. The raking danger I can sometimes forget, but it returned with an unpleasant scare last week. A fool of a girl thought she might be pregnant. Fortunately it has passed over, but we cannot be too careful.

On the practical issue, Jack insisted that we think of buying the farm. There would be great advantages from every point of view. Jack is certain it could be made to pay. It would make discretion easier. And I insist we have a right to our own world, unspied on and in peace of mind.

Also we must have money. Perhaps I have neglected it too long.

1 OCTOBER

Last night I crawled the pubs in the town. I don't remember ever doing this before. I have always kept these steam-blowing episodes for Nottingham. But what obligations do I owe Eden, after all? After my nine years' servitude.

Anyway, Roy Calvert and I and — (a young man in the group) got drunk and started home. By the post office we saw K. She hurried cringing down a side street. I stopped her. 'Yes – I know, you're drunk,' she said. The vision passed; and I was walking wildly, yelling with Roy, cheering – as we ran round the lamp-posts and crossed the streets.

Through 1931 the diary showed him more and more engrossed with Daphne, although it was not till the middle of the year that he broke off finally from Freda. The references to the purchase of the farm were continued: 'We have to go ahead. I have no alternative.'.... 'I propose to leave the whole business in Jack's charge, far more than I did the agency. There is no reason to occupy myself unnecessarily with it, now it is started, I have better things to do.' These entries both occurred in the autumn of 1931; after that time, during the nine months down to the last entry in my hands, he did not mention the farm business again.

I was forced to compare this silence with the long arguments to himself about the agency; I turned back to those pages which had given Daphne a reason for coming:

16 DECEMBER 1928

Tonight I went over the figures of the first month's business under the new regime (i.e. of the agency). They are satisfactory, and we shall be able to pay our way – but I still find the difficulty which has puzzled me before.★

16 JANUARY 1929

The agency is going well. Our profits are up by 10 per cent in the first month. At last Jack is justifying my faith in him (how it would have changed things if he had followed my advice four years ago and entered a profession. Even now I still feel I was right. I should not be fretted by this uneasiness which I cannot quite put aside).

★ There was no previous reference in the diary to this 'difficulty'.

17 JANUARY 1929

I cannot bear this difficulty any longer. There is no doubt that Martineau's statement of the circulation was fantastically exaggerated. On seeing our own figures there is no doubt at all. We are doing better business than they ever did; and we have not disposed of 1,100 copies of the wretched rag. This puts me in a false position. It devolves upon me to consider what is right for the three of us to do.

If I were to be censorious with myself, I should regret not acting on my earlier suspicions. I was amazed by the figure when Martineau first told me. But after all, I had his authority. What reasons could possess him, of all men, to deceive me? There was no justification for inquiring further. I was within every conceivable right in using his statement to help raise our money. There was one period when I came near to investigating the entire matter – that night, a fortnight before we actually completed the purchase, when I mentioned the circulation to Jack and Olive. Jack laughed, and would not explain himself. Olive said nothing. I began to take steps that night; but then it seemed unnecessary, and I decided to go ahead. I can still feel justified that I was right.

After all, what is the present position? We have borrowed money for a business. We have placed information about the business in front of those we persuaded to lend. All that information was given us on the best of authority; we transmitted it, having every rational ground to consider it true. Most of it was true; on one rather inconsiderable fact, it turns out that we were misled ourselves.

It would be an untenable position, of course, if this accidental misrepresentation had been a cause of loss to our creditors. That providentially is the converse of the actual state of affairs. Our creditors are safely receiving their money, more safely than through any similar investment I can imagine. They have done pretty well for themselves.

So what is to be done? There seems only one answer. No one is losing; for everyone's sake we must go on as we are. I do not consider it necessary to raise the subject with Jack. I have disposed of the moments of uneasiness. My mind is at rest.

18 JANUARY 1929

I am now able to feel that the difficulty is resolved. But there is one problem which I cannot settle. Why ever should Martineau have made a false statement in the first place? Can it have been deliberate? It seems unthinkable. I remember his curious manoeuvres about Morcom's flat just before he left the firm. But I could not believe that was done from selfish motives; still more I cannot believe anything so ridiculous of him now. After all, he did not touch a penny of the price we paid. He went straight off to his incredible settlement. Since then he has scarcely had a shilling in his pocket.

I suppose he was simply losing his grip on the world, and it is useless to speculate as though he were a rational being.

As soon as I read George's words, I did not doubt that his account of Martineau's statement was true. I wondered what Martineau had really meant; whatever underlay it all, his evidence might be essential now. On the whole, though, I was more distressed than before I knew as much.

Two things struck me most. George had certainly suspected the statement while they were still borrowing money; he had managed to shelve his misgivings for a time. Then at last he put his 'mind at rest'. I was not altogether surprised by his self-explanation; but it became full of meaning when we compared it to his silence over the farm.

He believed himself caught accidentally in a fog of misrepresentation over the agency – what about the other business? I could not help but imagine – was it something he could not reconcile himself to? Something he tried to dismiss from his thoughts?

And I knew what George's feeling for Jack had now become. The mention of the circulation, and Jack's laughter; George afraid, when struggling with his doubt, to speak to Jack again – those hints endowed some of George's words with an ironic, an almost intolerable pathos:

'It devolves on me to consider what is right for the three of us to do.'

31

Confidential Talk in Eden's Drawing-Room

I READ the diary all evening. At dinner Eden and I were alone, and he was kindly and cordial. We went into the drawing-room afterwards; he built up the fire as high as it had been the night of Morcom's slip; he pressed me to a glass of brandy.

Here I have to enter into a conversation which I reported, more subjectively, in a part of my own story.

'How do you feel about yesterday?' he said at length.

'It looks none too good,' I said.

'I completely agree,' he said deliberately, with a friendly smile to mark my judgment and to recognise bad news. 'As a matter of fact, I've been talking to Hotchkinson about it during the afternoon. We both consider we shall be lucky if we can save those young nuisances from what, between ourselves, I'm beginning to think they deserve. But I don't like to think of their getting it through the lack of any possible effort on our part. Don't you agree?'

'Of course,' I said. He was sitting back comfortably now, his voice smooth and friendly, as though I was a client he liked, but to whom he had to break bad news. He was sorry, and yet buoyed up by the subdued pleasure of his own activity.

'Well then, that's what Hotchkinson and I have been considering. And we wondered whether you ought to have a little help. You're not to misunderstand us, young man. I'd as soon trust a case to you as anyone of your age, and Hotchkinson believes in you as well. Of course, you were a trifle over-optimistic imagining you might get a dismissal in the police court, but we all make our mistakes, you know. This is going to be a very tricky case, though. It's not going to be just working out the legal defence. If it was only doing that in front of a judge, I'd take the responsibility of leaving you by yourself, if they were my own son and daughter. But this looks like being one of those cases where the legal side isn't so important – ' he chuckled – 'and it'll be a matter of making the best of a bad job with the jury. That's the snag.'

'Almost all my work's been in front of juries.'

'Of course it has. You'll have plenty more. But you know, as we all know, that they're very funny things. And in this case I should say from my experience of them that they'll be prejudiced against your people – simply because they're of the younger generation and one or two stories will slip out that they've gone the pace at times – '

'That's obviously true.'

'Well, I put it to Hotchkinson that they'd be even more prejudiced, if their counsel was the same kind of age and a brilliant young man. They'd resent all the brilliance right from the start, Eliot. You'd only have to make a clever suggestion, and they'd distrust you. They'd be jibbing from all the good qualities of your generation – as well as the bad, but they'd find the bad all right. The racketiness that's been the curse of these days – they'd find that and they'd count it against them in spite of anything you said. Anything you could say would only make it worse.'

'What do you suggest?' I said.

'I want you to stay in the case. You know it better than anyone already, and we can't do without you. But I believe, taking everything into consideration, you ought to have someone to lead you.'

'Who?'

'I was thinking of your old chief – Getliffe.'

'It's sensible to get someone,' I broke out, 'but Getliffe – seriously, he's a bad lawyer.'

'No one's a hero to his pupils, you know,' said Eden.

I persisted: 'I dare say I'm unfair. But this is important. There are others who'd do it admirably.' I gave some names of senior counsel.

'They're clever fellows,' said Eden, smiling as when we argued about George. 'But I don't see any reason to go beyond Getliffe. He's always done well with by cases.'

When I was alone, I was surprised that my disappointment should be so sharp. There was little of my own at stake, a brief in a minor case – for which, of course, I had already refused to be paid. Yet, when it was tested through Eden's decision, I knew – there is no denying the edge of one's unhappiness – that I was more wounded by the petty rebuff than by the danger to my friends.

I was ashamed that it should be so. But for some hours I could think of little else. Despite the anxieties of the case, the chances of Jack running, their immediate fate: despite being present at a time when George needed all the strength of a friend. Often, in the last days, I had lain awake, thinking of what would happen to him. But tonight I was preoccupied with my own vanity.

I went to London next morning and saw Getliffe. He said, alert, bright-eyed and glib after skimming through the documents: 'You worked with Eden once, of course.'

'I know him well,' I said.

'You've seen this case he's sent us?'

'I've watched it through the police court,' I answered.

'Well, L S,' his voice rose, 'it'll be good fun working together again. It's been too long since we had a duet, I'm looking forward to this.'

The preparation of the case gave me a chance to be more thorough than if I had been left alone. For there was the need to sit with Getliffe, to bully him, to ignore his complaints that he would get it up in time, to make him aggrieved and patronising. At any cost, he must not go into court in the way I had seen him so often, flustered, with no more than a skipped reading, a half-memory behind him, relying in a badgered and uncomfortable way on his inventive wits, completely determined to work thoroughly in his next case, fidgeting and yet getting sympathy with the court – somehow, despite the mistakes, harassment, carelessness, sweating forehead and nervous eyes, keeping his spirits and miraculously coming through.

I kept the case before him. He was harder-working than most, but he could not bear any kind of continuity. An afternoon's work after his own pattern meant going restlessly through several briefs, picking up a recognition-symbol here and there, so that, when a solicitor came in and mentioned a name, Getliffe's eyes would be bright and intelligent – 'You mean the man who – '

He left me to collect the witnesses. One of my tasks was to trace Martineau; it took a good deal of time. At last I found a workhouse master in the North Riding, who guffawed as I began to inquire over the telephone.

'You mean Old Jesus,' he said. 'He's often been in here.' He added: 'He doesn't seem mad. But he must be right off his head.'

He was able to tell me where 'that crowd' had settled now.

I returned to the town at the weekend. I had not been back an hour before Roy rang up to say that Jack seemed to have disappeared. For a day or two he had been talking of a 'temporary expedition' to Birmingham, to survey the 'prospects' for a new business as soon as the trial was over. Today no one could find him.

A few minutes after the call, Roy brought Olive and Rachel to Eden's house. For the whole afternoon Eden left us to ourselves.

Rachel was desperately worried. Roy also believed that Jack had flown. Of us all, Olive alone was unshaken.

'If you knew him better,' she said, 'you'd know that he fooled himself with his excuses – as well as you. He's really planning a new business. And he also thinks it's a good dodge for getting a few miles away.'

'He needn't stop there,' said Roy.

'I don't believe he's gone near Birmingham,' said Rachel.

'I think you'll find he has,' said Olive.

'I know I'm thinking of George all the time,' cried Rachel. 'We've got to sit by and watch Jack ruin him. And Olive, it's wretched to see you – '

'Go on.'

'I must speak now. I know it's hopeless,' Rachel went on. 'But if only you could see Jack for a minute just as we do – '

'You think he's a scoundrel. That he doesn't care a rap for me. And that he'll marry me because he can't get money some other way. Is that what you mean?' Before Rachel replied Olive added: 'Some of it's quite true.'

'You don't know what a relief it would be – to get you free of him,' Rachel said. 'Is there any chance? When this is over?'

'None,' said Olive. After a moment, she said: 'I don't care what you think of how much he's attached to me. But I'll tell you this. He knows he can live on my money. He may be forced to marry me in the end. But I shall be happier about the arrangement than he will. There'll be times when he's bound to think that I'm dragging him down. He's got more illusions than I have. You've got to persuade yourselves of that.'

Rachel tried to argue with her. She did not resent the obvious pretences and attempts to console her. She said, with a genuine smile: 'It's no use talking. You'll never believe a word I say.'

Rachel once more begged her to trace Jack – 'we can't let George be thrown away,' she cried.

Then the maid announced another visitor for me and Morcom came in. First he caught sight of Roy, and said: 'I can't find any news.'

At that moment, he saw Olive.

'I'm sorry. They didn't tell me – '

'Come and sit by the fire,' she said.

He sat down and spread out his hands. His face looked ill with care. We all knew that this was the first time they had met for months.

In her presence he would not say what he had come for. Roy talked more easily for a few minutes than anyone there could manage: then he took Rachel away.

Olive said to Morcom: 'You're not looking well, Arthur. You must take care of yourself.'

'I'm all right.'

'Promise me you'll look after yourself.'

'If I can,' said Morcom. Their manner to each other was still sometimes tender. Some casual remark made them smile together, and their faces, in that moment, rested in peace.

Soon Olive could not control her restlessness. She crossed to the window, and looked out into the dark; she returned to her chair again, and then got up to go. Her eyes caught the brief lying on the writing desk. She pointed to the words on the first page – Rex *v*. Passant and Ors.

'Is that us?' She was laughing without any pretence. 'I've never seen anything that looked – so far away.'

She stood still for a moment, and said goodbye. She put her hand on the back of Morcom's chair: 'Goodbye,' she said again.

As soon as the door closed, Morcom said: 'I came to say – you must force George to escape.'

'You think Jack has really gone?'

'I don't know. I advised him to.'

I broke out in angry recriminations, though as he spoke his face was torn with pain. I reminded him of my warning the night of the first inquiries: and how, after the police court, we agreed that I could not tell George to go.

'It's criminal to take the responsibility of persuading Jack – unless George was ready too,' I said.

'I had to speak,' said Morcom.

'You could not face telling me first.'

'Don't you understand that I was bound to speak to Jack?' Morcom said. 'You said I ought to have taken care of them before it happened. Do you think this was any more bearable? It means they will marry. They will stay abroad for years. They will be left with nothing but their own resources. That's what she longs for, isn't it? I've had to try to help it on.'

I looked at him.

'Will you tell George to go now?' he said at last.

'I shall have to try,' I said.

32

Visit to George

I TOOK a taxi to George's lodgings. He was alone, sitting in the same chair, the same position, as in the evening after the police court. He must have heard the taxi drive up outside, but he did not inquire why I had hurried.

He tried to stir himself for my benefit, however. Though his voice was flat, he asked after Sheila with his old friendly diffident politeness; he talked a little of a case that I had just finished in London.

Then I said: 'What do you think of our case, George?'

'It's gone more or less as I expected.'

'Has it?'

George nodded without any protest.

I hesitated.

'Look, George,' I said. 'I'm going to offend you. You'll have to forgive me. I don't care what has actually happened in this business. You know that perfectly well. I can't imagine any action you could do which would make the slightest difference to me. It wouldn't either make me think worse of you or better – it works both ways. Well, I don't know what's happened, you may be technically guilty or you may not, I don't know and, apart from curiosity, I don't care. You've told me you're not.' I met his eyes. 'I know you tell the literal truth more than most of us – but even so, I can imagine all sorts of reasons why you should lie here.'

He gave a resentful, awkward laugh.

'So I've got nothing to do with what really happened,' I said. 'The essential thing is what other people will think happened. That's all. I'm just talking as a lawyer about the probabilities in this case. You know them, you're a better lawyer than I am, of course, whenever you care. What should you say the probabilities are?'

'So far, they're not much in our favour.'

'If you came to me as a client,' I said, 'I shouldn't be as optimistic as that.'

I went on: 'Anyway, supposing you're right, supposing the chances were even or a bit better – ought you to risk it? If it comes down the wrong side –'

'We get a few months. And the consequences –'

'Is the risk worth taking?'

'What do you mean?'

'Jump your bail. I've spoken to the others who put up money. We all want you to please yourself.'

'What should I do?'

'You could be in South America in a fortnight. Nothing will touch you there, in this sort of case.'

There was a silence.

'I don't see how I'm going to live.'

'We can provide a bit. It won't be much, God knows – but it'd help you in a place where living's cheap. And in time it would be possible to make a little money.'

'It would be difficult.'

'Not impossible. You could get qualified there – if there's nothing else.'

'I should never have any security.'

'Think of the alternative.'

'No,' George burst out, in a loud, harsh, emphatic tone. 'I'm afraid it's completely impracticable. I appreciate the offer, of course.' (That 'of course' of George's which, as so often, was loaded with resentment.)

232

'But it's ludicrous to consider it. Apart from the practical obstacles – I should have to live in discomfort all my life, it isn't pleasant to condemn oneself to squalid exile.'

He added: 'And there's the question of the others.'

'I was coming to that.'

'Well?'

'Olive could go with a clear conscience. Her uncle's wealthy, she has enough to live on.'

He did not reply.

'I'll promise to readjust things with the others so that you won't have any responsibility,' I said. 'You come first. It's more serious for you. You stand to lose most. For me – I needn't tell you – you count very much the most.'

There was a silence before George replied: 'I appreciate the offer. But I can't take it.'

'There is one other thing,' I said.

'What?' His voice had returned to the lifeless tone with which he welcomed me.

'Jack may have gone already.'

'Are you inventing that to get rid of me?'

'I didn't want to tell you,' I said. 'But you've seen some indications, surely?'

'I didn't take them seriously.'

'This you must,' I said.

'I want to know exactly what basis you're going on.'

I told him the facts – that Olive believed Jack would return to stand his trial: that no one else did.

'If he doesn't,' I said, 'you recognise what your chances are?'

'Yes,' said George.

His face was heavy as he thought.

'I don't necessarily accept the view that he won't come back,' he said. 'But if he doesn't – I can't alter my position. I shan't go.'

'For God's sake think it over,' I said. 'We'll make it as easy for you as we humanly can.'

He was silent.

'I've a right to ask you to think it over tonight,' I said. 'I beg you to.'

'I'm sorry. There is no point in that,' George said. 'I shall stay here and let them try me.'

Part Four

THE TRIAL

33

Courtroom Lit by a Chandelier

THE morning of the trial was dark, and all over the town lights shone in the shop windows. In front of the old Assize Hall, a few people had gathered on the pavement, staring at the policemen on the steps.

It was still too early. I walked into the entrance hall, which was filling up. George came in: when, after a moment, he saw me in the crowd of strangers, his face became suddenly open and bewildered.

'There are plenty of people here,' he said.

We stood silently, then began to talk about the news in the morning papers. In a few minutes we heard a call from inside which became louder and was repeated from the door.

'Surrender of George Passant! Surrender of George Passant!'

George stared past me, buttoned his jacket, smoothed down the folds.

'Well, I'll see you later,' he said.

In the robing-room Getliffe was sitting in his overcoat taking a glance at his brief. As I came in, he stood up hurriedly.

'Time's getting on,' he said. 'We must be moving.'

I helped him on with his gown; he chatted about Eden.

'Pleasant old chap, isn't he? Not that he's as old as all that. He must be this side of sixty. You know, L S, I was thinking last night. First of all I was surprised he has been contented to sit in a second-rate provincial town all his life – and then I realised one could be very happy here. Just limiting yourself, knowing what you've got to do, knowing you're doing a useful job which doesn't take too much out of you. And then going away from it and remembering you're a human being. Clocking in and clocking out.'

He was speaking more breathlessly than in normal times. This nervousness before a case – which he had never lost – was mainly a physical malaise, a flutter of the hands, a catch in the voice: perhaps it had once been more, but now it was worn down by habit. He was putting on his wig, which, although it was faintly soiled, at once gave his face a greater distinction. He stared at himself in the mirror; his bands were awry, he was still a little dishevelled, but he turned away with a furtive, satisfied smile.

'All aboard,' he said.

He led the way into court. Olive and George were in the dock, looking towards the empty seats on the bench, which spread in a wide semi-circle round the small, high, dome-shaped room. It had been repainted since the July afternoon when George won a verdict in it; otherwise I noticed no change.

We came to our places, two or three steps beyond the dock; I turned and glanced at it. Jack was not there. I heard Porson, the leader for the prosecution, in court ten minutes early, greet Getliffe, in a rich, chuckling voice: I found myself anxious about nothing except that Jack should appear for the trial.

The gallery was nearly full. The case had already become a scandal in the town. Suddenly, I heard the last call for Jack and saw him walk quickly towards the dock. The judge entered, the indictment was read, they pleaded. George's voice sounded loud and harsh, the others' quiet.

'You may sit down, of course,' the judge said. His eyes were dark, bright and inquisitive in a jowled, broad face. There was only a small bench in the dock, barely enough for three. 'Why are there no chairs for them? Please fetch chairs.' His voice was kindly but precise.

The voice of the clerk swearing the jury fell distantly on my ears, deafened by habit. I looked round the courtroom. Eden was sitting upstairs, near the benches set aside for the Grand Jury; Cameron, the Principal of the School, had a place close by. Beddow, the chairman of that meeting over seven years before, bustled in, fresh and cheerful, to an alderman's seat. In the small public space behind the dock, several of George's friends were sitting, Mr Passant among them; Roy Calvert was looking after Mr Passant, and stayed at his side throughout the trial.

Just before Porson opened, a note was brought to me from Morcom. 'They say I've just missed rheumatic fever. There is nothing to worry about, but I can't come.' That was all. I kept looking at it; the oath had reached the last man on the jury. In the diffused light of the winter morning, added to by the single chandelier of bulbs hanging over our table, our fingers made shadows with a complex pattern of penumbra, and faces in the court were softened.

The case for the prosecution took up the first two days. It went worse for us than we feared.

Porson's opening was strong. From the beginning he threatened us with George's statement over the circulation of the *Arrow*.

'We possess a piece of evidence that no one can deny,' he said. He drew everyone's attention to a sheet of notepaper which was to be produced at the proper time. He concentrated much of his attack on the agency; then he pointed out how, when they had 'obtained some practice' in their methods, George and the others had gone 'after bigger game'. The farm business needed larger sums, but they had found it easy to misrepresent what its true position was. 'They didn't trouble to change their methods,' said Porson. 'They had learned after their little experience with the *Arrow* that it was child's play to give false figures. This time they needed larger sums, and you will hear how they obtained them from Miss Geary, Mrs Stuart and – '

He finished by telling the jury that he would produce a witness, Mrs Iris Ward, who would describe an actual meeting at the farm when the three of them decided they must buy it – 'decided they must buy it not only as a business, but because they had reasons of their own for needing somewhere to live in private, out of reach of inquisitive eyes'.

Porson did as he threatened.

The only point which Getliffe scored was made before lunch on the first morning. One of the witnesses over the agency, a man called Attock, said that, before he lent Jack money, he had looked over all the figures of the firm with an accountant's eye. He was a masterful, warm-voiced man, with a genial, violent laugh: Getliffe saw through him, and brought off an ingenious cross-examination. In the end, Getliffe revealed him as a man always priding himself on his shrewdness and losing money in unlikely ventures: and as one who had never managed to finish his accountant's examinations.

At lunch on that first day, Jack and Olive were more composed than before the trial. Even George, sunk in a despondency which surprised those who remembered his optimism but did not know him well, referred to Getliffe's handling of Attock.

It was, however, a false start. First thing in the afternoon, Porson produced the quiet kindly witness of the police court, who told the same story without a deviation. Then two more followed him, with the same account of the acquaintanceship with Jack, the meetings with George, the statement of the circulation of the *Arrow*. They testified to a statement written by George, which now, for the first time, Porson produced in court. It read:

'We are not in a position to give full figures of the Agency's business. So far as we have examined the position they do not seem to exist. One important indication, however, we can state exactly. The advertising paper run by the Agency – *The Advertisers' Arrow* – has had an average circulation of five thousand per issue. This figure is given on the authority of Mr Martineau, now retiring from the firm.'

Porson gave the sheet of paper to the jury. They passed it round: at last it came to Getliffe and myself. It was as neatly written as a page from the diary. We knew there was no hope of challenging it.

Pertinaciously, good-temperedly, Getliffe worked hard. Questions tapped out in the room as the sky darkened through the lowering afternoon. The illuminated zone from the chandelier left the judge half in darkness. Getliffe did not shake any of the three witnesses. He tried to test their memory of figures by a set of numerical questions which he often used as a last resource. Several times, still good-

240

tempered but harassed, he became entangled in names, that odd but familiar laxness of his – 'Mr Pass*more*,' he said, 'you say you were met by Mr Pass*more*.'

Then Porson called Exell, Martineau's partner in the agency. Getliffe, breathing hard, sweat running down the temples from under his wig, asked me to take him.

'You know, of course, the state of your business just before it was sold?' Porson was asking.

'Yes,' said Exell. He had grown almost bald since I last saw him, at the time of Martineau's departure.

'Was it at its most prosperous just then?'

'Nothing like it. Times had got worse,' said Exell.

'When was it at its most prosperous?'

'Just about the time that Mr Martineau entered it.'

'You would regard the circulation of your paper, the *Arrow*, as some indication of the state of the firm?'

'I'm not certain.' A series of questions followed, in which Porson tried to persuade him. He gave at last a rather unwilling and qualified assent.

'Now you have accepted that figure as an indication, I want to ask you – when did it reach its highest point?'

'At the time I told you. Seven years ago, nearly.'

'What was the circulation at the highest point?'

'Twelve hundred.'

'I should like you to repeat that. I should like the jury to hear you say that again. What was the circulation at the highest point?'

Exell repeated the words.

'There is just one thing else you might tell us, Mr Exell. The jury may find this important. We have been told this afternoon that the circulation at some time – never mind who told us or what the reason was – was estimated at five thousand. Was that ever a conceivable figure?'

'Never. I have told you the highest.'

'And just before the end it didn't rise for any reason?'

'It must have been lower.'

I tried everything I could invent. I asked him about the agency's books. Weren't they singularly carelessly kept? Hadn't he neglected them for years before Martineau joined him? Wasn't it Martineau's task to supervise the books during the months he was a partner? Wasn't it true that Exell could only have a vague knowledge of the agency's finances in general, this circulation in particular, during Martineau's time? Wasn't it true that he was always concerned – and his partner also – with activities outside the ordinary run of business? That Martineau was entirely preoccupied with religion? That Exell himself gave much time to eccentric causes – such as spiritualism and social credit? Wasn't it possible his estimate of the figure was simply a guess without any exact information? He was uneasy, but we gained nothing. His tone grew thinner and more precise. Once his eyes dropped in that mannerism of hampered truculence which in some men is like a child beginning to cry. He would not budge from his figure. 'Twelve hundred's correct,' he said.

When I had finished, Porson said: 'I want the jury to be certain of the figure, Mr Exell. First of all, you have no doubts whatever, despite anything that has been hinted?'

'No.'

'That's right. You have been telling us, with expert authority, the largest figure that the circulation can ever have reached. Now will you let the jury hear it again – for the last time?'

'Twelve hundred.'

As I left the court on that first night, Porson threw me a word, friendly, triumphant and assertive. I saw George hesitate in front of me; then Jack called him, and he walked away with the other two. Having dinner with acquaintances, I heard speculations going on, coolly and disinterestedly, over George and the others: I kept thinking of their evening together. It made me escape early, back to useless work on the case.

The farm evidence took up all the next day. It was heavy and suspicious, as Porson had promised, though there was nothing as clear as George's statement of the circulation. It was a story of Jack mixing in odd company, making friends, inspiring trust: meetings of his new friends with Olive and George: talk of the farm as a business, mention of accounts, figures on the table.

The stories fitted each other: Getliffe could not break any of them: it only needed those figures to be preserved for our last hope to go. But no one possessed a copy. Miss Geary, the witness who gave the sharpest impression of accuracy, said that in her presence no written figures had ever been produced; the whole transaction had been verbal. She obviously blamed herself for a fool, she was bitterly angry with Jack in particular, and she showed herself overfond of money. Yet I thought she inclined, even now, to the side of George and Jack when she was not entirely sure. Once or twice, certainly, she seemed pleased to put Porson off with a doubt.

Her very fairness, though, acted against us. And she was followed by Iris Ward, whom Porson kept to the last.

As her name was called 'Mrs Iris Ward! Mrs Iris Ward!' I caught sight of George's face. She had once been, before her marriage, an obscure member of his group; she was Mona's half-sister, but George had never paid much attention to her. Now he showed an anxiety and suffering so acute that it was noticed by many people in the court.

Her face was pleasant-looking, a little worn and tired. She was a year or two from thirty. She smiled involuntarily in a frank and almost naïve manner when Porson addressed her.

'Mrs Ward,' he began, 'did you hear Mr Passant and his friends talk about buying the farm?'

'I did.'

'When was this?'

'The last year I ever went there. I mean, to the farm itself. Nearly three years ago.'

'That is,' Porson remarked to the jury, 'ten months before the farm was actually bought. Can you describe the occasion for us?'

'I went over one Saturday evening.'

'Who was there?'

'Mr Passant, Mr Cotery, Miss Sands (Rachel) – ' She gave several other names.

'Was Miss Calvert there?'

'No.'

'Can you tell us anything that was said at that meeting – about the transaction?'

'We were sitting round after supper. They were all excited. I think they had been talking before I arrived. Mr Cotery said: "It would be a good idea if we ran this place. So that we could have it to ourselves whenever we wanted it. We shan't be safe until we do." '

Porson stopped her for a moment: then he asked: 'What was said then?'

'Mr Passant said it would be useful if we could, but he didn't see how it could conceivably be managed. Mr Cotery laughed at him and called him a good old respectable member of the professional classes. "Haven't I got you out of that after all this time?" he said. "Of course it can be managed. Do you think I can't raise a bit of money for a good cause?" and he went on arguing with Mr Passant, saying it was for an absolutely essential cause. He said: "It takes all the pleasure away. And it's dangerous. I don't propose to stand the strain if you do. Just for the sake of a little money." '

Her voice was quiet, clear and monotonous. Everyone was believing her story. It sounded nothing like an invention: she seemed to draw on one of those minutely accurate memories, common among many people with an outwardly drab and uneventful life.

'What did Mr Passant say?'

'He argued for a while – he talked about the difficulties of raising the money. He said he didn't propose to find himself the wrong side of the law.'

Getliffe made a note. She continued: 'Mr Cotery said how easy it would be to raise the money. "You see," he said, "as soon as we own the place we can kill two birds with one stone. We can make a good deal of money out of it ourselves. It would be a good investment for the people we borrow from. And it's child's play persuading them. We've got all the cards in our hands. We've been here more often than everyone else put together. No one else knows how many people might use a hostel like this. We can tell people what its possibilities are." '

'From that remark,' Porson said, 'you gathered Mr Cotery was suggesting they should give false information?'

'I can't say.'

'That's what you understood at the time, isn't it?'

'I'd rather not say. I may have got a wrong impression. I'm certain of what was said, though.'

'Very well. What happened afterwards?'

'Mr Cotery went on at Mr Passant. No one else said much. At last Mr Passant said: "It would be magnificent! It will have to be done! I've respected my obligations long enough and they go on ignoring me. Besides, the suspense is wearing us down." '

'We are hearing about this suspense again. What suspense did they both mean?'

Getliffe objected. He was getting on better with the judge than Porson was, and had begun to play on Porson's truculence. He also knew that the case was important in Porson's career, which hadn't been a lucky one.

Porson turned to the judge. 'I have just supplied what the jury will consider a discussion of a future conspiracy. I wish to carry this line further.'

The judge smiled perfunctorily. 'You may ask the question.'

'What suspense did they mean?'

'He meant – they were afraid.'

'What of?'

'Some of their relations being discovered.'

'You had no doubt of that at the time?'

'None at all.'

Porson's tone was comradely and casual: 'You mean some of them had immoral relations with each other?'

'Is this necessary?' put in the judge. 'I take it you only want to demonstrate that they had a strong reason for attempting to get this farm to themselves? Surely you have asked enough to make the position clear.'

'I consider it's desirable to ask one or two more questions,' Porson said.

'I don't think I can let you proceed any further along this line,' the judge said.

'I wish to make the jury aware of certain reasons.'

'They will have gathered enough.'

'Under protest, I should like to ask one or two relevant questions.'

'Go on,' said the judge.

'Well, Mrs Ward. I shan't keep you long in the circumstances. Can you just tell us whether there was any change in the attitude of Mr Passant and his friends – the attitude of these people whom we have learned to call the *group* – when strangers came to the farm?'

The judge was frowning. Getliffe looked at him, half-rose, then did not object.

'There was a great deal of talk about discretion after the scares began.'

'What were these scares?'

'You may not ask that,' said the judge.

'I should like – '

'You may not ask that.'

Porson turned round to the witness box.

'I hope the jury will have understood how afraid these people were of any discovery of their activities. Although I haven't been permitted to establish the point to my own satisfaction. However, perhaps I'm allowed to ask you whether you thought any of them, Mr Passant for example, were afraid of having their careers damaged if their activities came out?'

'I thought so.'

'Would you say any of them felt an even more compelling fear?'

'I can't answer that,' she said.

'Why can't you?'

'I'm not certain.'

All of a sudden, Porson was back in his seat, leaning against the bench, his legs crossed and his lids half over his eyes.

Getliffe cross-examined at length. She had left the School and George's company months before the farm was bought. This conversation was long before they made any attempt to raise money?

She had not been in their confidence at the critical time? The conversation might have been utterly at random? Obviously this danger which had been so much stressed could not have been urgent – as they went on for months without acting on it?

She answered the questions as straightforwardly as Porson's; she did not seem either malicious or burdened by her responsibility. I had learned only a few random facts about her; she had become a Catholic since she married, the marriage was apparently happy, she now lived in the school house of a country grammar school. She had always been intimate with her half-sister, Mona. None of us understood her part in the trial.

Getliffe finished by a number of questions on the after-supper conversation. Had she never heard people making plans for the fun of it? Had she never made plans herself of how to get rich quick? Had she never even heard people speculating on how to commit the ideal murder? For a moment, her answers were less composed than at the direct and critical points. Then Getliffe asked her about George's remark: 'I don't propose to find myself the wrong side of the law.' 'You are quite certain that was said?' Getliffe said.

'Yes.'

'You believed it at the time?'

'It struck me as a curious remark to make.'

She replied to Porson's re-examination just as equably. Now, however, with people excited by the scandal, he raised several bursts of laughter: it was, for the first time, laughter wholly on Porson's side. It was a sound which George could not escape. A wind had sprung up, the windows rattled, and at times the sun shone in beams across the room; in that rich, mellow, domestic light the court grew more hostile through the afternoon.

34

Dinner Party After a Bad Day

AS soon as the court adjourned, we heard a great deal of talk upon Iris Ward's evidence. Everyone who spoke to us seemed to have believed her account; there was a continuous stir of gossip and curiosity about the lives of George and his friends. They were disapproved of with laughter and excitement: people thought that Porson had been right to force a scandal into notice. 'He's won the case and shown them up at the same time,' someone said in my hearing.

Getliffe himself was unusually grave. He kept talking of Iris' evidence, and seemed both moved and despondent. He was anxious over the result, of course – but something else was taking hold of him.

Though we were to meet at Eden's house for dinner, he kept on talking in the robing-room long after the court had cleared. Then I went straight to George's and stayed for a couple of hours. The three of them were there alone; they had eaten every meal together since the trial began; only my presence tonight prevented an outburst of reproaches – my presence, and the state into which George had fallen.

He scarcely spoke or protested; yet, as his eyes saw nothing but his own thoughts, his face was torn with suffering – just as when he heard the call for Iris Ward.

When Jack spoke now, he assumed that George would obey. Only once did George make an effort to show himself their leader still. He heard me say that Martineau, who had promised to be in the town by that afternoon, had still not arrived. George stirred himself: 'I insist on your tracing him at once. I tried to make Getliffe realise that it was essential to keep in touch with Martineau – on the one occasion when Getliffe spared me a quarter of an hour. He didn't trouble to recognise that my opinion was more valuable than theirs.' He looked at the other two.

When I returned to Eden's house, I rang up Canon Martineau, to ask if he had any news of his brother: and also Martineau's housekeeper in his old house in the New Walk. Neither had heard from him.

As I hurried downstairs to Eden's drawing-room, there came a jolly and wholehearted peal of laughter. Eden and Getliffe were waiting for me, glasses of sherry standing by their chairs on the broad rail by the fireside. I was five minutes late for dinner, and Eden was a little put out; though, when I said that I had been trying to find Martineau, he smiled at Getliffe's jokes at my expense.

Getliffe, so dejected at the end of the afternoon, was in high spirits now, and as we sat down to dinner Eden looked at him with a broad and happy smile. He enjoyed entertaining him. He liked the reflection of the busy and successful world, and also the glow that Getliffe brought to so many people. With an aftertaste of envy, not unpleasant or bitter, Eden at times insisted on his own travels and tastes.

'I want you to try another wine,' he said, 'I brought it from a place just behind Dijon when I was there – why! it must be five or six years ago.'

Getliffe said: 'One doesn't ask any better than this, you know.' He took a gulp at his glass.

'I don't want you to miss the other,' said Eden. 'I can't let you leave without having something a little unusual.'

'Yours to command,' Getliffe answered.

Getliffe held his glass up to the light.

'I could go on drinking that,' he said. Then he chuckled. 'When I think of all the wine in my ancient Inn I always think it's a shame that there are chaps like me – who could drink any of it and not be much the wiser. But as for this you've given us – well, L S, you and I can tell our host that if he gives us nothing worse we don't care who's getting amongst the bottles at out respective ancient halls.'

'I've got up another bottle,' Eden said. 'We must finish it before the night's over.' He talked contentedly on, though he looked at me once with kindly concern. 'Those days' came in often, he told stories of counsel he had met at the Assizes, men of the generation in front of Getliffe's. They listened to each other with enjoyment; Getliffe began telling anecdotes about judges. 'That reminds me,' he said, in a few minutes. 'It reminds me of the best remark ever made by a judicial authority within the Empire of His Britannic Majesty. It was actually made by the Chief Justice of a not unimportant Colony, you understand. He was delivering judgment. You must guess the sort of case for yourself when you've heard the remark. He said, "*However* inclement the weather, His Majesty's police stations must in no circumstances be used for the purpose of fornication." '

Getliffe was still contented with the joke when we returned to the drawing-room. Then he and Eden found another pleasure in talking of London streets, dark during the war.

'I remember going across to the Inn one night when I was home on leave,' said Getliffe.

'I had to go up to see one of your men in the Temple,' Eden replied, 'it must have been the same year.'

'We might have run across each other,' said Getliffe. 'Perhaps we did for all you know.'

At last I could not help coming back to the trial.

On the instant Getliffe's face was clouded.

'I'm worried,' he said. 'I don't mind saying I'm worried – '

Eden broke in: 'Of course we've noticed that it's on Eliot's mind. But I'm afraid I am going to forbid you to discuss it now. We are all exercised about it. I dare say it's specially so with Eliot, because he's been friendly with the three of them for a few years now – '

'I'm worried on their account,' said Getliffe. 'Of course, one likes to win one's cases – but they count more – ' He looked at me. 'I'm asking you to believe that,' he said.

'You mustn't begin discussing it,' Eden continued. 'You must keep your minds off it tonight. I can't give either of you much advice, but I'm going to make sure that you follow this.'

His mouth was curved in a firm, kindly, gratified smile. But circumstances were too strong for him. He was himself rung up twice within half an hour. The second call was from Martineau, saying that he had arrived and would come round to Eden's house at ten o'clock. Seeing my relief, Eden said: 'Well, I didn't mean to let you worry tonight. I decided to guard you from some depressing news. But perhaps you'd better hear it now. That first conversation over the phone – it was with Cameron, the Principal at the School.'

'Yes?'

'He was just informing me, as a matter of courtesy, that if Passant couldn't deny the immorality stories, they would be obliged to dismiss him from the School. That applies, of course, whatever the result of the case.'

'I suppose you'd expect them to,' said Getliffe.

'You can't blame them,' said Eden. 'After all they're running an educational institution. They can't be too careful. They're entitled to say that Passant has abused a position of trust.'

I remembered George using exactly those words before the committee years ago: I remembered how he repudiated a suggestion by Jack in Nottingham that same night.

'Shall you get rid of him yourself?' said Getliffe.

Eden considered, and answered deliberately: 'I don't regard that as quite on the same footing. If he's convicted, of course, the question doesn't arise. But if you get them off, I don't think I should feel entitled to dismiss someone who's been found innocent in a court of law. It's true that his private life will have damaged the firm; but I set off against that the good solid work he's done for me in the past. I think, taking everything into account, I shall have to let him stay.

Though naturally I shouldn't be able to give him so much responsibility. It would mean harder work than I want until I retire.'

'I must say, you're more tolerant than most of us would be,' said Getliffe. 'I respect you for it.' He broke off: 'As for getting them off, I don't know. We may as well try to find out what Martineau has to say.'

'He'll be here in half an hour,' said Eden.

'Can I get a word with him?' said Getliffe.

'It's not exactly correct, is it?' Eden was frowning.

'But if you're there? I've done it before, believe me.'

'I'd rather Hotchkinson was here too. But maybe in the circumstances there'll be no harm done.'

'Not that I hope for much,' Getliffe said.

'I'm beginning to be sorry I inflicted it on you,' said Eden.

'Never mind that. One's got to do one's job,' Getliffe said. Then he added: 'I wish one of you would tell me what those three were trying to do. It's getting me down.'

'I'm afraid it isn't very difficult. They wanted money to go the pace,' said Eden. 'They weren't the sort to keep within their means. It's a pity.'

'I should have thought they could have made it like the rest of us. If they were as keen on it as all that. Or do you mean, they didn't care a cherub's apron for the way the money comes? With all due respect, I don't see them quite that way. God knows, I don't think much of them – '

'I've sometimes thought,' said Eden, 'that the greatest single difference between our generation and theirs is the way we look at money. It doesn't mean anything like the same as it did when we were starting. You can't altogether blame them, when you look at the world that's coming.'

'That's not true,' I said, 'of two of them at least. George Passant always had strict views about financial honesty, though he throws his own money about. And Olive – she would be perfectly sensible and orthodox about it.'

'I've generally found that people who are loose morally – are loose the other way too,' said Eden.

'You're meaning Cotery was the centre of the piece?' Getliffe said to me.

'I've always rather taken to him,' Eden put in. 'He's a bit weak, that's all. He's the sort of man who'd have done well in different company. Somehow I can't see him just sweeping the other two along.'

'Can you, L S?' Getliffe said.

'As for Passant,' Eden went on, 'you've always had too high an opinion of him, you know. As you get older, you'll lose your illusions about human nature. I dare say he did have strict views about financial honesty – when people he disliked were making the money.'

'I believe,' I said, 'that he's been as ashamed of the money part as you would have been yourself.'

'I must say,' said Getliffe, 'that it makes more sense if you take our host's line. It looks as though Passant went in up to the neck right at the beginning. He had no sooner talked to this man Martineau than he was ready to cook his figures. It doesn't leave you much to stand on, L S.'

I told him, as I had done before, that I believed George's own account; somehow Martineau had let him take away the idea of a large circulation. We had already arranged for him to press this story of George's when Martineau gave evidence. At first Getliffe had welcomed it as a glimmer of hope: tonight he did not pretend to accept it.

'There's only one chance of excusing them that I've been able to believe in,' said Eden. 'That is, Martineau may have been vague when Passant approached him. You must remember he was slightly eccentric at the time. You'll see for yourself soon. You'll find him a very likeable fellow, of course. But, you know, I've been trying to keep that doubt in their favour – and, between ourselves, I can't credit it for a minute. Martineau was always a bit queer – but he was the sharpest man on money matters I ever knew. It's very peculiar, but there – there's nowt as odd as fowk. I don't believe he had it in him not to know exactly what the paper was doing – even if he was going to give it away.'

'And if he was vague – you can't really console yourself with that,' said Getliffe. 'There's too much difference altogether. Passant would have to misunderstand on purpose.'

For a time they talked about the farm. 'If I'd been Porson, I should have given us more of that little business. Just our friends raising money, that's all,' said Getliffe.

Just before ten, I went up to my room. I heard Martineau being received below a few minutes afterwards. Getliffe had told me to be ready to join the interview; nearly an hour passed, but they did not send for me. At last footsteps sounded on the stairs. I opened my door, and from below heard Eden saying: 'Goodbye, Howard. We shall see you tomorrow, then.'

I went back into my room, and walked up and down, unable to keep still. On his way to bed, Getliffe looked in.

'It wasn't worthwhile bringing you down. I didn't get anywhere,' he said. He looked jaded and downcast.

'What happened?'

'I couldn't get anything out of him.'

'Did you tell him Passant's story? Did you let him see that some of us believe it?'

'I went as far as anyone could,' said Getliffe.

'Shall I see him?'

'I told him you'd satisfied yourself about Passant's version. I tried to make him believe I had too. But' – Getliffe's voice was tired – 'he simply didn't seem interested. He didn't remember it very well. It was all hazy. He couldn't have told Passant anything but the real figures. Even though he didn't have any recollection of it now.'

'You mean, he's going to deny Passant's story?'

'As near as makes no matter,' said Getliffe. 'All I can do is try to make him say that he's forgotten.' He added: 'I never thought Passant's side of it would hold water for a minute.'

35

The Park Revisited

AFTER Getliffe left me, I tried to read. Then I heard the front door bell ring below: it was just before midnight. There was a long delay: the bell rang again. A maid scampered down the stairs. In a moment a heavy tread ascended towards my door. George came in.

'Has Martineau been?'

'Yes.'

'What did he say?'

'I didn't meet him.'

'Why not?'

'He saw Getliffe,' I said. 'Getliffe couldn't get anything out of him. It seems – unpromising.'

'I must see him tonight,' said George. 'I should like you to come too.'

It was the first time George had visited me since the inquiries began. For weeks before the trial he had scarcely left his lodgings. Now his angry questions seemed like life stirring in him again – but a frightening, persecuted life. As we walked from Eden's house into the town, he said twice: 'I tell you I must see him tonight.' He said it with an intensity such as I had never heard from him before.

Since the preliminary inquiries he had shown only rare moments of anything like open fear. Instead, he had been sunk into the apathetic despair which many of us had noticed. For much of the time, he was shut away from any other person. He had been living with his own thoughts; often with reveries of the past, the meetings of the group at the farm; 'justifications' still came to his mind, and even sensual memories. In his thoughts he sometimes did not escape quite trivial shames, of 'looking a fool' to himself.

But tonight he could no longer look inwards. His thoughts had broken open, and exposed him to nothing but fear.

George made for Martineau's old house. There was a light in what used to be the drawing-room: the housekeeper opened the door.

'I want to see Mr Martineau,' said George.

'He's not in yet. I'm waiting up for him,' she said.

'I'm afraid that it's essential for us to see him tonight,' said George. 'I shall have to wait.'

Then she recognised him. She had not seen him since the morning we came to bid Martineau goodbye.

'It's you,' she said. 'When I heard of your goings-on, I said that I always knew you'd driven him away.'

'I shall have to wait,' said George.

She kept her hand on the latch. She would not ask him into the drawing-room. 'I'm alone,' she said, 'and until he tells me, I can please myself who I let in – '

We argued; I tried to calm her, but she had brooded on losing Martineau all these years; she took her farcical revenge, and we had to wait outside in the raw night.

We walked up and down the end of the New Walk. From the park we could see the gate of Martineau's and the light in the drawing-room, just as we had done that night of Jack's confession.

George, his eyes never leaving the path to the house, began to talk. He had heard, not many minutes after Eden, of the intention to dismiss him from the School. It had leaked out through an acquaintance on the staff; his friends at the School already knew. Then I told him what Eden had said about his position in the firm. He hardly listened.

'You might as well see something. Another sheet of paper,' he said.

256

I had to light a match to read it. As the flame smoked, I thought of the other sheet of paper, the bill of the little plays which Jack had produced beside these trees. But he did not mean that. He meant the sheet of paper on which he had written down his statement on the circulation – the sheet of paper which lay before the court.

In the match light, I read some of this letter.

Dear George,

We are writing in the name of twelve people who have known you at the School, and who are indignant at the news tonight. We wish there was something we could do to help, but at least we feel that we cannot let another day go by without saying how much you have meant to us all. Whatever happens or is said, that cannot be taken away. We shall always remember it with gratitude. We shall always think of you as someone we were lucky to know…

There were four signatures, including those of a young man I had met at the farm in September.

'They meant it,' I said.

'It's too late to be written to now,' said George. With desperate attention he still watched for Martineau. 'Though I don't entirely accept Jack's remarks on the letter.'

'What were they?'

'That the people who wrote it didn't realise that he and I weren't so very different nowadays – '

Without interest, George mentioned a quarrel over the letter. Jack had laughed at George's devotion to his protégés; he took it for granted, he expected George to take it for granted also, that it was just a camouflage to get closer to the women.

George was listening only for footsteps: he had no more thought for Jack's remark. Yet he had resented it little – suddenly, in this park where he might have finished with Jack, I saw their relation more closely than I had ever done.

Jack's power over George had grown each year. It was not the result of ordinary affection or admiration. It did not owe much to the charm which Jack exercised over many people. At times, George actively disliked him. But now, in the middle of this night of fear, George submitted to having his aspirations mocked.

The fact was, from the beginning Jack had never believed in George's altruistic dreams. For a time – until he had been an intimate friend for years – Jack entered into them, and in George's company talked George's language. But it was always with a wink to himself; he judged George by the standard of his own pleasures; by instinct and very soon by experience he knew a good deal about the erotic life. He saw the sensual side of George's devotion long before George would admit it to himself. Jack thought none the worse of George, he took it as completely natural – but he was often irritated, sometimes morbidly provoked, by the barricade of aspirations. He had spoken of them tonight as 'camouflage'; he had never believed they could be anything else. As soon as George 'got down to business' – his affair with Freda – Jack showed that he both knew and had suspected it all along.

From then onwards, in their curious intimacy, George seemed to be almost eager to accept Jack's valuation – to throw away all 'pretence' and to share his pleasures with someone who was a rake, gay, frank, and unashamed.

That mixture of intimacy and profound disbelief was at the root of Jack's power over George. George was paying a sort of spiritual blackmail. He was, in a fashion, glad to pay it. Very few men, the Georges least of all, are secure in their aspirations; it takes someone both intimate and unsympathetic to touch one's own doubts – to give one, for part of one's life at least, the comfort of taking oneself on the lowest terms. At times we all want someone to destroy our own 'ideals'. We are ready to put ourselves in the power of a destructive, clear-eyed and degrading friend.

The light in the drawing-room went out. Immediately George ran to the house, rang the bell, hammered on the door.

'Where is Mr Martineau? I've got to see him,' he shouted. His voice echoed round the road.

A light was switched on in the hall. The housekeeper opened a crack of door, and said: 'He's not coming home tonight.'

'Let me in,' George shouted.

'He's rung up to say he's sleeping somewhere else.'

She did not know where, or would not say. I thought she was speaking the truth, and did not know.

George and I were left outside the dark house.

'Why didn't you see Martineau? Why wasn't I sent for myself?' George cried.

Afraid also, I tried to give him reasonable answers.

'Getliffe was absolutely clear on the importance. We were talking about it at dinner.'

'With Eden?'

'Yes.'

'Do you think I'm going to be deluded for ever? You can't expect me to believe that Eden is devoted to my welfare. I tell you, I insist on being certain that Getliffe is aware of the point at issue. And that someone whom I can trust must be present with Getliffe and Martineau when this point is being made. You ought to see that I'm right to insist on that. Are *you* going to desert me now?'

'You don't believe we've missed anything so obvious,' I said. 'I know Getliffe was going to ask Martineau about the figure. He's very good at persuading people to say what he wants them to say. It's his chief − '

'And he doesn't think that he's persuaded Martineau?'

'No.'

'Don't you admit he would if there had been any serious attempt on my behalf? You come to me saying he's so good − and then apparently he wasn't interested enough to get the one essential piece of information. And then you think I ought not to insist that he's taken every step to get it.'

'It's no use − '

'You know what depends on it,' George cried. 'Do you think I don't know what depends on it?'

'We all know that.'

'But none of you will lift a finger,' he said. 'I'm beginning to realise why Eden imported Getliffe – '

'That's nonsense.'

'I'm not going to listen to that sort of defence. There's one thing more precious than all your feelings,' he shouted. 'It's got to be settled tonight.'

'What do you want to do?'

'I want to hear Getliffe and Martineau discuss the figure of the circulation. With you and myself present.'

I repeated the arguments: it had all been done. We did not know where Martineau was. He attacked me with bitterness and violence. At last, he said: 'I knew you would do nothing. I can't expect any help.'

We argued again. He began to repeat himself. He accused me of taking everyone's side against him. Nothing I said could bring him even a moment's relief.

36

Martineau's Day in Town

WHEN I turned out of — Street towards the court next morning, George and Martineau were standing on the pavement, outside a newspaper shop. Martineau cried: 'Ah, Lewis! You see I've come! I ran up against old George two minutes ago!' His cheeks were sunburnt and half-hidden by a rich brown beard. His skin was wrinkled with laughter, and his eyes looked clear and bright. In George's presence his gaiety was oppressive; I began a question about his evidence, but he would not reply; I asked quickly about the journey, how did he travel, how was the 'settlement'?

'They're shaking down,' he said. 'Soon they will be able to do without me. I might be justified in making a move –'

To my astonishment, George laughed; not easily – by the sound alone, one would have known him to be in distress – and yet with a note of genuine amusement.

'You don't mean that you are going to start again?'

'I'm beginning to feel I ought, after all.'

'What ought you to do? What more can you do along those lines? There's simply nothing left for you to give up –'

'It doesn't seem to me quite like that –' Martineau began.

I had to leave them, as I saw Getliffe climbing the hall steps.

The court was not so full as the afternoon before. Getliffe opened, and from his first words everyone felt that he was worried and dispirited. He told the jury more than once that 'it may be difficult for you to see your way through all the details. We all feel like that. Even if you've been forced to learn a bit of law, you often can't see the wood for the trees. You've got to remember that a few pieces of suspicion don't make a proof.'

Much of his speech was in that dejected tone.

The first witnesses before lunch were customers of the advertising agency. Getliffe's questions did not go beyond matters of fact; he was untidy and restless; several times he took off his wig and the forelock fell over his brows. Porson, resting back with his eyes half-closed, did not cross-examine.

As I met the three at lunch, Jack said: 'How was that?'

'He's trying to begin quietly, and go all out in the last speech. It's his common-man technique,' I said.

Olive looked into my face.

'Why are you lying?' she cried. 'Is it as bad as that?'

Jack said: 'It's got no worse. What do you expect him to say?'

'It's your own examination that matters most,' I said. 'Not anything he says. You've got to be at your best tomorrow – '

'We can put a face on it. If you tell us the truth,' she said.

'You've got to be at your best,' I said to George, 'you above all.'

He had not spoken to the others. Once he looked at a stranger with a flash of last night's fear. On the outside, his manner had become more indrawn than before. It was seconds before he replied to me: 'It's scarcely worthwhile him putting me on view.'

After lunch there was one other witness, and then Martineau was called.

'Howard Ernest Martineau!' The call echoed in the court, and was caught up outside: it occurred to me inconsequently that we had never before heard anyone use his second name. When he mounted into the box he apologised with a smile to the judge for being late. He took the oath and stood with his head a little inclined; he was wearing a suit, now creased, dirty, and old-fashioned, that I thought I had seen in the past.

'Mr Martineau, you are a qualified solicitor?'

'Yes.'

'You've practised in this town?'

'Yes.'

'How long were you in practice here?'

'Quite a long time.' Martineau's voice made a contrast to the quick, breathless question; he seemed less self-conscious than anyone who had spoken in the court. 'Let me see, I must think it out. It must have been over twenty – nearly twenty-five years.'

'And you gave it up a few years ago? How long ago, exactly?'

There was a pause.

'Just over six years ago.'

'And you joined Mr Exell in his advertising agency?'

'Yes.'

'What were the arrangements, the business arrangements, I mean, you understand, Mr Martineau – when you joined that firm?'

'I think we worked out the value of the business roughly, and I bought half of it from Mr Exell.'

'How much did you pay?'

'Five hundred pounds.'

Getliffe had asked the question at random. The answer went directly against us: George and Jack had borrowed half as much again.

'You ran the business yourself for a time?'

'I helped, I can only say that. I was also interested in – other fields.'

'You remember the little paper, *The Advertisers' Arrow*, which the agency used to publish?'

'Yes, I do.'

'Your other interests didn't leave you much time to keep acquainted with it, I suppose?'

Martineau hesitated for a moment.

'I think they did, on the whole. I think I knew more about it than anyone else.'

Many people noticed the dejection and carelessness that Getliffe had shown at the beginning of the examination; only a few realised the point at which his manner changed. Actually, it was when he heard this answer. He immediately became nervous but alert, pertinacious, ready to smile at Martineau and the jury. No one understood completely at the time; myself, I suddenly felt that he must be getting a different response from his last night's talk with Martineau.

'How long were you busy with the agency?'

'Not quite a year, not quite a year.'

'And towards the end of that time you received suggestions that you might sell again?'

'Not quite, not quite. It was after I had already got on the move once more. We talked over the possibility of other people buying it. You must forgive me if my memory isn't perfect – but it's some time ago and my life has changed a little since.' He turned to the judge, who smiled back. 'I think that was the first step, though.'

'Whom did you talk over the matter with?'

'Mr Passant, chiefly.'

'What kind of conversation did you have with Mr Passant?'

Martineau laughed.

'That's rather a tall order, I'm afraid. I talked to him a great deal then,' he looked in a friendly way at George, 'and I have talked a good deal since of different things, you know. I can't guarantee to remember very exactly. But I think we discussed the natural things – that is, whether Mr Passant ought to try to buy this business, and the state it was in, and its prospects in the future. My impression is, we touched on all those things – '

'You touched on the *Arrow*, did you?'

'Yes, we certainly did that.'

'Did you come to the conclusion that Mr Passant ought to try to buy the agency?'

'I think we did.'

'Can you recall what you said about its state just then?'

'That's a little difficult.'

'You stated that you did discuss the – condition at that time?'

'Naturally he was interested in those matters, I told him all I could.'

'You must have discussed profits and the turnover and the expenses – and the circulation of the *Arrow*, I expect?' Getliffe was still eager and excited.

'I think so, I think we did.'

'I'm afraid I've got to push on about the circulation. We should all be clearer if you could remember, do you think you can remember? – if you gave him a definite figure?'

'I may have done, but I can't be certain.'

'Is it likely you did?'

'I should have thought I told him in general terms, so that he could make an estimate of the possibilities for himself. I should have thought that was the most likely thing.'

'You think you told him that the circulation was, say, large – or in the thousands, or very small?'

'That was the way. I'm sure that was the way.'

'Now, Mr Martineau, can you think what indication you actually gave him? Did you say that it was very small?'

'No, no.'

'That it was reasonably large?'

Martineau smiled.

'I think I said – something of that nature.'

'If you put it in numbers?'

'I don't believe we were absolutely exact.'

'But if you had to, what would "reasonably large" have meant? More than a thousand?'

'Yes, surely.'

'Several thousand?'

'Something like that, perhaps.'

'You don't mind repeating that, Mr Martineau?'

'Of course not.'

'You're fairly certain that was the kind of number Mr Passant gathered from your discussions?'

'Yes, yes.'

'Thank you very much, Mr Martineau,' Getliffe said. He sat down, and as he took up a pencil to write a note his fingers were trembling. He leaned close to me: 'That's something, anyway,' he whispered.

Porson began in a level voice, spacing the words out: 'You said you gave up your profession as a solicitor six years ago?'

'Yes.'

'How are you earning your living at present?'

'I'm scarcely doing so at all.'

'You mean, you've retired?'

'No, no, I mean almost the opposite. It's only since I've left that I've become active – but that hasn't helped me much to make a living.' Martineau smiled.

'Come, Mr Martineau, where are you living now?'

'I've been living in a little settlement. We try to support ourselves and earn our luxuries by selling what we have left over. But, as I said, that doesn't always do so well.'

'You've been there for long?'

'Nearly two years. But perhaps I may not stay much longer.'

'I think the jury will understand your *temporary* association with the agency if you will tell us something about your movements. From the time you gave up your profession – first of all, you had a short period with the agency, and then – ?'

Martineau mentioned his changes: the 'Brotherhood of the Road', the solitary vagrancy, some of his humiliations and adventures (someone in the gallery laughed as he mentioned he slept in casual wards; Martineau turned towards him and laughed more loudly), the settlement. He did not say any word about his future. As the story went on Getliffe stiffened into attention. The whole court was tense.

'Very well,' said Porson, 'I suppose we can take it for granted you performed this very eccentric behaviour on religious grounds?'

Martineau nodded his head. 'Myself, I should call it trying to find a way of life.'

'Well – you were already trying to do that when you bought part of Mr Exell's business?'

'I think I was.'

'You weren't entirely interested in it as a business?'

'Not entirely.'

'Scarcely at all, in fact?'

'I couldn't say that.'

'You had every reason not to trouble to get any accurate knowledge of it at all?'

'I'm afraid that isn't true,' said Martineau. 'I knew it – pretty well.'

'You won't pretend you seriously thought of this paper, for instance – as a business proposition? You don't deny that you wrote religious articles for it?'

'I thought perhaps I should find others – well, who were trying to find the way too.'

'I'm glad you admit that. You'll also admit, won't you, that you weren't in touch with more prosaic things – like its circulation?'

Martineau shook his head. 'No. I was in touch with them. They were still very close.'

'I hope you'll admit, though, that Mr Exell still had something to do with it?'

'Yes.' Martineau smiled again.

'Perhaps even more than yourself?'

'Very likely he had.'

'Well, then, Mr Martineau, will it surprise you to know that Mr Exell has given the court exact information upon the circulation of this paper, and his information was very different from that which you remember – you vaguely remember – giving to Mr Passant?'

'It doesn't surprise me so very much,' Martineau said.

'So I put it to you that you were incorrect in your recollection of your talk to Mr Passant? You told him a figure very much less than you suggested a few minutes ago?'

'That's not true. Not true.'

'You realise you are contradicting yourself? You have told us you were thoroughly acquainted with the state of the firm.'

'Yes.'

'You've also agreed that Mr Exell knew it well, as well and better than yourself? I've told you that he gave evidence that the *Arrow* at no time had a circulation of more than twelve hundred.'

'Yes.'

'Then, Mr Martineau, I put it to you that either your recollection of your talks with Mr Passant is untrustworthy or – '

Martineau broke in: 'No, no, no. Those talks are returning more and more.'

'In that case, you were never acquainted with the real figures? You've been misleading us?'

'No. I knew them not so badly, not so badly.'

'How can you possibly justify what you have just said?'

Martineau replied: 'Because I should have agreed with Mr Exell.'

There was an instant of silence.

'Yet you said you remembered telling Mr Passant an absolutely different state of affairs? Is it true that you gave Mr Passant to understand that the paper had a large circulation?'

'That is also true.'

'While you yourself knew, with Mr Exell, that it was quite otherwise?'

'That's true as well. As well.'

'You're now saying, Mr Martineau, that you were responsible for telling a dangerous lie. You realise you're saying this?'

'I do.' He smiled. 'Naturally I do.'

The judge coughed, and said quietly: 'Would you mind telling us whether you actually knew the position of your paper in detail at this time?'

'Yes.'

'On the other hand, you gave Mr Passant a different estimate, a very much larger figure?'

'I think I never gave him a figure exactly. I've said before, I don't remember too well. But I let him get an impression of something much larger. I certainly let him get that impression.'

'Can you explain why you did that?'

'I think so. I've already said, m'lord, that the little paper contained some of my plans to find others on the same – well, "exploration" as myself, and it wasn't always easy in those days to confess how unsuccessful I had been.'

The judge pursed his lips into a smile of recognition (not his friendly smile), inclined his head, and made a note.

Porson kept on, his tone angrier and more hectoring.

'Was there any reason why a man who had apparently given up something for his beliefs should go in for indiscriminate lying?'

Martineau said: 'I'm afraid I found there was.'

Could he expect the jury to believe this 'extraordinary thing'? It was not part of his 'new religion' to damage and mislead his friends? The lie might make it more possible to obtain money from his friends, but that was scarcely likely to enter his thoughts? Was the only explanation that Martineau could offer for his 'completely pointless lie' simply his own 'vanity and conceit'?

It was commented on as the bitterest cross-examination which the trial had so far seen; Porson seemed full of personal antipathy. Many people in the court felt pleased at the tranquillity with which Martineau answered. He was still calm when Porson asked his last questions.

'In fact, your *way of life* has made you a person with no respect for the truth as the jury and all honest men must understand it?'

'I don't feel that's true.'

'You're aware, of course, that if the jury believe this story of your lie it may be of some slight advantage to your friend, Mr Passant?'

'Yes.'

'There's no more reason for them to trust you now than Mr Passant had – according to your story?'

'I hope they will trust me now.'

When Porson sat down, Martineau rested a hand on the box. Getliffe asked him the one question: 'You can say for certain, Mr Martineau, that you gave Mr Passant to understand that the circulation was a largish number, in the thousands?'

'I'm certain,' said Martineau, in a full, confident and happy voice.

37

Night With the Passants

TWO more witnesses were called before the judge rose. I stayed with Getliffe in the robing-room after Porson had gone out, leaving us with a loud laugh and a goodnight. Getliffe sat on the edge of the table.

'Old Martineau did us proud,' he said. I nodded.

'You're lucky to have known him,' he said with a warm, friendly smile. 'He's the sort of man who sometimes makes me want to do something different. You can understand my wanting that, can't you?' He was speaking with great eagerness.

'I knew you would,' Getliffe said. We took up our cases and walked through the empty hall. Suddenly Getliffe took my arm. 'I knew you'd understand,' he said. 'You pretend not to be religious, I know that, of course. But you can't get away from your own nature, whatever you like to call it. You can't pull the wool over my eyes. It's something we've got in common, isn't it?

'I don't mean we're better people in one way,' he went on. 'You know I'm not. You've seen enough of me. I can do – things I'm ashamed of afterwards. You can too, can't you? I expect we can both do more bad things than people who've not got the sense of – "religion". In many ways I'm a worse man than they are. But somehow I think there are times when I get a bit further than they manage to. Because I want to, that's all, L S.'

He laughed. 'Take Porson, for instance. I know what they say about his morals; I'm not taking any notice of them. If you rule that out, he's a better man than I am. He's more honest, he wouldn't have to watch himself as I do. Yet there isn't a scrap of anything deep in him. I'll swear there isn't. He's never prayed. He's never wept at night.'

As we walked on through the street, crowded with the first rush of the evening, Getliffe said: 'What happened to old Martineau, anyway? Did he lie to Passant or did he think of that later?'

'I think he lied to Passant,' I said. I told him of the entry in George's diary: and of that inexplicable chicanery over Morcom's flat years ago — when George had protested, angrily and loyally, that Martineau could never do a dishonest act.

Getliffe said: 'I don't know. He's not got much to lose now, of course — and Passant might gain a good deal. He liked Passant, I could tell that. Anyway, it's given us a chance. With our friend Porson going all out after that set of figures on paper. He never ought to have made so much of it. But as for Martineau — you know, he might have invented it for Passant's sake.'

'It's difficult to believe,' I said. 'He was always fond of George Passant — but personal affections mattered less to him than anyone I've ever met. His own story — '

'What about it?'

'You believed him last night?'

'I fancy I did,' said Getliffe. 'It went just as I told you. It was all a long time ago, he said. He did just remember talking to Passant, but he hadn't any recollection of what they said. He never knew much about the agency or the paper. He had forgotten the little he ever knew. He obviously wasn't going to make any effort to remember, either.'

'Was that all?'

'That was all I got him to say. Once or twice I did wonder whether he really had forgotten. He seemed to be making it too vague altogether. But I tell you, L S, I'm certain of one thing. *Last night he hadn't the slightest intention of saying what he did today*. I don't believe he had any intention of doing it — until he got into the box. It just came to him on the spur of the moment. I should like to know whether he invented it.'

'I'm certain he lied to Passant,' I said. 'Of course, if he did, Passant would believe him. He would never be suspicious of a friend, particularly of Martineau – '

'I don't think I should have been,' said Getliffe. He smiled at me. Because of these last hours, we were on better terms than we had ever been.

'I don't know,' I said. 'You might have believed him for the moment, but as soon as he went away you'd have taken care to find out.'

'We've got to remember,' said Getliffe, 'that Passant himself must have had his suspicions. He's too able a man not to have seen some snags and – they must all have *known* for certain there was something wrong. Very soon – '

'When?'

'We can both make our own guess, can't we?'

Before the money was borrowed, he was thinking. But his imagination had been caught by Martineau.

'The old chap must have gone through a good deal,' he said, 'getting no one to believe in his faith, at that time. I know you will say this is all too cut and dried, L S – but I fancy there is one thing he held on to longer than most. That's his self-respect. And I fancy his performance today had something to do with that.'

'You mean, he might have been trying to free himself – even from self-respect?'

'At times – I can imagine doing it myself.'

'But still,' I thought aloud, 'it's stronger with him than most men – even after today. There's part of it he never will lose. He would be the last man to be able to get free.'

Getliffe laughed affectionately.

'Anyhow, he got rid of a dash of it today.'

At Eden's Olive and Jack were waiting: their solicitor had sent for them, to have a last word before their examination the next day. Olive told me that Martineau was leaving the town within the hour.

Soon I left them, and took a taxi to the omnibus station. George, his father and Roy were standing close to a notice of the services to the North.

Martineau was on the steps by the conductor, and as I hurried towards them he went inside. The engine burred, they lurched off; Martineau was still standing up, waving.

'It's a pity he had to go away tonight,' Mr Passant said. Then he burst out: 'He never ought to go without an overcoat, going right up there in this weather. He ought to know it isn't doing any good – '

We were all sad that he could leave so casually, before the end of the trial. They were angry that he was free of their sorrows. Mr Passant said several times on the way to the Passants' house: 'I should have thought he might have stayed another day or two.'

He repeated it to Mrs Passant, who was waiting in her front room. 'I didn't expect much of him,' she said.

'He used to flatter you very nicely, though,' said Roy, who had replaced Jack in her favour. For one instant her face softened in a pleased, girlish smile.

'He couldn't have made any difference – ' Mr Passant began.

'If he had been a decent, sensible man everything would have been different. I shall always say it was his fault. He ought to have looked after you properly,' she said to George. She got up and put a kettle on the fire; since I last saw her, her movements had grown stiff, although her face had aged less than her husband's.

'But he wasn't worried by them this afternoon,' said Mr Passant. 'They couldn't get him to say anything he didn't mean.'

Mrs Passant was saying something in an undertone to George. Mr Passant looked at them, then said to me: 'I couldn't follow what Mr Martineau had been doing himself. I'm not pretending I could help him because I haven't fallen into the same mistakes or misunderstandings. It isn't that, Lewis.'

'No one followed what he'd been doing,' said Roy. 'Believe me. That is so.'

'The main thing is, we ought to be grateful to him,' said Mr Passant. 'When I heard them getting at him this afternoon – '

'I suppose we ought to be grateful to him,' George broke in.

'Of course we ought,' said Mr Passant. 'It's contradicted all they were saying.'

'It's very easy to exaggerate the effect of that.' George turned round to face his father. 'You mustn't let it raise false hopes. There are a great many things you must take into account. First of all, even if they believe him, this is only one part of the case. It isn't the chief part, and if they hadn't been wanting to raise every insinuation against me, they could have missed it out altogether.'

Mr Passant questioned me with a glance. I replied: 'It'll have some effect on the other, of course. But perhaps George is right to – '

'What's more important,' George went on, 'is whether they believe him or not. You can't expect them to believe a man who has left his comfort and thrown his money away, and who would sooner sleep in a workhouse than fritter away an evening at one of their houses. You can't expect them to take him seriously. You've got to realise that they'll think it their duty to put him and me in the same class – and feel proud of themselves for doing it.'

'No, that's not quite right,' Mr Passant said.

'You don't know.'

'I've been watching and listening – '

'You don't know what to listen to. I've had to learn. I've been fairly competent at my profession. If you want anyone to tell you whether my opinion is worth having, you had better ask Eliot.'

'I know it, you can't think I don't know it – '

'It can't be much of a consolation for you,' George said.

He was hoping more from Martineau's evidence than he could let his father see. During their argument, I felt it was one of the few occasions on I had seen George deliberately dissimulate. Perhaps he had to destroy his own hopes. I wondered if he also consciously wanted to keep up the pretence that there was nothing in the case; and so told Mr Passant that his persecutors would disregard favourable evidence, just as they had invented the whole story of the fraud.

Yet, listening to him, we had all been brought to a pitch of inordinate strain. He had started out to dissimulate, but his own passion filled the words, and he did not know himself how much was acted. Before he stopped, he could not conceal an emotion as violent as that of the night before.

We all looked at him. No one spoke for a time. Then George said: 'Where are you preaching on Sunday?'

'I don't know for certain.'

'The trial will be over,' said George. 'Whatever happens, I want you to preach. Where's the circuit this week?'

Mr Passant mentioned the name of a village.

George said: 'It's grotesque that they always give you the furthest places. You've got to insist on fair treatment.'

'It doesn't matter, going a few miles more,' said Mr Passant.

'It matters to them and it ought to matter to you. But anyway, this place is presumably fixed for Sunday. I want you to go.'

Mrs Passant suddenly tried to stop their pain.

'That's the place old Mr Martineau started his acting tricks, isn't it?' she said. 'I should like to know what culch he's getting up to now.'

'I don't know,' said George.

Mrs Passant said: 'He ought to have looked after you. He used to think you would do big things. When you went to Mr Eden's, he used to think you wouldn't stay there very long.'

'If I had wanted, I could have moved.'

'I never thought you would, somehow,' she said.

'Because I found something valuable to do,' George said.

'You found something you liked doing more. I always knew you would. Even when I told people how well you were getting on.' She spoke in a matter-of-fact tone, with acceptance and without reproach. George looked at her with something like gratitude. At that moment, one felt how close she had been all his life. She understood him in the way Jack did; she, too, did not believe in the purpose and aspirations, she had always seen the weaknesses and self-deceit. Like Jack, she had discounted the other sides of his nature, and possessed a similar power, the greater because of the love between them.

38

Impressions in the Court

FOR a time the next morning, the feeling of the court was less hostile. Martineau's evidence had raised doubts in some onlookers; and they responded to Getliffe's new zest. Jack's examination went smoothly and he soon made a good impression. The touch of genuine diffidence in his manner seemed to warm people, even in court, to his frank, spontaneous, fluent words. As he answered Getliffe, I thought again how there was a resemblance between them.

He gave an account of his positions in the years before they bought the agency – he was twenty-nine, a year older than he used to tell us in the past, a fact which I should have known if I had studied the register of our old school. He said of the transaction over the agency: 'I wanted money very badly, I'm not going to pretend anything else.'

'About the information you gave to people when you were borrowing money,' said Getliffe, 'that was never false?'

'No. I'd got a good thing to sell, and I was selling it for all I was worth.'

'You told them what you believed to be the truth?'

'Yes. Naturally I was as enthusiastic as I could honestly be.'

'You were certain it was a good thing, weren't you?'

'I put every penny I had got into it, and I spent every working hour of my time improving it for months.'

'You felt like that yourself after you had received Mr Martineau's information?'

'Yes,' said Jack. 'If I'd heard – for instance, that the circulation of the *Arrow* was much smaller – I shouldn't have become as keen. But even so, I should have known there were possibilities.'

'It was a perfectly ordinary business venture, wasn't it? That is how you would look at it?'

'It was a good deal sounder than most. It did quite well, of course. There's a tendency to forget that.'

Once or twice he drew sympathetic laughter. He kept to the same tone, responsible and yet not overburdened, through most of Porson's cross-examination. He denied that he had known the real state of the agency.

'I was a bit puzzled later, but all sorts of factors had to be taken into account. I set to work to put it right.' About the farm he would not admit anything of the stories of Miss Geary and the others. It was noticed on all sides that Porson did not press him. But after several replies from Jack, Porson said: 'The jury will observe there are two accounts of those interviews. One was given by several witnesses. The other was given by you, Mr Cotery.' He added: 'Incidentally, will you tell us why you gave different people so many different accounts of yourself?'

Getliffe objected. Porson said: 'I consider it essential to cross-examine this witness as to credit.'

The judge said: 'In the circumstances, I must allow the question.'

Porson asked whether Jack had not invented several fictitious stories of his life – one, that he had been to a good school and university, another that he had been an officer in the army? Jack, shaken for the first time, denied both.

'It will be easy to prove,' said Porson. He looked at the jury. He had given no warning of this surprise. 'Do you deny that – '

'Oh, I don't deny that I've sometimes got tired of my ordinary self. But that had nothing to do with raising money.' Jack had recovered himself. He replied easily to Porson's questions about his stories: some he just admitted.

At last Porson said: 'Well, I put it to you, Mr Cotery, that you've been living by your wits for a good many years?'

'I think that's true.'

'You've never settled down to a serious occupation? If you like, I can take you through a list of things you've done – '

'You needn't trouble. It's perfectly clear.'

'You've spent your entire time trying to get rich quick?'

'I've spent my time trying to make a living. If I'd been luckier, it wouldn't have been necessary.'

Porson asked a number of questions about the ways in which he had made a living. To many, there was something seedy and repellent in those indications of a life continuously wary, looking for a weakness or a generosity – they were identical when one was selling an idea. But most people actually in court still felt some sympathy with Jack; he was self-possessed, after the moment of anger about his romances, and he answered without either assertiveness or apology. Once he said, with his old half-comic ruefulness: 'It's harder work living by your wits than you seem to think.'

Porson said, after a time: 'You don't in the least regret anything you've done? You don't regret persuading people to lose their money?'

'I'm sorry they've lost it – just as I'm sorry I lost my own. But that's business. I expect to get mine back some day, and I hope they will.'

Porson finished by a reference to Olive's part in the transactions; she had been trying to raise money for the purchase, he suggested, at a time when Jack was taking other women to the farm.

'She was already your mistress as well, wasn't she?'

'Need I answer that?'

As Jack asked the question, several people noticed the distress and anger in his face, but they nearly all thought it was simulated. The general view was that he had chosen his moment to 'act the gentleman'; curiously enough, some felt it the most unprepossessing thing he had done that morning.

'I don't think you need,' said the judge.

Jack's reputation with women was well known in the town, and it was expected that Porson would make a good deal of it. To everyone's surprise, Porson let him go without another question.

Olive entered the box: Getliffe kept to the same lines as with Jack. All through she was abrupt and matter-of-fact; she made one reply, however, which Porson later taxed her with at length. It happened while Getliffe was rattling through his questions over the agency.

'You had considered buying other businesses?'

'Several.'

'Why didn't you go further with them?'

'We wanted a run for our money.'

'But you became satisfied that this one was sound?'

'It was a long way the best we had heard of.'

'Can you tell me how you worked out the possibilities?'

'On the result of Mr Passant's talk with Mr Martineau.'

'You didn't actually see Mr Martineau yourself, I suppose?'

'I didn't want to know any more about it.'

Very quickly, Getliffe asked: 'You mean, of course, that you were completely satisfied by the accounts Mr Passant brought? Obviously they convinced all three of you?'

'Of course. There seemed no need to ask any further.'

Many people doubted whether there had been a moment of tension at all. But when Porson cross-examined her, he began on it at once.

'I want to go back to one of your answers. Why did you say that "I didn't want to know any more about it"?'

'I explained — because I was perfectly well satisfied as it was.'

'Do you think that's a really satisfactory explanation of your answer?'

'It is the only one.'

'It isn't, you know. You can think of something very different. Just listen to what you said again: "I didn't want to know any more about it." Doesn't that suggest another phrase to you?'

'Nothing at all.'

'Doesn't it suggest — "I didn't want to know too much about it"?'

'I should have said that if I meant it.'

279

'I suggest you meant exactly that, though – before you had your second thoughts?'

'I meant the opposite. I knew enough already.'

Porson kept her an inordinately long time. His questions had become more slowly and truculently delivered since Martineau's evidence, his manner more domineering. It was his way of responding to the crisis of the case, of showing how much he needed to win it: but that would have been hard to guess.

He left no time to begin George's examination before lunch. Irritating the judge, he involved Olive's relations with Jack into his questions over the farm. He brought in a suggestion, so over-elaborate that it was commonly misunderstood, about her raising money in secret, without Jack's knowledge; Porson's insinuation being that she was trying to win Jack back from other women, and using her money as the bait.

But, though he had confused everyone by his legal argument and annoyed the judge, Porson had not entirely wasted his time. Olive was often admired at first sight, but seldom liked: and it had been so in court. Porson had been able to whip up this animosity.

As we went out for lunch, the crowd was full of murmurs about her evidence. Rachel met me, her face full of pity. She said several times – 'If only she'd thrown herself on their mercy.' Her pride had made many people glad to hear Porson's attack. And the impassiveness with which she had received the questions about 'running after a man who didn't want her' had added to their resentment.

Olive and Jack walked slowly together into lunch; they were not speaking when they arrived. George stared at her.

'What did you think of that?'

'Not much. They're waiting for you now.'

We tried to keep up a conversation, but no one made the effort for long. About us all, there hung the minute restlessness of extreme fatigue. Before the meal was finished Jack pushed his chair back.

'I want some air before this afternoon. I'm going for a walk,' he said to Olive. She replied:

'It'll be better if I stay here.'

Without smiling, they looked at each other. Their faces were harassed and grave, but full of intimacy.

'You'd better stay too,' Jack said to George. 'You'll want to get ready.' George inclined his head, and Jack asked me to go with him into the street.

We found people already on the pavements, waiting for the afternoon's sitting to begin. Jack walked past them, his head back. He was wearing neither overcoat nor hat, and many of them recognised him.

'We gave them something to listen to,' he said.

'You did pretty well.'

'You would expect me to, wouldn't you?'

'Yes, I should.'

'Do you know,' he said, 'when I was in the box and saw them looking at me – I felt they were *envying* me, just like these people who're staring now?'

Even then, he was drawing some enjoyment from the eyes of the crowd. But a little later he said: 'There isn't so much to envy, is there? I still don't know why I have never pulled things off. I ought to have done. A good many others would have done in my place. I might have done, of course I might – ' He began speaking very fast, as though he were puzzled and astonished.

'Lewis, if I'd been the man everyone thinks, this would never have happened. Do you realise that? I know that I've done things most men wouldn't, clearly I have. But I could have saved myself the trouble if I had lived on Olive from the start. She would have kept me if I'd let her. The man Porson struck something there. But I just couldn't. Why, Lewis, a man like you would have found it infinitely easier to let her than I did!'

'Yes, I should have taken her help,' I said.

'I couldn't,' said Jack. 'I suppose I was too proud. Have you ever known me to be too proud in any other conceivable circumstances before? It's incredible: but I couldn't take the help she wanted to give.'

Jack was reflecting. I recalled how Olive knew that he was struggling against being dependent on her – when we were afraid that he might run. We turned back towards the steps. He again felt curious eyes watching him, and casually smoothed back his hair.

'They think I'm a man who lives on women,' he said. 'It's true that I haven't lost by their company, in my time. The curious thing is – the one occasion when I ought to have let a woman help me, I couldn't manage it.

'I'm not the man they think,' said Jack. 'I've always envied people who've got the power of going straight ahead. I don't think there's much chance I shall learn it now.'

39

The Last Cross-Examination

WHEN George walked from the dock to the witness box, the court was full. There were acquaintances whom he had made at the School and through Eden's firm; as well as close friends, there were several present whom he had quarrelled with and denounced. Canon Martineau, who had not attended to hear his brother, was in court this afternoon, by the Principal's side; Beddow and Miss Geary were also there, of that committee which George once attacked. Roy's father was the only one of the five who had not come to watch. Roy himself stood at the back of the court, making a policeman fetch chairs for Mr and Mrs Passant. Daphne and Rachel stood near to Roy. Eden sat in the place he had occupied throughout the trial. And there were others who had come under George's influence – many of them not ready to believe what they heard against him.

As he waited in the box, the court was strained to a pitch it had not reached before. There was dislike, envy and contempt ready for him; others listened apprehensively for each word, and were moved for him so that their nerves were tense.

At that moment, just as Getliffe was beginning his first question, the judge intervened with a businesslike discussion of the timetable of the case. 'Unless you finish by tomorrow lunchtime,' (Saturday) he said to Porson, 'I shall have to leave it over until Monday. I particularly want to have next week clear for other work. If you could cut anything superfluous out of your cross-examination this afternoon –

then perhaps you' (he turned to Getliffe) 'could begin your final speech today.'

Getliffe agreed in a word; he felt the suspense in the court, tightened by this unexpected delay. But Porson argued for some minutes, and said that he could not offer to omit essential questions. In fact, George's evidence took up the whole afternoon.

Throughout the hours in the box George was nervous in a way which altered very little, whether it was Getliffe who questioned him or Porson. Yet he was, in many ways, the best witness the trial had seen. His hands strained at the lapels of his coat and his voice kept breaking out in anger; but even here, the rapidity and coherence of his mind, the ease with which his thoughts formed themselves into words, made the answers come clear, definite and undelayed.

In the examination, George gave a more elaborate account of their businesses, and one far more self-consistent and complete than either of the others or Getliffe himself in the opening speech. The answers explained that he and Jack heard of Martineau's leaving the town and wanting to sell the agency. He, as an old friend, undertook the task of asking Martineau about it, in particular whether it was an investment they would be justified in inviting others to join. Martineau told him the agency was in a particularly healthy state – and that the *Arrow* had a circulation of about five thousand. His memory was absolutely precise. There were no vague impressions. He had not thought of any misrepresentation ('It would have been fantastic,' George broke out, 'to inquire further'). Jack and Olive had approached Attock and the others; the firm was bought; it had brought in a reasonable profit, not as large as they expected. He had been puzzled for some months at the small circulation of the *Arrow* after they took it over. They had not been able to repay more than a fraction of the loan, but had regularly raised the interest. The disorganisation of industry in the town during the economic crisis had also diminished the business, just as it was becoming established. But still, they had maintained some profit and paid the interest regularly. The agency would still have been flourishing, if, in George's words, 'I had not been attacked'.

After the steady results of the agency, they had thought of other ventures. The farm, which he knew through visits with his friends from the School, struck him as a possibility, and he examined its finances together with Jack. They decided that, running it with one or two smaller hostels, and finally a chain, they could make it give profits on a scale different from their first attempt with the agency. They were anxious to make money, George said vehemently, in answer to Getliffe's question: it was also a convenience to manage the farm, as he and a group of friends spent much of their time there. Essentially, however, it was a business step. He gave a precise account of the meeting with Miss Geary and others.

In the middle of the afternoon, when the windows were already becoming dark, Porson rose for the last cross-examination of the trial. He wrapped his fingers in his gown and waited a moment. Then he said: 'In your professional career, haven't you done a good deal of work on financial transactions, Mr Passant?'

'Yes.'

'You would consider yourself less likely than most to make a mistake through ignorance – or vagueness – or any incompetence that a man can fall into out of inexperience?'

'I should.'

'Thank you for admitting that. I don't want to take up the court's time questioning you about the financial cases – very much more complicated than the ones you engaged in yourself – which you handled for Mr Eden during the last five or six years. So, with your knowledge of financial matters, what was your first impression when Mr Martineau described the state of the agency?'

'I accepted it as the truth.'

'You didn't think it remarkable that an agency of that kind – at that time – should be flourishing so excessively?'

'I was interested that it should be doing well.'

'With your experience and knowledge, it didn't occur to you that it might be said to be doing too well?'

'I was told it on the best of authority.'

'I suggest to you, Mr Passant, that if you had been told anything so remarkable, even by Mr Martineau, you would naturally, as a result of your knowledge of these matters, immediately have investigated the facts?'

'I might have done if I hadn't known Mr Martineau well.'

Porson continued with questions on George's knowledge of the agency. He kept emphasising George's competence; several times he seemed deliberately to invite one of the methodical and lucid explanations. Many, however, were now noticing the contrast between the words and the defensive, bitter note in George's voice.

'Obviously, Mr Passant,' Porson said, 'you would never have believed such a story. Whoever told it to you. I put it to you that this tale of Mr Martineau telling you the circulation as a large figure – actually never took place?'

'You've no grounds for suggesting that.'

At last, as George's tired and angry answer was still echoing in the court, Porson left the agency and said: 'Well, I'll put that aside for the present. Now about your other speculation. You gave some explanation of why you embarked on that. Will you repeat it?'

'I wanted money. This looked a safe and convenient method.'

'That's what you said. You also admitted it had some connection with your work at the Technical College and School of Art' – he gave the full title, and then added – 'the institution that seems to be referred to as the School? You admitted this speculation had some connection with your work there?'

'It had.'

'Let us see what your work at the School really amounted to. You are not a regular member of the staff, of course?'

'I've been a part-time lecturer – '

'For the last nine years your status, such as it is, hasn't altered? You've given occasional classes in law which amount to two a week?' By chance, he exactly repeated the Principal's phrase of over seven years before.

'That is true.'

'That is, you've just been a casual visitor at the School. Now can you explain your statement that one reason for buying the farm was this – itinerant connection?'

'I have made many friends among pupils there. I wanted to be useful to them. It was an advantage to have a place to entertain them – entirely at my disposal.'

'Surely that isn't a very important advantage?'

'It's a considerable one.'

'I suggest there were others a good deal more urgent, Mr Passant. Wasn't it more important to keep the activities of your friends secret at this time?'

'It was not important in the sense you appear to be insinuating.'

'Do you deny,' Porson asked, 'after all that's been said – that you wanted to keep your activities secret?'

'I saw no reason to welcome intrusion.'

'Exactly. That is, you admit you had a particularly urgent reason for buying the farm at this time?'

'It was no more urgent than – since I really became interested in a group of people from the School.'

'You know – you've just admitted that you were afraid of intrusion?'

'I knew that if strangers got inside the group, then I should run a risk of being attacked. That was also true since the first days that I began to take them up.'

'You are trying to maintain that that was the same several years ago as in the summer when you bought the farm?'

'Naturally.'

'There is no "naturally", Mr Passant. Haven't you heard something of these scares among your friends – the fear of a scandal just at the psychological moment?'

'I've heard it. Of course. I believe they've all missed something essential out of the idea of that danger.'

Porson laughed.

'So you admit there was a danger, do you?'

'I never had any intention of pretending there wasn't.'

'But you're pretending it was no greater the summer when you wanted very urgently to buy the farm than it was years before?'

'It was very little greater.'

'Mr Passant: the jury has already heard something of the scandals your friends were afraid of when you were buying the farm. What do you expect us to believe, when you say there was no greater danger then?'

George cried loudly: 'I said the danger was very little greater. And the reason for it was that the scandals were only the excuse to destroy everything I had tried to do. Some excuse could easily have been found at any time.' His outburst seemed for a moment to exhaust and satisfy him. He was left spent and listless, while Porson asked his next question.

'I shall have to ask you to explain what you mean by that. Do you really believe anyone threatened your safety for any length of time?'

'I should have thought that events have left little doubt of that.'

'No. You had good and sufficient reasons for fear at the time you wanted to buy the farm. What could you have had before?'

'I was doing something which most people would disapprove of. I didn't deceive myself that I should escape the consequences if ever I gave an excuse. And I wasn't fool enough to think that there were no excuses during a number of years. I was vulnerable through other people long before Mr Martineau himself acquired the agency.'

'You say you were doing something most people would disapprove of. That' – Porson said – 'is apparent at the time I am bringing you to. The time the scandals among your friends were finding their way out. But what were you doing before, what are you referring to?'

'I mean that I was helping a number of people to freedom in their lives.'

'You'd better explain what you mean by helping people to "freedom in their lives".'

'I don't hope for it to be understood. But I believe that while people are young they have a chance to become themselves only if they're preserved from all the conspiracy that crushes them down.'

Porson interrupted, but George did not stop.

'They're crushed into thinking and feeling just as the world outside wants them to think and feel. I was trying to make a society where they would have the chance of being free.'

'But you're asking us to regard that – as the work which would bring you into disrepute? That was the work you seemed to consider important?'

'I consider it more important than any work I could possibly have done.'

'We're not concerned with your own estimate, you know. We want to see how you could possibly think your work a danger – until it had developed into something which people outside your somewhat unimportant group would notice?'

'Work of that kind can't be completely ignored.'

'I suggest to you that it would have remained completely unknown – if it hadn't just one external result. That is, this series of scandals.'

'I do not admit those as results. But there are others which people would have been compelled to notice.'

'Now, Mr Passant, what could you imagine those to be?'

'The lives and successes of some of my friends.'

'Do you pretend you ever thought that those would be very easy to show?'

'Perhaps,' George cried loudly again, 'I never credited completely enough how blind people can be. Except when they have a chance to destroy something.'

'That's more like it. You're beginning to admit that you couldn't possibly have attracted any attention, either favourable or unfavourable? Until something was really wrong – '

'I've admitted nothing of the kind.'

'I'll leave it to the jury. In any case, there was no serious scandal threatened until somewhere about the time you considered buying the farm? For several years you had been giving them the chance of what you choose to call "freedom in their lives" – but nothing had resulted until about the time you all got alarmed?'

'There were plenty of admirable results.'

'The more obvious ones, however, were that a good many of your friends began to have immoral relations?'

'You've heard the evidence.'

'Most of them had immoral relations?'

George stood silent.

'You don't deny it?'

George shook his head.

'Your group became, in fact, a haunt of promiscuity?'

George was silent again.

Porson said: 'You admit, I suppose, that this was the main result of your effort to give them "freedom in their lives"?'

'I knew from the beginning that it was a possibility I had to face. The important thing was to secure the real gains.'

'You don't regret that you brought it about? You don't feel any responsibility for what you have done to your – protégés?'

'I accept complete responsibility.'

'Despite all this scandal?'

'I believe it's the final example of the stupid hostility I'd taught them to expect and to dismiss.'

'You have no regrets for these scandals?'

'They are an inconvenience. They should not have happened.'

'But – the happenings themselves?'

'I'm not ashamed of them,' George shouted. 'If there's to be any freedom in men's lives, they have got to work out their behaviour for themselves.'

'So your only objection to this promiscuity was when it became a danger? The danger that suddenly became acute at the time you said, in Mrs Ward's hearing: "If we don't get secrecy soon, we shall lose everything".'

'I should feel justified if much more had happened.'

'You also felt justified in practising what you preach?'

George did not answer. Porson referred to Iris Ward's evidence, the hints of Daphne and other girls. There was a soft, jeering laugh from the court.

George said: 'There's no point in denying those stories.'

'And so all this,' Porson said, 'is the work of which you were so proud? Which you told us you considered the most important activity you could perform?'

There was another laugh. With a flushed face, the judge ordered silence. 'You needn't answer that if you don't want,' he said to George, a kindly curious look in his eyes.

'I prefer to answer it,' said George. 'I've already described what I've tried to do. I can't be expected to give much significance to these incidents you are bringing up – when you compare them with the real meaning they mattered very little one way or the other.'

Porson drank some water. When he spoke again, his voice was a little husky, but still full of energy and assertion.

'You've told us, Mr Passant, that *work* with your group of friends was a very important thing in your life?'

'Yes.'

'And you always realised it might involve you in a certain danger? Shall we say in social disapproval?'

'Yes.'

'You still repeat, however, that the danger at the time of these alarms – just before you considered buying the farm – seemed to you little greater than in previous years?'

'It was an excuse presented to anyone wishing to be hostile. Before, they would have been compelled to invent one. That was all the difference.'

'I'm asking you again. You still deny that the danger really was desperate enough to affect your actions? To force you to make an attempt to buy the farm at all costs?'

'I deny it, naturally.'

Porson paused.

'How then do you explain that you were willing – just about that time – to give up your group of friends altogether? To have nothing more to do with work that you've told us was the most important thing in your life?'

'It's not true.'

'I can recall a witness to prove you said *these words also* at the farm.'

There was a silence. George began speaking fast.

'In a sense I grant it. It was the only course left for me to take. I'd finished as much as I could do. I'd tried to help a fair number of my friends from the School. I'd given them as much chance of freedom as I could. Doing it again with other people would merely mean repeating the same process. I was willing to do that – but if it was going to involve me in continual hostility with everyone round me, I wasn't prepared to feel it a duty to go on. I'd done the pioneer work. I was satisfied to let it go at that.'

As he spoke, George had a helpless and suffering look. This last answer scarcely anyone understood, even those of us who knew something of his language, and the barrier between his appetite for living and his picture of his own soul. He was alone, more than at any time in the trial – more than he had ever been.

For a moment, I found myself angry with him. Despite the situation, I was swept with anger; I was without understanding, as though I were suddenly much younger, as though I were taken back to the night of his triumph years before. For all his eagerness for life – I felt in a moment so powerful that no shame could obscure it – for all the warmth of his heart and his 'vision of God', he was less honest than his attackers, than the Beddows, Camerons, and Canon Martineau's, the Porsons, Edens and Iris Wards. He was less honest than those who saw in his aspirations only the devices of a carnally obsessed and self-indulgent man. He was corrupt within himself. So at the time when the scandal first hung over him, he was afraid, and already dissatisfied, tired of the 'little world'. But this answer which he made to Porson was the manner in which he explained it to himself.

At that moment, he suddenly seemed as alien to me, who had been intimate with him for so many years, as to those who laughed in court the instant before. I was blinded to the fire and devotion which accompanied this struggle with himself; through that struggle, he had deceived himself; yet it had also at moments given him intimations such as the rest of us might never know.

Even our indignations and ideals tend to be made in our own image. For me, to whom a kind of frankness with myself came more naturally than to George, it was a temptation to make that insight and 'honesty' a test by which to judge everyone else – just as an examiner, setting his papers and marking his questions, is always searching to give marks to minds built on the same pattern as his own.

I was blinded also to something as true and more simple. His words sounded less certain to him than to any of his listeners; they were more than anything an attempt to reason away his own misgivings. I ought to have known that he, too, had lain awake at night, seeing his aspirations fallen, bitterly aware of his own fear and guilt, full of the reproach of failure, remorse and the loss of hope. He too had 'wept at night', in a suffering harsher than Getliffe would ever feel, with all excuse seeming useless and remote; he had felt only degrading fear and the downfall of everything he had tried to do.

Yes, there had been self-reproach. I did not know, I couldn't foresee the future, whether it would last, or for how long.

Porson passed on to the money transactions over the farm. Nothing unexpected happened in the rest of the cross-examination, which ended in the early evening.

40

Confession While Getliffe Prepares His Speech

I WENT from the court to some friends who had invited me to drink sherry; a crowd of people were already gathered in the drawing-room. Many of them asked questions about the trial. No one there, as it happened, knew that I was so intimate with George. They were all eager to talk of the evidence of the day, discussing Olive's infatuation for Jack, the kind of life they had both led. Several of them agreed that 'she had done it because he was involved already'. It was strange to hear the guesses, some as superficial as that, some penetrating and shrewd. The majority believed them guilty. There was a good-humoured and malicious delight in their exposure, and the gossip was warm with the contact of human life.

From the point of view of the case, they were exaggerating the day's significance. People there felt that George's cross-examination 'had settled the business. He can't get away with that'; just as, in the street, I had overheard two men reading the evening paper and giving the same opinion in almost the same words. Yet, for all the talk of his 'hypocrisy', 'the good time he had managed for himself', there were some ready to defend him in this room. 'I can believe it of the other two easier than I can of him,' one of them said. 'I shouldn't have thought swindling was in his line.' But no one believed that he had ever devoted himself to help his friends.

I returned to dinner at Eden's. Getliffe told Eden that he thought it was 'all right'. He added: 'I'd be certain if it weren't for this prejudice

294

they've raised. I must try to smooth that down.' Yet he was not so cheerfully professional as he sounded; something still weighed on him. As soon as he had finished eating, he said: 'I had better retire now. I must get down to it. I've got to pull something out of the bag tomorrow.'

'I've heard people wondering what you will say,' said Eden.

'One must take a line,' said Getliffe. Soon afterwards, without drinking any wine, he left us. Eden looked at me and said: 'It's no use worrying yourself now. You can't do any more, you know.'

I went to my room, and lay down on the sofa in front of the fire. After a time, footsteps sounded on the stairs, then a knock at the door. The maid came in, and after her Olive. At once I felt sure of what she was going to say. She stood between me and the fire.

'You've worn yourself out,' she said. Then she burst out: 'But you've finished now, it doesn't matter if I talk to you?'

She threw cushions from the chair on to the hearthrug, and sat there.

'There's something – I shall feel better if I tell you. No one else must know. But I've got to tell you, I don't know why. It can't affect things now.'

'It couldn't at any time,' I replied.

She laughed, not loudly but with the utter abandonment that overtook her at times; the impassiveness of her face was broken, her eyes shone, her arms rested on the sofa head.

'Well, I may as well say it,' she went on in a quiet voice. 'This business isn't all a mistake. We're not as – spotless as we made out.'

'Will you tell me what happened?'

Without answering, she asked abruptly: 'What are our chances?'

'Getliffe still thinks they're pretty good.'

'It oughtn't to make much difference,' she said. 'I keep telling myself it doesn't matter.' She gave a sudden sarcastic laugh, and said: 'It does. More than you'd think. When I heard you say there was still a chance I was more shaken – than if I suddenly knew I'd never done it at all.'

She was silent for a moment. Then she said: 'I'm going to tell you some more. I can't help it.' She broke into a confession of what had happened between the three of them. She was forced on, degraded and yet relieved, just as Jack had been that night in the park years ago. Often she evaded my questions, and more than once she concealed a fact that she clearly knew. There were still places where I was left baffled, but, from what she said and what I already knew, their story seemed to have gone on these lines:

They actually did begin to raise money for the agency in complete innocence. George believed Martineau's account, and Olive took George's opinion; so probably did Jack, for a time. Jack had suggested the idea of taking over the agency – for him it was a commonplace 'flutter', and it was easy to understand George catching at the new interest. He was genuinely in need of money, compelled to see that he had no future in the firm, and, though he would not yet admit it to himself, tired of the group in its original form.

Olive, less clear-sighted on herself than on any other person, gave confused reasons for joining in. I thought that, even so early, she had wanted to control Jack – and that also, as she half-saw, she had been dissatisfied with herself for going back to her father and reverting to the childish, dependent state. This business seemed a 'hand-hold on real things'.

They borrowed their first amount, still believing in their own statements. George and Jack seemed to have realised the true position at about the same time. Neither said anything to the other. All through the transactions, the pretence of ignorance was kept up. Jack only made one hint to Olive (this happened, of course, some time before they were lovers): 'You might get some interesting information if you called on Exell. But it's always safer to wait until we've got the money in.'

As soon as he knew the truth, George passed through a time of misery and indecision. He thought for weeks that he alone had discovered it. He still wanted to consider himself responsible for the other two. At times he came near to stopping the entire business. He went so far as to call a meeting of the others and two of their creditors:

and then made an excuse to cancel it. No doubt he was justifying himself: 'after all, we still have Martineau's authority' ...'anyway, we have raised most of the money now. The harm's done, whatever we do.' He could also tell himself that, despite the false statement, they would make a success of it and bring money to their creditors. Most of all, perhaps, he was afraid of disclosing his knowledge to the others: because he dreaded that Jack's influence would be too strong – and that Jack would force him through it with *both of them knowing everything*.

George had few illusions about Jack. He remembered Jack's early attempt at something like fraud over the wireless company. But he could not escape from the power which Jack had obtained over him, as their relation slowly developed through the years.

As George went through this period, Jack looked on with a mixture of contempt, anxiety, and even amusement. Himself, he was enjoying the excitement of raising the money and 'putting it across'. He found the same kind of exhilaration that a business deal had always given him – but now far more intense. Often he seemed little more affected than when he first invoked George's help. He told Attock the false story with the same single-mindedness, the same sense both of anxiety and of life beating faster, that he had once experienced when going round, Roy's present in his pocket, to call at George's house.

'He enjoyed it. It was part of the game,' said Olive. She did not talk, however, of the pleasure and authority which Jack now felt completely in George's presence. At last he had become the real leader. Though George still talked as though they all accepted his control, each of them in secret knew what the position was.

Olive said that, about this time, she hated Jack and found herself on George's side. She wanted to break up the whole business. She told Arthur Morcom something of it; she wondered how she could withdraw without throwing suspicion on the others. 'Arthur tried everything he knew to get me out of it. But I couldn't trust him then. If I had been on my own, I should have had more chance of escaping.'

At that time she was not yet living with Arthur, and it was a few months before Jack seduced her. Throughout the confession, her tendency was to see her immersion in the business as a result of her relations with these two. I thought she always undervalued how much she needed to influence and manage and control. As she watched Jack at the drunken party after the police court, she had seen herself more clearly and tonight, with a flash of penetration, she said: 'You used to tell me that I insisted too much on how I liked being someone else's slave, didn't you? I used to say how I wanted someone to make me feel small and dependent. Yet that's always been true. At least it's seemed true. But as soon as I looked at what I'd done, I had to see myself trying to get the exact opposite. I still wanted him to order me about. But in all the big things I was trying to make sure that I should have him in my hands.'

For all her passions of subjection, she actually – in another aspect of her nature – was a strong and masterful person. Perhaps stronger than either George or Jack. Those passions were so important to her that they often obscured her insight. She did not realise how violently she wanted her own kind of power.

Neither she nor George could face easily the actual thought of fraud. All three were often seized by anxiety and almost physical fear – from their first realisation of Martineau's lie down to tonight. But there was something different in Olive and George; they were sometimes conscience-stricken in a way which Jack did not know. They could not excuse themselves for these dishonesties over money. They felt cheapened in their own eyes. They did not even possess a 'rational' excuse to themselves. It was different from their sexual lives; for there, when they acted in an 'irregular' fashion, they had at least a complete rationale to console them. Many of the people whom they had known for long talked and acted against the sexual conventions. On the surface, George, Olive and Morcom would, each of them, recognise them only 'out of convenience'. On the levels of reason and conscience, they were completely at ease about the way they had managed their sexual lives; one had to penetrate beyond reason and conscience, before one realised how misleading George's 'justifications' were.

Over their affairs with money, however, they possessed nothing like these justifications. Even superficially, they had not been accustomed to reason away the conventions. In particular, Olive had been brought up to a strict moral code in money matters – in a circle where openly confessing one's income was improper and brought a hush into the room. As I told Eden and Getliffe, George, though himself prodigal, had always 'recognised obligations over money', and felt a genuine and simple contempt for dishonesty. I remembered in the past hearing him say, after looking through one of Eden's cases: 'Bellwethers on the make again! And I'm supposed to see they do it safely.' Once or twice, years ago, he was shocked and angry when the waitress came up after tea in a café and asked: 'How many cakes?' – and Jack looked at her and deliberately undercounted.

And so, as they went on borrowing money on Martineau's statement, there were times when they winced at their own thoughts.

However, the agency was bought and Jack worked hard to make it a success. It was the best continuous work of his life, and Olive said: 'It shows what he could have done if he had had the chance. Or a scrap of luck.' In a small way, it was a remarkable achievement, only possible to a man of unusual personal gifts. He was glad to be doing 'something solid at last', Olive said. 'He kept telling me that.'

George and Olive were overcome with relief as they watched the interest steadily paid off. They were reminded less and less often of what had happened. It had still never been mentioned between the three of them.

After their first perfunctory affair, Olive saw little of Jack. Yet her attitude to him was changing during the months she lived with Arthur. From Arthur she had expected more than their relation ever gave her. If he had been described without her knowing him, she would have thought 'that's the man who'll give me everything I've longed for'. While actually she found herself half-pitying and half-despising him, and her imagination began to fill itself with Jack again.

It was not, as one might have thought, Jack the adept lover that she missed. As a matter of fact, she was excitable in love, and, perhaps as a consequence, she did not feel for either Jack or Arthur the kind of exclusive passion which can overwhelm less nervous temperaments. She missed something different. For now she realised or imagined that in Jack she had found what she would never have believed: someone who satisfied two needs of her nature: someone who made her feel utterly submissive and dependent, and yet whom – she thought this less consciously, but it helped to fill her with a glow of anticipation – she could control. She had seen what he could do; she was quite realistic about his character. And yet, he was the only man she had ever known who could imbue her with passionate respect.

In the end she went to Jack. For a long time he would not 'accept her terms', as they both told me. It was on this point that Jack had been provoked to his outburst today. She had tried, not once but several times, to make him live on her. He had to defend himself there: his romantic attitude represented his one streak of aspiration, his one 'spiritual attempt', and was precious in his own eyes on that account.

Meanwhile, George had given way to Jack's influence and had become engrossed in Daphne; in the autumn of 1930 they all wanted to buy the farm. The 'scares' deeply affected George, and the scene recounted by Iris Ward took place; but, although at that gathering Jack spoke as if frightened of a scandal himself, he probably only acted the part to play on George's fears. Himself, he wanted the farm as another business venture, and this was a way to bring George in. He was also exercising his power over George for its own sake.

When George said that he did not propose to get on the wrong side of the law, he was referring to the agency and half-excusing the way it had developed. But the remark bore for himself, and Jack and Olive, a deeper significance. He meant that, if they adopted Jack's suggestions, they would be acting with full knowledge from the beginning. Each would be going into fraud with his eyes open and *knowing the others were aware of it.*

From the moment that remark was made, they all three knew this business could not be done like the other. Iris Ward's evidence suggested that they decided to proceed the same night. That must have been a mistaken impression. George said the words when she remembered, but she did not realise how violently he would retract them the next day.

For weeks Jack kept the fear of scandal in front of him – and all the time suggested that he knew George's objections were sham fighting. He said that he knew George wanted the farm for his own pleasures. He assumed in Olive's presence that George felt no deeper objections than he felt himself. He often took the line that they were in complete agreement.

Olive said: 'I made myself argue for George. But I began to see him just as he looked this afternoon.' (She meant, when he answered Porson's question on why he was willing to give up the group.) 'I knew Jack was the better man. I knew I should always think that.'

This was the time when she tried most strenuously to finance and marry Jack. She found him obstinate. From her account, she went through a mood of complete mistrustfulness of her own intentions. 'I knew there had been sharp practice over the agency, so I told myself I was saving him from trying some more. But it wasn't that. If he had been trying the most creditable object in the world, I should have wanted to buy him out just then. I didn't want him to get on top of the world – and then marry me on his own terms.' Uncertain of herself, she withdrew her opposition to the farm scheme. Then George gave way.

That night, George said, apathetically after the bitter arguments: 'We may as well follow your plan, I suppose.' As soon as he spoke, they were all three plunged for hours into an extraordinary sense of intimacy. They felt exhausted, relieved, and full of complete understanding. They made schemes for Jack to bring in the 'victims'. They discussed the methods by which they could alter the farm's record of visitors. They laughed, 'as though it were an old joke', about the way they had borrowed money for the agency. 'I never felt three people so close together – before or since,' said Olive. 'We forgot we were separate people.'

The mood of that night did not visit them again. They went ahead with the plans, but for days and months their relations were shifting and suspicious. At times, in those days, Olive was overtaken by 'morbid waves' of dislike for Jack. She repeated to herself that she had always admired George, and that he was now not much to blame. George did not once try to withdraw from the arrangement; but he broke into violent personal quarrels with Jack. 'I insist on being treated with respect,' he complained to Olive one night. He needed that she herself should behave towards him as she had done in earlier days.

They did not take long to gather in their money. Jack found most of the investors, but he never settled down to manage the farm. He treated it differently from the agency. He did not make the same effort towards an honest business: he was thinking of extending their hostels into a chain and raising more capital. With a mixture of triumph and pity, he used to talk to George of the 'bigger schemes ahead'.

Now – with the admitted fraud behind them – their relations advanced to the state which I had noticed during the trial. George felt himself undermined and despised, half with his own consent. He obtained moments of more complete naturalness in Jack's company than anywhere else. But much of his nature was driven to protest. As in his cross-examination, he broke out in private and claimed his predominance. It seemed possible that he would be able to cut away from Jack in the future. Since there was no affection left on George's side, I could imagine that after the trial he might suddenly put Jack out of his mind.

Olive had already shown a similar change of feeling towards George. Or rather, her cold and contemptuous words tonight indicated openly something which had been latent for long. She already felt it that orgiastic night after they had been committed for trial: when, with a gesture that was disturbing to watch, she went to his side as he lay drunk on the sofa. She was thrusting her loyal comradeship in our faces – insisting on it, as one insists on a state which has irrecoverably passed. Just as George himself had most insisted on his devotion to his protégés when, in its true form, it was already dead.

During the first days of the fraud, when Olive felt repelled by Jack, she tried to restore her former admiration and half-dependence on George. But that had gone; and when she could not help still loving and respecting Jack, she transferred to George a good deal of hate and blame. He should have stopped it all. If he had been equal to his responsibilities, this would never have happened. He had made great pretensions to guide her life and Jack's, and he had proved himself to be unavailing and rotten. When she compared him with Jack, frank and spontaneous despite all they were doing, she felt that the one quality which she once admired in George now seemed only a sham. The aspirations which he still talked of appeared to her, as they did to Jack, simply a piece of self-deceit. She had no more use for him.

While Getliffe prepared his speech in his room close by, I defended George against her. This night of all nights, I had to defend him, who had lost the most, against those who had helped to bring him where he was. She was not moved by his fall. At last I said, angry and desolated, 'Whatever happens, Jack won't be much harmed. But George – he will never be able to endure looking back to what he once was. Do you remember telling Roy one afternoon years ago – "he is worth twenty Jack Coterys"? Even if this was inevitable, I believe what you said then. Do you think that such a man will forget this afternoon?'

'You're being sentimental,' she said, and was not even interested. She now thought only of her future with Jack. She realised that, if they got off, he would not be much scarred. If they could move to another town, he would soon put it all behind him. She knew he would become restless with ideas again. Left to himself, he might in time break the law in some similar fashion. She would keep him from that, now.

He would have to marry her. His gratitude and immediate respect for her – they would soon disappear. She talked about the prospect, forcing herself to sound matter-of-fact. She knew that she desired it. In a way, she believed that the life she wanted was only just beginning.

41

Getliffe's Speech

GETLIFFE'S final speech, which lasted for two hours on Saturday morning, surprised us all. It was in his usual style, spasmodic, still bearing the appearance of nervousness, interjected with jerky asides, ill at ease and yet familiar; he was showing all the touch which made men comfortable with him. He was showing also the fresh enjoyment which seldom left him when he was on his feet in court.

But there was another note which made many of us feel that he was deeply moved. For those, like Eden and myself, who had been close to him through the week, there could be no doubt that something had affected him personally; and as we heard him reiterate a phrase — 'the way in which Mr Passant's freedom has worked out' — we knew at last what it was. He kept using these words, slurring them in his quick voice. Last night, we had heard him promise 'to pull something out of the bag'. We knew that he had chosen this line to divert the jury's prejudice. Yet — I was certain — it was not only as an advocate he was speaking. I had never seen him so possessed by seriousness in court.

He began, in his simple, emphatic, salesman's way, hammering home the division of the case to the jury. The three of them were being tried for a financial offence, and, on the other hand, their manner of life was being used against them. 'First of all,' said Getliffe, 'I'm going to put the financial business out of our way.' He went over the transactions again, quickly, full of impatient liveliness, once or twice forgetting a figure; he described the agency and came to George's buying it from Martineau. 'A lot of this is dull stuff to you and me,' Getliffe smiled at the jury, 'but about that incident we had what I at any rate found an unforgettable experience. I mean, the evidence of Mr Martineau. Now we have all knocked about the world. We know that there are reasons why we're all capable of telling lies and even giving false evidence in a court of law. We all know that, though sometimes we pretend we don't. I'm going to admit to you now that some of the witnesses for the defence, in this case, have had *reasons* which would explain their telling lies. You would know that even if I hadn't told you. You're able to judge for yourselves. But in Mr Martineau we had someone – I think more than any witness I've ever had the privilege of calling – who is completely removed from all the pettiness that we are ashamed of and that we never manage to sweep out of our lives. You can't imagine Mr Martineau lying to us. You heard all about his story, didn't you? He's *done* something that most of us, if we are ordinary, decent, sinful men' – he laughed again – 'with one foot in the mud and one eye on the stars – have thought of at least once in our lives. That is, just cutting away from it all and trying to live the things we think we believe. Of course, we never manage it, you and I. It isn't our line of business. I'm not sure it would be a good thing for the world if we could. But that isn't to prevent us recognising something beyond us when we do see it – in a life like Mr Martineau's, for instance. I don't mind saying – whatever you think of me – that there's something saintly about a life like his. Renouncing, deliberately renouncing, all the things you and I worry about from the time we are young men until we die. I'm not going to persuade you that his evidence is true. It would be insulting you and me and all we hope for if it wasn't true.'

Some thought that this was an example of the craft, apparently naïve but really subtle, which made him, for all his deficiencies, a success at his profession. But they had not heard his confidence on the night of Martineau's examination. If this was subtle, it was all instinctive. He believed what he was saying; he did not need to persuade himself.

He spent a long time over the details of the agency and the farm. Martineau's evidence, he repeated again and again, acquitted them on the first. On the second – this was far vaguer than the agency; if it had not been for 'that curious definite figure of the circulation', then the second charge could never have been brought. He dealt with the figures of the farm, sometimes wrapping them round and complicating them.

All this, both the complication and the air of authority, was not much different from an ordinary defence. It was done with greater life and was less well ordered than most speeches at the end of such a case; but, if he had finished at that point, he would have done all that was expected of him. Instead, he began his last appeal, and for a quarter of an hour we listened in astonishment.

'I submit that you would never think of convicting these three on the evidence that has been put forward, neither you nor I would think they were guilty for a moment – if it were not for something else we have all had in our minds this week. I mean, the way Mr Passant's freedom has worked out. That is, you've heard of some people who have been breaking a good many of the laws that are important to decent men. I don't mean the laws of this country, I mean the laws which lie behind our ordinary family way of life. I won't try to conceal it from you. They haven't shown any shame. I don't know whether it's to their credit that they haven't. They have been living what some would call "a free life". Well, that's bound to prejudice them in your eyes, in the eyes of anyone older who doesn't believe a thing is good just because it is new. I don't mind confessing that it upset me when I discovered the pleasures they took for granted – as though there was nothing else for them to do. I think – I'm positive we think alike – that they are all three people of gifts. But chiefly I want to say something about Mr Passant, because I think we all realise that he has been the leader. He is the one who set off with this idea of freedom. It's his influence that I'm going to try to explain.

'You've all seen him. You can't help recognising that he's a man who actually made his way up to a point, who might have gone as far as he wanted. He could have done work for the good of the country and his generation – no one has kept him from it but himself. No one but himself and the ideas he has persuaded himself to believe in: because I'm going a bit further. It may surprise you to hear that I do genuinely credit him with setting out to create a better world.

'I don't pretend he has, mind you. You're entitled to think of him as a man who has wasted every gift he possesses. I'm with you. I look on him like that myself. He's chased his own pleasures. I'll go as far as any of you in accusing him. I'll say this: he's broken every standard of moral conduct we've tried to keep up, and he's put up nothing in their place. He is a man who has wasted himself.

'I know you're feeling this, and you know I am. I'm reminding you what one has to remind oneself – that he is not on trial, nor are the others, for having wasted himself. But if he was? But if he was? I should say to you what I have thought on and off since I first took on the case. I should say: he started off with a fatal idea. He wanted to build a better world on the basis of this freedom of his: but it's fatal to build better worlds until you know what human beings are like and what you're like yourself. If you don't, you're liable to build, not a better world, but a worse one; in fact you're liable to build a world for one purpose and one only, that is just to suit your own private weaknesses. I'm certain that is exactly what Mr Passant has done. And I'm certain that is exactly what all progressively minded people, if you'll let me call them that, are always likely to do unless they watch themselves. They usually happen to be much too arrogant to watch themselves. I don't think we should be far wrong to regard Mr Passant as a representative of people who like to call themselves progressive. He's been too arrogant to doubt his idea of freedom: or to find out what human beings are really like. He's never realised – though he's a clever man – that freedom without faith is fatal for sinful human beings. Freedom without faith means nothing but self-indulgence. Freedom without faith has been fatal for Mr Passant himself. Sometimes it seems to me that it will be fatal to most of his kind in this country and the world. Their idea of progress isn't just sterile: it carries the seed of its own decay.

'Well, that's how I think of Mr Passant and progress or liberalism or anarchy or whatever you like. I believe that's why he's wasted himself. But you can say – it's still his own fault. After all, he chose this fatal idea. He adopted it for himself. To that, I just want to say one thing more.

'He's a man on his own. I've admitted that. But he's also a child of his time. And that's more important for the way in which he has thrown himself into freedom without faith. You see, he represents a time and generation that is wretchedly lost by the side of ours. It was easy to believe in order and decency when we were brought up. We might have been useless and wild and against everything round us – but our world was going on, and it seemed to be going on forever. We had something to take our places in. We had got our bearings, most of us had got some sort of religion, some sort of society to believe in and a decent hope for the future.' Eagerly, he laughed. 'We'd got something to stick ourselves on to. It didn't matter so much to us when the war – and everything the war's meant since – came along. We had something inside us too solid to shift. But look at Mr Passant, and all the generation who are like him. He was fifteen when the war began. He had four years of chaos round him just at that time in his life, just at the time when we had quietness and discipline and hope all round us. It's what we used to call "the uncounted cost". You remember that, don't you? And I'm not sure those four years were the worst. Think of everything that has happened in the years, it's nearly nineteen years now, since the war began. Imagine people, alive and full of vitality and impressionable, growing up without control, without anyone believing in control, without any hope for the future except in the violence of extremes. Imagine all that, and think what you would have become yourself if you'd been young during this – I've heard men who believe in youth at any price call it an "orchard time". I should say it was one of the swampy patches. Anyway, imagine you were brought up among these young people wasting themselves. That is, if you're one of us, if you are a normal person who could go either way, who might go either Martineau's or Passant's. Well, if you were young, don't you think you could have found yourself with Passant?

'That's what I should have said. I've let it out because it's something that has been pressing inside me all through this trial, and I couldn't be fair to Mr Passant and his friends unless I – shared it with you. You see, we're not trying them for being wasted. Unless we're careful we shall be. The temptation is to feel they're pretty cheap specimens anyway, to give the benefit of doubt against them. We've got to be careful of our own prejudice. Even when the prejudice happens to be absolutely right, as right as anything we're likely to meet on this earth. But we're not trying them for their sins and their waste of themselves. We're not trying them for a fatal idea of freedom. We're not trying them for their generation. We are trying them for an offence of which there is scarcely a pennyworth of evidence, and which, if it were not for all this rottenness we have raised, you would have dismissed and we should all have been home long ago. You've got to discount the prejudice you and I are bound to feel...'

42

Fog Outside Bedroom Windows

AS soon as Getliffe finished his speech, the court rose for the weekend. He had created an impression upon many there, particularly the strangers and casual spectators. Even some who knew George well were more disturbed than they would admit. Someone told me that he thought the whole speech 'shoddy to the core'; but by far the greater number were affected by Getliffe's outburst of feeling. They were not considering whether it was right or wrong; he was reflecting something which had been in the air the whole week, and which they had felt themselves. Whatever words he used, even if they disagreed with his 'ideas', they knew that he was moved by the same emotions as themselves. They were certain that he was completely sincere.

I went to George's house after lunch. We did not mention the speech. For a time, George talked in a manner despondent and yet uncontrollably nervous and agitated. He had received that morning from the Principal the formal notice of dismissal from the School.

He took a piece of paper and began drawing a pattern like a spider's web with small letters beside each intersection. Some time later, Roy arrived. George did not look up from his paper for a moment. At last he raised his head slowly.

'What is it now?' he said.

'I just called in,' said Roy. He turned his head away, and hesitated. Then he said: 'Yes, there is something. It can't be kept quiet. They've gone for Rachel.'

'What?'

'They've asked her to leave her job.'

'Because she was connected with me?'

'It's bad,' said Roy.

'How is she going to live?' I said.

'I can't think. But she mustn't sit down under it. What move do you suggest?' He looked at George.

'I've done enough damage to her,' said George. 'I'm not likely to do any better in the present situation.'

Roy was sad, but not over-anxious: melancholy he already fought against, even at that age, but anxiety was foreign to him. He and I talked of the practical steps that we could take; she was competent, but over thirty-five. It would be difficult to find another job. In the town, after the trial, it might be impossible.

'If necessary,' said Roy, 'my father must make her a niche. He can afford to unbelt another salary.'

We thought of some people whose advice might be useful; one he knew well enough to call on that afternoon. George did not speak during this discussion, and when Roy left, made no remark on his visit. I turned on the light, and drew my chair closer to the fire.

'How is Morcom?' George asked suddenly. 'Someone said he was ill, didn't they?'

'I've not heard today. I don't think he's much better.'

'We ought to go and see him.'

For a moment I tried to put him off. I suggested that Morcom was not well enough to want visitors, but George was stubborn.

We walked towards Morcom's; a fog had thickened during the day, and the streets were cold and dark.

Morcom's eyes were bright with illness, as he caught sight of George.

'How are things going?' George said, in a tone strangely and uncomfortably gentle.

'It's nothing.'

I walked round to the other side of the bed. Morcom lay back on the pillow after the effort to shake hands. Beyond the two faces, the fog was shining through the window; it seemed to illuminate the room with a white glare.

George made Morcom tell him of the illness. Unwillingly, Morcom said that when he had last seen me at tea with Olive, he had not been well: a chill had been followed by a day of acute neuritic pain; then the pain lessened, and during the trial he had been lying with a slight temperature.

George sympathised, with his awkward kindness. Their quarrels of the past had been patched up long since; they had met as casual acquaintances in the last few years. Yet, with an inexplicable strain, I remembered the days when Morcom played a special part in George's imagination – the part of the disapproving, persecuting world outside. Now George sat by his bed.

It was strange to see: and to remember how George had once invented Morcom's enmity. Still, more or less by chance, Morcom had done him some bad turns. George did not know that if Morcom had conquered his pride and intervened, the trial might never have happened. Perhaps – I suddenly thought – George, whose under-standing sometimes flashed out at random, felt that Morcom also was preyed on, was broken down by remorse.

'This illness is a nasty business,' George was saying. 'You'll have to be careful of yourself. It's a shame having you laid up.'

'You're worrying too much. Your trouble isn't over yet?'

George's face was, for a moment, swept clear of concern and kindness; he was young-looking, as many are at a spasm of fear.

'The last words have been spoken from my side,' he said. 'They've said all they could in my favour. It's a pity they couldn't have found something more.'

'Will he save it – ?'

'He told them,' George said, 'that I probably didn't do the frauds they were charging me with. He told them that. He said they weren't to be prejudiced because I was one of the hypocrites who make opportunities for their pleasures, while persuading themselves and other people that they had the highest of motives. I've been used to

312

that attack since you began it years ago. It's suitable it should come in now – '

'I meant nothing like that.'

'He said I believed in freedom because it would ultimately lead me to self-indulgence. You never quite went to the lengths of saying that was the only object in my life. You didn't need to tell me I wanted my sexual pleasures. I've known that since I was a boy. I kept them out of my other happiness for longer than most men would have done. With all the temptations for sexuality for years, I know they have – encroached. You don't think there haven't been times when I regretted that?' He paused, then went on: 'Not that I feel I have hurt anyone or damaged the aims I started out with. But this man who was defending me, you understand, who was saying all that could be said in my favour against everyone there trying to get rid of me – he suggested that I have never wanted anything but sexuality, from the time I began till now. He said I thought I wanted a better world: but a better world for me meant a place to indulge my weaknesses. I was just someone shiftless and rootless, chasing his own pleasures. He used the pleasant phrase – a man who has wasted himself.'

'He was wrong,' said Morcom. He was staring at the ceiling; I felt that the interjection was quite spontaneous.

'He suggested I was "a child of my time".' George went on, 'and not really guilty of my actions because of that. As though he wanted to go to the limit of insulting nonsense. There are a lot of accusations they can make against me, but being a helpless unit in the contemporary stream – that is the last they can make. He said it. He meant it. He meant – running after my own amusement, living in a haze of sexual selfishness, because there's nothing else I wanted to do, because I have lost my beliefs, because there's no purpose in my life. I tell you, Arthur, that's what he said of me. It would be a joke if it had happened anywhere else. With that offensive insult, he dared to put up the last conceivable defence I should ever make for myself. That I had been guilty of a good many sins, that I had been a hypocritical sensualist, but that I wasn't responsible for it because I was "a child of my time". He dared to say that I wasn't responsible for it. Whatever I have done in my life, I claim to be responsible for it all. No one else and nothing else was responsible for what I have done. I won't have it taken away. I am utterly prepared to answer for my own soul.'

The echo died away in the room. Then George said to Morcom: 'Don't you agree? Don't you accept responsibility for anything you may have done?'

There was a silence. Morcom said: 'Not in your way.'

He turned towards George. I listened to the rustle of the bedclothes. He said: 'But after a fashion I do.'

'There are times when it's not easy,' George said. 'When you've got to accept a responsibility that you never intended. This afternoon I heard of the last thing they've done to me. They've dismissed Rachel from her job. Just for being a supporter of mine. You remember her, don't you? Whatever they say against me, they can't say anything against her. But she's going to be disgraced and ruined. I can't lift a finger to help. And I'm responsible. I tell you, I'm responsible. If they want to attack me any more they can say that's the worst thing I've done. I ought not to have exposed anyone to persecution. It's my own doing. There's no way out.'

Morcom lay still without replying. George got up suddenly from his chair.

'I'm sorry I've been tiring you,' he said. 'I didn't think – ' He was speaking with embarrassment, but there was also a flicker of affection. 'Is there anything I can do before we go?'

Morcom shook his head, and his fingers rattled with the switch by the bedside. The light flashed back from the windows.

'Are you sure there's nothing I can do?' George asked. 'There's nothing I can fetch? Shall I send you some books? Or is there anything else you'd like sent in?'

'Nothing,' Morcom replied, and added a whisper of thanks.

That night I woke after being an hour or two asleep. The road outside was quiet. I listened for the chimes of a clock. The quarters rang out; I could not get to sleep again.

The central fear kept filling itself with new thoughts. Beyond reach, beyond the mechanical working of the mind, there was not a thought but the shapeless fear. I was afraid of the verdict on Monday.

Sometimes, in a wave of hope, memory would bring back a word, a scrap of evidence, a juror's expression, a remark overheard in court. The fear ebbed and returned. One part of the trial returned with a distress that I could not keep from my mind for long; it was that morning, Getliffe's final speech for the defence.

I could look back on it lucidly and hopelessly, now. There might have been no better way to save them. He had done well for them in the trial; he had done better than I should ever have done; I was thankful now that he had defended them.

And yet – he believed in his description of George, and his excuse. He believed that George had wanted to build a 'better world': a better world designed for George's 'private weaknesses'. As I heard those words again, I knew he was not altogether wrong. His insight was not the shallowest kind, which is that of the intellect alone; he saw with the emotions alone. Yet what he saw was half-true.

George, of all men, however, could not be seen in half-truths. It was more tolerable to hear him dismissed with enmity and contempt. He could not be generalised into a sample of the self-deluded radicalism of his day. He was George, who contained more living nature than the rest of us; whom to see as he was meant an effort from which I, his oldest friend, had flinched only the day before. For in the dock, as he answered that question of Porson's, I flinched from the man who was larger than life, and yet capable of any self-deception; who was the most unselfseeking and generous of men, and yet sacrificed everything for his own pleasures; who possessed formidable powers and yet was so far from reality that they were never used; whose aims were noble, and yet whose appetite for degradation was as great as his appetite for life; who, in the depth of his heart, was ill-at-ease, lonely, a diffident stranger in the hostile world of men. How would it seem when George was older, I thought once or twice that night. Was this a time when one didn't wish to look into the future?

Through that sleepless night, I could not bear to have him explained by Getliffe's half-truth. And, with a renewed distress, I heard also Getliffe's excuse – 'a child of his time'. I knew that excuse was part of Getliffe himself. It was not invented for the occasion. It was the working out of his own salvation. Thus he praised Martineau passionately: in order to feel that, while most aspirations are a hypocrite's or a sensualist's excuse, there are still some we can look towards, which some day we – 'with our feet in the mud' – may achieve.

But there was more to it. 'A child of his time.' It was an excuse for George's downfall and suffering: as though it reassured us to think that with better luck, with a change in the world, his life would have been different to the root. For Getliffe, it was a comfort to blame George through his time. It may be to most of us, as we talk of generations, or the effects of war, or the decline of a civilisation. If one could accept it, it made his guilt and suffering (not only the crime, but the whole story of his creation and its corruption) as impermanent, as easy to dismiss, as the accident of time in which it took place.

In the future, Getliffe was saying, the gentle, the friendly, the noble part of us will survive alone. Yet at times he knew that it was not true. Sometimes he knew that the depths of harshness and suffering will go along with the gentle, corruption and decadence along with the noble, as long as we are men. They are as innate in the George Passants, in ourselves, as the securities and warmth upon which we build our hopes.

That had always appeared true, to anyone like myself. Tonight, I knew it without any relief, that was all.

43

The Last Day

PORSON'S closing speech lasted until after twelve on the Monday morning, and the judge's summing up was not quite finished when the court rose for lunch. The fog still lay over the town, and every light in the room was on all through the morning.

Porson's tone was angry and aggrieved. He tried to develop the farm business more elaborately now. 'He ought to know it's too late'; Getliffe scribbled this note on a piece of paper and passed it to me. The feature that stood out of his speech was, however, his violent attack on Martineau.

'His character has been described to you as, I think I remember, a saint. So far as I can see, Mr Martineau's main claim to the title is that he threw up his profession and took an extended holiday – which he has no doubt enjoyed – at someone else's expense. Mr Martineau told you he wasn't above deceiving someone who regarded him as a friend. In a way that might damage the friend seriously, just for the sake of flattering Mr Martineau's own powers as a religious leader. Either that story is true – which I don't for a moment believe, which you on the weight of all the other evidence can't believe either – or else he's perjuring himself in this court. I am not certain which is regarded by my learned friend as the more complete proof of saintliness. From everything Mr Martineau said, from the story of his life both in this town and since he found an easier way of living, it's

317

incredible that anyone should put any faith in his declaration before this court.'

From his bitterness, one or two spectators guessed that the case was important to him. Towards the end of his speech, which was ill-proportioned, he made an attempt to reply to Getliffe's excursion over 'a child of his time'. He returned to the farm evidence before he sat down, and analysed it again.

As we went out to lunch, Getliffe said with a cheerful, slightly shamefaced chuckle: 'He thought because I could run off the rails, he could too.'

Outside the court, most of those who spoke to me were full of the attack on Martineau. Some laughed, others were resentful. As I listened, one impression strengthened. For several Porson had spoken their minds, and yet, at the same time, distressed them.

The judge's face was flushed as he began his summing up.

'A great deal of our time has been spent over this case,' he said, the words spread out with the trace of sententiousness which made him seem never quite at ease. Despite the slow words, his tone held a smothered impatience, as it had throughout the last days of the trial. 'Some of you may think rather more time than was necessary; but you must remember that no time is wasted if it has helped you, however slightly, to bring a correct verdict. I propose to make my instructions to you as brief as possible; but I should be remiss if I did not clear up some positions which have arisen during this trial. First of all, the defendants are being tried for conspiracy to defraud and for obtaining money by false pretences – ' he explained, carefully and slowly, the law relating to these crimes. There was a flavour of pleasure in his speech, like a teacher who is confident and precise upon some difficulty his class has raised. 'That is the law upon which they are being tried. The only task which you are asked to undertake is to decide whether or not they are guilty under that law. The only considerations you are to take into account are those which bear directly on these charges. I will lay the considerations before you – ' At this point he broke off for lunch.

In the afternoon he gave them a competent, tabulated account of the evidence over the business. It was legally fair, it was tidy and compressed. It went definitely in our favour.

He came to Martineau: 'One witness has attracted more attention than any other. That is Mr Martineau, whom you may consider as the most important witness for the defence and whom the counsel for the prosecution wishes you to neglect as utterly untrustworthy. This is a matter where I cannot give you direct guidance. It is a plain question of whether you believe or disbelieve a witness speaking on oath. There is no possibility, you will have decided for yourselves, that the witness can be mistaken. It is a direct conflict of fact. If you believe Mr Martineau you will naturally see that a considerable portion of the prosecution's case about the agency is no longer tenable. If you disbelieve him, it will no doubt go a long way in your minds towards making you regard the defendants as guilty on that particular charge. If you believe him, you will also no doubt reflect that the most definite part of the prosecution's case has been completely disposed of.

'In such a question, you would naturally be led by your judgment of a witness' character. Here, if I may say so, you are considering the evidence of a witness of unusual character – against whom the leader for the prosecution was able to bring nothing positive but eccentricity and who has certainly undertaken, we must believe, a life of singular self-abnegation. I must ask you to consider his evidence in the light of all the connected evidence. But in the end you must settle whether you accept it by asking yourselves two questions: first, whether such a man would not estimate the truth above all other claims; second, whether even a good man – whom you may think eccentric and unbalanced – might not consider himself justified in breaking an oath to save a friend from disgrace.

'I think it necessary to remind you that, according to his own account, you are required to believe him capable of an irresponsible lie.'

One of the jury moistened his lips. The judge paused, passed a finger over his notes, continued: 'That is all I wish to direct your attention towards. But there is one matter which makes me detain you a little longer: and that is to require you to forget, while you consider your verdict, much that you have heard during the conduct of this case. You have been presented with more than a little talk about the private lives of these three young people. You heard it in evidence; both counsel have referred to it with feeling in their closing speeches. I ask you to forget as much of it as is humanly possible. You may think they have behaved very foolishly; you may think they have behaved very wrongly, as far as our moral standards allow us to judge. But you will remember that they are not being tried for this behaviour; and you must not allow your condemnation of it to affect your deliberations on the real charge against them. You must be as uninfluenced as though you accepted the eloquent plea of Mr Getliffe and believed that the world is in flux, and that these actions have a different value from what they had when most of us were young.' For a moment he smiled.

'That is not to say, though, because you are to assume what may be an effort of charity towards some of the evidence which you have heard, that you are to regard the case itself with lightness. Nothing I have said must lead you to such a course. If you are not entirely convinced by the evidence for the prosecution you will, of course, return, according to the practice of our law, a verdict of not guilty. But if you are convinced by the relevant evidence, beyond any reasonable shade of doubt in your own minds, then you will let nothing stand between you and a verdict of guilty. Whatever you feel about some elements in their lives, whether you pity or blame them, must have no part in that decision. All you must remember is that they are charged with what is in itself a serious offence against the law. It is the probity of transactions such as theirs which is the foundation of more of the structure of our lives than we often think. I need not tell you that, and I only do so because the importance of the offence with which they are charged must not become submerged.'

Several people later mentioned their surprise on hearing, after the tolerant advice and stiff benevolence of his caution upon the sexual aspect of the case, this last sternness over money.

As the jury went out, the court burst into a murmur of noise. One could distinguish no words, but nothing could shut out the sound. It rose and fell in waves, like the drone of bees swarming.

The light from the chandelier touched the varnish on the deserted box.

Getliffe and I walked together outside the court. He said to one of the solicitors, in his breathless confidential whisper: 'I want to get back to the house tonight. One deserves a night to oneself – '

My watch had jerked infinitesimally on. 'They can't be back for an hour,' we were trying to reassure ourselves. At last (though it was only forty minutes since they went out) we heard something: the jury wanted to ask a question. When we got back to our places, the judge had already returned; his spectacles stood before him on his pad, their side arms standing up like antennae; his eyes were dark and bright as he peered steadily into the court.

Through the sough of noise there came Porson's voice, unrestrained and full. 'It's inconceivable that he shouldn't send it before Easter,' he was saying to his junior. His face was high-coloured, but carried heavy purplish pouches under the eyes. He was sitting, one leg over the bench, a hand behind his head, his voice unsubdued, with a bravura greater than anyone's there. He laughed, loud enough to draw the eyes of Mr Passant, who was standing between his wife and Roy, at the back of the court.

The door clicked open. Then we did not hear the shuffle of a dozen people. It was the foreman alone who had come into court.

'We should like to ask a question. We are not certain about a point of law,' he said, nervously brusque.

'It is my place to help you if I can,' said the judge.

'I've been asked to inquire whether we can find one of them definitely had nothing to do with – with any of the charges. If we do that, can we leave out that person and consider the others by themselves?'

The judge said: 'I tried to give you instructions about the law under which they are charged. Perhaps I did not make myself sufficiently clear.' Again he explained. His kindness held a shade of patronage. Two of them could be guilty of conspiracy without a third. It was possible for any of them to be guilty of conspiracy and not guilty of obtaining money by false pretences. (If the jury considered that any of them had not, in fact, profited after joining in a conspiracy.) If they were not guilty of conspiracy, in the circumstances they could not be guilty of obtaining money under false pretences. Unless the jury considered only one person to be responsible – in which case there was no conspiracy, but one person alone could be found guilty of obtaining money by false pretences.

'You are certain you understand?' the judge went on. 'Perhaps you had better write it down. Yes, it would remove any uncertainties if you wrote it down and showed it to me.'

Many found this interruption the most intolerable moment of the trial. Someone said the most sinister – meaning perhaps the confusion, the sudden flash of other lives, of human puzzlement and incompetence.

Through the hour of waiting which still remained, it shot new fragments of thought to many of our minds. Whom did they mean? What were they disagreeing on? But none of us could go on thinking for long: we were wrapped in the emptiness of waiting. The apprehension engrossed us like an illness of the body.

The message came. The jury were coming back. The three were brought up, and took their seats in the dock again. George's arms were folded on his chest. His face was curiously expressionless: but his hands were as livid as though he had been hours in the cold.

The jury came in. Automatically I looked at the clock; it was after half-past four. Their walk was an interminable, drumming sound. The clerk read out the first charge – conspiracy over the agency – with a meaningless emphasis on the name of the town. 'Do you find them guilty or not guilty?'

The foreman said quickly and in a low voice, 'Not guilty.'

Then the second charge – conspiracy over the farm. Again the name of the town started out.

'Guilty or not guilty?' There was a pause. In the silence someone coughed. Suddenly – 'Not guilty.'

Then the individual charges of obtaining money by false pretences. There was a string of 'Not guilty' for Jack and Olive, and finally the charges against George were read out for the last time; the foreman replied 'Not guilty' twice again, in a manner by this time repetitive and without hesitation.

The judge pressed his lips together, and spoke to them with a stiff formal smile: 'You are free to go now.'

44

Walk into the Town

THE court seethed with whispers. The three were surrounded by
friends and walked to the door. I waited, with Porson and Getliffe,
until we could leave ourselves, watching Mr Passant come out of the
crowd and take George's hand. Gossip was already in the air. 'They
didn't expect – ' someone said as I went out with Getliffe. People were
laughing with excitement, face after face suddenly leapt to the eyes,
vivid and alive.

Getliffe talked in the robing-room until Eden fetched him.

'It's been nice to be together again.' And then: 'Well, one's pulled it
off for your people. It was a good case to win.' He smiled. 'We'll have
a crack about it in the train tonight. I've learned from it, L S, I've
learned from it.'

When he had shaken hands with Porson and followed Eden out,
we heard his voice, cheerful and a little strident, down the corridor. I
went across the room to say goodbye to Porson myself. His eyes were
narrow with unhappiness.

'I ought not to say it to you, I suppose,' he said, 'but it's incredible
these clods of juries should – ' then he stopped and laughed. 'Still,
goodbye, my boy. We'll run together again one of these days. I hope
the job goes well. Let me know if I can be of any use, I expect I
can.'

On the pavement outside the court, George and the others were
being congratulated by a large party. Olive and Jack had their arms

round each other's waists. Soon I was shaking Mr Passant's hand, listening to Olive and Jack and their friends, being invited to visit them later, saying goodbye. In the crowd, someone had put an arm through mine, our voices were raised, there was a great deal of laughter; simply by being together, we were filled with intimacy and excitement. We were careless with the relief, greater and unmixed because others were there to share it. It was only for a few minutes: then Olive took Jack to her car, and Daphne followed after making a sign to George.

The others scattered. I was leaving the town that night, and George told his mother that he would join them in an hour. Roy took the Passants home, and George and I walked up the street alone. The fog had cleared but the sky was low and heavy. Lights were shining in the windows. Neither of us spoke for a few minutes, and then George said: 'This mustn't prevent me doing the essential things.' His voice was sad and defiant. 'I've not lost everything. Whatever they did, I couldn't have lost everything.'

We walked on; he began to talk of his plans for the future, the practical necessities of making a living.

'I shall have to stay with Eden for a few months, of course,' he said. 'Unless they're going through with their persecution. After that – ' He became cheerful as he invented schemes for the years afterward: how he would leave Eden's, and get a job at some similar firm where he could work his way through to a partnership. 'I'm ready to leave this place,' he said. 'You used to try to persuade me against my will. I'm prepared to go anywhere. You won't find me so enthusiastic to spend myself without any return.'

It was strange to hear how he enjoyed developing the details of these plans, and the gusto with which he worked them out.

'I've still got time to bring it off. I mustn't leave anything to chance. I can work it out beforehand.'

It reminded me curiously of some of Martineau's happiness as he gave up his career, except that George's hopes were not wild, but modest and within his powers. He was inventive and happy, walking under a sky which seemed darker now we were in the middle of the town. He was in the mood, full of the future, and yet not anxious, which I had not seen since the nights when we first walked in these streets; years before, when he was delighted with the idea of his group of friends, luxuriously thinking of their lives to come and the minor, vaguer, pleasant plans for success in his own life.

After one bitter remark, when we were first alone, everything he said was hopeful and full of zest; several times he laughed, hilariously and without resentment. Just as we were passing a shop, a bicycle, which had been propped up by its pedal against the kerb, toppled over on to the pavement. At the same moment, we happened to notice a man with an unconcealed, satisfied, and cunning smile.

'I wonder,' said George, 'if he's smiling because that bicycle fell over?' Then he broke into a shout of laughter. 'No, it's not that, of course it isn't. He's smiling with relief because there was no one on it.'

We ended the walk at the café near the station, where we held our first conference over Jack. But the café had been respectabilised since then. There were now two floors, and neat waitresses. We went upstairs and sat by the window. We looked down the hill, over the roofs below, out to the grey, even sky.

George elaborated his plans, laughed, drank cup after cup of tea. Then, when I spoke to him, I found his face grown preoccupied. He replied absently several times. At last he said: 'I've got to show them that I've not lost everything. They've got to realise that I've not lost anything. Not anything that I put a value on. They mustn't think they've dispensed with me as easily as that. I shall keep the essentials. Whatever happened, I couldn't be myself without them. I mean, one way or another. I'm going to work for the things I believe in. I still believe that most people are good, if they're given the chance. No one can stop me helping them, if I think another scheme out carefully and then put my energies into it again. I haven't finished. You've got to remember I'm not middle-aged yet. I believe in other people. I believe in goodness. I believe in my own intelligence and will. You don't mean to tell me that I'm bound to acquiesce in crippling myself?'

His expression was strained and haggard, the opposite of his words. By contrast to the trial, when often he looked young with fear, now his face was older than I had ever seen it.

'I don't deny that I've made mistakes. I gave too much opportunity for jealousy. It's natural they should be jealous, of course. But I shan't leave so many loopholes this time. I didn't make enough concessions. Perhaps I oughtn't to have confined myself to a few people. That was bound to make my enemies hate me more. Whatever I do, it won't have the same completeness this has had for me. But we've got to accept that this is finished. I'm willing to make some concessions now. The main thing is, I shall be keeping on. Everyone would like me to live as they do – shut up in their blasted homes. I'm not going to give them the satisfaction.'

He had not said a word about the substance of the case; he seemed to have dismissed the transactions and charges from his mind.

After a time, feeling he had spoken himself out, I asked about Daphne. As he replied, his voice was quieter.

'I hope she'll marry me,' he said. He smiled in a friendly, almost bantering way. 'It's a pity I didn't find her when you found Sheila.' (He didn't know it, he hadn't guessed it, but that night, as we talked, I was thinking how I could break my marriage.) 'I didn't expect to find everything I wanted in one person then, did I? Still, I ought to have married someone by now, I ought to have made myself.'

'As a result of this trouble –'

George broke out again: 'They've tried to insinuate that everything I've done was because I was sex-crazy. They've tried to explain away the best years of my life – by saying I spent them doing nothing but plot to get a few minutes of pleasure. I ought to have known they would do it. I trusted them too much. It's senseless letting your faith in goodness run away with you. It would have been easy to shape things differently. I shall profit by it now. Marriage with Daphne will leave me free. As it was, I shan't blame myself. It was bad luck things went the way they did. It wasn't my fault – but when they did, well, they were all round me, I'm not a celibate, my taste is pretty wide. And so I gave them the chance to destroy everything I'd spent all these years in building.'

He paused, then said, in a flat voice, with all the bitterness gone: 'That's why, you see, I've got to show them that it hasn't affected me. I've got to show them for certain that I'm keeping on.'

I could not help but feel that he meant something different and more tormenting. It was himself in whose sight he needed to be seen unchanged. In his heart a voice was saying: 'You can't devote yourself again. You never have. Your enemies are right. You've deceived yourself all this time. And now you know it, you can't begin deceiving yourself again.'

There were to be times – I felt at this moment – when he would want to give up struggling against that voice. There were to be times, darker than now, when he would have to see himself and ask what was to become of him. Yet, in those dark moments, would he – as he was now – be drawing a new strength from his own self-searching, even from his own self-distrust?

After his last remark, both he and I were still eager for what life would bring him. He could still warm himself and everyone round him with his own hope.

C P Snow

A Coat of Varnish

Humphrey Leigh, retired resident of Belgravia, pays a social visit to an old friend, Lady Ashbrook. She is waiting for her test results, fearing cancer. When Lady Ashbrook gets the all clear she has ten days to enjoy her new lease of life. And then she is found murdered.

'An impressive novel, as elegant and capacious as the Belgravia houses in which it is set' – *New Statesman*

The Conscience of the Rich

Seventh in the *Strangers and Brothers* series, this is a novel of conflict exploring the world of the great Anglo-Jewish banking families between the two World Wars. Charles March is heir to one of these families and is beginning to make a name for himself at the Bar. When he wishes to change his way of life and do something useful he is forced into a quarrel with his father, his family and his religion.

C P Snow

Homecomings

Homecomings is the sixth in the *Strangers and Brothers* series and sequel to *Time of Hope*. This complete story in its own right follows Lewis Eliot's life through World War II. After his first wife's death his work at the Ministry assumes a larger role. It is not until his second marriage that Eliot is able to commit himself emotionally.

In Their Wisdom

Economic storm clouds gather as bad political weather is forecast for the nation. Three elderly peers look on from the sidelines of the House of Lords and wonder if it will mean the end of a certain way of life. Against this background is set a court struggle over a disputed will that escalates into an almighty battle.

C P Snow

The Light and the Dark

The Light and the Dark is the second in the *Strangers and Brothers* series. The story is set in Cambridge, but the plot also moves to Monte Carlo, Berlin and Switzerland. Lewis Eliot narrates the career of a childhood friend. Roy Calvert is a brilliant but controversial linguist who is about to be elected to a fellowship.

'A novel written with the intuition of a woman and the grasp of broad essentials generally reserved for men... As full of life as life itself' – *John Betjeman*

The Search

This story, told in the first person, starts with a child's interest in the night sky. A telescope begins a lifetime's interest in science. The narrator goes up to King's College, London, to study. As a fellow at Cambridge he embarks on love affairs and searches for love at the same time as career success. Finally, contentment in love exhausts his passion for research.

Printed in Great Britain
by Amazon.co.uk, Ltd.,
Marston Gate.